PRIME TIME

LIZA MARKLUND
PRIME TIME

TRANSLATED BY
INGRID ENG-RUNDLOW

**SIMON &
SCHUSTER**

London · New York · Sydney · Toronto · New Delhi

A CBS COMPANY

First published in Great Britain by Simon & Schuster UK Ltd, 2006
This edition published by Simon & Schuster UK Ltd, 2011
An imprint of Simon & Schuster UK Ltd
A CBS COMPANY

3 5 7 9 10 8 6 4 2

Simon & Schuster UK Ltd
1st floor
222 Gray's Inn Road
London WC1X 8HB

www.simonandschuster.co.uk

Simon & Schuster Australia, Sydney
Simon & Schuster India, New Delhi

A CIP catalogue record for this book
is available from the British Library

ISBN: 978-1-84983-513-8

Printed and bound by CPI Group (UK) Ltd, Croydon, CR0 4YY

I can't take this, Annika thought. *I'm dying.* She pressed her palms against her forehead, forcing herself to breathe regularly and calm down. The pile of baggage by the front door mushroomed before her eyes, a shapeless blob threatening to conquer the hall and the entire world that was impossible to take stock of. How on earth would she figure out what she had forgotten?

There were the kids' clothes, the beach bag, the packets of formula and jars of baby food, the rain gear and the rubber boots, the tent, the baby carriage and its rain hood, the sleeping bags, the backpacks with her own and Thomas's stuff, the security blanket and the cuddly toys . . .

'Is Ellen supposed to look like that?' Thomas wondered on the other side of the bedroom door.

Annika looked at the one-year-old toddling over by the beach bag.

'What do you mean?'

'Don't you have something nicer for her to wear?'

She felt her brain short-circuit.

'What's wrong?' she roared.

Thomas brushed his hair off his forehead and blinked in astonishment.

'I was only asking – what's your problem?'

Feelings of inadequacy, always lurking right below the surface, bubbled up and boiled over.

'I've been busy packing all morning,' Annika said, 'but I didn't pack any frilly dresses. Was I supposed to?'

He snorted.

'I only wondered if the kid had to look like a construction worker.'

Five rapid steps brought her face to face with him and she glared.

'A construction worker? What's going on here? Are we going out to your parents' summer place by the seaside, or is this some fucking final exam in being well adjusted?'

Thomas's surprise was genuine: Annika hardly ever challenged him. The force of the rage that enveloped him was paralysing – he opened his mouth to yell at her, but no sound emerged. Instead, one of the countless electronic devices that they owned sounded off, insistently and increasingly louder.

'Is that mine or yours?' Annika asked.

Thomas turned and went into the bedroom to check his pager, his cellphone and his Palm Pilot. Annika's gaze surveyed the chaos in the hall without being able to locate the source of the signal.

'It's not anything in here,' Thomas called out.

Annika started to rummage through their belongings. The muffled buzzing was coming from somewhere in the pile. Ellen tried to stand while holding on to Annika's bag, but it slipped away and she fell face first on the floor.

'Oh, my goodness! Mommy's going to kiss that, boo-boo, and make it better . . .'

The terrified sobs of the child drowned out the buzzing. With a soothing murmur Annika pulled her daughter close, inhaling her sweet scent, feeling her softness and warmth. They sat on the shoe stand and the small figure relaxed, thumb in mouth. By the time the crying had ceased, the buzzing had stopped too and the phone started ringing instead. Still holding her daughter, she got up and wedged the phone in between her shoulder and her ear while continuing to comfort Ellen.

'Heard the news?' Spike, the news-desk editor, demanded.

Annika rocked and soothed her daughter.

'What?'

'Out in the province of Sörmland, Michelle Carlsson.'

She stopped her soothing motions and flicked her tongue quickly over her dry lips. The paper she worked for, *Kvällspressen*, barrelled into her hall with all the delicacy of a tank – totalitarian and omnipresent.

'We're talking about your old hunting grounds, right?' the news-desk editor said. 'The photographer's already left. It was Bertil Strand, right?'

The last sentence was directed at someone else, presumably the news editor, and Spike came back on the line.

'Berra's on his way, he'll be picking you up in five minutes.'

'Did you pack the nappies?' Thomas asked, taking Ellen.

Annika nodded and pointed at the pile of stuff, trying to get a grip on the situation.

'What's up?' she asked.

'Don't you have a flash?'

Damn, the pager with the built-in newsflash service from TT. She grabbed her bag and rummaged through the contents without finding it.

'Um,' she mumbled, 'I heard it go off, but I haven't had time to check it.'

'Michelle Carlsson's been murdered. In a control room on the outskirts of Flen, shot in the head.'

The words didn't register, comprehension eluding her again. Thomas set Ellen on the floor and the girl headed straight for Annika, wobbling along with outstretched arms.

'You've got to be kidding,' she said.

'Carl Wennergren's at the scene. It seems he was there when they were taping the show yesterday, so we have a head start. Talk about timing.'

The admiration in Spike's voice was pure and unreserved. Annika heard him take a deep drag on his cigarette, the sounds of the newsroom coming across as an indistinguishable backdrop of noise. She sank back down on the shoe stand.

'Berit's over in Öland doing a piece about juvenile drinking sprees. She's dropping everything and driving up there, so she should be there late this afternoon. Langeby's vacationing in the Canary Islands, so you're the only one left. You've got to leave on the double. Bertil Strand's bringing everything we've got so far from the news agency, which amounts to virtually nothing, so you'll have to call in on the way. Are you familiar with the Sörmland police force?'

Annika closed her eyes, trying to bring her separate worlds together as she felt her daughter's warm hand clasping her leg.

'Pretty familiar.'

'Talk to Wennergren, get a feel for the situation and call me . . . like around noon?'

'Sure,' she replied.

Thomas stared at her, his shoulders going rigid.

'What was that all about?'

Annika hung up and met his gaze.

'No,' he said. 'I don't want to hear it. Not another fucking assignment, not today.'

'Michelle Carlsson's dead,' Annika said, feeling incredibly empty.

'That girl on TV?' Thomas asked. 'Anne's friend?'

She nodded, the adrenalin reaching her brain and bringing out goose bumps on her upper arms. Leaning against her mother's knees, Ellen gurgled.

'How? How did she die?'

Annika moved the child away, got up and got a change of perspective. The baggage cluttering her hall shrunk and disappeared; all that remained were her computer and her big bag. With a thud, Ellen flopped down on her behind and started to cry again. Thomas picked her up.

'They're already on their way over to pick me up,' Annika said.

For two seconds, Thomas stared at her uncomprehendingly.

'The boat leaves at eleven,' he told her.

Annika took their daughter, carried her over to her crib and kissed the top of her head. The relief she felt at getting out of the visit to her in-laws and the island cottage was replaced by a sense of loss.

'Oh, baby,' she whispered into Ellen's hair, 'Mommy loves you so very much.'

Not wanting to nap, Ellen resisted. Annika couldn't make herself let go of the baby.

'Mommy will be back later. You and your daddy and your big brother will be together, and you'll have a great time. I know this is for the best.'

The child turned her face away from the lie, tucked her legs in under her and put her thumb in her mouth. Annika stroked Ellen's hair awkwardly, her hands and her heart suddenly lacking grace. She quickly left the bedroom, bumping into the doorpost on her way out. The soundtrack noise of Scooby Doo being chased by a ghost trickled in from the living room. Kalle's sweet little singing voice was there, behind the wall of noise.

Everyone else can do it, Annika thought. *I can do it too, I have to.*

'Are you serious?' Thomas demanded when she came back into the hall. 'Are you really going to work? Right now?'

The last words boomed loudly. She looked down at the wooden floorboards.

'There isn't anyone else. I'm on call, and you know how understaffed—'

Red in the face, he leaned forward and shouted: 'Come on! Fifty people are waiting for us out at Gällnö, and you're not going?'

The gamut of emotions ranging from panic to relief to loss passing through her now exploded into unexpected and unreasonable rage.

'Waiting for *you*,' Annika said, 'not *me*. They couldn't give a damn about me, and you know it.'

Kalle came into the hall, the raised voices of his parents leaving him wide-eyed. He slipped into Annika's arms, throwing his arms around her neck. His softness threatened to undo her.

'You really are something else,' Thomas said.

'Don't make it any worse,' Annika said in a low voice while crouching down to embrace her son. 'Go out to the island, party with your buddies and your brother and let the kids play, and everything will be just fine.'

Her son nuzzled her ear.

'Buddies? You make it sound like this was some kind of pleasure trip. Buddies! We're talking about my parents and my aunts here.'

Annika tore herself away from the warm embrace,

kissed her three-year-old son on his velvety cheeks, and gazed up at Thomas.

'What happens next is up to you,' she said. 'I'll be here when you get back on Sunday.'

She set the boy down, got up and pulled on her raincoat.

'You can't be serious,' Thomas exclaimed. 'You can't leave me like this.'

'There's going to be so many people around that no one will miss me, not even the kids. Have a good time.'

Annika put on her boots, slung her bag over her shoulder and picked up her laptop in its black case. Watching Thomas the whole time, her expression reserved.

'Well, wasn't this convenient,' he remarked tersely.

'It's not like we haven't discussed this,' she countered. 'It's not easy for me. You know that I have no choice.'

'A fine mother you are!'

Annika blanched.

'Do you think I like to do this?' she asked him breathlessly. 'That's awfully unfair of you.'

'This stinks,' Thomas said, his back rigid and his face red. 'I'm never going to forgive you for this. Damn you!'

Annika blinked, at one level stung by his words, at another, untouched. The armour that protected her working persona had locked into place and made her impervious. Slowly, she turned around, hugged her son, whispered something into his ear and left.

Bertil Strand had been assigned a new company car, another Saab, while she had been on maternity leave. Annika presumed that he was even fussier, if such a thing could be possible, about this car.

'You sure took your sweet time,' he said as she tossed her bag and her laptop in the backseat.

The expression on the photographer's face told her that she had shut the car door too hard.

'What lousy weather,' she murmured.

'It's Midsummer,' Bertil Strand remarked. 'What do you expect?'

He shifted into first gear and left the bus stop right before the No. 62 bus pulled up. Annika's mouth was dry as she wriggled out of her raincoat and clumsily fastened her seat belt.

'Got those telegrams?'

The photographer pointed at a thin stack of papers at her feet.

'Seeing as our reporters are scattered halfway across the globe, this won't be easy. We're damn lucky that Wennergren was at the scene.'

Annika bent over to pick up the papers and the seat belt she had just fastened kept her from reaching them. Irritated, she unbuckled it again.

'Right,' she said. 'And just what do you mean by that? Am I invisible even though I'm right here in the front seat beside you?'

The photographer gave her a quick glance out of the corner of his eye.

'It's a crying shame we aren't prepared to accommodate situations like this – poor planning and no forethought. Schyman ought to take charge instead of bickering with Torstensson. Put your seat belt on.'

Annika didn't have the energy to care about the power struggle between the managing editor and the editor-in-chief. She buckled up again, then closed her eyes and felt how the lack of power teamed with the longing for her children made her stomach churn. Her mother-in-law would certainly have a field day. Poor Thomas – why did her son's life have to fall apart? Annika forced herself to exhale, then she opened her eyes wide and focused on the news-agency printouts. The telegrams, all five of them, had been set at one-minute intervals. Flash 09:41 a.m.: TV journalist Michelle Carlsson dead. 09:42: Michelle Carlsson killed by a shot to the head. 09:43: Michelle Carlsson found in a mobile control room near Yxtaholm castle. A weapon was found next to the victim. 09:44: The police suspect that Michelle Carlsson was murdered. 09:45: Several individuals are being interviewed by the police with regard to the murder of Michelle Carlsson.

'They were taping a series that was going to be aired next week,' Bertil Strand said.

'*Summer Frolic at the Castle*,' Annika said. 'My friend Anne Snapphane has been working on the production team since March . . .'

She stopped talking and stared at the tracks of the raindrops on the side window, small streams that converged and diverged, relentlessly pressed back towards the rear until they smashed into the chrome strip of the car door. She remembered her friend's rage and despair when Anne, after working for this production company for six years, was demoted from producer to researcher and studio hostess. This new position meant that Anne Snapphane would clean up the site after the shoot, take care of the taped material and file it, and do all the tiresome dirty work. This meant that she was probably still at the castle. Annika turned around and fished out her pen and her pad from her bag in the back seat.

'Who are the suspects?'

'I haven't the vaguest,' Bertil Strand replied and groaned.

The Saab had reached the Essinge highway, Stockholm's ridiculously undersized beltway which, naturally, was clogged with cars at a standstill.

'This is going to take for ever,' he sighed as he put the car in neutral.

Annika couldn't contain herself.

'What did you expect?' she said. 'It's Midsummer Eve.'

The photographer closed the vents and the windows started to fog up. The windshield wipers maintained a steady beat, the left wiper squeaking every time it reached the top of the windshield. Annika closed her eyes, forcing Thomas's voice and her sense of failure to recede and concentrated on the rain, the windshield wipers, and the asthmatic wheezing of the climate control system.

'*Summer Frolic at the Castle*', she thought. The big family extravaganza slated for the TV Plus channel, filled with entertainment and discussion panels, guest stars and artists. Michelle Carlsson's prime-time comeback, the TV star's chance to show who was boss. Actually, Annika reflected, Carlsson was pretty good.

'What do you think of Michelle?' she asked.

Bertil Strand's head was swivelling back and forth as if operated on ball bearings while he looked for an opening in traffic.

'Fluff,' he said. 'No credibility. Fine in kids' programmes and game shows, but that discussion forum she had wasn't anything to write home about. She was so ignorant.'

Annika was surprised by the protests that welled up inside her.

'Well,' she said. 'Michelle spent ten years working with radio and TV broadcasting. She must have learned something.'

'How to smile for the camera,' Bertil Strand said. 'Now how hard could that be?'

Annika shook her head, holding back tired protests. Still, she had often reasoned along the same lines when she and Anne Snapphane discussed journalism.

'My best friend has worked with television broadcasting for the past six years now,' she said. 'Everything's a lot more complicated than you'd think.'

Bertil Strand cut in front of a rough-and-ready Land Rover. The man behind the wheel of the Land Rover slammed on his horn.

'It seems like one hell of a strange job,' the photographer remarked. 'All that technical junk that never works and droves of conceited morons running around.'

'Sounds sort of like *Kvällspressen*,' Annika said and looked out the window again, grinding her teeth. The man in the Land Rover gave her the finger.

What am I doing here? Here I am, with a pompous ass of a photographer, on my way to the scene of a senseless violent crime, leaving Thomas and the children behind, the only people who really matter. I must be out of my mind. She sniffed at her hands; the scent of Kalle's hair and Ellen's tears still lingered. Her throat closed up. She turned around, got her cellphone and some paper towels out of her bag and wiped her hands.

'I see an empty slot ahead,' Bertil Strand exclaimed and stepped on the gas.

Annika dialled the number.

The police had ordered everyone to switch off their cellphones. Anne Snapphane was sure that she had obeyed orders, so the vibrations emanating from her jacket pocket came as a bit of a shock. She quickly sat up in bed, her pulse throbbing at the base of her throat and right above her eyes, and realized that she must have dozed off. Her phone buzzed like a gigantic insect hidden in the inside pocket of her rain jacket. Dazed, she brushed her hair off her face with her hands. Her tongue tasted mouldy. She dragged herself across the chaotic tangle of covers, throw pillows and bedspreads, unearthed her jacket and pulled out her phone. She regarded the display with distrust. No number had come up, making her hesitate. What was going on? Some kind of test?

She pressed the button and said in a whisper:

'Hello?'

'How are you?' she heard Annika Bengtzon say, her voice sounding distant and indistinct. 'Are you alive?'

A sob escaped Anne Snapphane's lips. Covering her eyes with one hand, she pressed down hard to relieve the pain in her head and listened to the wireless connection. It whistled and rattled, there were engine noises and the wobbly moans of passing car horns.

'Just barely,' she whispered.

'We've heard about Michelle,' her friend said, speaking slower than usual. 'We're on our way over. Can you talk?'

Anne started to cry, softly and silently, salty tears dripping into the receiver.

'I think so.'

Her reply came out as a gasp.

'. . . Lousy traffic jams . . . you out there now?'

The connection broke up and went fuzzy; Annika's sentences came out in fragments. Anne Snapphane took a deep breath and felt her pulse slow down.

'I'm not allowed to leave my room in the South Wing. They've detained us all and I guess they'll question us one by one.'

'What's happened?'

She swiped away the tears with the back of one hand, clutching her phone in the other hand and pressing it to her ear, her end of a lifeline.

'Michelle,' she whispered. 'Michelle's dead. She was in the OB and the back of her head was blown away.'

'Are there lots of cops around?'

Anne Snapphane's heart stopped racing and approached a manageable rate. Annika's voice represented normality and the real world. Her knees sore, Anne got up and looked out the window.

'I can't see much from here, just a bridge over a channel and a few archery targets. I've heard a few cars and a helicopter landed a while ago.'

'Did you see her?'

Anne Snapphane shut her eyes and pinched the bridge of her nose while the images flashed past, piercing through her wooziness.

'I saw her. I saw her . . .'

'Who did it?'

There was a knock on the door. Anne froze and stared at the door, paralysed. Her lifeline snapped – confusion swallowed her up once more.

'I've got to go,' she whispered into the phone and hung up.

'Anne Snapphane?'

The voice on the other side of the door was commanding. She tossed the phone under the covers and cleared her throat. Before she had the chance to reply, the door swung open. The officer standing in the doorway was young and obviously nervous.

'Right, you can come along now.'

She stared at him.

'I'm pretty thirsty,' she said.

The policeman didn't see how unreal she felt, he didn't see her as a person at all. He looked right through her.

'Go out through the door and to the left. Hurry up.'

The rainy weather and all the closed doors left the hallway dark. The walls seemed to billow – she wasn't quite sober yet. In order to gather some physical and emotional support, she walked down the hallway with one hand touching the wall. No other members of the TV team were in sight.

When the policeman opened the front door, the chill

and the damp slapped at her like a wet towel. She gasped, swaying there in the doorway and looking up at the castle. Policemen and police cars were blurred by the curtain of grey rain.

'You wouldn't happen to have an umbrella, would you?'

Her guard replied by pointing to the corner of the house. Anne Snapphane hunched up her shoulders and reluctantly walked out on the stone steps. Water seeped inside her collar in no time at all.

'Where am I supposed to go?'

'To the house down by the water. Right now.'

A cold rivulet ran down her spine and she had water in her eyes. She blinked to get rid of it, started weaving her way down the three steps to the gravel path and followed the boxwood hedge over to the herb garden. She followed the whitewashed wall that led her to the New Wing, passed a small group of enamelled cast-iron furniture items and stopped. The wall encircled a small courtyard: it had arches and was topped with red tile. It wouldn't be hard to escape from here, she thought.

'Straight ahead, keep moving.'

Anne Snapphane looked away from the wall and focused on the door.

The police lieutenant was seated at a table in the large conference room. Right behind him, on the other side of the window, the OB bus was parked. Unconsciously, Anne shrank back, stepping on the guard's toes. The bus stood out like a cardboard cut-out, white than white and emblazoned with the extremely flashy company logotype.

I wonder if she's still in there, she thought. *I wonder if she's gone cold by now.*

'Have a seat.'

Anne sank down on the chair that the officer had indicated, wiped the rain out of her eyes, blinked and noticed that the lieutenant was wearing a colourful Hawaiian shirt. A sense of relief washed over her.

'Oh my God,' she said. 'It's you.'

The man didn't seem to have heard her.

'We've met, in Stockholm,' she told him eagerly. 'Annika Bengtzon was there.'

'You were one of the people who found her,' he said.

Confused, Anne blinked.

'Um,' she said. 'Yes, I was one of them.'

Suddenly, the sense of unreality returned, the floor began to rock under her feet and she grabbed hold of the desk.

'Could I . . . please have some water?'

An officer came over with a pitcher and a glass. With shaking hands, she poured herself a glass of water and greedily downed the entire contents of the glass, spilling some.

'Got a hangover?'

Waves of nausea swept over Anne Snapphane as she leaned back in her chair.

'I think I'm going to have an asthma attack.'

'Is it customary to have a blow-out when you wrap up a TV show?'

She smoothed her hair and noticed how damp it was.

'Why am I here? When do I get to go home?'

The lieutenant got up.

'We're going to interview the whole group of you today, one by one. So far, no one is more of a suspect than anyone else but, naturally, we have to ask you all about last night. I hope you understand.'

Trying to make sense of what he was saying, Anne looked at the man, her mouth half-open.

'Until we have finished these interviews, you will be

restricted to your rooms. You will be summoned at our convenience. You are not allowed to talk to each other, or communicate in any other fashion. Is that clear? Anne Snapphane, did you hear what I said?'

She forced herself to nod and thought of the cellphone under the covers in her bed. The man pushed a button on a tape recorder and sat down on the table in front of her. His jeans were worn at the knees.

'This is a record of the interview with Snapphane, Anne, born . . .'

He stopped and fixed Anne with his gaze. She swallowed and mumbled her date of birth.

'. . . Conducted by Q at Yxtaholm castle, in the conference room of the New Wing, on Friday, 22 June, at 10:25 a.m. Anne Snapphane is being interviewed with regard to the probable homicide of Michelle Carlsson.'

Silently, the police lieutenant studied Anne.

'Why are you here?'

Anne drank some more water.

'I'm being interviewed by the police,' she said softly.

Lieutenant Q sighed.

'I'm sorry,' Anne Snapphane said and cleared her throat. 'I'm a researcher at Zero Television – a production company that makes TV programmes that are aired by various networks. I've also been a studio hostess this week, while we've been taping these shows.' She grew silent and looked around the room. There were police officers in front of her and behind her, and the broadcast bus was outside the building.

'Shows?' the police officer asked. 'In the plural. Does that mean there are several of them?'

She nodded.

'Eight shows in a row,' Anne replied, her voice a bit steadier now. 'Two whole shows a day for four days running, and it's been raining the whole fucking time!'

Suddenly and inappropriately, she laughed shrilly. The policeman didn't react.

'And how did it go?'

'How did it go?'

Anne bowed her head.

'More or less as expected, apart from the weather. We hadn't counted on having to put up canopies to be able to shoot the various slots and segments. And that meant that we had to keep rearranging the shooting schedule – some of the artists had to perform up in the music room on the second floor of the manor house. But apart from that, everything went according to plan.'

She tried to smile.

'Any conflicts?'

'What do you mean?'

She finished the water in her glass.

The policeman spread his hands in a tired gesture.

'Fights,' he explained. 'Arguments. Threats. Unruly behaviour.'

Anne Snapphane closed her eyes again and took a deep breath.

'Some, I guess.'

'Could you be more specific?'

She took another sip of water, noticed that her glass was empty and waved it to get a refill.

'Millions of things can go wrong in a big production like this,' she said, 'and there's just no room for it. If everyone's stressed, things can get out of hand.'

'Could you spell that out for me?' Q asked.

Her heart started racing again and she began to shake.

'Michelle,' she began, 'could be a real pain. For the past few days she's locked horns with every single member of the team.'

'Including you?'

Anne Snapphane nodded a few times and swallowed. The policeman sighed.

'Could you please give us a verbal answer?'

'Yes,' she said, her voice booming much too loudly. 'Yes, including me.'

'When was that?'

'Last night.'

The policeman studied her closely and didn't lower his gaze.

'What happened?'

'It was nothing, really. We got into this argument over money, about what things are worth. It all started with a discussion about the stock market, and I'm principally opposed to an economy based on speculation, while Michelle insisted that it was an essential cornerstone of democracy, and then we went on to discuss salaries. According to Michelle, corporate managers and other people in public positions were worth their high salaries and pension deals, and she mentioned Percy Barnevik and all the other high-rollers, even though she was really talking about herself, as usual.'

She stopped short and her cheeks started to burn. The policeman regarded her, his face a mask.

'Were you angry?'

I'll lie, Anne Snapphane thought. *I can't tell it like it is, they'll think I did it.*

The man in front of her studied her, examined her, read her mind.

'Lying will only complicate things,' he said.

'I wanted to throttle her,' Anne said, looking away, tears burning in her eyes. 'But we were drunk.'

The lieutenant got up, walked around the table and sat back down again.

'Drunk,' he repeated. 'How drunk? Does that go for the whole film team?'

She shrugged her shoulders, suddenly exhausted and fed up with the whole business.

'Words, please.'

Her brain short-circuited, signalling error and overload.

'How should I know?' she shouted. 'How could I know such a thing? It's not like I went around picking up the empties, even though certain people seemed to think that was my job.'

'Like who? Did Michelle think you ought to clear away the empty bottles?'

'No,' she replied in a somewhat more subdued voice.

The silence deepened, her nausea increased.

'Were there any other disputes as the night wore on?'

Out of breath, Anne Snapphane swallowed hard.

'Maybe,' she whispered.

'Who was involved?'

'Ask the others. I don't know, I wasn't listening.'

'But there was some sort of commotion around here last night, wasn't there? Things got kind of rowdy.'

'Ask around and you'll find out,' Anne replied. 'Ask what it was like over at the Stables.'

'Were you there?'

'Not for long.'

'But you were one of the people who found her, right?'

The lieutenant didn't insist on hearing her affirm this.

'Apart from you, who else entered the bus?'

She closed her eyes briefly.

'Sebastian,' she said, noticing how feeble her voice sounded.

'Sebastian Follin, Michelle Carlsson's agent?'

Anne nodded. Then she remembered something.

'Yeah,' she said. 'Oh, he's her manager. Sebastian Follin is Michelle's manager.'

Confused, she stopped.

'How should I put that? That he is? Or was . . .?'

'Anyone else?'

'Karin. Karin Bellhorn, the producer. She was there too.'

'Anyone else?'

'Mariana and Bambi. They can't stand each other.'

'Why were you up all night?'

Anne laughed, a single short bark.

'There was still some booze left.'

'Who are Mariana and Bambi?'

'Mariana von Berlitz is a feature editor for *Summer Frolic at the Castle*, we work for the same production company. Bambi Rosenberg, the soap actress, was a guest on the next to last show. She and Michelle were pals.'

'Right,' the policeman said. 'The manager, the producer, the editor, the friend and you. Would that be everyone?'

Anne considered the question briefly.

'Well, Gunnar was around too,' she said. 'He had the key. His last name's Antonsson. He works in the bus and you should have seen him.' A fit of the giggles bubbled up inside her, passing through her brain and over her lips, oozing like green poison. 'He was more upset about the mess than . . .'

She motioned with a hand and grew silent.

'What do you mean?'

'It bugged Gunnar more that Michelle had messed up his equipment than that she was dead.'

'Messed up?'

'Yeah, all that grey goo, you know . . .'

The image flashed before her, filtered through intoxication and shock: the slim body sprawled in a grotesque position, enormous eyes that would never see again.

'I can't do this . . .' Anne Snapphane murmured and passed out.

The pier in front of the Grand Hotel was clogged with people. The passenger boats to Stockholm's archipelago bobbed like whales behind a curtain of rain, the wind whipping the bunches of birch branches embellishing the bow and stern of each vessel. *This is impossible*, Thomas thought. *There won't be room for us.*

'Gällnö? That's the boat at the far end. Have a nice Midsummer.'

Thomas tried to smile at the employee from Waxholmsbolaget shrouded in raingear, gripped the handle of the stroller firmly, ploughed through a deep puddle and managed to ram a young woman in the legs from behind.

'It's customary to apologize, you know,' she hissed at him.

Thomas averted his gaze and felt how the plastic handle on the package of diapers cut into his wrist and the frame of his backpack slammed against his hip bones.

'I want ice cream,' Kalle declared, pointing at the stand behind them on the pier.

'Once we're on the boat, I'll get you some ice cream,' Thomas promised, his forehead breaking out in a sweat. A gust of wind splattered rain against his face. Ellen whined. His heart sank as he gazed down the pier.

The old steamer *Norrskär* was tied up at the far end, and it was pitching and rolling. She looked like a hump-backed old lady next to the potent modern brutes. In this weather, on this boat, it would take them more than three hours to reach his parents' place out in the islands.

One of the last passengers to make it aboard, Thomas stashed the stroller, their bags and his backpack indoors, under the bridge.

'Come on, time for a snack,' he said, hearing how feeble he sounded.

The sea was pretty rough. Kalle was seasick before they even passed the first islands on the route, Fjäderholmarna. He threw up all over the table in the cafeteria and dropped his jumbo ice-cream bar in the slimy puddle.

'My ice cream!' the boy sobbed, trying to pick up the slimy stick while wiping his mouth on his sleeve.

'Hang on,' Thomas exclaimed while Ellen tried to wriggle out of his arms.

The other passengers edged away from them as inconspicuously as possible.

'Clean it up yourself,' the girl behind the counter said resentfully, handing Thomas a roll of paper towels.

'Don't worry,' he said, sensing how the stares of the other passengers were growing more disapproving. 'It's okay, Ellen, Kalle, everything's going to be fine . . .'

Thomas fled out on deck, clutching his daughter under one arm, the stroller under the other and urging a tearful and unwilling Kalle on in front of him.

There, in a shelter by the stairs, he deposited his children. He pulled off his raincoat, wrapped it around the boy and sat him down on the bench. The boy stopped crying at once and fell asleep in less than a minute. Thomas lowered the backrest of the stroller, tucked his daughter in snugly with a blanket and began to rock the stroller quickly back and forth, back and forth. Aided by the rolling motion of the boat, it did the trick. She too fell asleep.

Thomas applied the stroller brakes and made sure that his children were protected from the rain before going up to the railing to be embraced by the spray and the wind. A sudden and inexplicable sense of loss engulfed him. There was something here that he no longer had.

It struck him that it was the sea water, the semi-salty water found in this part of the world. The way it felt, its characteristic scent.

Something he had grown up with. The sea was a part of his frame of reference, it had always been there. Its pure transparent depths were not only a feature of Thomas's childhood and the summer season, the sea had been a presence in Vaxholm as well, where he had lived until the age of thirty-two. That facet of his life had only slipped away during the past few years, and he had forgotten one of the cornerstones of his life.

She isn't worth it, he thought.

And suddenly another thought struck him with full force: *I regret it.*

Thomas gasped, never having allowed these feelings to surface before. The acknowledgement of his deceit tied his stomach up in knots, threatened to bring him down.

He had betrayed Eleonor, his wife, all because of a fling with Annika Bengtzon. He had left his fine house, his home and his life to go and live in Stockholm, in Kungsholmen, in Annika's ramshackle apartment building that was scheduled to be torn down, where there was no hot water. He hadn't kept his promise to God and to Eleonor, he had let his parents, his friends and his neighbours down. In Vaxholm, he and Eleonor had been important members of the community, involved in the church and various societies. She was a bank manager and he had been employed by the local authorities as a chief financial officer.

'All for a piece of tail,' he told the wind.

Then the pendulum of guilt swung back again, striking him with the same shattering force.

Oh, Kalle, he thought. *I'm sorry, I didn't mean it that way.*

Turning his back on the sea, Thomas studied the

children asleep in the shelter. They were fantastic, and they were his. His!

Eleonor didn't want to have children. He hadn't really given it much thought until Annika had turned up on their doorstep that night right before Christmas, pregnant and weeping. How long ago was it? Three and a half years ago? Not longer than that?

It *felt* like much longer. After that scene, he had only been back to the house once, accompanied by the movers. Eleonor had kept the house and he had put his share of the settlement into the stock market, into the Tech sector that his broker had so warmly recommended.

'Don't buy junk like that,' Annika had said. 'What's the point of broadband connections when they can't even make computers that work, for God's sake?'

Then she'd dropped her laptop on the floor and stomped on it.

'Now that's mature,' he had told her. 'Your analysis of the stock market is truly confidence-inspiring.'

Of course, in the end she was right. A month later, the market took a nosedive, and his stocks took the worst beating of them all.

Thomas moved out of the wind and noticed that he was cold and wet.

And they hadn't even passed Gåshaga yet.

'Why isn't the elevator working?' Anders Schyman wheezed as he reached the fourth floor of the paper's high-rise office building.

Tore Brand regarded him with a sulky expression.

'It's the damp weather,' he said. 'The repairman will be here on Monday.'

The managing editor tried to catch his breath, deciding that he wouldn't broach the subject again until some other member of the maintenance staff was on duty.

All on his lonesome, Spike was parked at his desk: feet up and the phone practically glued to his ear. He jerked in surprise when Schyman put his hand on his shoulder.

'I'll get back to you,' he said, slamming down the receiver.

'Where's Torstensson?' Schyman asked.

'With his family in the province of Dalarna, playing the fiddle. Ever see him gussied up for traditional folk music?'

Spike grinned. The boys in the newsroom had absolutely no respect for their editor-in-chief. Schyman knew it was of secondary importance. As long as the boys could push Torstensson around, make him do their bidding, the man would stay on the job.

Schyman sat down facing the news-desk editor and leaned back. He knew that the boys respected his know-how and experience, but that was of little consequence as long as he didn't have the executive power.

Suddenly Annika Bengtzon's name for the newsroom editors popped into his head. 'The Flannel Pack', she called them, due to their virtually interchangeable dark-blue flannel jackets. He grinned.

Then he cleared his throat.

'So what do we do about poor Miss Carlsson?'

'Annika Bengtzon was supposed to call me around noon, but she hasn't.'

Schyman raised his hands in a gesture of impatience.

'Who's she riding with?'

'Bertil. They left not long after ten.'

'Then I bet they've hardly passed the city limits. The traffic is unbelievable.'

'Damn right,' Spike exclaimed. He lived in Solna and drove his company car four kilometres to work every day. 'Now that would be something to start a crusade about.'

Schyman stifled a sigh.

'You're aware that Michelle Carlsson had filed two court cases against us for defamation of character, aren't you?'

'So what?' Spike countered. 'Are we supposed to hold back at a time like this because some broad was a legal disaster while she was alive?'

Schyman regarded his news editor in silence for ten seconds.

'Who's doing what?' he finally asked.

In a somewhat agitated manner, Spike leafed through stacks of paper, his upper lip beaded with perspiration.

'Like I said, Annika Bengtzon and Bertil are on their way to Flen, and Berit Hamrin is on her way from Öland. She was supposed to write a piece about kids boozing it up and causing Midsummer mayhem. We booked a photographer for the assignment and I've spent the better part of an hour on the phone with the guy. He's pissed off now that the assignment's been canned.'

'It goes without saying that we'll pay him anyway,' Anders Schyman replied and extracted a newspaper from the mess on Spike's desk.

'All right, but the guy wasn't doing it for the money, he was after a byline in the paper. I told him to shoot something anyway and send it over to us with details about the names and ages of the people in the photos.'

'I'd like to see those pictures before we use them,' the managing editor said. 'We've had our fill of faked shots of trashing teens.'

Spike went pink. Last year he had sent two reporters who weren't on the regular staff to Öland, and they'd brought in some fabulous material. The only drawback was that the reporter and the photographer had been hitting the bottle as hard as anyone else, and they had forgotten to tell their new-found friends that they would be immortalized barfing, crying and defecating in the

pages of *Kvällspressen*. The result of this episode had been
that the Swedish Press Council found the paper guilty of
unethical behaviour in five instances, and therefore liable
for damages of more than SEK 150,000 to keep things out
of court. *Kvällspressen* would have won in court, but the
whole business was so sordid that it was better to buy out
the Council and preserve whatever was left of the paper's
good name.

'That's why we sent Berit this year,' Spike replied
curtly and clicked on his computer screen. 'I only said that
crap about the photos to get that freelancer off my back.'

'Just make sure that he doesn't clog up the modem
with five hundred useless pictures five minutes before
deadline,' Schyman countered drily and got up. 'I want to
talk to Bengtzon when she calls.'

'*If* she calls,' Spike said. But by then Anders Schyman
had already left the room.

The holiday motorcade inched its way along Route 55.
Rain was coming down in buckets and the car's windshield wipers creaked. The slow monotonous pace
charged the atmosphere in the Saab with tension, and the
silence was oppressive. Annika tried to get comfortable,
but the seat belt chafed and the seat itself was designed to
support the small of a taller person's back. She realized
that her discomfort had nothing to do with the seat, really;
her feelings of insecurity were the culprit. Her maternity
leave was over and she had only worked a few weeks so
far, but she could tell that the others were already
questioning her presence on the crime-desk team.

During her pregnancy, Annika had been posted to
other departments – Women's Issues and stupid trivia
assignments. Despite feeling demoted and dismissed, she
hadn't raised a fuss. Naturally, she was fully aware of
management's attitude towards young women who got

pregnant soon after being made a permanent staff member. She knew that in their eyes she had let them down, that she was seen as deadbeat, as using the system to get paid maternity leave and leave the paper in the lurch. Adding insult to injury, a very pregnant crime reporter was something to joke about. One, it was presumed that she went brain-dead as soon as one of her eggs had been fertilized, and two, she had to be punished for letting everyone down. She could still remember the bitter tears that she'd shed and how Thomas, unable to really understand, made clumsy attempts to comfort her.

'You'll feel better soon, you'll see,' he had said, bringing her a glass of milk.

Annika never told him that she wasn't crying because she felt sick to her stomach.

Her neck ached. She massaged the uppermost vertebra and tried to unclench her jaw muscles. During most of the trip she hadn't been able to use her cellphone: her worthless service provider, Comviq, didn't have enough coverage out in the sticks.

The tiny morsels of information that she had told her that both the Eskilstuna police force and the national homicide division had been called in, a fact she found simultaneously comforting and disturbing. Annika was pretty familiar with the national homicide division, particularly Q, who was often in charge of these investigations. Her relationship with the Eskilstuna police force was somewhat more complicated. They had investigated the death of Sven Matsson in Hälleforsnäs, and she was certain that they hadn't forgotten her.

She stared out the car window, saw the blur of pine trees flash by; the same lush green landscape that she had been chased through all those years ago. Escaping from her stalker.

It had been a chilly autumn day, the air crisp and clear.

She had left Sven the night before, had broken off their sadistic relationship once and for all. His response had been to threaten to kill her, and he had chased her through the woods with a hunting knife and then attacked her cat, gutting the animal.

Annika closed her eyes and let the poorly paved road in combination with the new Saab suspension rock her, concentrating on relaxing. Eyes closed, she saw Sven's head being crushed by an iron pipe by her own hand. Saw him slowly crumple and fall over the railing into the blast-furnace and disappear. She started breathing rapidly and the skin of her legs was crawling, so she forced the image to recede.

She had been convicted of manslaughter. The Eskilstuna County Court sentenced her to two years of probation. The court determined that she had acted in self-defence, so the charge had not been second-degree murder. She wasn't certain that the verdict was the right one – she had wanted to kill Sven. Cradling her dying cat in her arms, its intestines spilling from its belly, she had been convinced that she had done the right thing.

'Is this the right exit?'

Annika looked up.

'Yeah. Make a left.'

They followed the long avenue leading to the drive at Yxtaholm. As they reached the side road leading to the stud farm, the drive was sealed off by a large road barrier.

Bertil Strand groaned.

'Now isn't that just damn typical?'

Annika looked over to the left and caught a glimpse of the white walls of the castle through the foliage. Further up the drive she could see people walking around and an uplink bus pulling up in the parking lot next to the Stables.

'Everyone in the whole fucking media sector is here already,' the photographer said.

'Quit complaining,' Annika said.

She opened the door and got out while Bertil revved up the car to leave.

Calling out to the police officer at the barrier Annika asked: 'How much of the area is sealed off?'

'The whole point.'

'Why were the others allowed to enter?'

Pretending not to hear Bertil Strand's angry protests, she slammed the car door.

'We're going to seal off and clear the entire area bit by bit,' the officer replied in authoritative tones that were belied by his behaviour; his Adam's apple bobbed nervously and he gazed out uneasily over the lake. He was a local, probably a member of the Katrineholm police force.

Annika decided to try an aggressive approach. She whipped a press card out of her pocket, marched up to the policeman, shoved the card in his face and glared.

'Are you trying to interfere with my work?'

The officer gulped.

'I have my orders,' he replied, gazing intently at Lake Långsjön.

'Do they include obstructing the press? I don't think so.'

The officer looked at Annika.

'Say, aren't you from Hälleforsnäs?' he asked.

Annika recoiled. Then she spun around and got back into the car, landing in the front seat with a thud.

'We won't be getting in this way,' she said, slamming the door.

'Damn it, how many times do I have to tell you—?'

Bertil Strand released the clutch carefully to avoid a spray of gravel that would scratch up the paint job.

'Hang on,' Annika said. She closed her eyes, smoothed her brow, and felt the adrenalin start pumping away. 'There's got to be some other route.'

The photographer revved up the car and put it in second gear, skidding slightly on the wet gravel.

A sense of failure felt like a stone slab on Annika's chest.

'Stop the car,' she pleaded. 'We've got to think.'

Bertil Strand parked next to a faded traffic sign.

'There's got to be some other way to get in,' she said.

The photographer gazed out over the lake.

'Is it possible to approach this place from the other side?'

'The castle's on an island located between two lakes,' Annika told him. 'This is Lake Långsjön. On the other side, Lake Yxtasjön continues quite a long way up to the left. I don't think there are any public roads there. There could be a tractor path, but they're usually gated.'

She scanned across the lake and caught a glimpse of Finntorp Farm through the foliage. When she'd been a teenager, she'd been to riding camp there, jumping her horse Soraya and winning ribbons. Impressions flashed through her mind: the scent of new-mown hay, the warmth of the horse between her thighs, the dust of the dirt road, the love and the sense of utter harmony she felt in the mare's company.

Suddenly she knew.

'Go left,' she said, 'and then make another left.'

Without questioning her, the photographer did as she said; either he trusted her or he was pissed off. It made no difference, she decided.

'Where do we go now?' he asked when they reached Finntorp.

'Make a right turn,' Annika said. 'Head for the Ansgar Centre.'

They made their way carefully up the hill, past the paddocks and the 'closed to all vehicles' sign. Red-painted wooden houses emerged from the gloom like huge building blocks.

'What is this place?'

'A Christian centre and retreat, I think it's owned by the Swedish Missionary Society. Drive down the hill, there's a parking lot in the back.'

Apart from an RV at the far end, the lot was empty. They parked at the edge of a substantial lawn.

'What are we doing here?' Bertil Strand asked.

'There's a beach beyond that hill,' Annika replied, 'and there should be a lifeboat next to the jetty. I figure we could borrow it.'

The rain showed no sign of letting up. They put on raingear and Bertil Strand packed his cameras in plastic bags and put them in a watertight backpack.

'Cover that computer,' the photographer said. 'I don't want anyone to break into my car.'

Annika gritted her teeth and tossed a blanket over her computer bag in the back seat. Break in? When you're parked in an empty parking lot at a Christian centre?

The boat was there, half-filled with water. The oars had been tossed into the reeds, but they couldn't find a bailer. They pulled the boat ashore, turned it over and watched the water carve a creek in the sand.

'Do you know how to row a boat?' an uncharacteristically timorous Bertil Strand asked.

'I hope they haven't sealed off the beaches,' Annika replied.

It was farther than she'd thought. The tiny rowboat bobbed like a float on the waves; at times it felt like they weren't getting anywhere. The boat began to fill up with water again, and it wasn't only coming from above.

A lifeboat, huh? Yeah, right, she thought when they were halfway across the lake.

As they rounded the point, the full force of the wind hit them. Annika's arms started to cramp up.

'Do you really think we'll make it today?' Bertil Strand asked, wet as a drowned dog.

This made Annika row faster and more vigorously. Right when she was ready to give up, she caught sight of the sauna and the beach house.

'We're almost there,' she said, squinting to see the island where the castle was located behind its cloak of rain.

Something was going on there on the beach. She could make out some little black figures milling around outside the buildings. She could also see a large and colourful logotype on a white wall near the canal inlet.

Pulling out a camera from a plastic bag, the photographer said: 'That's the outside-broadcast bus, isn't it? Could you hold the boat steady? I might as well snap a few shots in case they run us off the place . . .'

Annika paid no attention to Strand and rowed the boat further from shore, almost grateful for the bad weather. If they were in luck they could row clear around the island without being seen, land by the flagpole and make their way up to the estate.

It worked. Chilled through and exhausted, Annika was shaking all over by the time they pulled the boat ashore through the reeds and up on the lawn.

'Do you know your way around this place?' Bertil Strand asked.

She spent a few seconds gasping for air and tried to suppress a cough.

'My grandmother used to bring me here every year, on her birthday. We would take a walk in the park and then have a three-course meal in the dining room.'

'What fancy habits,' Bertil Strand said as he wriggled into his backpack.

'Gran was the matron of Harpsund. It's less than ten kilometres away, through the woods. She knew the former manager at Yxtaholm. The meal was a gift.'

Annika pointed to the right, into the mists.

'The terrace,' she said. 'That must be where they taped the shows.'

She waved to the left.

'The North Wing: suites and two-room apartments. Straight ahead there's the manor house, the dining rooms and the different lounges. Let's go.'

The manor house towered in front of them like a glistening palace, white and slick with rain. They approached the house from the direction of the north gable, its mansard roof blacker than the stormy sky. Halfway up the slope leading to the house, a bed of roses was on the verge of blooming. Three police cars were parked along the drive.

'What kind of a place is this, anyway?' Bertil Strand wondered as he unpacked a camera.

'It's an old country seat,' Annika replied, 'dating back to medieval times. Now it's a conference centre and a hotel owned by the Swedish Employers' Confederation. It was built in 1753.'

The photographer shot her a quick glance.

'Not 1754, then?'

'Check it out,' Annika said, pointing to the year written over the entrance. It struck her that she hadn't ever seen it closed before, the double doors had always been wide open and welcoming. Now the solid brown doors seemed massive, heavy and dismissive.

She pointed across the slope, past the South Wing.

'The first buildings were made of wood and they were located over there. The castle and the annexes have a core of brick that was fired in a furnace over there behind the trees. Want to see the crime scene first?'

Bertil Strand nodded.

They walked around the castle, progressing slowly and carefully from tree to tree through the park. They passed the terrace with its well-tended gravel paths, manicured lawns, hedges and flower beds. With a side-ways glance, Annika looked at the exterior of the building – so austere and whitewashed, tidy rows of windows. The hundreds of intricately mullioned windows in their lead frames reflected the silvery surface of Lake Yxtasjön.

'You can almost see people running around in crinolines,' the photographer said, shooting away.

They went down to the lake, passing the small labyrinth of hedges and walls and the jetty, and reaching the gable of the New Wing, the one that faced west.

Pointing, Annika said: 'There's the bus.'

Bertil Strand switched cameras and stretched out on the grass. Supporting the telephoto lens with his left hand, he triggered the winder motor with his right.

Annika stood behind him, observing the scene of the murder. The broadcast bus didn't really look like a bus, more like a gigantic Mack truck. It opened up lengthwise on one side, which created twice as much space. The entrance was facing them, and five metal steps led up to a narrow door to the left of the cab. She saw a policeman in uniform standing there, his back to them, talking to someone inside the control room.

'Do we need to move in closer?' she asked in a low voice.

Even though Annika didn't get on particularly well with the photographer, she respected his professional opinion.

'Not really. I got a few shots from the other side, from the boat. We could move down to the right and try to get a shot of the annexes in the background. Stall them if they try to get rid of us.'

Bertil Strand got up, slung his backpack over his left shoulder and walked along the beach. Scanning the white buildings, Annika followed him. The castle nestled at the top of the hill: the annexes, the walls, the lush trees – each one a different type – the contrast between the warm golden light emanating from the windows and the gloomy weather.

I can see why Oxenstierna wrote the words 'as beauteous as Eden' in his diary here after staying here, Annika thought.

'Got it,' the photographer said and turned to face the lake.

They went back the same way they'd come, Bertil Strand taking pictures along the way.

When they reached the top of the drive they walked straight into a police officer from Eskilstuna whom Annika had met before.

'What are you doing here?' the man said in a commanding voice.

Annika whipped out her press card and waved it in the officer's face.

'We're looking for a colleague of ours, Carl Wenner-gren. He was present at the taping of the shows yesterday and presumably he's still on the premises.'

'He's being interviewed,' the police officer replied and came up very close to Annika. 'Would you please leave the premises and join the other reporters?'

'Is he a suspect?'

'I am not at liberty to disclose information of that nature at the present time.'

The policeman prodded her.

'Watch it,' Annika exclaimed sharply. 'You can't just detain journalists for questioning. If the police have detained or arrested a reporter working for one of

Sweden's major newspapers, you are required to report this fact to his employer.'

This wasn't true, but the officer didn't know that for sure.

'I honestly don't know,' he said. 'I have no idea.'

'How many people have been interviewed?'

'Everyone who stayed here last night.'

'How many people would that be?'

'A dozen. And another associate of yours is here too – that older woman who writes a column.'

Annika gaped.

'Barbara Hanson? What's she doing here?'

Leaning in close, the policeman lowered his voice.

'There haven't been any arrests, at any rate,' he said. 'I would have been told.'

'Has the staff here at the castle been interviewed too?'

'Not at the present time. None of them were here last night.'

'Anything else?' Annika hurried to ask.

A man in a raincoat and tall boots was heading in their direction, unsettling the policeman.

'You've got to go,' he said, taking her arm and turning her away from the castle.

They walked slowly towards the bridge, back to where the other journalists were waiting. Annika pulled out her cellphone and called Spike.

The news editor appeared to be eating at his desk. She could hear him chomping away and trying to talk in between bites.

'What does Wennergren have to say?'

'I don't know, he's only allowed to talk to the police.'

'What the hell, have they arrested Wennergren? He's a journalist, for God's sake!'

There was a sound of something moist landing on the receiver, Annika grimaced.

'I didn't say he'd been arrested, he's only been detained for questioning. Anyhow, he's in good company. Barbara's here too.'

'Hanson? Damn it, Schyman ordered her to quit writing any more crap about Michelle Carlsson.'

Annika felt slightly stupid; she didn't know what Spike was referring to. To be honest, she hadn't really kept up to date during her maternity leave, particularly when it came to Barbara Hanson's nasty gossip columns. She changed the subject.

'A total of twelve people have been detained for questioning.'

'Who are they?'

The news editor had apparently finished his meal. He burped and lit a cigarette.

'Mostly people from the TV team, I suppose, but I'll find out.'

'We want their names and pictures,' Spike said, and began composing headlines. '"Survivors of the castle bloodbath. One of them is a murderer – and then they were twelve . . ." Great stuff!'

'Pure poetry,' Annika remarked and hung up.

'What do we do now?' Bertil Strand asked.

'Head for the parking lot,' Annika replied.

They crawled under the police tape at the end of the bridge and joined the rest of the media representatives.

'How did you get in?' one of their competitor's reporters asked, a tall blond man in a wet leather jacket.

'We hid in the grounds last night,' Annika said and started to head for the Stables.

She relaxed. Her body was starting to return to normal. The cramps in her arms had gone away and the knot in her stomach had relaxed. The water that had trickled down the back of her neck had been warmed up by her skin and she walked around a bit to limber up her stiff joints.

A policeman in uniform came out from the Stables and fiddled with the lock. He hurried off in the direction of the castle without acknowledging the presence of the journalists. Annika followed his progress and felt some more rain trickle down the back of her neck. The ground was spongy and waterlogged, creating puddles at her feet. She stared at the surface: brown, spotty gravel and debris. It smelled musty and sour.

Sweden, she thought. *What a lousy country it is.*

Shocked at her thought, she focused on the positive aspects.

Our ice-hockey team is good, at least when Peter Forsberg is on it, and the social welfare system is good, and the countryside. The countryside. Annika tried to make it out behind the pouring rain. All she could see were various smudgy shades of brown and grey. There were no mitigating circumstances on a day like this. She wiped her nose, forcing the sour smell to recede.

Several people had made it to the scene before it had been sealed off. In addition to the competition she noticed there were representatives from the national broadcasting service; the local radio station, Radio Sörmland; the regional news show *Öst-Nytt* and her old paper, *Katrineholms-Kuriren*. Their cars were all more or less sloppily parked up by the Garden Wing. She pulled out a pad and a pen and looked over the cars in the lot.

A golden Range Rover, the largest and most expensive SUV on the market. Annika jotted down the licence-plate number. She continued: a VW Polo, red, with a black soft top; a rusty Fiat Uno; a black sports car that looked pretty ritzy until she realized that it was a Chrysler; a green Volvo S40; a bronze-coloured Renault Clio with a 'Jesus Lives' sticker on the rear window; a blue BMW and a brown Saab 900 that had seen a good decade or two.

Her cellphone was working – well, thank you, Mr

Stenbeck – and she got hold of a guy at the Department of Motor Vehicles in Stockholm within a minute or two.

'Could you run a few licence-plate numbers for me?'

The giant SUV belonged to TV Plus; the German convertible was listed as belonging to Barbro Rosenberg, a resident of Solna; the Fiat belonged to a Hannah Persson, Katrineholm; the sporty Chrysler belonged to Build&Create in Jönköping; the Volvo was the property of a Karin Andersson, Hägersten; the Renault belonged to a Mariana von Berlitz, Stockholm; a Carl Wennergren owned the BMW; and the Saab belonged to a Stefan Axelsson, who lived in Tullinge.

Purposely disregarding the fact that hundreds of kronor would be racked up on her cellphone bill, Annika decided to check out the owners' phone numbers.

'There is no Barbro Rosenberg living in Solna, only a Bambi Rosenberg with an unlisted number,' the operator, who introduced herself as Linda, drawled.

The actress, Annika wrote on her pad.

Linda had no listing for a Hannah Persson in Katrineholm.

'Lots of people only have a cellphone without a subscription nowadays,' she told Annika. 'And then they wouldn't be on our records.'

Build&Create had scads of numbers and Annika wrote them all down. The first number belonged to Sebastian Follin, a manager. The name sounded vaguely familiar.

Karin Andersson Bellhorn had dumped her middle name in the phone book and was listed as a TV producer. Annika knew who she was: they had met a few times at the office where Anne Snapphane worked.

Mariana von Berlitz had an unlisted number, but Annika knew who she was too. Six years ago, they had shared a desk at *Kvällspressen* and had had a falling-out about who was expected to clean up. Mariana was Carl

Wennergren's girlfriend. And Stefan Axelsson was listed as a technical director.

Annika made a quick calculation. She was fairly sure of seven people, if the manager guy was the right one. And she knew that Anne Snapphane was there. That made eight. Anne had travelled by train, and Annika guessed that Barbara Hanson had done the same. Nine. Who were the others? The Range Rover belonged to TV Plus, so it must be a bigwig's company car, maybe it even belonged to the head honcho himself. Anne Snapphane only ever referred to him as the Highlander.

'Because he thinks he's immortal and invincible,' Anne had explained.

Who could the other two be?

Annika gazed out over the park. Soaking wet and hungry, a flock of sheep bleated on the opposite side of the avenue. Out on the island, a couple of police officers guarded the bridge. The broadcast bus was hidden by the buildings.

The bus, she thought. Somebody had to be in charge of the bus, some technical wiz. Eleven.

She couldn't figure out who number twelve could be. It was time to make contact.

She picked up her phone and dialled Anne Snapphane's number. It was busy.

'Annika, Annika Bengtzon . . . Annika Bengtzon!'

The voice came from the direction of the cars over by the Garden Wing. She turned, peering through the rain to make out who it was.

It was Pia Lakkinen, one of her former associates at *Katrineholms-Kuriren*. The reporter had just got out of her car. Pia pulled up the hood of her raincoat and hurried over to Annika.

'It's been ages!' she exclaimed. 'It's great to see you.'

They shook hands and Annika tried to smile. But she

didn't share Pia's enthusiasm. As a rule she disliked overly friendly approaches by fellow reporters when they were at the scene of a murder, and the fact that they had worked on the same paper at one time made things worse. Annika had quit her job in order to work for *Kvällspressen* in Stockholm, and many of her associates at *Katrineholms-Kuriren* had seen this as her passing judgement on their paper.

'Well, how are things at *KK*?' Annika asked.

Pia sighed theatrically.

'Oh, it's the same old grind. Lousy planning, no leadership, all that . . . and now all this rain too. Has it let up at all, you think?'

Annika searched for the right words, a platform to stand on, to no avail. The other reporter didn't notice Annika's uneasiness, she was adrift herself and rattled away nervously.

'And now this,' Pia said, 'right in the middle of the holidays. A murder, here in Flen. It's totally unreal – you never expect something like a killing to happen in a quiet place like this . . .'

Annika looked around her, searching for Bertil Strand, or anyone at all, just to escape from her former associate. Pia Lakkinen noticed the dismissal without accepting it.

'I guess this kind of stuff happens all the time in Stockholm,' she said.

'Actually, the most brutal murders tend to be committed in rural areas, in small towns and communities,' Annika countered coolly.

Her statement had the desired effect. Pia suddenly looked shocked and worried.

'Do you think they'll catch the killer soon?'

'Hard to say,' Annika replied. 'Twelve people are being interviewed up at the castle as we speak.'

Pia Lakkinen's eyes opened wide.

'Really?'

Despite the pouring rain, Annika stood up straighter: she was the one in the know. And *KK* wouldn't hit the shelves until Monday, so she could afford to be generous.

'Nearly all of them belong to the TV team involved with the show,' she continued. 'A few are guests or reporters on the job. I know who all of them are but one.'

The small-town reporter looked defeated.

'It's hard to get information when you don't know the police officers,' Pia said. 'I don't know what the Crime Squad from Stockholm is doing here.'

'It's an old tradition that Stockholm is prepared to assist police forces all over the country,' Annika explained. 'But these guys are from the Homicide Division. They're pros.'

Pia Lakkinen glanced over at the castle.

'As far as I can see, they just seem to be milling around.'

'They always start by searching the grounds,' Annika said, 'for shoeprints and stuff like that. They work from the outside in, you could say. Do you know what time the police were called in?'

The reporter shook her head.

'The news flash was sent at 9:41 a.m.'

'Yeah, but someone was already on the scene by then, probably regular beat cops from Katrineholm or Eskilstuna. They established the fact that there was a dead body in an OB bus parked behind the New Wing. By the time the news flash was dispatched they probably had sealed off the crime scene and isolated the witnesses already. I don't think Forensics or any detectives had made it here by then, but they were on their way.'

Pia Lakkinen looked impressed.

'Is she still in there?'

'Probably. They were working inside the bus a little

while ago when I was over there. I don't think they'll move her before the rain eases up. It would destroy too much evidence.'

'Have you been inside the bus?'

Her ex-colleague sounded sceptical.

Annika could hear the critical edge to her voice when she continued: 'A struggle would complicate matters. They have to investigate the bus and the body. They examine her clothing and see if the body has been moved to the bus or if the crime was committed there. When they're done and it's stopped raining, they'll move her.'

'Move her? Where to?'

'Someplace where there's a medical examiner. My guess is Karolinska: it's the closest hospital with facilities like that. A forensics team and a pathologist will remove her clothing. You know, to check for matter under her nails and stuff like that . . .'

'Yuck,' Pia said with a shudder, followed by an attempt at a laugh. 'Well, how's life treating you?'

Annika took a deep breath.

'I'm just fine. It's nice to be back on the beat. I've been away on maternity leave twice, so I'm getting back into the swing of things.'

'So, I guess the kids are spending Midsummer with their daddy.'

Annika smiled.

'Of course.'

'How are the kids taking it?'

Pia Lakkinen looked sympathetic, Annika kept smiling.

'They're fine. They're out at Gällnö Island visiting their grandparents. We were supposed to stay in a tent, but in this weather I hope they won't have to.'

The reporter regarded Annika searchingly for a few seconds.

'We? Were you supposed to be there too?'

'That's right,' Annika said, laughing briefly. 'But since it's pouring down, it doesn't bother me to be here.'

Pia's face reflected disappointment and distrust.

'Then you haven't split up?'

Annika's smile faded.

'Split up? Me and Thomas?'

Pia laughed.

'Well, you hear a lot of stuff, you know. Somebody said you'd split up, that he'd left you and the kids.'

Annika turned pale.

'Who said that?'

Pia Lakkinen backed away, an embarrassed smile on her face. Annika interpreted her expression as derision and maliciousness.

'You know how people talk in a small town like Katrineholm – I think it was a checker at the supermarket. But I have to run now and join my photographer, we're supposed to write about the Midsummer celebrations in Bie and then interview the prime minister out at Harpsund too, so you take care now and give my love—'

Annika turned away, the weight on her chest rotating a full 360 degrees. Her sense of loss returned and it mingled with the degradation she felt.

In her home town no one was impressed by her work, her career and ambitions. They felt sorry for her.

Gunnar Antonsson crawled out of bed in his stuffy room in the South Wing and glanced at his watch. No wonder he was hungry. He got his little French press coffee-maker, went over to the sink and rinsed out the old grounds. Then he filled it with fresh water that he then poured into the electric kettle. He dumped four scoops of coffee into the press. While the water hummed and whistled in the kettle, he looked out the window at the lacy crowns of the trees, the impenetrable greyness of the sky behind its cloak of rain.

When the kettle had boiled, he poured the hot water into the press, pushed down the filter and poured some of the resulting beverage into his tooth glass. He looked at himself in the mirror above the washbasin while he took a sip. The coffee was scalding so he put down the glass, causing it to clink against the porcelain. Rubbing his chin he felt the rough stubble there. He could use a shave.

Antonsson should have been on his way to Dalarna in the bus. They were supposed to broadcast a Midsummer special from the abandoned chalk mine, a huge opera concert including works by Wagner, Alfén and Beethoven. The Royal Philharmonic, directed by Uno Kamprad and featuring Scandinavian soloists.

He had looked forward to the concert, and not only because it would generate incredibly welcome revenue for his company. He was also a Wagner fan.

Michelle Carlsson liked opera music, he suddenly recalled. She would have enjoyed coming along to see the concert live.

The thought was strangely arousing. Unseeingly, Gunnar Antonsson looked again at his own reflection in the mirror. In his mind's eye he saw the white legs, the well-tended bush between Michelle's legs, the moisture that still glistened on the inside of her thighs. He felt aroused and then ashamed. What was wrong with him?

He hadn't slept a wink after 6:12 this morning. That was when he had put the key in the lock of Outside Broadcast Bus No. Five, opened the door and encountered that odd smell. He'd never smelled anything quite like it before in his whole life. Sweet, sour and faecal at the same time. The absurdity of the situation struck him only after he had opened the door and the unbearable smell had enveloped him.

'Why are you guys here?' he had asked the crowd behind him, their faces displaying various degrees of inebriation and haggardness.

'We've got to talk to Michelle,' the scrawny one had said, the manager guy. He had tried to push past him, but Gunnar had blocked the way.

'The sets have been struck and the equipment has been stowed. No one has any business being here.'

'But Michelle's in there,' Anne Snapphane had said, and when Anne Snapphane spoke, he listened.

'She can't be. I just unlocked the door.'

Dazed and half-asleep, Gunnar had stood there in his slacks, unbuttoned shirt and shoes with no socks and realized that the others hadn't even been to bed. They'd woken him up so that he would unlock the bus. That was when he'd got angry.

'What's going on?' he had demanded. 'What kind of monkey business is this?'

He had put his keys back in the left-hand pocket of his slacks and felt the familiar weight near his groin, sensing the jagged points of metal through the lining. Then he had stepped into the control room, blinking in the dim light. A few monitors faintly lit the narrow path leading to the production room, the rack on the right, the electrical control unit; he had popped in and checked out the CCDs, opened the door to 'Technology Row', looked into the video room and gazed at the tape recorders, beta, digital, and VHS, and all the profilers. Everything was packed and secured.

He had stepped out into the hallway again, and Anne Snapphane had been in the doorway, the others crowding behind her.

'Please, Gunnar darling, it's raining cats and dogs,' she had said, and he always had a hard time resisting Anne.

He had muttered something that she interpreted as an invitation, so she had walked in, the crowd following in her wake.

The lighting inside the production area was patchy and weak and emanated from the tiny lights on the monitors and controls. The smell was pungent and the soft grey shades of the walls swallowed up the shadows. Gunnar blinked a few times before he caught sight of Michelle Carlsson.

She had been lying in the narrow space between the front and rear production consoles, right in front of the seat used by the technical director. The first thing he had noticed was that she was nude from the waist down. The second thing was that her bare legs were bent at an inexplicably unnatural angle. The third thing was that she was way too still. Then it had hit him. Even before he saw what was left of her head, he had known. Gunnar went hunting, so he knew what death looked like. Even so, this wasn't the same – it was an utterly foreign sensation, the smell so overwhelmingly different. A wave of sorrow and tenderness had crashed over him. He had heard himself gasp and he had fallen to his knees.

Coming up behind Gunnar so that he hadn't been able to stop her, Anne Snapphane had asked: 'What is it?' Then she had turned on the overhead lamps, bathing the entire place in light. White and bloodless, Michelle's legs had stood out sharply against the dark blue carpeting. The revolver by her foot was large and clumsy-looking. A scream echoed in his mind.

Gunnar Antonsson shut his eyes, not wanting to remember anything more. Quickly turning away from the mirror, he shook off the memory of the smell and walked over to the window. The rain kept coming down just as hard, pattering loudly against the windowsill and making a sound like an engine running. He looked out the window and saw two policemen walking around the bus in a seemingly aimless and irrational manner.

Suddenly he was fed up.

He had put on his poplin jacket, retied his shoes, smoothed his hair and left the room.

The policeman looked up in surprise when he approached them, standing around as if the bus was theirs, not his.

'How long is this going to go on?' Gunnar asked.

'What?' a young man in uniform and with peach fuzz on his cheeks replied.

'When do I get my bus back?'

'I'll go get the lieutenant,' the fuzzy one said.

The other officer stood a short distance away, a watchful expression on his face.

'I was supposed to have left at eight this morning,' Gunnar Antonsson said through the rain.

The policeman turned away.

Then the first officer returned with a man dressed in street clothes.

'Let's go inside the bus,' the new arrival said. He was dressed in a leather jacket and a colourful shirt and shook Gunnar's hand like a regular guy. The words left Gunnar speechless and teary-eyed. Feeling grateful and relieved, he mounted the five metal steps and walked in through the door, out of the rain, only to stop short. The passage leading into the production area was starkly lit and packed with people. At least, that was how it seemed to him at first.

'As you can tell, we're going over the place with a fine-tooth comb, looking for evidence,' the man in the colourful clothes explained.

Gunnar nodded curtly and asked in an unsteady voice:

'Is she still in there?'

Mr Colourful pulled a pack of cigarettes out of the breast pocket of his shirt, fingered it and looked at Gunnar.

'Yeah,' he said. 'She's still there. Exactly as you found her.'

Gunnar Antonsson fixed his gaze on the floor.

'It must have been awful,' the policeman said. 'And in your bus and everything.'

'It's not my bus,' Gunnar said, suddenly belligerent. 'It belongs to the company. And I liked her. I was one of the few people here who did.'

The policeman started to pull out a cigarette, then stopped and put the whole pack back into his pocket.

'What do you mean?'

Hearing his voice starting to shake, Gunnar Antonsson replied: 'She was nice. She always had something nice to say. The others were just jealous.'

Then he could no longer stop himself and tears began to roll down his cheeks. Embarrassed, he swiped them away with the back of his left hand.

'What's your occupation?' the officer asked.

Gunnar took a deep breath and tried to pull himself together.

'I'm a TOM, a Technical Operations Manager, and this is Outside Broadcast Bus No. Five. I was in charge of the technical operations, and the OB vehicle, while all the TV Plus summer specials were taped.'

'This is a marvel on wheels,' Mr Colourful said.

Gunnar Antonsson cleared his throat.

'A vehicle this size can be used in lots of different ways, from larger sports events like World Cup soccer or hockey, to spectacular performances and entertainment programmes. Last year, we taped the Eurovision Song Contest and the MTV Music Awards in the Globe Arena in this bus.'

The lieutenant whistled.

'This was the last thing you needed,' he said. 'And you were the person who unlocked the door?'

Gunnar nodded.

'They woke me up not long after six a.m.'

'Who did?'

He thought for a while.

'A crowd of people,' he said. 'Anne Snapphane, the manager guy, Karin, the producer and a few others, I think. Is it important?'

'Yes, it is,' the policeman said. 'But it can wait until we can conduct a real interview up at the house. For now, just give me a brief account of what happened.'

Gunnar Antonsson took a deep breath.

'I unlocked the door, and there she was. Everybody reacted in a different way: the manager howled, he screamed like an old lady. Karin just walked out, Annika Snapphane bent down and touched Michelle's legs and then sat there staring, I had to drag her away. Mariana and that other girl couldn't have seen much, I got them out of there right away.'

'So you took care of things?'

Gunnar stared at the carpet.

'I went in and called Emergency Services at 6:22, told them a death had occurred in the broadcast bus.'

'But you didn't tell them it was a murder?'

'I didn't want to interfere, that would be up to the police to determine.'

One of the policemen in the bus excused himself, pushed past them, walked out in the rain and went down the steps. Gunnar Antonsson noticed that he was carrying small plastic bags containing some indeterminate matter.

'What did you do after that?' Mr Colourful asked.

'I made myself a cup of coffee in my room, using the French press I brought with me. Then I sat and waited for the police. It took a while, I waited until 8:16.'

'The police on duty were out in Vingåker, investigating a rape case,' the lieutenant said. 'Since no one knew that a murder had been committed, this case wasn't high on the list of priorities.'

Gunnar said nothing.

'What did the others do?' the policeman asked.

Gunnar swallowed and hesitated.

'I mind my own business.'

'So you have no idea?'

The forensics team pushed past then, empty-handed this time. Gunnar Antonsson was fed up with the conversation and with the entire situation.

'They sat in the lounge and talked. Some of them cried. How long is this going to take? I was supposed to be on my way hours ago.'

'I'm afraid this will take a while.'

'How long?'

'A few weeks.'

Gunnar did a double take.

'A few *weeks*? Are you out of your minds?'

The lieutenant was calm and collected.

'We will be impounding the bus,' he said, pulling out his cigarettes again. 'I'd say that it will be in our garage, on standby, for at least a fortnight.'

Indignation made Gunnar Antonsson's ears grow hot and red.

'The whole financial future of the company is riding on this unit,' he said in a somewhat strangled voice. 'Do you realize how much it costs us every single hour it's not on the road? We've got to be in Denmark on Monday – we're involved in a big trade fair. How are we supposed to cover it now?'

The brightly dressed man sighed sympathetically and put a cigarette in his mouth.

'Well,' he said, 'talk to the DA. She's the person in charge of impounds.'

Gunnar Antonsson shot one last glance over his shoulder in the direction of the production area, but all he could see were the backs of officers in there. Snidely, he remarked:

'How can you find any evidence with all these people all over the place?'

'That wouldn't have been a problem,' the lieutenant shot back, 'if people hadn't been running in and out of here all night.'

He wasn't the kind to back down, this officer.

'Nobody's been running around in this bus,' Gunnar Antonsson stated with absolute conviction. 'I struck the sets myself, I kept watch while they loaded the stuff in and secured it, and I locked up when we were done.'

Nodding, the lieutenant mulled this over.

'Then there's only one thing that bothers me,' he said. 'How did Michelle get in? Not to mention the killer.'

Gunnar Antonsson stared, the shock of awareness causing his blood to drain instantly into his feet.

'You can't possibly believe that I . . .?'

'If you want to talk about beliefs, go see a clergyman,' the policeman replied. 'Are there any more keys to the bus?'

Dumbstruck, Gunnar merely shook his head.

'So, what's the explanation? How did they get inside a locked control room? And how did the killer lock up afterwards?'

The Technical Operations Manager jammed his hands in his pockets, roughly and jerkily, fishing around for the familiar weight of the key chain in his left pocket without finding it and then remembering that the police had it.

A split second later he knew exactly what had happened. He studied the policeman's face, imagining that he saw arrogance and malice there.

'Well, I guess you have something to think about, don't you?' he said and walked back out into the rain.

Nearly all the other passengers got off at either Grinda, Boda or Puttisholmen. The rest were headed for Gällnö. Thomas thought he recognized two groups of people, but he avoided their gaze.

By the time he could see Söderby Farm through the mists and the rain, he had started to feel like he was coming down with a cold. The scene unfolding behind the sheets of rain was so tremendously familiar. It had been almost a year since he'd been here, yet he was familiar with every tuft of grass along the shore, every slant to every house and every rusty roofing plate in sight. The barn on the left-hand side of the dock still needed a paint job, the rust on the boathouse to the right was worse than ever. The colour scheme was a greyish greeny-brown, the way it always was when it rained. The only contrast was the standard-issue blue road sign. He took a deep breath and was filled with expectancy and nostalgia.

This trip was going to be fun after all.

Thomas woke the children. They were cold and upset. He felt a stab of guilt – Annika always made sure the kids were warm and dry. He gathered the two of them in his arms and carried them down to the cafeteria, letting them wait indoors until he had taken their things ashore.

By the time they finally started heading down the dirt road leading to the village, the rain had let up. The drops turned to droplets and remained suspended mid-air, shimmering and transparent. He had bribed the kids with ice cream, which meant that he would have to change every last item of clothing they had on, from head to toe, when they arrived. But he didn't care. He was rapidly approaching the end of his tether. The relief he felt when his parents' large red wooden house next door to the store came into view was enormous.

'Thomas. Oh, Thomas, we're so glad to see you. Why are you so late?'

His mother hurried awkwardly down the steps, her sweater draped over her shoulders and fastened with the top button.

'Now watch that hip of yours, be careful, don't fall, Mother . . .'

His mother clasped his face with both hands, kissing first one cheek and then the other.

'You're so cold.'

Then she looked around.

'Where's Annika?'

Thomas tried to compose himself, compressing his lips briefly before he answered her.

'She had to go to work.'

His mother's dismay was genuine and monumental.

'Work? Today? Well, I never . . .!'

'I'm sorry we're late, but we had to take the Norrskär, and I had so much stuff to lug along . . .'

Suddenly, he felt wretchedly abandoned. Damn Annika.

'Oh, dear! Have you dragged all that all this way? Come, let me give you a hand . . .'

Ellen's ice cream had melted. It fell on the garden path and the girl howled and reached for it.

'I didn't manage to bring the tent,' Thomas said, 'but I've got to change the kids. Is there anywhere we can stay?'

'Now that you're alone, you can stay in the house with us.'

She smiled and patted his arm, a well-organized paragon of kindness and consideration.

'Leave those things out here, Dad and Holger will bring them in. You don't have to lug all that stuff. Come and have a nice hot cup of coffee and I'll take care of the kids. Kalle, Ellen, come to Granny. My, you're dirty, honey-bun, you need a bath.'

Thomas took a long shower while his mother changed his kids' clothes and treated them to Danish pastries with custard filling. The heat spread throughout his limbs, making him feel at ease. Everything would be all right, they would take care of him here. When the kids had gone to sleep he could knock back a few with his brother, maybe go fishing at dawn.

Feeling confident, he went into the living room, wrapped in his father's king-sized burgundy robe. The spirit of summer embraced him, the light from the sea filtered in through the large handmade glass windows and the smooth wooden floors caressed his bare feet.

'Well, look who we have here. If it isn't the handsome man from Stockholm,' his aunt Märta exclaimed as she slowly and deliberately got up from the sofa to greet him.

She too kissed him on the cheek and patted his arm.

'Doris told us about your trip out here. I'm impressed that you made it. All by yourself, with the children and all. I do declare, modern men are fantastic. Taking care of their families and packing and all . . .'

Slightly embarrassed, Thomas laughed and dried his ear with the towel.

'Annika did the packing,' he admitted. 'I guess my brother's already made it out here?'

Aunt Märta's smile expressed sympathy.

'Poor Thomas,' she said. 'Your wife deserts her family in the middle of the holidays. Can't you keep her in line?'

Rage welled up inside him. His body went rigid and he jerked his arm away from her grip.

'She's on call this weekend, we knew this could happen.'

As soon as he uttered the words, he knew it was the truth, that he had just blocked it out earlier.

'Writing about violence and crime, is that really a suitable job for a woman?' Aunt Märta demanded.

He didn't reply and started heading for the kitchen.

'Märta, please,' his mother said in a disapproving voice. 'These days women can do anything a man can do.'

She turned to Thomas and said:

'Holger arrived this morning.'

'Daddy,' Ellen crowed while kicking her legs and reaching her arms out to him. 'Da-da-daddy!'

Thomas removed his daughter from his mother's lap and swung her up to ride on his shoulders. Then he set off on a wild gallop around the whole floor while she gurgled with delight above him and Kalle clung to his robe and squealed: 'Me too, Daddy, me too!'

'Playtime's over, kiddies!' Holger informed them as he entered the house. 'It's time we had ourselves a pick-me-up!'

Anne Snapphane sat bolt upright in bed, woken by a sound that she couldn't quite recall. Her heart hammered away in her chest, her hair was glued to her temples and her bare feet were cold. For a few seconds she was suspended in a void. Then it all came crashing down on top of her and she fell back against the pillows, groaning. The room had closed in on her even more. Under the down duvet it was hot and damp. Apart from socks and shoes, she was fully dressed and her clothes smelled.

I don't want to, she thought. *No more . . .*

Her hangover had receded and had been replaced by another kind of malaise. Maybe it was shock or fear. She listened to the sounds of the old building – the faint creaking of the beams, the rain as it beat against plaster and tiling – and sensed the presence of the others nearby. Curling up on her side, she concentrated on directions and distances.

Upstairs Gunnar Antonsson paced slowly back and forth. In the room on the right, Bambi Rosenberg never stopped crying. The sound rose and fell, and Anne Snapphane turned over to shut the noise out. In the room on her left she could hear the radio muffling Mariana's murmured words. Anne understood what was going on – Mariana had turned on the clock radio to drown out the sound of cellphone calls. Pretty transparent.

She kicked off the sweaty covers, pushing them to the foot of the bed, then burrowed her feet into the damp mass while she stared at the ceiling. Restlessness churned inside her. This waiting was sheer torture.

Anne closed her eyes and breathed shallowly, listening to the chirpy backdrop of sound on the other side of the thin wall: two radio-show hosts were squabbling good-naturedly. The music in the background faded and was replaced by jingles followed by the news.

The flat tones of the woman in the news studio signalled how nervous she was about filling in on a holiday when most people had the day off. Anne heard about a terrorist attack on a bus in central Jerusalem without really listening and the spot gave way to a statement that the government was expected to finalize this autumn. The next item was Michelle's death. Anne Snapphane concentrated on this, but the announcement was so short, matter-of-fact and without speculation that it almost seemed indifferent. Michelle Carlsson, the journalist, had been found dead in a control room after participating in a TV programme. The police suspected foul play. Investigations had not yet been concluded, and the police spokesman had declined to make further comments at this time.

The newswoman paused for a split second before moving on to the story of two men who had been reported missing after their boat was found drifting keel up on Lake Vänern. Then came a report of a flood in Poland, and a weather forecast. The cold front would continue to move south and would be followed by new low-pressure zones coming in from the Atlantic. The province of Svealand could expect a steady downpour of rain and some local thunderstorms during the day. These would clear up, beginning in the northernmost regions, this evening.

Suddenly, Mariana turned down the volume, and the weather conditions of Norrland disappeared somewhere halfway into the wall.

Anne Snapphane felt the wallpaper close in on her, as though it was pressing up against her lungs. She struggled to get up, walked around the bed to reach the window and looked out over the bridge and the small canal. The room needed airing, so she opened the window, gasping when the wind and the rain threatened to tear the window frame out of her hand. Alarmed, she shut it again, latching it with trembling fingers. She rested for a minute or so, sitting on the desk with her back to the rain. Then she went over to the door, sure that it would be locked.

It wasn't. Opening it a crack, she heard the murmur of voices in the lounge. The hall was dark and empty, muffled sounds coming from all different directions. The light from her window fell on the door on the opposite side of the hallway, Karin Bellhorn's room.

It was a split-second decision. Without making a sound, Anne closed her door, tiptoed a couple of steps in the darkness over to Karin's door and opened it.

The producer was seated at the desk in her room, and she looked up in surprise, her eyes swollen and lips cracked, as Anne Snapphane entered the room and closed the door behind her.

'What on—?'

She got halfway out of her chair. Anne put her finger to her lips.

'I've got to talk,' she whispered, 'or I'll go nuts.'

'We're not allowed to talk,' Karin whispered back to her. 'Go back to your room.'

Anne Snapphane's lower lip began to tremble and so did her hands and arms.

'Please,' she said, 'I can't take it any more.'

The producer came up to her, studied her briefly, then took her hands.

'You poor thing,' she said softly. 'Sit down for a while.'

Anne sunk down on the bed, buried her face in her hands and cried. The tears felt softer now, not as sharp and piercing as in her lonely room.

'Shit,' Anne sobbed. 'This is so fucking awful! How could it happen?'

Karin Bellhorn sighed, a deep and ragged sound that bordered on a sob.

'I don't know,' she said. 'I can't make sense of it.'

'Did you see her?'

Anne looked up at the producer. Karin smoothed her grey hair and averted her gaze.

'I saw enough.'

'She was still warm, but it was hot inside the bus. Did you see the gun?'

The older woman swallowed and nodded.

'Nothing this awful has ever happened to me before,' Anne Snapphane continued, the words tumbling like the waters of a brook in springtime. 'I've never even seen a dead person before, and there she was, somebody I've worked with for nearly four years. A person who had been alive a few hours earlier . . . murdered. Shot! Did you see the grey stuff? Did you see the mess on the wall and on the monitors? That was her brain. Christ, that was her fucking brain coating the TV screens. It's disgusting – her memories, her childhood, her feelings, everything she was – all that was left was a sticky, yucky, blown-away mess . . .'

Anne bowed her head and cried some more, louder this time, the sobs almost like screams. Karin placed a warm, dry hand on the back of her neck.

'Anne,' she whispered urgently. 'Please, Anne, you aren't supposed to be here, the police would flip if they found you here, please pull yourself together.'

With tears streaming down her cheeks, nose and chin, Anne Snapphane took a few deep breaths.

'Shit,' she whispered, 'Karin, it's so fucking awful . . .'

'I know,' the producer said and put her arms around her. 'I know . . .'

They remained like that for quite some time, the older woman holding the younger one.

'I'm so ashamed,' Anne whispered as soon as she had calmed down. Karin released her. 'I was always so nasty to Michelle.'

'No, that's not true,' Karin said. 'You weren't nasty.'

'Yes, I was,' Anne Snapphane said, wiping her nose with her sleeve. 'I couldn't stand her, all because she was prettier than me, and better.'

'That's not true,' the producer protested. 'You were always a much better journalist than Michelle was.'

'I mean better on TV,' Anne said. 'She had more screen presence than I ever had. You do know that both of us were up for the *The Women's Sofa* gig, don't you? She got it. And I never forgave her for that.'

'So she got rich and famous at your expense?'

Anne hesitated and then nodded.

'Something like that.'

Karin Bellhorn smiled wryly.

'Well, see how much good it did her.'

Anne looked up at her with a shocked expression on her face. She met the producer's gaze and began to giggle hysterically.

'I certainly prefer being me today,' she said.

The two women sat in silence on the bed. Anne Snapphane felt a melancholy calm start to radiate throughout her chest.

'That was some night,' she said after a while.

Karin Bellhorn sighed.

'Not to mention the taping session; I've never seen such chaos and I've been around the track a few times. Those anarchists were just too much – who dug them up?'

'Mariana, I think. And did you hear her talking to Bambi Rosenberg about nude pictures at two a.m. in the lounge? What a racket they made!'

'Then Highlander showed up and had a fight with Michelle.'

'The boss himself? What did they fight about?' Anne Snapphane asked.

'He fired her.'

'You're kidding me!'

Karin put her finger to her lips.

'Careful . . . I saw them, he went up to her as soon as we had wrapped. Michelle wasn't receptive, you know how hyper she gets after a show, and particularly after a special like this.'

'Highlander's nuts,' Anne Snapphane said.

'He certainly knew exactly what he was going to say. But his timing wasn't very appropriate.'

'Well, what *did* he say?'

'That she was too old.'

'Too old? She just turned thirty-four last Monday.'

Karin smiled with a trace of bitterness.

'First it didn't register: Michelle was still pretty buzzed after the show. Then I was afraid she was going to pass out – her face went all white and she was chewing her tongue. And suddenly she went berserk, yelling that Highlander was a pathetic fool who made his way up by sucking dicks, cleaning toilets and making coffee for the big shots in London.'

'There is something to that,' Anne interjected.

'And that she wouldn't accept orders from a conceited, power-crazed moron who didn't have brains or balls. And she went on and on like that.'

Anne Snapphane giggled.

'It was almost funny,' the producer conceded.

'Highlander felt that Michelle should be grateful that he had taken the trouble to talk to her in person. He wasn't obligated to do anything beyond sending her written notice. Apparently, that's in her contract. Naturally, she'd be paid for the duration of her contract, a little more than one and a half years, as long as she respected the terms of the quarantine clause.'

'In other words, even though she had been fired, she wouldn't be able to work for anyone else?'

'Exactly,' Karin Bellhorn replied. 'If she hosted some other network's shows, they could sue her for breach of contract. And that's not all. After the showdown at the Stables, Michelle kicked out her manager. She called him a leech, a millstone, and a lot of other nice things.'

'Did Follin get fired too?' Anne asked.

Karin Bellhorn lit a cigarette and fingered her lower lip.

'I don't know,' she said. 'Right now I don't know one damn thing for certain.'

Suddenly Anne felt like crying again.

'What *are* we involved in?' she whispered.

They sat for a while in silence. Sounds seeped in through the walls: Sebastian Follin was running water in the sink upstairs. To the right, Highlander's radio blared. To the left, Barbara Hanson coughed.

'Listen,' Anne Snapphane said. 'Who do you think did it?'

Karin gave this some thought, the tip of her tongue in the corner of her mouth.

'I don't know,' she said. 'Who do *you* think it was?'

'Do you think it was one of us?'

Anne's whisper was barely audible.

The producer's gaze drifted off towards the window, her eyes glazed and vacant-looking.

'The technical staff left as soon as the bus was packed,' she said. 'Gunnar was the only one left. Apart from us.'

'Could someone else have come, an outsider?'

'In the middle of the night?'

Turning with an unfathomable expression in her eyes, Karin looked at Anne and shook her head.

'No,' Anne whispered. 'So it was one of us.'

The sound of Anne Snapphane gulping resonated in the room.

'I agree, so be careful about who you talk to,' Karin said, 'and think of what you say.'

Anne nodded, her eyes wide with renewed fear.

'Did you see anything?' Karin asked. 'Anything strange?'

Suspicion dropped like a stage curtain. Anne Snapphane felt doubt take root, felt how it drove a wedge into the foundation of trust. Her emotions were reflected in her eyes, and she felt how she distanced herself and grew watchful.

'No,' she whispered. 'Did you?'

Karin shook her head and Anne saw her own emotions reflected in the producer's eyes.

'I'd better be going,' Anne said, and got up to leave with a brand-new sorrow in her heart.

They wouldn't be confiding in each other again.

Editor-in-chief Torstensson didn't call in. A restless Anders Schyman sat in his glass cubicle at one end of the newsroom and felt irritation well up inside him. There was a pile of documents on his desk: legal action was being taken against *Kvällspressen* and the executive editor responsible for the publication. The charges ranged from defamation of character to libel.

And the person legally responsible for the publication was Torstensson. As executive editor he had the final say in controversial issues. It didn't matter what the rest of the newsroom team felt, Torstensson called the shots. After a great deal of pussyfooting around, Schyman had made sure that he, the managing editor, was registered at the Patent and Registration Office as Torstensson's deputy. This meant that Torstensson could delegate decisions to him, but only if the editor-in-chief expressly wished to do so. Whenever this occurred, the information listed in the corporate heading would be changed. This was simply a cosmetic change, but one that gave Schyman in-house clout. It didn't happen very often.

Anders Schyman tore his hair. The situation was unpleasant. Michelle Carlsson had caused *Kvällspressen* a lot of trouble for a long time, and if truth be told, *Kvällspressen* had caused Michelle Carlsson trouble too. Some of his associates at the paper had decided that the TV personality didn't cut the mustard, something they delighted in telling their readers. For two years running, she had topped the 'Worst-dressed women of the year' list. She had been called 'The most over-hyped Swede of the millennium', a 'TV bimbo' and other even less flattering names that Schyman couldn't immediately recall. They jeered at her shows and lampooned her in the culture section of the paper, they gave her scathing reviews in the TV column and poked fun at her when she was given *Kvällspressen*'s People's Choice award. Her landslide victory caused the paper to revise the rules for the award. The readers were no longer allowed to vote for anyone they wanted. A jury at the paper, led by Barbara Hanson, nominated four TV personalities that the readers could choose between. The last time around, Anders Schyman had never even heard of two of them.

As long as the criticism and the antics had remained at that level, Michelle Carlsson and her representatives had kept their distance.

She started suing them when the articles about her alleged shell-company dealings were published. As far as Anders Schyman could tell, the paper was going to go down for this.

The second time Michelle sued them was when they published nude photos of her and a man who was claimed to be an escaped convict. Michelle Carlsson was offended by the inference that she would have anything to do with a criminal. And to make matters worse, the paper had got the man's identity all wrong – he was a Norwegian film star, and he decided to sue the paper as well. The film star was a married man with children and he claimed that the nude pictures had violated his privacy. The paper's strategy in the two different cases was somewhat schizoid.

With regard to Michelle, they claimed that her companion was clearly identifiable as being the Norwegian film star, which meant there was no reason for her to take offence even if the paper had happened to infer that the man was a criminal.

With regard to the film star, the paper claimed that the photos did not depict the star at all, that the man in question was alleged to be an escaped convict, a criminal, which meant that they could not possibly constitute a violation of the film star's privacy in any way.

Anders Schyman sighed and rubbed his forehead.

The third court case, which was almost settled, concerned Michelle Carlsson's mother. A reporter had found the TV star's lush of a mother at a hotel in Riga where she, with limited success, supported herself as a prostitute.

'These days there are too many young and good-looking girls in the business,' the woman complained on the front page of *Kvällspressen*.

She had also been allowed to beg Michelle to get in touch with her, since she missed her little girl so much and their falling-out had pained her to such an extent that she had succumbed to drink and drugs. Schyman's cheeks burned with shame when he remembered the headline: 'Help me, my beloved Michelle!'

The fact that Michelle Carlsson's mother had abandoned her husband and daughter when the girl was three was never mentioned. The only reason they had been able to reach a settlement at all was because of Michelle's reluctance to discuss her mother publicly. Naturally, this was an expedient solution for the paper, and one that was cheaper than paying a lawyer for a protracted court case. The reason they hadn't settled the other cases out of court in a similar way was because Michelle Carlsson had refused to do so, and now it was too late.

The managing editor stacked the summonses. The poor air quality of the room had left him feeling sluggish. He knew he would have to remain at his desk for hours to come. Every single word about Michelle Carlsson destined for tomorrow's paper would have to be closely reviewed by him. The last thing they needed was another court case, and this time the charge would be the defamation of a deceased person's character.

The mechanism groaning under his weight, Schyman leaned back in his chair. His wife was celebrating Midsummer with friends out in Vikinghill. He closed his eyes and pictured her there, seated on a patio under an awning, with flowers in her hair, singing and indulging in a schnapps or two.

Why the hell did he take this lousy job?

Because he was tired of superficial pursuits. Frustrated by the limited financial and expressive scope provided by Sweden's public service television network back when he produced and hosted shows that reviewed society in a critical manner. He was fed up with the celebrity that came with the job. When he accepted the position as managing editor at *Kvällspressen*, he was shooting for something bigger, something more hands-on, responsible and well conceived. Many times he'd wondered if he'd made the right choice.

The show he had walked out on was doing just fine. Mehmed was a better host than he'd ever been.

Schyman got up and restlessly paced the floor.

Well, he had a fire to put out, so he'd better get down to it.

The rain was driving Annika crazy. Bertil Strand was a regular poster boy for geniality as he sat in the car belonging to the competition, laughing and being amusing. She would never stoop that low just to be warm and dry. Instead, she looked around, searching for some kind of shelter or a roof, her gaze lingering on the greenhouse beyond the parking lot. Did they usually lock those things?

The door didn't even have a lock. Sliding a glass panel to one side, Annika entered a lush green world. The heat and the smells were so intense that her head began to swim. It struck her that she hadn't eaten all day. Dizzy and soaked, she sat down on a gravel path between two rows of tomato plants in bloom, leaned back against a big wooden planter and gazed out through the glass wall. She had a pretty good view of the parking lot and the bridge leading up to the castle.

The words she'd tried to push away all day came back to haunt her. Thomas's voice, choked with rage:

'Well, wasn't this convenient!' 'A fine mother you are!' 'I'm never going to forgive you for this. Damn you!'

Slowly, she exhaled until every last particle of air had left her lungs.

'I'm sorry,' she whispered. 'I'm so sorry, but you knew I might have to . . .'

For a few minutes Annika succumbed to guilt and self-pity. Both emotions struggled to gain the upper hand and left her feeling drained and miserable. Conjuring up the faces of her children, she felt strangely unaffected by the thought of them just then.

She got up, found a tap and drank until her thirst was quenched. Then she browsed through rows of arugula and sugar-snap peas, trying to pick some without leaving any noticeable gaps.

I'll treat Thomas to dinner here, and I'll leave a big tip, she promised herself to make up for her pilfering ways.

Somewhat less dizzy now, she returned to her seat by the planter, hesitated a moment and then called Anne Snapphane. Right before the answering service kicked in, her friend picked up.

'You sound blue,' Annika said.

'I wonder why,' Anne whispered and turned up the volume of a radio in the background.

'How are you doing?'

Anne Snapphane's voice was feeble and flat.

'I'm having a hard time breathing,' Anne replied. 'Do you think you can develop asthma overnight?'

Not wanting to encourage her friend's hypochondriac tendencies, Annika said nothing.

'It's so awful,' Anne went on. 'I see her in front of me all the time, I feel like I'm to blame.'

'Well, you can't possibly—'

'Don't you tell me what I can or cannot feel. You're not the one shut in here like a goddam killer.'

Anne started to sob into the phone and Annika wished she hadn't called her.

'Do you want me to hang up?' she asked gently. 'Do you want to be left alone?'

'No!' Anne whispered back. 'Please don't hang up.'

They sat in silence for quite a while, listening to the rattling base tones of the clock radio.

'Have they told you when you'll be able to go home?' Annika asked.

'No. All they've said was that they'll let us leave as soon as they've finished questioning us. By the way, Q is here. He interrogated me. What a mean son of a bitch.'

'Have you talked to Mehmed?' Annika asked.

Her friend sighed.

'No. Could you give him a call and tell him I've been detained here? God, I miss Miranda.'

'I bet she's doing just fine,' Annika said in her most soothing voice as she kept watch over the parking lot. 'Are you allowed to use your cellphone?'

'Not really. Are you out there somewhere?'

'It's pissing down, so I hid in a greenhouse. How about it, do you dare talk to me?'

Annika heard her friend moving around, the sound of her footfalls and how she fiddled with the radio.

'For a while, I guess.'

'Could you help me out?' Annika asked. 'I've been

through the cars in the parking lot and think I know who
most of your companions are. Could you tell me if I'm
right?'

Anne Snapphane gave a tired laugh.

'Always the journalist. So what do you want to know?'

'Highlander, is he there?'

'Roger.'

'Mariana von Berlitz and Carl Wennergren?'

'Absolutely.'

'Is Mariana a born-again Christian?'

'When it suits her. How did you know that?'

'She has a "Jesus Lives" bumper sticker. And then
there's a girl from Katrineholm called Hannah Persson.'

'That's correct.'

'What's she doing here?'

Anne Snapphane took a deep breath. When she spoke
again her voice contained at least a modicum of life, as if
it was invigorating to talk about something humdrum.

'She's the secretary of the Katrineholm NP, the neo-
Nazis. She was on the panel of the final show along with
two anarchists, and they really kicked up a fuss. The
anarchists attacked Michelle and this girl and left the Nazi
with a bloody nose. Me and one of the sound technicians
had to break up the fight. My chin got scratched.'

'Why did she stay on after you wrapped?'

'Free booze. No one had the energy to get rid of her.
Anyone else?'

'Barbara Hanson?'

'That bitch? Sure, she was here to sneer at Michelle, as
usual. She got stinking drunk, of course, and passed out
before midnight.'

'What about Karin Bellhorn?'

'I just talked to her. She's in the room across the
hall.'

'Anyone by the name of Sebastian Follin?'

'That would be Michelle's manager, the guy who takes care of all her contracts, public relations, and appearances and stuff. They had some kind of falling-out last night.'

'Bambi Rosenberg, the babe from the soaps?'

'Bambi the bimbo? Yeah, she's Michelle's best friend. She was on the next-to-last show and she stayed for the wrap party. Michelle definitely needed to have a good friend around, that's for sure . . .'

'What about Stefan Axelsson, the technical director?'

'He took care of the whole shebang from the bus all day long. A very talented technical director, but a real sourpuss; he complained non-stop about everything and everybody. He's here.'

'And then there's you and some technical wiz in charge of the bus.'

'That's right – Gunnar Antonsson. He loves that bus more than his life.'

'Do you think they'll talk to me?'

Anne Snapphane managed to laugh.

'That depends on which one you approach,' she said. 'Sebastian definitely will. Steffe? No way. Michelle herself would have spat in your face. She detested *Kvällspressen* after all the garbage you guys wrote about her, claimed she was being persecuted. And you know what? I almost agree with her.'

'Come on,' Annika countered, 'she could take it. Being in the public eye like that. So who is the twelfth person?'

Annika noticed that Anne was referring to Michelle as though the murder victim could still express her views, which gave her pause.

'He's left already.'

'How could that be possible? The police have roped off the entire island.'

'He left real early, before Michelle's body was found.'

'Who? Who is this person?'

Anne inhaled so sharply that she made a whistling sound.

'Well, I guess it can't stay a secret for ever.'

'What are you talking about?'

'No one was supposed to know until the show was aired. We recorded his stuff in the music room in the Castle, so the other guests never saw him. It's John Essex.'

Annika couldn't help but gasp.

'Are you for real? Is that on the level?'

'It most certainly is. He's so hot, we were drooling.'

'Are you serious? How did you manage to get him to come to Yxtaholm?'

'Karin gets the credit for that – her ex-husband is the band's producer. Essex was going to be the highlight of the series.'

Annika was so excited that she had to stand up.

'This is fantastic,' she said. 'John Essex was at Yxtaholm when Michelle Carlsson was murdered and he left before she was found.'

'The band left around nine last night, but John hung around and partied. I saw him right before one o'clock, but I don't know when he left. He could have been out of here way before she was killed.'

'Does anyone know when she was shot?'

'I saw her at two-thirty. I didn't hear any gunshot, but then again, I didn't go anywhere near the bus. It was packed and locked. And there were several pretty fierce thunder showers all night.'

'That means they hadn't detained twelve people, only eleven. And the twelfth little Indian did a runner.'

'I guess.'

'What kind of gun was used?'

Anne paused again.

'It belonged to the Nazi girl,' she finally said. 'A silly kind of revolver, humongous and fussy-looking. She had been showing it off all night. Promise me you'll call Mehmed?'

'I will, don't worry. I don't expect we'll be staying here much longer.'

'Are there lots of media people around?'

'A lot less than you'd expect. They've closed off the entire point; only a few of us managed to get in. As soon as they have some officers to spare they'll make us leave too.'

They grew silent again, letting themselves be lulled by the faint buzz of the connection. Annika watched the irregular tracks of the raindrops as they slid down the glass walls and remembered other Midsummer weekends spent with Anne Snapphane in her apartment in Stockholm's historic Gamla Stan district. The rain had been pouring down then just like it was today and they had watched sci-fi movies about life in space.

'Funny that we should be spending Midsummer together again, you and I,' she remarked.

Anne Snapphane couldn't help laughing, a sad laugh that quickly died out.

'You know what?' Annika said. 'I ran into Pia Lakkinen, from my old paper, *Katrineholms-Kuriren*. Guess what she said? That everyone in Katrineholm thinks that Thomas has left me and the kids.'

'Really?' Anne Snapphane said. 'What about it?'

'It was such a nasty thing to say. Don't you agree?'

'No, why?'

They went back to being silent again. Family was one of the two subjects where their opinions clashed. The other subject was TV journalism.

'Listen,' Annika said, 'do you know who shot her?'

Anne Snapphane started breathing heavily. The nightmarish feeling was back.

'I heard an awful fight right after midnight,' she said.

'Over at the Stables, the place is a shambles.'

'Who was involved?'

'Mariana and Michelle,' Anne said in a whisper.

'Christ, that's unpleasant,' Annika said.

'I know,' Anne Snapphane said. 'Hey, something's happening outside my door. I've got to go.'

They hung up and Annika reflected on their conversation for a few seconds before she called the newsroom.

Anders Schyman looked up when Spike jerked open his sliding glass door.

'Heard anything from the Music Man?'

Schyman sighed.

'No, not so much as a minor chord. We'll have to get someone from the night shift to trace him. How are we doing?'

Spike raised one arm and swept his right hand across the imaginary headlines.

'*The suspects: The entire list.* The sub-heading: *A dozen celebrities and the witching hour at the castle.*'

He lowered his hand.

'And one of them happens to be John Essex.'

The managing editor whistled and got up.

'The Elvis Presley of our day,' he said. 'This is shaping up into a world-class story.'

Schyman walked past Spike out on the newsroom floor.

'Have they arrested them all?'

'Not yet,' Spike replied, one hand jammed in a pocket.

'Then we better steer clear of calling anyone a suspect. Hey, Pelle. We're having a brief meeting over by the desk.'

The picture editor was holding a receiver in one hand and made a thumbs-up gesture with the other. Spike shuffled after Schyman with mixed feelings of humiliation and respect. Schyman was a mean bastard, but he was a good mean bastard.

'Is Jansson in yet?'

'He was just—'

Anders Schyman dismissed the rest of the sentence with a wave.

'Tell me what's on the way in.'

He sat down on a vacant chair that belonged to the foreign correspondent and was located at the heart of the newsroom. Spike went to his own spot, cleared his throat and polished off the dregs of a cup of coffee.

'We have a list of the twelve people who were at the castle that night. As far as Bengtzon could figure out, all of them are still on the premises except for John Essex. He left before Michelle was found.'

Eyebrows raised in surprise, Anders Schyman took notes.

'That's excellent,' he said. 'I haven't seen this on the news agency flash. Is it official information?'

Jansson, the night-desk editor, rushed in, spilled some coffee and grinned.

'Not at all,' he said. 'Our source is Annika Bengtzon. We might even have an exclusive.'

Anders Schyman saw the coffee drip down into a waste-paper basket.

'How did she get hold of the list?'

'The cars in the parking lot. And she has a source she doesn't want to reveal.'

'Picture' Pelle and Spike rolled their eyes.

'John Essex,' Schyman continued. 'What was he doing there? He's too big for the Globe Arena these days. That's an article in itself – have the showbiz section check it out.'

Spike took notes.

'So what do we do about the list?' Jansson asked. 'What do we call the dirty dozen?'

Anders Schyman tapped his pen on his pad.

'Not suspects, at any rate. Friends, maybe, or witnesses. Let's read the story and see where it takes us.'

'*Mates meeting with murder*,' Pelle Oscarsson suggested in the background, with rhythmic emphasis.

'Naturally, we've got to cover the police manhunt,' Schyman said.

'And then there's the castle itself,' Spike added, 'Yxtaholm. It's supposed to be quite a place. Only a hundred kilometres from Stockholm, but very secluded all the same.'

The managing editor nodded.

'That's right,' he said. 'The government uses the place for secret negotiations. I know that the Colombian government held negotiations with the FARC guerrillas there a few years back.'

'They say that Arafat and the Israelis have been there too,' Jansson said.

Spike nodded in approval.

'It would work as a separate piece, for page twelve,' he said. 'Who's going to do it?'

'Annika Bengtzon was the one who told me about the place,' Schyman said, 'so I think she's the most suitable choice. And how's our man in the trenches? Wennergren? Has anyone talked to him?'

Spike squirmed a little.

'Not yet – seems he can't call in right now, not with the police interrogations and all that . . .'

'Is it true that Barbara is there too?'

The acid tone of Schyman's voice caused Spike to pause.

'Well, Barbara does whatever she wants,' Jansson explained. 'I talked to her before she left and she told me she'd write whatever she felt like in her columns as long as she has the support of the executive editor.'

'And the blessing of the family that owns the paper,' Picture Pelle said.

'She belongs to it,' Jansson retorted.

'What do we do about Michelle?' Schyman said.

A dense silence hovered over the news desk. Picture Pelle leafed through the prints, Jansson focused on drinking his coffee, Schyman noticed how Spike hesitated before taking the plunge.

'The best angle would be to run her entire background,' he said. 'Her mother was an alcoholic whore, her father died in a car crash, the many lovers – she's controversial and rich, much talked-about and much disliked . . .'

Anders Schyman had raised his right hand and Spike stopped talking.

'Just for starters, this paper has already paid fifty thousand kronor in damages,' the managing editor said. 'All because we published the story of her drug-addicted whore of a mother. In addition to that, we've signed an agreement stating that we would never write about her again, ever. Our archives are not authorized to sell those old articles. And, Spike, those other adjectives you used to describe Michelle, they weren't generally used by the police, now, were they? Practically no one outside this paper used them.'

Beads of perspiration had formed on the news-desk editor's upper lip.

'We can't pretend we never gave her a bad press.'

'That's true,' Schyman said. 'But we don't need to keep heaping on the dirt after her death, either. I want to see a restrained and dignified account of Michelle Carlsson's life. And death too, by the way. All the awards she won, how much audiences loved her – the story about her dad is tragic but good . . .'

Suddenly Schyman felt drained.

Death and destruction: the words flashed through his mind. *Terror and tragedy, murder and mayhem, that's what puts the daily bread on the table.*

'Anything else?' he asked in a dull voice.

'What about Torstensson?' Spike asked. 'Isn't he the one who should be making these decisions?'

'I'll be in the fish tank,' Schyman said. 'Let me know if there are any calls, like from some musician or something . . .'

He slumped slightly as he headed towards the glass cubicle.

The reporters from *Katrineholms-Kuriren* had left to cover the Midsummer festivities in Bie, but the people from the regional TV news team were still around. They had thermoses full of coffee, which they consumed inside their minibus. The TV team from the state-owned public service broadcasting service were somewhat superior in their uplink bus, and the reporter from Radio Sörmland was taking a cellphone call over by the Stables.

Bertil Strand was still keeping warm inside the competition's car, where the motor had been kept running, when Annika knocked on the front passenger window. The photographer opened the window a mere two centimetres.

'It's time,' Annika said.

One second later, the photographer had left the car, and so had the other journalists.

'A meat wagon!' the reporter from their capital's other major evening paper shouted and rushed over to the police-line tape by the canal. Shaky and speechless, Annika remained where she was. She looked up at the castle. On the other shore a flagpole was like a landmark for the community. The small boat bobbed at the water's edge.

She was hit by a nasty flashback of the first time that she had seen the police remove the body of a dead person. It was in Kronobergsparken in Stockholm, just a few blocks away from where she lived. Shielded by tall trees, the small Jewish cemetery had been dark and in a state of neglect. The heat, the stench, the wide-open eyes and the slightly screaming mouth of the dead woman. Her name had been Josefin. Josefin Liljeberg. She died because she loved too much. *It could have been me*, Annika thought.

Then she caught a glimpse of the hearse between the trees over by the smithy and the beach house. Slowly, it pulled up at the roadblock where the reporters were waiting. Cameras whirred and clicked, photographers stepped on each other's toes and heels. Annika wasn't standing with the crowd; she saw the car roll up and the policeman drive the media pack away. The tape was pulled back to allow the hearse to accelerate across the bridge, the white body-bag barely visible through the tinted glass windows, and head for the drive. The reporter from the local radio station ran after the vehicle, pointing his mike at the wheels. Annika blinked – talk about tasteless!

Bertil Strand followed the car with his telephoto lens until it disappeared from sight over by the stud farm.

'There are two things I'd like you to tell me,' he said to Annika. 'How do we get out of here, and how do I get my car back?'

Annika stared at the photographer.

'Is that all you need help with?' she asked. 'Anything else I can do for you?'

She picked up her cellphone and dialled a preprogrammed number.

'I've reached Flen,' Berit Hamrin said, using the hands-free feature of her cellphone. 'Where's Yxtaholm?'

Annika exhaled with relief.

'You're coming by way of Norrköping, right? Drive across town, take the 55, turn left, then make a right at the sign . . . Yeah, we're inside, but I doubt they'll let you pass. We rowed over. That's right, we used a rowboat.'

She laughed as she hung up.

'Berit will be here in ten minutes. As soon as we're done here, she can give you a lift over to your car.'

'What are we waiting for?'

'For the twelve people who were detained to put in an appearance. Or eleven, as the case may be. If we stay here at the parking lot, we'll have the best shot at getting to them before they leave.'

'Something's happening up at the castle,' Bertil Strand said, peering over her head.

A policeman wearing a leather jacket and a Hawaiian shirt was crossing the bridge. The rest of the press representatives were gathered on one side of the barrier. The policeman stopped on the other side.

'Okay,' he said. 'The press officer just informed me that he won't be coming, so I have some information to impart to the press. Let's make this short and sweet.'

Annika fished a pad and a marker out of her bag. She saw her colleagues repeatedly click their ballpoint pens. They never learned. Ballpoint pens were useless: water made the ink run and if it was cold enough, the ink would freeze. When it was as damp as this you couldn't even use a pencil, only a waterproof marker.

'Michelle Carlsson was found dead in a mobile control room parked behind the New Wing in the grounds of Yxtaholm. She had been shot in the head. Death was instantaneous . . .'

'Were there any signs of a struggle in the control room?' one of the TV reporters called out. Annika recognized the woman, knowing that she always prided herself on winning press conferences. In other words, the reporter thought she showed the world how good she was by being loud and by butting in first as soon as the opportunity presented itself.

Lieutenant Q sighed.

'Could we take this nice and easy? Thank you. The victim has been taken to the medical examiner's office in Solna. Pathologists and investigators will continue their work there. During the day we have interviewed a number of people who were in the vicinity of the castle at the time of the murder. There are no suspects at present, but the police will continue to investigate this case and conduct interviews, here and at other locations. Naturally, this means that I will not, at this point in time, reveal details such as if there were any signs of a struggle in the control room. Any questions?'

'How long will the suspects be held at the castle?' the TV reporter bellowed.

Q paused a few seconds before answering.

'As I just mentioned,' he said slowly and deliberately, 'there are *no* suspects at present. No one is being detained at the castle involuntarily. The individuals who have been interviewed today elected to stay on in order to assist the investigation, something they are anxious to do.'

'Will the witnesses want to go home this evening, or will they elect to spend another night at Yxtaholm?' Annika asked in a polite voice.

Q almost smiled.

'My assessment is that the witnesses will all elect to spend the night at the castle,' he replied. 'Are there any more questions?'

And, naturally, there were. The different news teams had to ask their questions one at a time, since their inquiries were so tremendously special and required an exclusive answer. In other words, Annika watched Q say the exact same thing three times in a row. He began by talking into the large, unwieldy camera operated by the national broadcasting network, since TV is superior to radio and national trumps being local. Next came the small digital camcorder provided by *Öst-nytt*, the local TV news show. Finally, he spoke into the mike of the local radio station.

Annika prowled back and forth behind them and waited. Once all the broadcasting media had had their shot, she approached Q.

'Damn, you're wet,' he exclaimed.

'Have you got hold of Essex yet?' she asked.

The lieutenant sighed and hauled out a pack of cigarettes from the inside breast pocket of his leather jacket.

'Anyone wanting to get hold of John Essex just needs to follow the trail of screaming teenage girls,' he replied, lighting up and taking a long drag on his cigarette. 'Of course we have.'

'Is that who you were referring to when you said interviews conducted elsewhere?'

The officer grinned in reply.

'And . . .?' Annika said.

'We don't suspect him more than anyone else.'

'When was she found?'

Exhaling a cloud of smoke, Q glanced at her.

'Can't tell you that.'

'So it took a while before you got here?'

'It would be nice if you wouldn't put it that way in print,' the policeman said.

'Then spill.'

He sighed.

'Emergency Services received a report about an unconfirmed death. Michelle Carlsson was found shortly after six a.m. The beat cops arrived two hours later.'

'Lots of time for everyone involved to synchronize their stories,' Annika observed.

'We haven't noticed anything like that,' the captain retorted.

'How did neo-Nazi Hannah get hold of that fancy monster of a revolver she was packing?'

'Well-informed, as always,' the lieutenant acknowledged. 'What else do you know?'

'Apart from the bit about the gun?' She shrugged. 'I know who you've interviewed, that the whole bunch were at each other's throats all night long, and that one of those twelve people is probably the killer.'

'Someone could have crossed the lake,' Q said, a smile lurking in his eyes.

'Sure,' Annika said. 'That's why the government uses Yxtaholm for secret peace negotiations, because it's so easy for potential killers to sneak in here at night.'

The lieutenant laughed out loud, jammed his hands in his pockets, turned away from Annika, and started to walk towards the castle, the cigarette dangling from the corner of his mouth.

Laugh as much as you like, she thought to herself triumphantly. *I managed to cross the lake without being discovered, in full daylight.*

'Annika?'

The voice came from the barrier over by the stud farm. Berit was standing under an umbrella next to one of the paper's cars.

'What's going on?' she called out.

Waving in relief, Annika hurried over to her.

'They're not going to release the witnesses,' she told Berit, 'but I'd like to hang around for a while longer. Could you come back for me later?'

Berit flashed her a thumbs-up. Annika acknowledged her gesture with a quick grin and ran over to the photographer, taking him aside.

'Go with Berit, get the car and check into the motel at

the Statoil station in Flen. It's called the Loftet,' she said. 'Berit will come back for me later on. I want to do some snooping around.'

'What? What are you going to do?'

Annika shrugged and looked around.

'There are a few things I'd like to check out,' she said.

'Like what?'

She turned away, leaving the parking lot and passing the bell tower before turning a corner and reaching the building known as the Stables. Down by the shore of Lake Långsjön there was a hen house, some laundry facilities and a few tennis courts.

The door to the laundry facilities was locked. Annika leaned against the wall and surveyed her surroundings. It had almost stopped raining; all that remained was a mist hovering around the buildings.

Suddenly she was aware of the scents of summer: newly mown grass, roses in bloom, the dampness and the crispness. She dumped her bag on the steps, flipped her pad to a fresh page and placed it on the steps to protect her jeans from getting wet. Then she sat down on it and leaned her back against the door. At least two cars drove off. All she had to do was wait.

'A fine mother you are! I'm never going to forgive you for this. Damn you!'

Annika swept back her hair. He hadn't meant what he'd said. It was the kind of thing you said when you were disappointed and upset. He would come around, and it wasn't all that strange that he had overreacted. He'd had a rough time at work. The project he had been working on, one that had taken three and a half years, had to be wrapped up by the end of the month, only he wasn't ready. And he had no idea if the end of this project signalled the end of his employment with the Swedish Association of Local Authorities. His supervisors had mentioned a few possible future projects, but they hadn't said anything definite.

Annika sighed, knowing how hard it was on Thomas to be unable to plan. He couldn't accept her assurances that it would work out and he wouldn't listen to her analysis of the situation. That there were other jobs out there, other employers. Whenever she showed him an ad in the paper for a position such as a senior accountant within the Social Services sector or a financial officer, he got testy and sullen.

Actually, she knew what the problem was. Thomas wanted to have a fancy job. He wanted to have a position that topped being the chief financial officer of the city of Vaxholm. He wanted to show his parents and his old friends that his career had moved up a notch or two, even though the rest of his life might have gone downhill.

Annika looked out over the park and noticed that it had stopped raining. She was aware that Thomas saw his life in this light. She was a step down. Nothing she was, had or did could compete with Eleonor, his wife, the banker, in that sumptuous house in Vaxholm. They had never discussed it, but a certain tenseness around his mouth told her that was how he felt. Her efforts weren't good enough, and never would be.

For the first two years they had lived together in her apartment, in an old building that the landlord was planning to tear down, where there wasn't any elevator. In addition to this there was no toilet inside their flat and no hot water. As long as it had been just the two of them living there, it had worked out. But once Kalle was born things had become almost intolerable. Annika had worked like the dickens and had done a lot of crying, but she had never complained. She knew that the day she complained would be the day when Thomas walked out. She was the one who stayed home on maternity leave, never demanding anything from him. She did the dishes, heated the water, breastfed the baby, did the shopping and cleaning, changed the diapers, and made love – all with the same dogged determination. As long as she could take it, they would make it. To help ensure that they could stay on, she acted as an unpaid apartment-block superintendent. She changed light bulbs in the stairwells, made sure there was toilet paper and paper towels in the bathroom that the tenants shared in the part of the complex that faced the street, and called the landlord whenever her neighbours complained of leaks or cracks in the dilapidated building.

When the building facing the street was eventually remodelled, she was the spokesperson for the tenants, negotiating solutions that were acceptable to all.

She was six months pregnant with Ellen when the letter arrived. They were offered a contract for a four-bedroom apartment in the remodelled building. It was on the fourth floor, and there was an elevator, an old-fashioned tile stove and a balcony facing the courtyard. She had cried tears of joy when she read it, but Thomas's comment still rang in her ears to this day:

'The rent's so steep that we could afford three houses.'

He was probably right. It was expensive, but the apartment was fabulous. Panelling, old-fashioned doors, freshly refinished oiled wooden parquet floors in all the rooms, a range with a ceramic cooktop, two bathrooms with heated floors.

The first time that Thomas's parents came to see their new place they had said the same thing:

'What did you say the rent was? You could pay for a house with that kind of money.'

Thomas's mother found it hard to like Annika – she couldn't forgive her for disrupting her life. Eleonor had been the daughter she'd never had. As far as Annika knew, the two women still socialized a great deal. Not even the children made much of a difference to her standing with her mother-in-law.

'Poor children,' Thomas's mother would exclaim, 'having to live in the city.'

No matter what Annika did, it was never good enough.

'Oh dear,' her mother-in-law might say, 'the children are so skinny. Aren't they eating right?'

What she meant was: 'Aren't you feeding them?' Followed by: 'Let's hope they won't be as skinny as you.'

Annika had no relationship at all with her father-in-law. Whenever he came to visit, he quickly buried his nose in a paper or magazine and only replied absent-mindedly in monosyllables. Sometimes he would go and lie down on their bed and sleep through dinner.

A sharp thunderclap caused Annika to jump to her feet. Once again, the sky was overcast: a dark and ominous vault suspended over the white buildings. The air crackled with electricity and a gust of wind pushed her forward. Irritated, she shoved the damp pad in her bag and slung it over her shoulder. A second later the entire landscape exploded in a bluish-white light, followed by another thunderclap a split second later. Any moment now the rain would assault her.

Noiselessly, she made her way behind the hedges, hugging close against the back of the old stable building. A glance at the parking lot told her that the other reporters had left. The police officer over by the barrier who had been guarding the path to the castle had disappeared. Another bolt of lightning split the heavens. The delay before the thunderclap was heard was slightly longer this time – the storm was moving away. She quickly retraced her steps. A basement window of the laundry facilities was banging in the wind. She hoped she wouldn't have to crawl in through it. Gingerly, she pressed down on the handle of the kitchen's back door. It squeaked a bit and opened with an unoiled groan. Then the first raindrops hit her. They were as big as tennis balls. Without reflecting more on the matter, Annika went into the scullery and closed the door behind her.

The darkness enveloped her immediately. The torrents of rain pulled down a grey blind outside the only window in the room. She could make out a washing machine and a dryer, a small stainless-steel sink and piles of dirty bedlinen. A door led into a small kitchen and she went in: a dishwasher, a coffee-maker, a kitchen table covered with a plastic tablecloth and surrounded by six chairs. The place was littered with empty bottles, rubbish and dirty dishes. There was a window facing the backyard and a door appearing to lead to the parlour was ajar. Annika opened the door fully and stopped short, utterly perplexed.

Practically every single stick of furniture had been knocked over: a sofa, two armchairs, and a dining table. A few chairs were broken and had been piled up near the front door. A vase of flowers had been smashed to smithereens in front of the fireplace, the lupins now wilting in a welter of splintered china and spilled water. The rugs were all scrunched up and a picture had fallen down from the wall.

A thought flashed through Annika's mind: *I shouldn't be here. I really ought to leave.*

But she remained nailed to the spot, staring at the mess. A giant had ploughed through this place, tipping, tossing and crushing everything in its path. Fascinated, she tried to picture the scenario of this destruction, the strength of the arms that had splintered the backs of the dining-room chairs. Cautiously, she picked her way through the mess, approaching the upended table, noting the playing cards and broken glasses on the other side. The awareness that she shouldn't be there made the adrenalin course through her system and she moved on, picking up her pace.

There were papers behind one of the armchairs, computer printouts with blocked diagrams. Annika bent over, picked one up and read the words 'Schedule for show no. 7, *Summer Frolic at the Castle*'. She skimmed through the paper. It contained instructions for someone on the TV team but the words didn't reveal who it could be: 'Opener, card, video segment, live, closing words, music, intro, guest, card . . .' She dropped it so that it landed more or less where it had been before. Then she walked over to the fireplace, a bolt of lightning creating razor-sharp shadows round the room.

Someone went on a rampage, she thought, feeling uneasy and strangely excited at the same time.

Next to the broken vase there was a dark bundle. Annika stole closer, picked up a corner of cloth with a pinching motion and held it up to the light from the window. An item of clothing, black. It was a skirt, slightly damp from the rain or from the water in the vase. She dropped it again and looked around. A thought struck her and she put her hand in the ashes of the fireplace. They were cold, no heat remaining from the night before.

She brushed her hands together to remove the soot and dust when the sky exploded overhead. The peal of thunder shook the whole house, bolts of lightning flashed, and she backed against the wall in alarm. The smell of the electrical discharge filled the air, its sulphurous odour making Annika gag slightly.

I can see why people believed in Thor, she thought.

A second later she heard a noise from the front door on the other side of the room. Paralysed, she stared at the door handle. The next flash of lightning revealed the handle being pressed down and the door opening slowly.

Annika gasped, took three quick steps over to the kitchen and peered back from her hiding place behind the door. It was a man. He quickly entered the parlour and closed the door. When he pushed back the hood of his raincoat she was so relieved that her legs shook briefly. *That bastard!* What was he doing here?

She stayed where she was, concealed by the door, and watched him rifle through the mess. He moved cautiously, stopping during the most violent thunderclaps, then going back to sifting through the jumble of items and tossing them aside. Crouching down, he looked under certain items, lifted others up and felt around with his hands in the darkest corners. When he was about a metre away from the kitchen door she opened it wide and said:

'Lose something?'

Carl Wennergren jumped up and flew backwards. His face was chalky white while his eyes were as big as saucers and shone with terror. Annika leaned against the door; she couldn't help but smile.

'What the—?' Carl Wennergren sputtered. 'Where the hell did *you* come from?'

'The paper sent me,' Annika said. 'Have you talked to Spike yet? He's been going on like a madman about you all day.'

'How the hell did you get in?'

'What are you looking for?'

Wennergren's breath came out in gasps. He was soaked through, Annika noticed.

'That's none of your damn business.'

Annika looked at her colleague. She'd never seen him like this. Carl Wennergren was the newsroom hunk, the paper's charmer, management's pet, the son of the chairman of the board. Over the years there had been quite a few clashes between them. In Annika's opinion, Carl was spoiled and had questionable ethics. What he felt about her she could only guess. Right now he wasn't particularly arrogant or cool, and it suited him.

'Have a seat,' she said and sat down at the kitchen table. 'Have you talked to Schyman or anyone else at the paper?'

Carl Wennergren stared at her, his fear beginning to subside. 'No,' he said. 'I've been interviewed by the police.'

'What luck that we ran into each other,' Annika said. 'Now you can tell me what happened yesterday.'

Her colleague snorted, a sound that was supposed to come out as a laugh.

'Tell you? Why should I tell you anything?'

He really hates me, Annika thought. The sulphurous fumes tore at her nostrils.

'Because we work for the same paper,' she replied, hearing to her dismay that her voice was quavering. 'If we collaborate we'll have a leg up on everyone else. I know some things, but you know so much more. We could work out what we can go to press with and what needs to be suppressed for the good of the investigation. This is going to be the biggest news item of the summer, and your story would put us way ahead of the competition.'

Annika looked up at her colleague, biting her lip when she realized that she'd been pleading.

'Of course it would,' Carl Wennergren said. 'But my story is mine. Not yours. Why should I hand over a headline to you?'

She felt rage blaze through her body. His rejection of her suggestion made her stomach wrench. Carl Wennergren grinned. His self-confidence and arrogance had returned. Annika gritted her teeth and met his gaze.

'All right,' she said and got up. 'Then I won't be

keeping you – you seemed so awfully busy. Would you like me to help you?'

She paused and looked up at him.

'You know what I think?' she said. 'I think the police have already found it, whatever it may be.'

The grin was wiped off his face. Annika pushed past him, picked up her bag and headed for the back door.

'What do you want to know?'

She paused and looked up at him.

'What went on in here, for one thing.'

Carl Wennergren stared out into the gloom and swallowed audibly.

'There was one hell of a row,' he said.

Annika suppressed the urge to make a snide comment.

'Sebastian Follin walked in on Michelle and John Essex while they were getting it on. He went crazy.'

'Getting it on?'

'Well, you've got two kids, so you must know the drill.'

Annika felt her cheeks grow hot.

'So, did Sebastian Follin tear the place up?'

Carl Wennergren looked down at the floor. Annika saw his mouth tense up, but she wasn't sure what that meant. Was he struggling with a lie or with the truth? Was he embarrassed about not knowing even though he had been there? Was he trying to protect someone? Was he the killer?

Involuntarily, Annika backed away from him. She realized that she couldn't trust anything he said. So she slung her bag over her shoulder and pulled out her cellphone to call Berit on her way out.

As soon as Annika and Berit had parked in front of the Loftet motel in Flen, the rain ceased as suddenly as it had begun.

'Well, it's not exactly the Grand Hotel,' Berit Hamrin said.

'Are you kidding?' Annika said. 'My mother celebrated her fiftieth birthday here. Afterwards she claimed that the pork roast had given her food poisoning, but the rest of us knew why she'd been throwing up.'

Berit smiled wryly.

It was so much easier to breathe now. The thunderstorm had cleared the air and washed it crispy clean. Golden shafts of evening light filtered down on the asphalt. Apart from Bertil Strand's and Berit's cars, the parking lot was empty. On the other side of the road, Katrineholmsvägen, Annika could see a few young men talking over by the Statoil filling station. Feeling vaguely uncomfortable, she studied them for a second or two. All the kids from Hällefors had been bused into Flen, to attend secondary school at Stenhammarsskolan, and the locals had treated them like country bumpkins. This feeling of inferiority lingered when she encountered people of her own age in Flen. She thought she recognized at least two of the guys.

Then it struck her that they were ten years younger than her.

Oh my God, she thought, *I'm getting old.*

'Can I get you something to eat? A schnitzel or a schnitzel?'

Annika smiled.

'With fried potatoes?'

'Or how about fried potatoes?' Berit joked. 'Now go upstairs, you're in room three. The key's in the door. I'm in room number one, Bertil's in number four . . .'

The room was as lacklustre as the menu, but there was plenty of hot water in the shower. Annika had just slipped back into her clothes when Berit walked in with a tray.

'*Voilà, mademoiselle*,' Berit said as she set down the meal on one of the night-stands. 'It is still "miss", isn't it?'

Annika rolled her eyes and started tucking into the tough pork.

'I've been in touch with Schyman and Spike,' Berit said as Annika chewed away. 'We agreed that you and I would split the story as much as possible. There are a few reporters on the night shift up in Stockholm, but they're rookies filling in for the holidays. Is it true that John Essex was there?'

Annika took big gulps of her cola and remembered how frustrating it was to fill in as a reporter: you were never included and never good enough.

'Yes, indeed,' she said.

'The entertainment team has gone bananas. They're hunting down his crew all over Europe for comments, so they'll take that story. Let's see . . .'

Berit checked different items off a list.

'I've ordered copies of every story there is on Michelle from the paper's morgue – they're on their way as we speak. In addition to the crime stuff we have to write a cradle-to-grave version of the Michelle Carlsson story.'

'*The girl from the wrong side of the tracks became Sweden's biggest TV star*,' Annika said somewhat indistinctly, her mouth full of food. 'The sub-header: *Her life a sad fairy tale.*'

Berit smiled.

'Then there's the crime bit,' she said. '*A star is killed: the death of Michelle Carlsson shocks Sweden's entertainment community*. The hunt for the killer, the clues, how could it happen, all that.'

'I can do it,' Annika said and tried to remove a bit of gristle stuck between her molars. 'The murder weapon belonged to one of the guests on the show, I'll put that in.'

Berit nodded appreciatively.

'The final show, facts about the series, the taping sessions, the guests – do you know anything about those things?'

'Not much, but that's easy. The entertainment department has got to have some material. If nothing else, the press rep over at TV Plus should be able to provide something for us. Why not let the entertainment department handle it?'

'I'll ask Spike,' Berit said, taking notes. 'They want a piece about the castle, too. They say you know all about it.'

'That's an overstatement,' Annika replied and downed the last of her cola. 'How much do they want?'

'Two thousand characters, tops. Unlimited when it comes to the crime stuff. What else do you have?'

'The last night at the castle, the survivors.'

'Right,' Berit said, pointing her pen skywards. 'That's the biggest story for tomorrow, that and the John Essex thing. Use whatever you've got, just be careful when it comes to the wording about suspects and potential killers.'

'*This is how we will remember Michelle* – well-known Swedes saying nice and utterly pointless things?'

'The night shift in Stockholm is on to that,' Berit said.

There was a knock on the door. It was the receptionist, loaded down with a huge stack of papers.

'This came in over the fax,' she said, staring at the headlines with wide eyes.

Berit relieved her of her burden, closed the door in the receptionist's curious face, and spread the clippings across the double bed.

'Schyman wanted us to check these out before we got started,' she explained.

'Good grief,' Annika said. 'Have we written all that about her?'

'Where have you been the past few years?' Berit asked.

'Stuck in Nappyland,' Annika retorted, picking up an article.

It was a little over a year old and dealt with the fantastic new contract that Michelle had landed when she switched from the prosaic public service network to the hard-driving commercial cable outfit TV Plus. Michelle was beaming with joy and looked forward to meeting her new colleagues. Her manager, Sebastian Follin, who had negotiated her record-breaking contract, was giving Michelle a hug on the happy picture that illustrated the story.

Annika picked up another clipping at random, a *People are Talking* segment that had been published when Michelle had remained number one in the ratings for fifteen weeks in a row.

They spread out the clippings; the older stories went on the bedspread, the newer ones were put on the floor, where they were soon soiled by the women's shoes and bags.

A small info box caught Annika's attention. Michelle's entire life was summarized.

Born in Belorussia: mother, Latvian; father, Swedish. She had grown up with her father, an oil driller, until his death, then she had spent some time in foster care. High school in Växjö, then a job as a tourist guide in Jönköping. Likes Japanese food, enjoys a glass of wine, is interested in yoga and water sports. Currently the host of *The Women's Sofa*.

'Did you know that she was an immigrant?' Annika remarked.

'Well, I would hardly call her that,' Berit said. 'She's

lived in this country since she was three. Pass me that pile, would you?'

Annika passed her the requested pile, made herself comfortable and skimmed through some of the articles. The ones that dated back a year or so seemed, generally, to concern successful ventures, prizes, positions on lists and good-natured gossip. After the network switch, the tone changed. Michelle's show didn't do as well as TV Plus had hoped. Anonymous sources from the management level of the network spoke of multimillion kronor losses and ratings that kept plummeting. Suddenly, the star was criticized for every single trait that used to be seen as an asset. Where once she was 'unaffected', she was now perceived as being 'gushing'. The one-time 'charmer' changed to 'silly', 'mellow' became 'sloppy'. A trade union attacked her for making appearances on radio and TV game shows free of charge. 'We realize that she doesn't need the money,' a union rep acknowledged, 'but she's undermining the market for others.' The next clipping was about a radio station executive who was furious with Michelle for having billed them five hundred kronor for expenses after participating in a show. 'There's no end to the greed of some people,' the executive claimed.

'No matter what you do, you're screwed,' Annika observed.

'Just wait until you see the columns,' Berit said.

Columnist Barbara Hanson had devoted miles of paper to the harassment of Michelle Carlsson. Hanson called for Michelle's resignation, as if she had been appointed to office. The columnist harangued the TV star for committing tax fraud, even though the information was erroneous. She criticized Michelle's appearance, her diction, her salary, her morals, her capabilities and her relationships.

However, the truly massive onslaught of criticism didn't start until Michelle hosted an analytical news review, a concept that TV critics found positively ridiculous. When the series was taken off the air after only five shows, the maliciousness took on new heights: 'Michelle's Fiasco' and 'The fall of the TV Queen' were some of the headers, and a nice publicity shot of Michelle was captioned, 'Bad deal for Sweden'. Highlander was quoted as saying that the network regarded Michelle's contract as a long-term investment that would begin to show results in the appropriate demographics in a few years' time.

'This is insane,' Annika said, resting a stack of papers in her lap. 'Why have we written so much about this girl?'

Berit shrugged, pushed a few clippings into a pile and sat down on the bed. The articles slid down towards her behind, getting all disorganized.

'She sold papers. Everyone knew who she was, and at first she didn't mind getting personal or being controversial. She let us shoot her for the cover of an insert while she was wearing nothing but gold paint. She told the story of how she lost her virginity, talked about a lesbian encounter she'd had in high school, granted an interview at the hospital when she broke her leg – you know, stuff like that.'

'But it didn't last,' Annika observed.

'No,' Berit agreed as she rummaged through the faxed material. 'After a while Michelle started to cause trouble, which naturally made her even more interesting. That was when she started being the favourite celebrity screwup in the news. Anybody who wanted to beef about Michelle Carlsson got in the headlines, and Michelle was forced to defend herself. I think you're sitting on one of those articles, there you go . . .'

Annika pulled out a paper near her knee and skimmed through it. A middle-aged male TV personality from one of the other networks attacked Michelle Carlsson and claimed that she was a flop and a fraud. A million other Swedes could conduct TV interviews as well as Michelle, while no one else could compete with *him*.

'What a buffoon,' Annika said as she studied the picture of the conceited man-with-a-tan.

'These are the articles she sued us for,' Berit said, handing over a stack next to the bed. 'We'd better read them a little more carefully, just so we know what to avoid.'

Annika looked at the world war-like magnitude of the headlines:

'*Michelle Carlsson – a white-collar criminal*' covered the entire front page. The picture accompanying the headline was a passport photo of Michelle Carlsson that must have been nearly ten years old. She had an apprehensive look on her face, she was wearing too much make-up and her dated hairstyle was unflattering. *She looks like a carjacker*, Annika thought.

The story inside covered eight pages. The piece was written by Carl Wennergren. '*From celebrated star to white-collar criminal – Michelle moves from the top of the ratings to the courtroom*' was the creative inside headline.

Michelle Carlsson was alleged to be the subject of an investigation involving a shell-company scandal. Her company was one of many that had been bought and sold by a group of corporate raiders that the police had dubbed 'Sweden's smartest criminals'. Michelle, it was claimed, had commissioned their services in order to evade taxes. She was supposed to have earned twelve million kronor on the deal and was now being charged with fraud. A police superintendent at the Fraud Squad confirmed the facts in essence, while pointing out that no charges had been brought against the woman who owned the company. However, that was expected to take place before the end of the week.

The next spread was dominated by complicated graphics that illustrated the different transactions and deals. Annika blinked, understanding nearly nothing of what she was reading.

The next spread dealt with the outrage that well-known Swedish figures felt about Michelle Carlsson's greed, and went on about how a TV star like herself should be a role model. The universal opinion was that even if she didn't end up being convicted of a crime, it was morally reprehensible to exploit legal loopholes like that.

On the last page, Michelle Carlsson was asked to account for this fraudulent and criminal behaviour. The picture was shot at an angle from below that distorted her appearance and made her look grotesque.

'I have no idea what you're talking about,' Michelle was reported to have said to *Kvällspressen*'s journalist Carl Wennergren.

His questions made up the bulk of the text and were printed in boldface above the brief replies. Many of the questions had a moralizing tone, such as 'Do you think it's right that rich people should break the law to evade taxes?' Her replies reflected her bewilderment and irritation. Annika doubted that Michelle Carlsson had realized that she would be quoted.

When she was asked 'What prison would you prefer to do time in?', the TV star had had enough. She reportedly screamed: 'This is insane! What the hell is wrong with you?' The second part of her statement had been used as the header.

'I'm sorry,' Annika said, 'but I seem to have missed this. How did the trial go? Was she convicted?'

Berit sighed heavily.

'As you can see, Wennergren had a good source when it came to the fraud charges. He even managed to obtain the corporate registration number for several of the companies involved, and that's where things went wrong.'

'In what way?'

'No one knows how it happened, but somehow some of the digits were mixed up.'

Annika closed her eyes.

'Oh, no . . .'

'Oh, yes. Michelle Carlsson wasn't involved in *any* corporate raiding scam. Wennergren claims that either the police or the Patent and Registration Office mixed up the digits, and our management chooses to believe him.'

Seeing as she had a lot of faith in police sources, Annika asked: 'What about the police officer?'

'No names were mentioned when he and Wennergren discussed the case. There were just references to the female suspect, the owner of the company.'

'But didn't he check out her identity?'

'According to the Patent and Registration Office, the woman's name was Karlsson, with a "K", and her initials were M and B. As it turns out, she was just a patsy, some nutcase who agreed to be a figurehead for the raided company in exchange for a bottle of booze.'

'Holy moley!' Annika exclaimed. 'What did the paper do about it?'

'They offered Michelle the opportunity to write her own account of the events and promised to publish it.'

'You're kidding me! But the whole story was inaccurate!'

'That's right,' Berit conceded, 'but just think of it: if Michelle gave us her account, we'd have another headline. *The tax scam in Michelle Carlsson's own words.* We would have been handed an article by Sweden's biggest celebrity, and anyone who had missed the story the first day would catch it on day two.'

'I've been gone too long,' Annika observed.

Berit shrugged.

'Naturally, Michelle refused to give us anything. She demanded that we publish a disclaimer and an apology. Torstensson flatly refused. He had offered her the opportunity to answer in kind, and that was that. She went to the Press Ethics Committee and filed a complaint, but they let us off the hook, amazingly enough.'

'That's unbelievable,' Annika said.

'Well, consider who's got the spot as the Press Ethics Arbitrator. He used to host Studio 69, and he'd never pass judgement on a paper for stuff they'd published about a celebrity.'

'How could we wriggle out of that one?'

'Because we offered her a chance to be heard. It was her call to refuse to do it. The statement was pretty snidely worded.'

'So now she's suing us? Or *was* suing us, at any rate.'

'That's right, and Torstensson could go down.'

Annika quickly skimmed through the other cases. As far as she could tell, they could be found guilty of defamation of character or libel in both instances.

'We reached a settlement in the case about her mom,' Berit told her as she scooped up the papers. 'Now, what was it like over at the castle?'

Annika got up, stretched her legs and flexed her knees cautiously, leaning against the small desk.

'Unpleasant, of course,' she said. 'Kind of nasty at times. Anne Snapphane had her cellphone on and we talked a few times. She's pretty damn scared.'

'What about Wennergren?'

Annika pictured the ravaged room and recalled the smell of sulphur in the air.

'I ran into him in one of the surrounding buildings. He was looking for something, but he wouldn't tell me what.'

'Carl's a strange guy. Did he mention anything at all about what had happened?'

Annika shook her head.

'I could figure out that there had been a fight. The lounge at the Stables was completely trashed, and it seems that Michelle Carlsson had been getting it on with John Essex.'

Berit tapped her pen against her front teeth.

'Looking for something, you say . . . Something large or small?'

Annika mulled this over.

'Small. He was feeling under a sideboard, and he picked up some small items and looked under them.'

'A sheet of paper? A pad? Something even smaller? It could be anything. Cigarettes. A lighter. A pocket flask. An item of clothing. An address book. A cellphone. Who trashed the room?'

'Wennergren said that Sebastian Follin did it, but I'm not sure that's true.'

Berit got up, shook her head resignedly and headed for the door, holding her pen and her pad.

'This place doesn't have an in-house telephone line, so bang on the wall if you need me.'

She left Annika in the cramped room. As soon as she left, the voice returned.

Damn you! A fine mother you are!

Annika unpacked her laptop, looked for a wall socket, found one behind the drapes and turned her computer on, then stared unseeingly at the icons and start-up directions on her Mac.

Well, wasn't this convenient! I'm never going to forgive you for this.

She went over to her bag, pulled out her cellphone and dialled Thomas's number. Got the answering machine, so cold and scratchy. She hesitated, then hung up without leaving a message.

Next, Annika put a pillow on the uncomfortable chair by the desk to boost her up a bit and create a better angle for her forearms while she was typing. Then she rested her head in her hands for three seconds before getting to work. The short piece about the castle was the easiest one to do, so she did that first. Then she compiled what she had on the murder – it wasn't much, but no one else would have more facts. Before she got started on the list of names, she called Anders Schyman.

'One of them is probably the killer, right?' he asked.

'Probably.'

Her supervisor sighed loud enough to be heard in Flen without a telephone.

'Damn it,' he said. 'This is going to require a death-defying tightrope act. And as far as you know, there weren't any other people out there last night?'

'Nope.'

'But someone could have turned up and then left again.'

'Theoretically speaking, yes.'

'By car? On a bike? In a balloon?'

'Yes, or by boat.'

'By boat! That's good. Work with that. You could approach the castle by air, by land or by water. Anyone could have killed Michelle.'

'The companion piece about Yxtaholm describes its location as remote, since the government uses the place for secret negotiations.'

'Oh, shit!' Schyman said. 'Scratch that.'

Annika moaned silently.

'What do I run with?' she asked. 'That final night at the castle? The circle of friends? The witnesses? What am I supposed to call them?'

Her supervisor was silent for a while.

'What do you think?'

She swallowed, pushed her earpiece more firmly in place and let her fingers roam the keys.

'Quite a few people were present in the vicinity of Yxtaholm castle during the course of the evening,' she said tentatively as she typed the words. 'Guests from the shows that had been taped, journalists, artists, technicians and engineers, as well as personal friends and colleagues of Michelle Carlsson were there. And according to a police source, anyone could have reached the place during the night and left later on, either by car or by boat.'

'Is that true?' Schyman asked.

'More or less,' Annika replied and continued: 'No one is being detained at the castle against their will. The interviews conducted today were voluntary, and the subjects were eager to cooperate with the police in order to facilitate the investigation, according to Police Lieutenant Q. *Kvällspressen* is able to reveal the names of the eleven individuals who remained at the castle on the morning of Midsummer Eve, the people who were interviewed by the police today. The twelfth member of the party, John Essex, was interviewed elsewhere.'

'Are you sure about that?'

'Yup. Then I'll just list the names. Do we have photos of them all?'

'Not the girl from Katrineholm – she doesn't have a driver's licence or a passport.'

'She does drive, though,' Annika said tersely. 'Have you checked out the school pictures at Duvedholmsskolan?'

'I'll check.'

There was a pause. Annika felt her head buzzing with weariness.

'I saw Wennergren,' she said and sensed her supervisor's reaction.

'Why didn't you tell me that before?'

Surprise and reproach.

'Because he refused to talk to me,' Annika replied, struggling to keep her voice steady. 'He told me that his story was his. And asked me why he should hand me a front page.'

'How about because you both work for the same paper?'

Mortified by the way she'd been treated, Annika swallowed hard and felt herself get angry for being so submissive.

'That's exactly what I told him.'

This statement was followed by another silence between them.

'Good job,' Schyman said eventually. 'Don't let Wennergren get you down. You know what he's like.'

'So how long does he get to go on being like that?' Annika said frostily.

The managing editor paused for half a second.

'E-mail those articles directly to me.'

Annika hung up and closed her eyes. The events of the day whirled before her: the bus, the hearse, the trashed room, Pia Lakkinen's insincere show of sympathy, Thomas's features disfigured by rage.

She finished her pieces, e-mailed them, undressed, turned out the lights and crawled under the covers. There, in the dark, she watched the headlights of passing cars sweep across the walls and heard them roll along Route 55 – leaving Flen, venturing out into the world. Sleep eluded her. The images continued to dance in front of her eyes, but fatigue made them slow down. At last only one image remained. She picked up her cellphone, dialled his number, listened to the answering machine and waited for the tone.

'Hi there,' she whispered into the void. 'I love you. You're the best.'

SATURDAY, 23 JUNE:
MIDSUMMER DAY

The woods by the hostel resembled a roaring wall of fire. He struggled to breathe air as thick as porridge, passing Salströms Backe and heading down to the general store. The heat made the lush greenery sizzle and turn purple and the strict lines of the landscape had been obliterated, becoming coarse and twisted. The rocks scorched his feet. He hurriedly made his way towards the coolness of the sea, knowing that water would be his salvation, that the danger would disappear once he reached the shore. Gällnö would be saved, the houses would reappear, coolness and calm would return. But when he reached the beach, the sea was boiling. The sea water smelled of sulphur and soot, it bubbled like hot lava and closed in on his feet . . .

Thomas woke with a jerk. The sun was shining on his face, blinding him when he opened his eyes. His hair was dripping with sweat. He was lying fully clothed on the couch in his parents' living room, his body aching and stiff. The weight of his feet as they dangled over the armrest told him that he hadn't even removed his rubber boots. The nightmare lingered like a foul veil, a swallow conjured up a taste of fire and soot in his mouth.

Bloody hell, he thought.

He sat up and was afraid that his head would explode.

Never again, not so much as a beer.

The sound of children's voices entered the room, riding in on the wind by way of an open window and making him want to cry.

He was a lousy father.

Images zipped past; short and noisy sequences. He sang, bellowed and fell down, vaguely sensing the disapproval of the people around him, how they had turned away.

'So you're awake now,' his mother said, standing over by the kitchen door. 'Good. Then you can change your daughter's nappy. It's dirty.'

Thomas looked up at his mother. The curtness of her tone was reflected in her features. Her mouth was pale and pinched as she deposited Ellen on his lap. The stench from her dirty nappy hit him and he almost threw up.

'Sure,' he said, breathing through his mouth. But his mother had already gone.

The little girl whimpered – she wanted to stand up in his lap. He tried to get up, but lost his balance and had to try again. He weaved over to the bathroom with one arm around the child while supporting himself against the wall with the other, and kicked off his boots. Then he spread out a towel on the tiled floor and gently placed the girl on the hard surface. She met his gaze and laughed.

'Daddy,' she said. 'Da-dad-daddy.'

She patted him on the nose. Thomas smiled and undid the strips of tape that kept the nappy in place, the foul smell making him cringe. Just as he was trying to remove the dirty nappy the little girl tried to flip over on her tummy, smearing poop on the towel.

'Please don't move, Ellen.'

He held on to one of her legs to keep her from standing up in the gooey mess. Ellen howled and beads of sweat began to form on his forehead.

'Please, sweetheart, let Daddy—'

Ellen twisted her other knee so that it landed right smack in the middle of the poop. Thomas closed his eyes and sighed. Now he would have to bathe her.

Determinedly he got up, picked up the little girl around her waist, tossed the dirty nappy in the wastepaper basket under the sink, went over to the bathtub and turned on the shower.

Nothing but cold water. He opened the bathroom window and saw his mother there, sitting with Kalle out in the yard.

'Mother,' he called out, making himself heard above the sound of gushing water. 'There's no hot water.'

'I guess it's all gone,' she called back over her shoulder. 'Eleonor's taken a shower.'

Thomas blinked a few times, standing by the side of the tub, holding his squirming daughter, frozen. Eleonor? Here?

Without thinking he held out the baby and as the icy blast of water hit her behind she started screaming and squirming wildly to get away, nearly making him drop her. Sweat dripped into his eyes.

When he had finished washing and drying his daughter, she shot him a look of utter distrust. She didn't want him to hold her and she toddled away, heading for the porch. He sat down on the floor in the hall, put his head in his hands and felt dehydration burning in his veins.

'Thomas!' his mother shouted from the garden.

A second later he heard something tumbling down the porch steps with a thud, something soft and tiny. His entire body froze, he stopped breathing. His mother screamed:

'Dear Lord! Ellen, are you all right?'

Thomas's mind registered a heart-rending wail and he rushed out the door to see his daughter lying prone on the grass at the foot of the stairs. Disregarding her bad hip, his mother waddled quickly over to her granddaughter, a hostile expression on her face as she spoke to her son:

'What's going on, Thomas? Aren't you keeping an eye on the baby?'

He jumped down the steps in a single bound, reaching Ellen before his mother did, scooping the trembling baby up in his arms. She had banged her forehead and the blood was trickling into her eyes. She was crying so hard that she couldn't breathe.

'I'm sorry,' he whispered, tears of shame filling his eyes. 'Daddy's so sorry, honey. Are you all right?'

Feeling ashamed and inept, Thomas kissed Ellen and rocked her. His mother went to get a bottle of antiseptic from the bathroom. Over the baby's shoulder he could see Kalle sitting at a table in the garden set with lemonade and buns. The boy, upset and confused, locked eyes with him momentarily, then dropped his bun on the grass and decided to get down from the sofa. As he climbed over the armrest, he kicked over his glass of lemonade and his grandmother's cup of coffee.

'Do you think she'll need stitches?' his mother asked him and held out a cotton pad soaked in antiseptic.

He took the pad and gently wiped the wound. Ellen tried to turn her head away.

'No,' he said gruffly. 'It's just a scrape, it's not deep.'

Slowly, the crying subsided, turning into shudders that shook Ellen's tiny form.

'Daddy, I hurt myself too,' Kalle informed him as he stretched out a hand, sticky with lemonade and sugar.

'Oh my, I guess I'll have to kiss that boo-boo too,' he said. 'All right if I finish up with your baby sister first?'

The boy nodded and latched on to one of his legs, clutching a fistful of cloth.

'Hello, Thomas,' a voice behind him said.

His heart stopped. Wanting to die, he closed his eyes and quietly took a deep breath.

'Hello, Eleonor,' he said and turned around.

The first thing he noticed was her hair. She had cut it. It was short and spiky and she'd had it streaked. She was taller than he remembered, softer-looking.

Jesus, he thought, *she sure looks great.*

The woman he had been married to for thirteen years stretched out her hand and smiled.

'Good to see you,' she said.

Thomas moved the little girl to his left hip and clasped Eleonor's hand. It was warm and dry.

'Good to see you, too,' he said.

'So here are the little miracles,' she said without a trace of bitterness in her voice. She smiled at the children.

'Kalle and Ellen,' he said.

She smiled at him. The sun made her hair shimmer, her eyes were warm and brown.

'I know,' she said.

A man came out of his parents' house and went over to stand behind Eleonor. She put her hand on his arm.

'This is Martin,' she said.

'Pleased to meet you,' the man said extending a tanned hand and clasping Thomas's paler one in a firm hand-shake.

Thomas smiled so much that his jaws hurt. Martin? Who the hell was he?

'You had already conked out by the time Eleonor and

Martin arrived last night,' his mother said with a tinge of tartness. Then she patted their arms before she walked past them and went indoors. 'I expect you'd like some coffee.'

Thomas excused himself. He took refuge in the bathroom with his daughter in tow, set her down on the floor and started looking for Band-Aids in the medicine cabinet. He stopped short when he caught sight in the mirror of his own face. It was blotchy and flushed, his eyes were bleary and bloodshot, his hair was sticky-looking and he needed a shave. The roof of his mouth was burning, so he filled a toothbrush glass with ice-cold water and downed it greedily.

'Daddy,' the little girl at his feet said as she patted his leg and looked up and smiled, showing eight teeth.

Thomas peeled the plastic backing off a Band-Aid, bent down brushed a lock of hair off Ellen's face and put the sticking plaster in place.

'Ellen,' he whispered, 'Daddy's darling Ellen.'

He pulled her close, felt her warmth and breathed in the sweetness of her.

'Daddy,' she said and put her arms around his neck.

'Gunnar Antonsson?'

The Technical Operations Manager quickly rose to his feet. He hadn't heard the woman open the door.

'I'm Karin Lindberg,' she said, extending her hand. 'I'm the DA, and I'll be conducting the preliminary inquiry. All right if I sit down?'

The man composed himself, nodded, pointed at the bed and straightened the chair he occupied. The DA tugged at her skirt, sat down with her legs crossed and her hands resting in her lap.

What an elegant woman, Gunnar thought to himself.

'I understand that it's extremely important that the

duration of the impoundment of your trailer is as short as possible,' she said.

He nodded again, not bothering to correct her about the type of vehicle.

'Could you please explain why this is so important to you?'

Gunnar Antonsson swallowed audibly, feeling his Adam's apple bob as he searched for the right words. It wasn't just the money, it had to do with love – and with life too, somehow.

Tonight the concert in Dalhalla would open. He should have been seated in the stands of the natural amphitheatre, enjoying the power of the music while the money rolled in.

The thought made his chest constrict with rage.

'Times are tough,' he said curtly. 'For the business. We're booked until the end of next week and that's it. We've got to do these gigs, or . . .'

The sentence trailed off and his gaze wandered to the window.

He was going to miss Michelle. She had shown sincere interest in the bus and had listened to his speeches on technical matters. She'd made an effort to understand, and had wanted to explore new uses for the equipment. It had bothered some of the other members of the team that she paid so much attention to him, a technician.

'I've talked to the forensics team and the others involved with the investigation,' the DA said. 'And even though we intend to perform a thorough and systematic search of the bus it will be possible to release it at the beginning of next week. After all, the area in question is fairly limited. Unfortunately, we will have to seize the tapes of the show and run through them as well. They might contain information that could have some bearing on the case.'

Gunnar Antonsson cleared his throat.

'Help solve the murder, you mean?'

The DA smiled. Her lipstick was glossy.

'You never know. Maybe something got caught on camera.'

The TOM shook his head slowly.

'No,' he said. 'That's not possible. We dismantled the entire set right after we wrapped. Everything was packed and stowed, I supervised the process myself. After 10:45 p.m. there was no equipment left connected that could receive any kind of information.'

'How can you be so sure of that?'

Irritation made Gunnar Antonsson sweaty and uncomfortable.

'Every last camera, mike, transmitter pack and body-mike was packed into zinc cases and stowed in the storage space. There wasn't a single piece of electronic equipment left at the castle or in the bus that could record anything.'

The woman studied him intently, making him feel apprehensive. Her silence made him talk. The words tumbled out much too fast.

'I've packed this bus one hundred and thirty times, and I've never missed a single item. I was supposed to hit the road at eight sharp yesterday morning. The only thing left to do was close up the side with the hydraulic lift.'

He paused again, then got up and went over to the window to study the large vehicle.

Imagine the potential that this new technology held for sound and image broadcasting, whether you were talking about brilliant productions or horrible flops. The digital age, where images and sound were stored on hard drives instead of old-fashioned tapes, made it possible both to perform magic and to screw up royally. Anyone could fix a broken tape, while a profiler breakdown could ruin an entire series, all due to a bug in the program made in faraway Japan. Gunnar liked to hedge his bets and play it ultra-safe. No one took any notice – his efforts weren't worth a bean until they were stuck there with their spoiled betas and computers that had crashed. Then his colleagues most certainly did get involved, tearing their hair and griping loudly, mostly about the equipment, before giving Gunnar an earful. But Michelle never did that. She would ask: 'So, how did I do?' And he would run through things with her, explaining the details as they went along.

The DA got up too and came up to him, standing close to his back. She was a handsome woman, and tall as well.

'Lieutenant Q would like to talk to you again,' she said, 'and that will be it for the time being.'

Gunnar turned around. He could smell her perfume.

'What?' he said.

'You can go home,' she said.

'But what about my bus?' he said. 'I don't have a car.'

The woman's smile became a bit forced.

'Perhaps you can get a ride with someone, or call a cab.'

After the DA had gone Gunnar Antonsson stared at the door, trying to figure out what this interview added up to.

Number one: he would get his bus back next week. That meant there was still a chance they could do the gig in Denmark.

Number two: he was permitted to leave. That must mean that he wasn't a suspect.

Gunnar was greatly relieved by both of these conclusions.

After a stop at Flen's flamboyantly oversized railway station Annika took over the car that Berit had been driving. The station had been designed to create a suitable setting for the guests of Prince Wilhelm when they journeyed to Stenhammar Castle. There was no need for both Annika and Berit to stand around at Yxtaholm all day, waiting for the witnesses to show. Just like the body itself, parts of the story had been transferred to Stockholm: the autopsy, the John Essex angle, the 'grieving entertainment community' angle, and all sorts of other angles. Since Annika was familiar with the scene of the crime, it made sense to split up the story coverage. She took Flen and Berit took the train back to the newsroom.

'Things will have settled down a bit today,' Berit consoled her before getting out of the car.

Berit was right. The roadblock by the drive was gone, there were no guards in sight and Annika could drive all the way up to the parking lot. The castle, the surrounding buildings and the park were still taped off, but journalists moved freely around the Stables, the greenhouse and the buildings on the mainland. Bertil Strand was already there, along with the competition's reporter and photographer and the people from the national broadcasting Service Three teams. Annika could deal with that. Confronting the witnesses would be unpleasant, and a crowd would only make things worse.

The air was crisp and clean, cleared after the rage of yesterday's thunderstorm, cool without being chilly. The sun made the white castle gleam in its setting of birch trees, inaccessible behind the billowing police-line tape. Annika stopped by the car and leaned against the boot, feeling the cold metal through her slacks. She could stay put here all day and still not miss a trick. Anyone who left the castle would have to cross the bridge over the canal and their cars were all right here next to her.

Lake Långsjön shimmered, its surface surging languidly in the breeze. The leaves, still translucent at this point, rustled and whispered. Satiated sheep with matted wool wandered aimlessly around the area below the parking lot.

Annika closed her eyes, took a few controlled breaths and felt her pulse rate go down. An insect buzzed past her face and her nostrils were filled with the smell of wet soil.

I've got to remember to get that rowboat back to the Ansgar Centre, she thought.

The first person to leave the South Wing was a neatly dressed and somewhat perplexed-looking middle-aged man. He stopped short when he reached the blue and white police-line tape as if it was meant to block his path, not keep the journalists on the other side at bay.

Annika remained where she was, waiting, and watched the sunlight play over the scene in front of her. She saw the competition's reporter, pad in hand, ask the man something. He put up a hand to ward the media pack off and kept his gaze fixed on the ground. The national TV team followed him with their camera at a distance, making no effort to approach the man.

After a minute or so, the competition's reporter backed away and the man continued along the drive. He was in his fifties, a bit stocky, and he was wearing a well-ironed plaid shirt. Annika brushed the dust off the seat of her slacks and, on the opposite side of the wall, followed the man. When he passed the drive he stopped and looked around helplessly. Annika approached him.

'Excuse me,' she said. 'My name is Annika Bengtzon and I work for the paper *Kvällspressen*. Can I help you? Do you need a ride?'

The man's bewildered expression gave way to a smile.

'Yes,' he said, 'I need to get home. They're keeping the bus.'

Annika nodded, thrust her hands in her pockets and looked out over the lake.

'Did they say for how long?'

'It might be just until the beginning of next week. I've got this assignment in Denmark – I've even fixed the permits and everything.'

Excitement got the better of him and he put his suitcase down on the gravel.

'You know, that bus is almost longer than the legal limit – twenty metres. We need a permit to drive it in certain European countries. We're not allowed to pass through Denmark – we can only drive there if we have a Danish assignment – so we have to take the ferry to Sassnitz if we're headed for the Continent.'

Annika smiled and gazed out over the lake.

'Would you like me to drop you off at the station in Flen? There are trains to Stockholm almost every hour.'

The man's eyes widened and he picked up his bag.

'That won't be necessary,' he said, warding her off with his hand in a characteristic gesture that seemed to define his personality: restrained and wary. 'I'll be fine.'

'No problem,' Annika said. 'My car's right over here.'

Without waiting for the man to protest further, she went back up to the parking lot, jumped in her car and glimpsed the tall, slim form of the reporter for the competition out of the corner of her eye.

'All right,' she said, opening the passenger door next to the man. 'Jump in.'

He obliged and got in the seat next to her, holding his bag on his lap.

'My friend Anne Snapphane has told me so much about you,' Annika said.

He blinked in confusion.

'She has? Anne?'

'Like how well you take care of the OB and what a dependable guy you are to have on the team. You *are* Gunnar Antonsson, right?'

The man blinked and nodded.

'I'm the Technical Operations Manager of Outside Broadcast Bus No. Five,' he said. 'I'm in charge of the bus.'

Annika looked around and turned out on Route 55.

'You are one of the people who found her, weren't you? That must have been awful.'

Gunnar Antonsson blinked a few times and his chin quivered, possibly from holding back tears.

'Michelle was a nice kid,' he said. 'Don't let anyone tell you anything else.'

'Would anyone try to?' Annika asked.

The man sighed deeply and fingered his bag.

'Journalists always have it in for TV personalities,' he said. 'They always zoom in on what's bad instead of what's good. I guess the problem is that everybody wants to be on TV.'

'Except for you, right?' Annika said, smiling.

He actually laughed.

'No,' he said, 'it's not for me. Can you imagine me on screen?'

They turned off at Flen and passed the intersection leading to Hälleforsnäs.

'I took a look at the Stables,' Annika said. 'It looked like there had been a fight. Were you there?'

Gunnar Antonsson shook his head.

'I had to get up at seven, have breakfast, close up the bus and drive to the province of Dalarna. So I went to bed as soon as I'd seen *The Flying Doctors*.'

'And you didn't hear anything during the night?'

He shook his head sadly.

'What did she look like when you found her?' Annika asked and braked for the one and only stop light in town.

Gunnar Antonsson's expression became closed and distant.

'She wasn't wearing any pants,' he said, sounding puzzled. 'No underpants.'

Annika glanced at the man. He met her gaze.

'Why would she be in the bus without any underwear on?'

Images zipped past in Annika's mind, like a camera clicking away. She shook her head and pulled over.

'Here we are. I hope you don't have to wait too long.'

'Thanks for the lift,' Gunnar Antonsson said politely. He shook her hand, smoothed his hair and got out of the car.

Anders Schyman was on his way back from the coffee machine when he heard angry voices coming from the reception desk. He couldn't make out the words, but there was something about the voice's intensity and its particular dialect that made him check things out.

Tore Brand stood with his back to him, arms hanging limply at his sides, head protruding like a turtle's. He was facing a tall, red-faced man who was bristling with rage.

'Now how would that look,' the attendant demanded, 'if I just let people walk in off the streets?'

Schyman put a hand on Tore Brand's shoulder.

'It's all right,' he said and extended a hand to greet the paper's chairman of the board.

'I'm Anders Schyman,' he said, 'the managing editor. What can I do for you?'

Tore Brand snorted and returned to his sentry duty behind the desk.

Herman Wennergren pulled out a paper he had been holding under his arm.

'I would like to speak to Torstensson,' he said.

The managing editor expressed a concerned sigh.

'He isn't in yet.'

'Then I would like to speak to the executive editor.'

Schyman cocked an eyebrow and said:

'Well, that would be Torstensson: yesterday, today,

and every other day. Would you care to step into my
office for a while? Would you like a cup of coffee?'

The chairman of the board ignored the last question.

'You have a great deal of explaining to do,' he said
as he held out the most prestigious spread of the
paper, pages six and seven. It featured Annika
Bengtzon's balancing act about the twelve witnesses at
the castle.

'My office,' Schyman repeated, this time in the same
authoritative tones he used with members of his staff
when they made a fuss in public.

The floor rocked a bit under the managing editor's feet
as they headed towards his glassed-in corner office. As far
as he knew, Herman Wennergren had never set foot in the
newsroom before.

'Now, what can I do for you?' Anders Schyman asked
as he indicated a chair. The chairman of the board
remained on his feet.

'Where the hell do you get off, calling my son a
murderer? In our own paper, too?'

Schyman took a deep breath. He had his explanations
ready: how Carl Wennergren was not, in fact, indicated in
any way as being a murderer – rather, he was described
as a hero – and that there was a difference between the
words 'witness' and 'suspect'. Only suddenly something
clicked. A thought materialized, crystal clear and bril-
liantly refined. It appeared out of the blue, but was
actually the product of months and years of frustration.
Then all the reasons not to go for it assaulted him: the
moral implications, the risks involved, the possible conse-
quences. Schyman drew another breath and brushed
away these doubts.

'I'm very sorry,' he said. 'I wish I could give you a good
explanation. But decisions of this nature, such as those
pertaining to the publishing of names and pictures of

suspects in a crime or people with a criminal record, are the sole domain of the executive editor.'

'How dare you *do* such a thing?' Herman Wennergren roared, angrily pacing the confined office space. 'Portraying my son as a suspect, and his fiancée too! Carl and Mariana are upstanding young people – we could sue you for this. And where did you find that old picture of Carl? He looks like a gangster!'

Schyman slowly lowered himself onto his chair.

'The picture is Carl's byline shot. He selected it himself. With regard to publication issues, I'm afraid I must direct you elsewhere.'

The chairman of the board, accustomed as he was to being in charge, didn't give up that easily.

'What about the rest of you, like this Annika Bengtzon – what kind of person is she? How can she write garbage like this?'

'Our reporters are our foot soldiers,' Anders Schyman replied. 'They keep their ears to the ground and tell us what they hear. They don't decide what will be published. Only the executive editor can do that. But I do agree that the article in question constitutes a balancing act. It would have been appropriate if the executive editor had discussed it with us.'

'You mean he hasn't done that?'

'Not with myself nor with the reporter.'

'Get that bastard on the phone. Now.'

Schyman got up, picked up the phone and dialled the editor-in-chief's cellphone number. For the first time during the Midsummer holidays the call went through. Torstensson picked up after three signals.

'I'm glad I could reach you, Torstensson,' Schyman said as he caught Herman Wennergren's glare and pointed at the receiver. 'There's something we need to discuss. What do you think of today's paper?'

In the background Schyman could hear the sound of plates and utensils in use, conversations interspersed with laughter, and the distant strains of accordion music.

'I haven't read it yet,' Torstensson said. 'Was there anything in particular?'

'I see,' Schyman said, holding Herman Wennergren's gaze. 'All right . . . We've had a few reactions to the first news spread on pages six and seven. The pictures of the witnesses at the castle.'

'What witnesses?'

The man sounded uninterested. He seemed to be concentrating on a conversation taking place at his end.

'Journalistic decisions of this nature are always open for discussion,' Schyman continued in a deliberate voice and turned to survey the newsroom through his glass partition. 'It might be prudent to evaluate the situation.'

'What are you talking about?' Torstensson demanded, talking directly into the phone now.

Schyman paused, nodded silently and then shook his head.

'I don't agree,' he said. 'I think this issue is a relevant and timely one to discuss.'

Tortensson's confusion was giving way to rage.

'What the hell are you up to?' he demanded.

Schyman heard the scraping of a chair and the sounds of dining receded.

'I think we should pursue the matter,' the managing editor continued. 'But reflection and deliberation are certainly never counter-productive to ambition and determination.'

Schyman turned around and shot a glance at Herman Wennergren, who nodded in agreement.

'Are you putting me on?'

By now the editor-in-chief was enraged. The

restaurant sounds were gone, replaced by the humming of the outdoors wind.

'Absolutely not,' Schyman said. 'Not at all. But, you see, Herman Wennergren happens to be here, and he would like to share his views on the journalistic ethics exercised in today's paper. Would you like to talk to him?'

'Me? Right now?'

'Yes, I thought you would. I'll put him on.'

Schyman handed over the phone, his heart racing at a controlled pace. He noticed from the brief contact that Wennergren's hand was hot and moist.

'I never thought I'd read such a thing in my own paper,' Herman Wennergren said. 'It's an outrage, that's what it is! An outrage!'

Schyman swallowed, pricked up his ears and tried to refrain from staring. He couldn't make out the editor-in-chief's response.

'Carl!' the chairman of the board shouted, his face bright red. 'You've insinuated that my son is a murderer in today's paper. How dare you?'

Silence. A vein at the chairman's temple throbbed.

'What else would I be referring to, goddam it?!' he bellowed.

Schyman studied the dust on the panes of glass.

'Well, are you the executive editor or aren't you?'

The chairman of the board picked up the paper and started leafing through it.

'At this very moment I'm looking at the executive byline. Are you telling me that you don't take your responsibilities seriously?'

Schyman turned away, shut his eyes and began to breathe through his mouth. *It's all or nothing*, he thought.

There was a drawn-out silence. When the chairman spoke, his voice was calmer.

'Good. Of course. I'm looking forward to that.'

He hung up with a bang. Schyman turned around. Herman Wennergren's face was dark with rage.

'Is this some sort of conspiracy directed at the editor-in-chief?' he asked.

Schyman sighed, sat down at his desk again, then leaned back and relaxed.

'I wish it was as simple as that,' he said, folding his hands and placing them behind his neck. 'A plot would require an adversary with a pronounced set of values, an attitude to oppose. And that's not the case here at our paper.'

The chairman of the board blinked in confusion.

'What do you mean?'

Schyman leaned forward and fixed Herman Wennergren with his gaze.

'Torstensson is bringing this paper down. He doesn't have the faintest idea of what he's doing. The rest of us save his tail daily. He's a disaster as an editor-in-chief.'

Herman Wennergren stood utterly still, considering if he had possibly misunderstood what he had just heard. No subordinate had ever said anything vaguely like this about any editor-in-chief over the years. Schyman was breathing rapidly and didn't avert his gaze.

'Do you mean . . .?'

'The members of the board must have discussed this matter,' Schyman said, getting up again. 'All the lawsuits, the Press Ethics petitions, the dip in sales, the polls showing diminished credibility . . .'

'It's the recession,' Herman Wennergren countered. 'That and the increasing competition from broadcasting media and the Internet.'

Schyman shook his head.

'They are all relevant factors, but they're not the main problem. Our competitor's sales are up, ours are going down.'

'And you mean our editor-in-chief is to blame for that?'

'Not entirely, of course. There is a substantial collective responsibility factor as well. But *Kvällspressen* is a hierarchical organization, one that requires powerful and visionary leadership. I'm convinced that the arrangement is a winning concept in the long run. It provides everyone with the scope to pursue excellence, but only if management can deliver.'

The chairman of the board stared at Schyman, struck by something the managing editor hoped was insight and not distrust. There was a stand-off. Finally, Herman Wennergren averted his gaze, folded his paper, put it under his arm and headed for the glass door. As he passed Anders Schyman, he stopped and spoke in a low voice:

'No board has ever fired an editor-in-chief of this paper,' he said. 'Mine won't be the first to do it.'

Mariana von Berlitz had come and gone, passing Annika without a glance. Annika didn't have the strength to approach her – she couldn't face the humiliation that she knew it would involve. However, the competition got a soundbite, Annika noted, though she doubted they would use it.

'What a way to go,' Mariana von Berlitz had said, her voice reverberating with an emotion that Annika was unable, or unwilling, to place.

'I bet she arranged the whole thing herself, just to be front-page material again. It's been a while.'

The competition asked Mariana something that Annika didn't catch. But she heard the woman's shrill reply.

'She was making this documentary about her own life, produced by her own production company. I mean, can you get any more narcissistic and vain that that?'

Then the TV reporter flicked the locks of her snappy little Renault with her remote, tossed her bags in the front seat and drove off in a spray of gravel.

'Christ,' Annika said aloud and the reporter for the competition responded.

'She certainly didn't think much of Michelle Carlsson,' he observed and walked up to Annika, fishing out a pack of cigarettes and offering her one. She declined politely and he took one himself.

'One hell of a story we've got here,' he said.

Annika sighed theatrically.

'I'm not a huge fan of hers, I'll admit that,' the reporter went on, 'but no one should have to die like that.'

They both shook their heads – a bullet in the brain was a truly godawful way to go. They stood next to each other and looked up at the castle, waiting for the next witness, rocking slightly on their heels. Annika closed her eyes and turned her face up to the pale yellow sun. The air was so delicate after the rain.

'It's a beautiful day,' the reporter for the competition remarked.

'Why does almost everyone dislike TV show hosts?' Annika asked.

The reporter blinked.

'Do they? Who do you mean?'

She looked at him.

'You, me, Mariana von Berlitz. The entire staff of my paper. Why are we so opinionated about people we've never met?'

'They're in the public eye,' the reporter said tentatively, stubbing out his half-finished cigarette.

'Well, does that mean we have to hate them?' Annika countered.

'I guess it's the same deal as for columnists,' the man said. 'No one likes them, no one wants them around, and no one understands why they're entitled to write a load of crap each week and deserve a huge byline. But still, we read their stuff. To be honest, I guess all of us would like the power to make our voices heard like that.'

Annika stared at the guy, perplexed to discover that her competitor was no dummy.

'I'm Bosse,' he said, extending his hand.

Annika blushed a little and cautiously shook his hand.

'Here comes Bambi Rosenberg,' Bosse said, forgetting everything else, dropping Annika's hand and rushing over to the police tape.

She followed him with her gaze and looked up at the castle. A petite woman was walking towards the bridge, lugging a gigantic suitcase. The way her tiny torso slumped signalled defeat and frustration.

Michelle's best friend, Annika thought and moved forward to approach her. What if it had been Anne they'd found in the bus? She shook her head to throw off the thought.

'Bambi?' the reporter from the competition, Bosse, called out. 'Bambi Rosenberg, may I ask you some questions, please?'

The woman approached the tape and slowly made her way under it, pulling the huge bag behind her. She had a hard time walking on the gravel path in her high-heeled sandals and tottered slightly. Her hair was pulled back in a ponytail and her eyes were bloodshot and heavily made-up. When she saw the large cameras from the national broadcasting service, her hands instinctively flew up to yank off the elastic, releasing a cascade of blonde hair.

'Yes,' she whispered, so softly that Annika sensed her reply rather than heard it. 'All right . . .'

'How do you feel right now?'

The woman's eyes filled with tears that she carefully

brushed away with her fingertips to avoid smearing her mascara.

'This is so awful,' she whispered. 'It's the most terrible thing that's ever happened to me.'

'You knew Michelle well, didn't you?' Bosse asked.

Bambi Rosenberg nodded, then searched her pockets for a tissue and blew her nose.

'She was my best friend.'

Annika could barely hear her. She took a step forward and spoke without introducing herself, due to her paper's relationship with the deceased.

'Is there anything in particular that you'd like to say about Michelle?' Annika asked her in a soft voice.

The woman met Annika's gaze and appeared to be mustering up some courage.

Looking unseeingly up at the treetops, she finally said: 'There are a lot of people who should be taking a good look at themselves today.' The large TV camera whirred in the wind, the reporter for the competition had whipped out a tape recorder, Bertil Strand was focusing his camera and a fascinated Annika studied the young woman.

'Michelle Carlsson was a genuinely good person,' Bambi Rosenberg said. 'There aren't many out there. I knew her, so I know it's true. She wanted to make this world a better place. She had an obligation to the young women of Sweden – she wanted to be a role model, show them that you could make it on talent and ambition.'

She paused and took a few deep breaths, Annika wondered how much effort Bambi had put into preparing this speech.

'The malice that was directed towards Michelle over the past few years was unprecedented,' she continued, now looking them in the eye, one by one. Annika thought she held her gaze for an extra-long time and felt her cheeks grow hot.

'The begrudging attitude to Michelle that character-
ized Swedish journalists was vulgar, it bordered on the
disgusting. You enjoyed cutting her to pieces, you
sneered when she made mistakes, you wished her the
worst of luck, you wanted to hurt her. Now you've got
what you wanted. Are you satisfied?'

The last sentence came out as a shriek, and she could
no longer hold back the tears or save her make-up. Black
rivulets coursed down her cheeks while Bambi Rosenberg
bolted over to her red convertible, leaving the journalists
stunned and uncomfortable.

'There's some truth in that,' Bosse admitted, while the
woman from the national broadcasting service just
snorted.

'You can certainly tell why Bambi Rosenberg won't be
offered any parts in a serious production,' the woman
said, and her cameraman and sound technicians
snickered.

'What makes you think that she would want those
parts?' Annika heard herself ask.

The TV team looked at her. The reporter's expression
of surprise gave way to one of disdain and she turned
away.

'It's like assuming that I covet your job,' Annika said,
'just because you happen to think you're superior. But
you know what?'

The TV reporter turned around slowly and stared at
Annika as if she couldn't believe her eyes.

'Excuse me?' she said.

'I'd rather work the register over at IKEA,' Annika
informed her and walked back to the parking lot to write
down Bambi's little speech.

'Well, aren't we clever?' she heard Bertil Strand say
behind her. 'Do you have to antagonize everyone in the
business?'

'Get any good shots?' Annika asked him in a reserved voice. 'Or didn't you get enough notice beforehand?'

'What the hell is your problem?' the photographer demanded in a frosty voice, his eyes full of disapproval.

Annika sank down on the low wall by the parking lot, not caring that the seat of her pants would be soaked in no time.

'I don't know,' she replied quietly, a lump forming in her throat. 'It's all so terrible.'

'Pull yourself together,' Bertil Strand snapped back.

Anne Snapphane entered the conference room. It appeared to have shrunk since yesterday: the ceiling seemed lower. The bus was still parked outside the window and a sense of unease engulfed her again, broadcasting her lack of confidence as clearly as sweaty palms.

'Not as thirsty today, are we?'

Q had a different outfit today, a T-shirt instead of the Hawaiian shirt, khakis instead of jeans. Anne sat down and folded her hands, trying to appear calm and collected.

The police officer switched on the tape recorder and proceeded to rattle off: 'Interview with Snapphane, Anne, held by Lieutenant Q at Yxtaholm castle in the conference room of the New Wing on Saturday, 23 June at 12:55. Anne Snapphane is being interviewed with regard to the murder of Michelle Carlsson. This is interview number three.'

'People are going home,' Anne said as soon as he was finished.

'I would like to continue where we left off yesterday,' Q said and leafed through some papers.

'Why don't I get to leave? Why do I have to stay here? Am I a suspect?'

'If you answer my questions in the order that I ask them, you might get to go home too, at some point.'

'Do you really have the right to detain me here?'

Anne Snapphane was unable to control her voice – it went revealingly shrill.

'Let's get back to the run-in at the Stables . . .'

She jumped up, her chair scraping the wooden floor.

'What would happen if I walked out right now? What would you say? If I simply marched out the door, could you keep me here? Could you?'

Q remained expressionless.

'Sit down,' he said. 'This isn't funny. Now tell me what happened over at the Stables.'

Anne remained on her feet and screamed at the man.

'I've already told you that!'

'That's right, you have,' the policeman said. 'Only there's a catch. I think you lied.'

She stared at him. Sensing that her armpits were drenched in sweat, she held her arms stiffly at her side as she sat down again.

'I believe you are withholding vital details,' Q said. 'I'm not going to allow you to go until you tell me the truth. If that means I have to arrest you, I will.'

She forced herself to glare at him.

'You're bluffing.'

He shrugged, got up and called out into the corridor:

'Could you ask Karin to come in here?'

Panic spread throughout Anne's body, an icy sensation radiating from slightly below her navel.

'Karin?' she said. 'Who's Karin?'

'She's the DA,' Q told her. 'She's up at the castle right now.'

'No!' Anne Snapphane cried, getting up and taking a couple of steps towards the door in confusion. 'Christ,

I've got to go home. There's Miranda, my little girl, she's only two and I can't . . .'

She remained frozen in place, panic drilling a hole in her gut, feeling again as though she was going to pass out. Q waited for her to calm down, his arms folded across his chest, his face expressionless.

'All right,' she whispered and returned to her seat, trembling. 'What would you like to know?'

Completely deflated, she felt the ceiling closing in on her.

Q walked slowly around the table and sat down again.

'The Stables,' was all he said.

She kept her eyes shut for a few seconds, and breathed with her mouth open.

'Like I already told you, the fight was in full swing by the time I got there.'

'And who were the people involved?'

'Michelle and Mariana. They were both pretty wasted and they were screaming at each other when I came in.'

'What were they fighting about?'

'It had started over something to do with John Essex. As far as I could tell, Michelle had got it on with him, and that freaked Mariana out. But I'm not positively certain – that's just what I heard . . .'

'Was John Essex in the room when you got there?'

Anne shook her head and the policeman sighed and pointed at the microphone.

'No,' she said and leaned closer to the mike. 'No, he was in the kitchen, only I didn't know at the time.'

'Why did it bother Mariana that Michelle Carlsson had something going on with John Essex?'

Anne Snapphane snorted.

'Everything Michelle did bothered Mariana. She would almost go as far as sabotaging the taping sessions just to ruin things for Michelle.'

'How did Michelle feel about that?'

'She detested Mariana and tried to get her replaced on the set. Only Zero has been cutting back on staff – they've been affected by the recession, you know. And Mariana's terms of employment meant that she couldn't be budged. We just had to lump it. And that hardly improved their relationship.'

'What were they screaming about when you walked in?'

'Something about a contract. Michelle was coming apart at the seams, her voice was really high-pitched and shrill and she was reeling around like she was drunk as a skunk . . .'

Anne paused.

'What else?'

'From the waist down she wasn't wearing any clothes. It looked bizarre. She was reeling around the room half-naked, and . . .'

'And?'

'She was holding that revolver. It was pretty scary, even though we knew it wasn't loaded.'

'How did you know that?'

An ironclad door slammed shut somewhere deep inside Anne, sending tingling ripples to her nerves and fingertips, leaving her breathless.

'I . . . Well . . . I don't know.'

The policeman saw straight through her, his eyes fishlike, and he dropped the subject.

'What were they fighting about?'

Anne regained her ability to breathe, and searched her memory while slowly rubbing her forehead.

'It was something about a contract. I don't know how the fight got started, it was already way out of hand by the time I arrived. Michelle wasn't really all there. She was, how should I put this, incoherent. Went on about how

Mariana should be happy now, how everyone should be pleased tonight since they'd all got what they wanted, that she was headed for the garbage disposal, stuff like that . . .'

'Did you get the feeling that Michelle Carlsson was unbalanced?'

Anne cackled with laughter and then sighed.

'That's putting it mildly.'

'I would like you to keep this to yourself,' Q said, 'but could Michelle have taken her own life?'

Anne Snapphane gasped and felt her eyes open wide, a sensation followed by a wave of relief so strong she almost lost control of her bladder.

'You're asking could she have shot herself?' she whispered.

The detective nodded.

Yes, Anne thought. *She shot herself. It wasn't one of us. She did it, her death was her own fault. It had nothing to do with us.*

A second later realization hit her like a punch in the gut.

That would mean that we were even more to blame.

She shut her eyes in concentration. *Could Michelle have taken her own life?*

No.

She looked up at Q.

'No,' she said. 'No, someone else did it.'

Suddenly less sure, she asked:

'Why do you ask? Did you find a letter?'

The police officer's intense gaze nailed Anne to the backrest of her chair. Her body tensed and grew rigid.

'Did you see anyone else handle the gun?'

The silence grew oppressive. Anne forced oxygen into her lungs, her terrified thoughts shooting through her mind like bolts of lightning.

'Hmm,' she murmured. 'I don't know.'

Buying time.

'Think about it.'

Somewhere a clock was ticking. Anne turned her head to locate the source of the noise without success.

'We found your prints on the gun,' the lieutenant said. 'Could you explain that?'

Anne's mind went absolutely blank. The blood drained from her heard and she felt the colour drain from her lips.

'Here, have some water,' Q said, pushing a glass in her direction.

Anne Snapphane tried to take it, but spilled it and gave up.

'I didn't do it,' she whispered.

'Then who did?'

She shook her head. Her throat felt like it was coated with shards of glass.

'When did you handle the gun?'

'In the lounge over by the South Wing.'

Each word tore at her throat.

'Was that before or after the fight at the Stables?'

Anne closed her eyes and felt her tear canals start to burn.

'After, I think.'

'Why?'

'I wanted to feel how heavy it was.'

As soon as she had said the words, she regretted it, the flimsiness of her explanation mocking her.

'When did you see the gun for the last time, apart from in the bus, after the murder?'

The image bank of her *corpus collosum* was flooded with fuzzy pictures, the product of alcohol and fatigue, a photo album of blurry outlines and confused emotions.

'On the table in the lounge,' she said after a while.

'Are you sure of that?'

'Fairly sure.'

'What time could that have been?'

'I don't know. After the Stables. Maybe even after Mariana's and Bambi's argument about nudie pictures. Say, 2:30?'

She met Q's gaze. It was cold and aloof.

'And then what? Where did you go?'

Anne made an effort to remember.

'I tried to get some sleep, but there was too much of a ruckus going on so I got up again.'

'So, after three o'clock, you were in your room over in the South Wing?'

She searched her memory and nodded. 'Yeah, that's probably right.' And her breathing returned to normal.

'Then could you explain why you were observed in front of the bus at 3:15 a.m.?'

The room started reeling and Anne grabbed on to the table and tried to keep her voice steady.

'What?' she said. 'Who saw me?'

'Actually, several people did. Why would you go to the bus at three in the morning?'

Her head moved from side to side – no, no, no.

'I don't remember.'

The reply was like air being expelled.

'Come on. Your memory's been pretty good up to now.'

Frantically searching that memory Anne thought, dear Lord, what had she done? What had she said? Where had she been?

'I . . . went for a swim?'

'In the pouring rain? Come on, Anne Snapphane. If you're going to lie, at least try to make it a good one.'

The detective's words oozed contempt.

'I don't remember,' she said, feeling the tears well up

in her eyes. She looked up and let the tears flow. Her voice broke, wavering and indistinct.

'I don't remember. You've got to believe me! I was pretty drunk, I must have gone the wrong way or something. I was going to go to the South Wing and I guess I wandered around some. I didn't do it!'

The waiting left Annika hot and restless. The sunlight sliced pathways through the leaves and the air stood still. The sheep gathered around the journalists, smelling of wool and crap. She distanced herself from them all, the animals and her colleagues, strangely affected by the situation.

After Mariana and Bambi the parade of witnesses had ceased. The other journalists didn't seem to mind. They chatted, leaning against walls and rocks.

Annika walked over to the Stables and tried the door. Locked. Then she sat down on the steps and took a few deep breaths, trying to find some freshness in the breeze. She hesitated momentarily, then picked up her cellphone again. 'You have . . . no messages.' She swallowed her disappointment. He didn't have time to call, not with the kids and everything.

'Did you ever meet her?'

Confused, she looked up and was blinded by the sun, so she put her hand up like a visor. It was Bosse, the reporter who worked for Sweden's other major tabloid.

'Oh,' she exclaimed, realizing that she wasn't sure.

She let her hand drop and chewed on the inside of one cheek. Didn't she run into Michelle Carlsson once, on a job, or was it something Anne Snapphane had mentioned, or even something she'd seen on TV?

'No,' Annika said at last to the dark silhouette. 'I don't think so. But I do know Anne Snapphane, one of her associates, and I've been to Zero's offices now and then. It feels like I know her.'

Bosse sighed, sat down next to her without waiting for an invitation and stretched out his legs.

'I know what you mean,' he said. 'I've met Karin Bellhorn a few times at dinners and events like that, and she's told me stuff about Michelle. Like how hard it was for her to deal with her success. How it wore her down. How unbalanced she could be, touchy and weepy. How euphoric she would get when the camera was rolling or if she got some attention.'

'It's kind of sad,' Annika said. 'That success is such a big deal.'

The other paper's reporter picked up a small stick and traced figures in the dust on the stone steps.

'We feel the same way, you know. We love it when celebrities do good. It's almost as nice as when they fail.'

'Someone's coming,' Annika said.

They got up, and as if they had been given a signal the photographers shouldered their cameras and sharpened their gazes while Annika and Bosse felt for their pads and pens. Stefan Axelsson was tall, rangy and blond, and the stubble on his face was peppered with grey. Cautiously, Annika approached the technical director along with the rest of the group. When no one else made an attempt to communicate – everyone just stood there staring at him – she stepped up, introduced herself, and asked an innocuous question.

'Leave me alone,' he snapped, his eyes red and his forehead shiny. 'Leave *her* alone.'

'That was Axelsson, wasn't it?' Bosse asked.

'He's reputed to be quite a bastard,' Annika replied as the man drove off in his old Saab. 'But he's brilliant at his job.'

The other reporter nodded.

The dust on the road had barely settled before the next witness came sailing down the hill. Barbara Hanson needed no introduction. She kissed Bertil Strand on both cheeks and proclaimed in a loud voice that her bed had been uncomfortable, that the policemen were handsome, and that the weather had been frightful.

'Oh my God,' Bosse exclaimed. 'Is she always like that?'

Annika simply rolled her eyes.

A minute later, Carl Wennergren appeared. Annika could see him coming from a distance.

'Don't waste your breath on him,' she whispered to Bosse. 'I tried to talk to him yesterday, but he wouldn't tell me anything, even though we sit more or less next to each other in the newsroom.'

'Yesterday?' the reporter said in surprise. 'How did you manage to do that?'

She lifted her fingertip to her lips and smiled. Carl Wennergren got into his BMW and drove off without anyone trying to talk to him.

'Here comes the next one,' Bosse said, and pointed.

Even at that distance, Annika could recognize the CEO of TV Plus in spite of the fact that she'd never actually met him. He liked to be seen at parties with the in crowd and he promoted his own channel in commercials. Highlander, the immortal one.

He swiftly climbed over the tape; his hair was glossy and black, his suit was impeccable and he wasn't carrying any luggage. Annika joined the other reporters and approached him, intuitively anticipating an unpleasant situation.

The man tried to appear confident and relaxed, but his smile didn't quite reach his soul. Under his tan he was pale, and a lack of sleep had carved sharp lines around his eyes.

'I would like to start by saying that this is a tragedy for TV Plus,' he said without waiting for a question.

The small assembly of reporters and photographers gathered around him in silence, an impromptu press conference accompanied by bleating sheep.

'Naturally, this terrible loss will have an impact on our entire network. Michelle Carlsson was one of our most esteemed associates,' Highlander said as he fingered a creased piece of paper in one hand.

'On a personal note,' he continued, 'I would like to add that Michelle was a very dear friend, a very good friend, one whom I appreciated for her great . . . warmth, and her considerable . . . professional expertise.'

He faltered, paused and glanced quickly at his notes for a few seconds. Lowering the paper again, he looked up and wet his lips before speaking.

'We here at TV Plus will honour and cherish Michelle's memory,' he continued in a voice aimed at the birds and the treetops. 'History will prove that she was one of the great personalities of our time. Her shows will live on, a legacy to future generations of viewers and TV associates. This is a legacy that we here at TV Plus aim to hold in trust, and I promise you that we take this responsibility seriously.'

'Jesus,' Bosse whispered to Annika. 'Next he'll be sprouting wings.'

She bit her lip. The combined effect of the TV executive's pompous words and perfumed exterior made her want to giggle.

'What will happen to the shows you taped this week?' the woman from the national broadcasting service asked.

'Here's someone who's got her priorities straight,' the reporter for the competition said, leaning close to Annika. 'First things first – find out what happens to the shows.'

Suppressed laughter welled up inside Annika. She

turned around and tried to hide it by covering her mouth with her hands. Highlander, who had started to answer a question, was distracted and stared in her direction.

'Is . . . What's so amusing?' he asked, his eyes darting around the crowd.

''I'm sorry,' Annika replied, struggling to control herself. 'I swallowed my gum.'

The truly pitiful lie caused Bosse to start shaking with silent laughter himself. He turned and walked away from the group. Annika looked up at the treetops, taking in the bright, clear colours. None of this was actually happening; it was all a show, a bad reality-TV show.

'This series represents our TV Plus summer special,' Highlander said, his suit standing out like a silvery silhouette against the water. 'It was intended to give us an edge in the competition with the terrestrial networks, as well as with regard to the other satellite TV networks.'

'Will you be airing the shows, and if so, when?' the persistent female broadcaster continued.

Highlander wiped away a small moustache of perspiration on his upper lip.

'At the present time I'm unable to give you a reply,' he said. 'Naturally, I'll have to confer with the head office over in London first, and delineate our policy for the commemoration of Michelle's memory. The airing of *Summer Frolic at the Castle* is a part of our strategy and as such must be given due consideration.'

The man glanced down again, fingering his notes. His whole face had now broken out in a sweat, causing his waxed bangs to wilt. Suddenly Annika saw the man as he truly was, deathly pale and under strain, on the verge of tears.

'How are you holding up?' she heard herself ask.

He glanced up without looking at anyone in particular.

'The past few days have been rough,' he said. 'Really

rough. The entire future of the network hangs in the balance.'

'Actually, I meant you personally,' Annika said. 'What's your reaction to the fact that your associate was murdered while she was taping a show for you?'

Highlander crumpled up his notes into a ball, shoved it into his pocket and strode off towards the car. The photographers were hot on his heels, causing the man to break into a near-run. Annika remained where she was and saw him get into his huge vehicle and sit there for a while, slumped over the wheel.

'If you think he felt lousy, check *this* guy out,' Bosse said and pointed over her shoulder.

A short and rather corpulent man with thinning hair was on his way down the hill. His mouth was slack, the lips chapped and shiny, and he moved jerkily, almost reeling. Annika could sense his bottomless despair and desperation.

'Poor soul,' the reporter next to her said.

Sebastian Follin had clipped on dark sunshades over his regular glasses with metallic frames. His complexion was dull and grey, haggard-looking. They saw him make his way slowly towards the parking lot, somehow seemingly oblivious to his surroundings. The journalists left him alone until he reached his car. The national broadcasting team was the first to address him. He didn't catch the question and looked around in confusion, watching the reporters and photographers with dread.

'What?' he said. 'What do you want?'

'I'm sure you realize that we will be writing about Michelle's death in tomorrow's papers,' Annika said as she walked up to the man, took his hand and introduced herself. His hand was limp, cold and moist.

'I just can't understand it,' he said. 'I can't get it into my head that she's gone.'

'You worked with Michelle for many years, didn't you?'

Annika sensed how the other journalists were concentrating, how they were waiting expectantly for the words to issue from the man's trembling lips.

'She was mine,' Follin said. 'My very first client. We were a team. I made her what she was.'

Annika nodded and tried to catch the manager's eye behind the opaqueness of his glasses, sensing his gaze drifting off towards the lake.

'How did you meet her?'

Sebastian Follin took a few rapid breaths, still avoiding her gaze.

'It was at the National Road Association,' he said. 'Their public relations department. In Växjö. I was in charge there and we needed someone to present . . .'

He stopped talking and some saliva dribbled from the corner of his mouth down to his chin. Annika felt a tingling of uneasiness running up and down her spine.

'So you hired her to do a presentation?'

Follin quickly bowed his head and wiped his chin with amazing speed. Then he clasped his briefcase more firmly.

'She was incredible,' he said. 'It was the best press conference we ever had. She was funny, smart, beautiful – everyone listened when she spoke. It was magic.'

He nodded to confirm his words.

'It was magic. Afterwards I asked her how come she was so good, and she just laughed. That was the way she was. She was a natural. I used her for everything we did after that.'

He swallowed.

'Where did you find her?' Annika asked.

'She was working as a guide on the tourist train in Gränna, and she was a receptionist at Gyllene Uttern. That was . . . five years ago.'

'You've been around her for a long time,' Annika said.

'The whole time,' Follin said, looking at her for the first time. She could detect small pale blue eyes behind the dark lenses.

'Did you have contacts in the TV business?'

'My brother's wife worked at Zero. I negotiated her first contract as a host for a TV show. She was a star in no time at all.'

Annika nodded, realizing that it was true.

'What other clients do you represent?' the woman from the national broadcasting service asked.

Sebastian Follin was startled and jerked his head in her direction.

'I'm sorry . . .'

'You *are* a manager, aren't you? Do you only represent TV personalities, or do you have other clients as well?'

The man's expression hardened, the lines around his mouth tightening.

'What network do you represent?' he asked the woman, his voice now shrill.

She mentioned the name of the national news show.

'I refuse to work with you people,' he said, abruptly turning away and unlocking the door to his sporty American car.

He almost drove into the wall as he roared away from the parking lot.

Torstensson's complexion was both pale and blotchy as he walked into the newsroom. He was no longer clad in his traditional folk costume; he'd changed into a pair of warm-up pants and a turtleneck shirt. As always, he looked a bit lost among the computers and news bills, his eyes darting nervously around the newsroom and its staff. Schyman caught sight of him through the glass partition, noted how weak and confused the man seemed and felt a wave of compassion and misgivings.

I can't do this, he thought. *You can't treat people like this.*

Then he looked at the newsroom staff: editors and reporters, photographers and photo editors, rewrite people and proof-readers, news-desk editors and night-shift editors. He doubted whether Torstensson knew who they were or what they did.

The editor-in-chief caught sight of him through the glass and approached his corner office, his teeth gritted.

'I demand an explanation,' he said. 'What are you up to?'

Schyman left his desk, walked past the editor-in-chief and closed the glass door. Torstensson looked stooped in his baggy leisure clothes, much smaller than in the bulky suits he usually wore.

'I'm trying to get this paper on track,' Schyman replied.

He stood with his back to the door, forcing the other man to face the newsroom and the curious glances of his associates as they whispered to each other.

'What's the point of playing games with the chairman of the board? He thought I was the one who okayed the use of the names and pictures of those people.'

The editor-in-chief's lips were white and dry. He spoke with difficulty, as if talking was painful.

Schyman looked at the man for a few seconds, assessing his will to fight.

'You *should* have been the one to okay it,' Schyman said. 'Isn't that right? Only we couldn't get hold of you all day yesterday, even though we called every number we had. You didn't contact the office either, despite the fact that we left you a dozen or so messages. Did you check out the news at all yesterday?'

'I had the day off,' Torstensson said, his ear lobes burning.

The managing editor stared at his superior with

astonishment. The man's incompetence and inability to shoulder responsibility knew no bounds.

'This is unacceptable,' Anders Schyman said. 'The staff of this paper needs to know that they can depend on their management when the going gets tough. We need to be consistent on all levels when it comes to the issues.'

Torstensson wet his lips uncertainly.

'What do you mean?'

Anders Schyman walked past the editor-in-chief and sat down at his desk again.

'Barbara Hanson was at Yxtaholm when Michelle Carlsson taped her very last shows,' he said, looking intently at his boss. 'Could you please explain why she was there?'

A furrow appeared between Torstensson's eyebrows and he folded his arms as he turned to face the managing editor's desk.

'She asked to cover the event. It *is* her job, you know.'

Anders Schyman forced himself to not move a muscle and just look at the man.

'I expressly ordered Barbara Hanson to stop harassing this particular journalist. And you know that.'

'She wasn't harassing anyone,' Torstensson countered, shifting his weight from one foot to the other. 'She wrote about a public figure, and celebrities just have to deal with that sort of thing.'

'There are limits, though,' Schyman said. 'And Barbara passed them quite a long time ago.'

'I don't agree,' the editor-in-chief said.

Anders Schyman was overcome by a sudden wave of intense weariness, the same feeling of draining exhaustion that had hit him several times during the past few days.

I don't have the strength, he thought. *I won't even bother*.

'Barbara Hanson is one of this paper's most prominent

and esteemed reporters,' Torstensson said. 'She's known for her bold and feisty celebrity profiles, they're a distinctive feature—'

'Don't you try to teach me what this paper stands for,' Schyman interrupted the man, suddenly blazing with rage. 'Barbara Hanson is a lazy, spoiled and hard-drinking member of the family that owns this paper, and that's why you let her behave any way she damn well pleases.'

The editor-in-chief gasped. What little blood he had left in his face drained down into his stomach.

'You can't be serious,' he exclaimed.

'Well, don't we usually call a spade a spade when it comes to our other associates? You've called Hasse over at the sports department the Drunk Driver, and you've called Annika Bengtzon the Manslaughterer. Is Barbara Hanson more fragile than the others?'

'I'm not going to listen to this,' the editor-in-chief said tightly and spun around to face the door.

Anders Schyman got up.

'Where are you going? Could you possibly leave a telephone number where we can reach you? You can drop it off at Tore Brand's desk.'

He studied Torstensson's stooped back under the thin cotton fabric of his shirt. The man's spine protruded like a railroad track. His ribcage heaved with every breath as he paused. By the time he finally turned around, his face was convulsed with anger.

'I'm not going anywhere,' he said. 'I'm going to spend the night here, with the journalists.'

The managing editor looked into the other man's eyes, trying to fathom their cloudy depths.

He's going to fight, Schyman realized. *He's not going to let go. Did I really expect anything else?*

'You can go home now,' Torstensson said as he opened the door.

'I have some papers to go through,' Schyman said.

'You don't have to do that tonight.'

'Are you ordering me to leave?'

Schyman sat down heavily, leaned back in his chair with his hands cradling the back of his head and regarded Torstensson without flinching. Without uttering a word, Torstensson closed the door behind him.

Karin Bellhorn kissed Annika's competitor Bosse on both cheeks, holding his hands in hers, and then nodded to Annika herself.

'Awful business, this,' Bosse said.

The TV producer was pale and there were dark circles under her eyes. Her hair was gathered in a loose bun on the top of her head, secured by a purple plastic comb. A cardigan with pockets, a wrinkled blouse, wide slacks in an exotic print.

'The worst thing of all,' she said in a low voice, 'is that it was in the air. These past few days have been terrible.'

'Could you tell us more?' Bosse asked and glanced over at Annika.

The producer pulled her purse out in front of her, rummaged around in it, and managed to locate a pair of sunglasses and a crumpled pack of cigarettes. She put on the shades and, with the aid of Bosse's lighter, lit a cigarette and inhaled deeply as she looked out over the lake.

'It's beautiful here, isn't it?' she said, hardly exhaling a trace of smoke. It was as if it had been absorbed by her lung tissue.

Annika and Bosse nodded. It really was a beautiful place. A light breeze had started to blow, making the leaves of the treetops flutter gently so that the sunbeams filtering through the foliage danced. Little reflections skimmed the surface of Lake Långsjön and the sheep bleated.

'I felt so incredibly sorry for Michelle,' Karin Bellhorn said slowly, her gaze trained on the opposite shore. 'She had never been as stressed out as she was during this series.'

'Have you worked with Michelle for a long time?' Annika asked, her mouth slightly dry. The TV producer had a personality that commanded respect.

Karin Bellhorn glanced at them over her shoulder. She was holding her cigarette between two fingers next to her mouth and smiled wearily.

'On and off for four years,' she replied. 'I saw a star being born, and dying . . .'

Standing very still, she looked out over the lake again.

'Being in the public eye does strange things to people,' she said. 'It's like a drug, you get hooked. Once you've had a taste of fame, you would do anything to have more.'

'Not everyone,' Annika countered. 'A lot of people choose not to stay in the spotlight.'

Another over-the-shoulder glance accompanied by a sad smile.

'Not without experiencing withdrawal symptoms,' the TV producer countered. 'It takes its toll. Fame is like wounds in your soul – they can heal, but they leave scars. Anyone who's been there will pick at the scabs – they can't leave them alone.'

'Did Michelle have scars like that?' Bosse asked.

A tear escaped from the outer corner of one eye, and the woman let it roll down her face, past her ear and down her neck, without wiping it away.

'She was one great big bleeding wound,' Karin Bellhorn said very quietly. 'But please don't write that. Let her keep some shred of dignity.'

Both Annika and Bosse nodded wordlessly.

'Please tell us what we can write,' Bosse said.

Karin Bellhorn flicked some ash off her cigarette and sighed deeply.

'This whole taping session has been a mess, I'll tell you that. Partially because of the rain, you see. When everyone's constantly soaked to the skin, they lose their tempers. But there was so much at stake too. The series was a gamble for TV Plus, a lot of money, prestige hung in the balance, and it would have made or broken Michelle's career at this point.'

'How did she do?' Annika asked.

The producer inhaled the final greyish-blue puff of smoke, then stubbed out her cigarette against the sole of her shoe and put the butt in her pocket.

'She was absolutely fabulous,' she said quietly, turning towards them and taking her glasses off. 'Michelle had never been better. The whole show was tailored to suit her personality, she got to show off her entire range and she really pulled it off. If TV Plus decides to air the shows, Michelle's critics will have to eat crow. She had an enormous range and great expertise as a reporter, and her camera presence was magnificent. I believe she could have gained international fame in time . . .'

Karin Bellhorn's voice trailed off and she bowed her head.

'I'm sorry,' she said. 'This is so unpleasant.'

Annika glanced at the reporter standing next to her, noting how he studied the producer, memorizing her words and expressions.

'What happened here that night?' Annika asked. 'From what I understand, there was a pretty violent fight over at the Stables.'

The producer pulled out another cigarette, lit this one herself and greedily inhaled the nicotine.

'I wasn't there,' she replied, curtly now.

'Who found her?'

'Why?'

Annika shrugged.

Karin Bellhorn looked at her, her bright, transparent eyes inscrutable. She smoked for a while before she answered.

'I did,' she said. 'There were others. Like your friend Anne. Sebastian, Bambi and Mariana were there too.'

'And Gunnar,' Annika said. 'I expect he unlocked the door.'

'Why such a crowd?'

The producer looked at Annika again for a long time, then burst into laughter.

'That's a good question,' she said. 'Why were there so many of us? Well, I guess we were looking for her. We all needed to talk to her.'

'About what?'

'We had our reasons.'

Karin put out her cigarette, this time leaving the butt on the grass.

'See you around, Bosse,' she said as she threw him a kiss and headed for her car.

'That makes nine out of eleven,' Bosse said as Karin Bellhorn revved up her white Volvo and drove off.

'That leaves Anne and the neo-Nazi,' Annika said.

With a twinkle in his eye, Bosse turned to look at her.

'Well, what do you know . . .' he said. 'So this Hannah is a neo-Nazi? There was nothing about that in your paper today.'

Annika could have bitten her tongue.

He saw her dismay and chuckled.

'I would have found out anyway.'

When the girl put in an appearance, Annika realized that the reporter was right. Hannah Persson from

Katrineholm made no secret of her political affiliation: she had a swastika tattooed on her cheek.

'What a loser,' Bosse whispered.

Annika squinted to keep the sun out of her eyes and tried to study the girl's face behind the tattoos and gobs of black make-up.

Hannah from Katrineholm, shouldn't I be able to recognize you?

Then she became aware of the relentless-time factor.

Hannah had only been seven when Annika had graduated from high school. *She's still a child.*

Unlike the others, Hannah seemed to have been barely affected by her stay at the castle. She walked with a bounce and gazed at her surroundings with curiosity, shielded by a teenager's inability to fear the consequences of her experiences. Her expression was expectant, and she moved in a calflike manner. Annika detected the shadow of a smile on Hannah's face as she climbed over the tape, and felt slightly sick to her stomach for some reason.

'How well did *you* know Michelle Carlsson?' the woman from the national broadcasting service asked.

Hannah Persson stopped, tugged at one sleeve and smiled uncertainly, while the TV camera was less than an arm's length away. Slowly, Annika moved closer, noticing that the little Nazi had a bruise on her forehead and an abrasion on her neck.

'I was on one of the shows,' she said, her voice like silvery bells, a total contrast to her appearance.

'Why is that?'

The reporter's body language and tone of voice illustrated her scepticism and lack of respect.

This rattled the girl. She licked her lips and tried to keep smiling.

'There was this debate,' she said. 'A debate. About feminism and stuff.'

'Why were you detained? Are you a suspect?'

The questions lashed out at the girl, cold and blunt. The cameras buzzed in chorus with the wasps.

Hannah Persson took half a step backwards. The camera closed in on her and her chin began to quiver.

'What . . . Why are you asking me that?'

'You've been detained longer than anyone else. And a murder's been committed, you know. Have any charges been brought against you?'

A shadow passed across the girl's face. The feeling rooted itself and remained. Annika saw the expression in her eyes change, from anticipation to defiance. The next time she spoke her voice had changed; it was somewhat hoarser now and displayed traces of outrage.

'Bitch,' she said. 'I don't want to talk to you.'

The reporter didn't back down. She brandished her huge microphone like a weapon.

'Do you belong to a neo-Nazi organization?'

The girl tossed her head and pouted, looking even younger.

'I'm the secretary of the Katrineholm NP,' she boasted.

That's it, Annika thought. *The label. She is somebody.*

'How do you feel about immigrants?'

The girl shifted position, her feet further apart now, making her look more solid.

'I believe in white supremacy,' she said.

'Then you think we should throw all the immigrants out of this country?'

Something glittered in the girl's eyes, a reflection of their dark, destructive depths.

Stop it, Annika thought. *You're just digging a deeper hole for yourself.*

'I think Sweden belongs to the Swedes,' she said.

'Do you believe we should kill immigrants? Michelle Carlsson was an immigrant, right?'

The TV camera whirred. Darkness took hold of the girl's eyes. Her voice was as smooth as silk when she spoke:

'She was?'

Then she walked away from the camera, passing through the small group of photographers and reporters, and headed for her car. Swiftly, Annika went in the opposite direction, reaching the battered Fiat by walking along the wall.

'Where did you get the gun?' she asked the girl in a whisper.

Hannah Persson stopped short with the key in the car door, and looked up at Annika in surprise. For several seconds her eyes were expressionless. Then they came alive and her face brightened.

'Annika!' she said. 'Annika Bengtzon! You're from Hälleforsnäs!'

She let go of the car key and walked around the car, waving her arms.

'How . . .?' Annika said.

The white supremacist laughed.

'Of course I know who you are. Everyone knows who you are. I heard your husband left you.'

Annika was speechless and stunned. The words struck her full force in the solar plexus.

The girl walked up to her, close. Annika stared at the scratch on her neck.

'Hey,' the girl whispered in her tiny little voice, 'what's it like to kill someone?'

Annika gasped for air like a fish out of water and instinctively backed away a few steps.

Hannah Persson followed her, her eyes as beady as a predator's. Her teeth looked sharp and her breath was stale.

'Tell me. I've always wondered what it's like. Was it hard? How did it feel afterwards?'

Annika bumped into the wall that separated the parking lot from the grounds, staring at the girl. Suddenly, a wave of rage engulfed her.

'What the hell is wrong with you?' she shouted. 'Are you some kind of imbecile?'

The sullen expression returned to the white supremacist's face.

'Don't get mad,' she said, 'I didn't mean to piss you off. I just wondered what it was like, that's all.'

Hannah glared at Annika and returned to her car. Annika didn't move. Her heart was racing and her feet felt like they had lost contact with the ground.

Suddenly Bosse was leaning over her, concerned.

'Annika, are you all right?'

She closed her eyes for a few seconds and breathed with her mouth open, trying to return to normal.

'I'm fine,' she said. 'I tried to communicate with our little Nazi. Only the light's on but nobody's home . . .'

'Q is coming out.'

Annika looked at her fellow reporter and saw honest concern in his eyes, not a trace of craftiness or malice. She averted her gaze. She would have felt victorious if her competitor had missed a press briefing.

They went over to the canal together.

This time Q crossed the tape and stood in the shade of a huge oak tree.

'The first round of interviews with the witnesses who had resided at Yxtaholm castle on the night of 22 June is now completed,' he said and looked guardedly at the small group of journalists.

'We have a picture of the course of events that took place on that occasion. This is why there is no need to detain the witnesses any longer. As you have noticed, most of them have already left.'

Everyone except for Anne, Annika thought, worry lodging like a hot rock in her gut.

'The time of death has been established. Michelle Carlsson died somewhere between two and four a.m.,' the policeman continued. The wind died down and everything was silent.

'Since two witnesses independently confirmed that they saw her outside the castle at approximately 2:30, this interval can be reduced even further. We have concentrated on the events taking place around the castle building and in the grounds between 2:30 and 4:00 a.m.'

He paused for a few minutes before he continued.

'There was a great deal of activity during the night. We know that a car drove up the castle drive soon after 3:00 a.m. The two passengers were male; we have identified both the driver and the passenger. Both men have been interviewed, and neither of them is regarded as a suspect in any way.'

The journalists hung expectantly on his every word.

'In accord with the description provided by a member of the media present at this briefing,' Q said, looking directly at Annika, 'the murder weapon is a revolver which had been brought to Yxtaholm by one of the witnesses. A number of fingerprints have been secured from the gun, but they do not implicate a particular assailant.'

'Is it true that the weapon was stolen from the army?' the woman from the national broadcasting service asked.

Q looked genuinely surprised.

'The Swedish Army doesn't use revolvers,' he said. 'The murder weapon was brought into Sweden illegally.'

'What make is it?' Bosse asked.

'One that is totally unknown on the market in this country,' the policeman said. 'It's apparently home-made, and its country of origin is the US. Naturally, we will pursue this and find out how this weapon managed to reach Sweden, but this is of no interest to the murder investigation.'

'Do you have a suspect?'

The TV team again.

'We are pursuing the leads provided by forensic evidence and the information given to us by our witnesses,' Q said.

'Is an arrest imminent?' Bosse asked.

'Not at this point in time, but circumstances change constantly. We are confident that the murder will be solved.'

'Where is John Essex today?'

Dying of curiosity, the TV reporter's voice was a near-squawk.

'He's on tour in Germany,' Q replied, 'I think he's appearing in Cologne tonight. Any more questions?'

'Did any other kinds of transportation arrive here during the night?' Annika asked. 'Cars, boats, other vehicles?'

The policeman's eyes narrowed a bit.

'As far as we know, the car we mentioned is the only vehicle.'

'Do you believe that one of the twelve people who stayed at the castle is the killer?' Annika asked, not caring that the others would hear the answer as well. The policeman sighed, leaned back against the tree trunk, and felt for his cigarettes in his breast pocket.

'We cannot rule that out,' he said, watchfulness making his eyes gleam.

Annika concentrated on the expression in his eyes, trying to read the message behind his intense blue stare. *He's telling us this because he wants us to write about it, to pass it on. He wants us to spread the word that one of the guests at the castle could be the killer because it suits his purposes. And what could those purposes be?*

The policeman sensed her scrutiny and met her gaze. He lit a cigarette and swallowed the smoke.

It was impossible to speculate any further, she realized. Either it was true that one of the twelve guests really was the killer, and he wanted to throw that person off balance. Or he believed that the killer was an outsider, and in that case he wanted that person to be lulled into a false sense of security.

He saw right through her.

'All right,' the lieutenant said. 'We're getting ready to pack up and go back home to Stockholm. As of tomorrow, I hope our press representative will take over these briefing sessions.'

'Can't you tell us anything else?' Bosse pleaded.

Q stopped resting against the tree trunk and slowly walked over to the police tape. Was his body language resigned? Annika wondered. Or pretending restraint?

'Damn,' Bosse exclaimed. 'The guy doesn't give us a thing.'

'The stuff about the car and the time of death were news to me,' Annika said. As soon as she had uttered the words, she saw Anne Snapphane exit the South Wing, weighted down with luggage. A wave of relief flooded through Annika's system. Unconsciously, she took a few steps towards the tape and raised her arm to wave. But Anne didn't see her. Her gaze was fixed firmly on the ground and her back was bent. It looked as if her bags were extremely heavy.

'Can I give you a hand?' Annika asked Anne Snapphane as she crawled under the tape, her face white and beaded with perspiration.

Her friend looked up, her mouth half-open, her eyes frightened. Then she exhaled sharply and almost smiled.

'I thought you had left already.'

'Without covering the whole story?'

Annika looked at her friend. She had changed; something in her demeanour was very different from how it had been last Sunday, when the two of them had been out with Annika's children at Djurgården. Her hair had lost its lustre, even though it was freshly tinted, and her skin looked more transparent, thinner. There was fear in her eyes and something strangely evasive in the way her shoulders slumped under the weight of her bags.

'Has it been rough?' Annika asked.

Anne Snapphane didn't reply. Her gaze scanned the parking lot.

'How the hell am I supposed to get back home?'

Her voice was small and flat.

'I've got a car,' Annika said. 'Berit's company car. I can drop you off at the station, if you want some time alone. Or, if you can deal with it, you can come with me while I stop by my grandmother's grave and then I'll take you home.'

They both pitched in and carried Anne Snapphane's bags over to Berit's car. A fragile silence prevailed. Anne slipped into the front seat, locked the door and covered her face with her hands.

Annika walked up to Bertil Strand who was talking to the sound technician from the TV team. She stood right next to her photographer without getting his attention.

'We're done here, aren't we?' she said, interrupting him.

Bertil Strand stopped in mid-laugh and turned in her direction.

'Are you in a hurry?'

'I'll see you at the office.'

He nodded curtly and resumed his conversation with the sound technician.

'Are you leaving now?'

Bosse was standing behind her, tall, smiling. She

looked him in the eyes; they were so clear and bright that instinctively she backed away a step, away from his warmth.

'Soon,' Annika said, not knowing why. She should have said 'Yes,' or 'That's none of your business.'

The smile remained. His gaze drew her in, engaging her in a dance that began in her belly and whirled up through her chest, making her giddy.

'How about we grab a beer sometime up in Stockholm?'

Annika blinked a few times, her heart suddenly fluttering in her chest like a bird. When she spoke, she didn't recognize her voice.

'Sure, why not, maybe, I guess we could . . .'

'I'll call you.'

She turned around and fled to her car. Her breathing was so shallow that it barely made it past her larynx.

Anne Snapphane was crying as she sat in the car. Annika got into the driver's seat and looked at her friend who was leaning forwards, her hands up by the windshield. Anne was resting her forehead against the glove compartment, her shoulders heaving with soundless spasms. The unexpected and confusing impression of drunkenness evaporated in seconds.

Gently, Annika placed a hand on Anne's back.

'Everything will be all right,' she said. 'The worst part is over now.'

Thomas got out of bed carefully. His back was stiff and he straightened the sheet to cover the children. He hoped that Kalle wouldn't wet the bed during his nap – he couldn't face doing any more laundry. He stopped in the doorway and looked at them. The girl looked so much like Annika, while the boy was a copy of himself. Their downy hair was tousled by the wind that found its way behind the drawn curtains, and their bodies were shapeless blobs under the sheets. Desperately, Thomas tried to find the feeling of love and connection, the usual pride and fulfilment, but it slipped away, refusing to materialize. He knew why and gritted his teeth.

Doubt.

Were they really worth . . .?

He slipped out and quietly closed the door, a draught making the last ten centimetres slow going. He padded carefully across the hall and got two chairs to block access to the stairs.

'Holger?' he carefully called out in the direction of the kitchen. 'Mother?'

No reply.

The sun was almost hot. The sea's surface seemed to be covered with slivers of mirrors casting reflections that made his eyes smart. Thomas walked down towards the rocky shore, the ground so smooth to the touch, balancing along the waterfront. He caught sight of her too late. She was sitting on the rock out in the water, their favourite spot, and she was smiling at him.

'There you are,' Eleonor said. 'The others were wondering where you went.'

He stopped and cleared his throat, his embarrassment upsetting him.

'I was putting the kids down,' he said, aware that Annika would have told him off if she had known. You weren't supposed to lie down next to the kids to get them to go to sleep, she'd read that in some parenting manual – children were supposed to fall asleep on their own, in their own beds.

Eleonor patted the spot next to her, and without thinking Thomas sat down and put his left arm around her like he had always used to do. Her bare thighs burned his, causing a rush of blood to his loins.

'Gällnö must be paradise on earth,' she said as she looked out to sea, unaware of the effect she had on him.

Eleonor was much softer-looking than he remembered, taller and shapelier. It struck him that Annika was small and hard.

'Don't you miss this island?' she asked, looking into his eyes.

Thomas's diaphragm contracted. He had a hard time breathing and invested her words with a different message.

'Maybe I do,' he said.

She looked out over the water again, shaded her eyes and peered at Hägerön.

'They swam over there,' she said, 'those nuts. Can you see them?'

Thomas pretended to look, her presence making him feel faint. She raised an arm and waved, unintentionally hitting him on the nose with her elbow. He grabbed his nose, amazed at the pain, and she laughed.

'Isn't Martin nice? I'm so happy, Thomas. Aren't you happy for me?'

He blinked away the tears brought on by the punch in the nose, confused and angry.

'We met at a dinner that the bank had for the IT consultants who are going to build our new control system. Martin is one of the partners.'

Thomas checked his nose. It wasn't bleeding.

'Don't fuss,' Eleonor said with another laugh and jumped into the water, hiking up her shorts a little more. The waves lapped at her thighs and she walked carefully along the sharp rocks on the seabed.

'Has he moved into the house?' Thomas asked, suddenly territorial.

'No,' she said and smiled. 'But we have bought a sailboat. It's moored over at the marina in Torsviken.'

'What type of a boat?' he wondered, trying to sound polite.

Eleonor craned her neck in a preening gesture, a quirk she had when she was proud of something.

'It's a 2001 Beneteau Oceanis 36 CCCli, with a fully equipped centred cockpit, a wind-powered generator, sun panels, rubber raft davits, the works when it comes to navigational equipment, adjustable mainsheet rails, supersized Swedish Albatross sails, and waterborne heating. It had travelled seventeen hundred and fifty nautical miles when we bought it, one hundred and forty hours by engine.'

Thomas nodded, impressed but trying to conceal the fact.

'What kind of engine does it have?'

'A Volvo, thirty-eight horsepower. A 20:40.'

'How much was it?'

Eleonor came ashore, shook the water off her legs, slipped on her sandals and gave him a sideways glance.

'I told you it was a used boat.'

He motioned her to spit it out.

'One point three million kronor,' she said.

Thomas crowed with laughter, something he'd already decided to do no matter what the answer was.

'One point three? Talk about being shafted!'

Her joy evaporated and her body language showed it. She pouted, causing a double chin to appear.

'You don't even like sailing,' Thomas said.

She looked up at him with a condescending air.

'That depends on the company I keep,' she said. 'You criticized me all the time.'

Eleonor turned her back on him and walked along the bluff in the direction of the house. His protests remained stuck in his throat – *No, I didn't, you never wanted to learn.* In a flash he knew she was right; he had been impatient, getting upset when she was seasick, finding her weakness irritating.

Thomas saw her get something on the porch and then rush over to Hemfladen and wave at some heads bobbing in the water. The realization made his lungs sting.

I don't deserve her.

Tore Brand rapped on the glass door.

'You've switched off incoming calls,' he said disapprovingly when Anders Schyman opened the sliding door.

'Yes, and I did so for a very good reason,' the managing editor maintained.

'The police are on the line. They want to talk to you.'

Without waiting for an answer, the attendant turned away and went back to the front desk. Dread sunk its claws into Anders Schyman's gut, the same emotion that strikes anyone when the police come knocking on your door – the sense of not knowing what you've done wrong, a desperate and fruitless attempt at justification.

It was a woman.

'I'm calling from the Impound Department,' she said, 'to notify you that the DA has released your property. Do you have the number?'

Anders Schyman cleared his throat.

'There must be some kind of misunderstanding,' he said. 'We don't have any impounded material.'

'No,' the woman conceded, 'but we do. We've got rooms full of stuff. So you can pick up your property now.'

He leaned back in his chair and rubbed his eyes.

'I must say I don't quite understand this.'

'According to the inventory, this property was seized during the murder investigation at Yxtaholm Castle.'

Schyman heard the rustling of papers.

'It's a camera,' the woman said, 'and it has no bearing on the case. The DA's office is anxious to return all impounded property as soon as possible. We don't want to have this stuff here all summer.'

'And it belongs to us?'

'I must request that you pick it up as promptly as possible. Go to our offices on Bergsgatan 52, tell the staff why you came, and you will be able to sign for the release of your property.'

The managing editor jotted down the address on his blotter.

'Are you certain that you won't be needing it?'

'Obviously, we've made copies of the pictures that we deemed were of interest.'

Schyman thanked the woman and hung up, his hand lingering on the receiver.

Then he asked Tore Brand to go and pick up the camera as soon as possible.

Twenty-five minutes later he was holding the impounded object in his hand. It was sealed in a plastic bag and labelled with a police code, a registration number, the case designation, and a serial number. Tearing the bag open, Schyman hefted the device; it was small, compact and heavy. A digital camera bearing a nameplate on the back declaring that it was the property of the *Kvällspressen* Picture Department. He pressed the button marked *power* – the device sprang to life with a ring tone, and the word 'Hello!' appeared on the orange display.

He studied the buttons, which were logical. He had never used a camera like this before, but he had attended the meeting when the paper decided to buy a few for the Picture Department. It wasn't much different from a conventional camera, only the images were stored on a device a bit like a floppy disc instead of on film. The great advantage was that no processing was required; you could view your pictures straight away.

Anders Schyman made a selection and the first shot appeared. The subject was a young woman whom he vaguely recognized as a friend of Annika Bengtzon's. She was laughing and holding a beer, a slightly fuzzy look in her eyes. A man he didn't recognize was sticking his tongue out at the camera. The next shot showed Carl Wennergren in an easy chair, his feet propped up on a dining table.

He clicked through a few more shots, one party picture after another flashed by. He was just about to turn the camera off when he stopped short.

Picture number seventeen showed two people having sex on the dining-room table, in a position that could only be described as advanced. It was obvious who they were: Michelle Carlsson and John Essex. For a few seconds, Anders Schyman stared at the image in disbelief before switching to the next shot. It was out of focus and dark, but he could tell that the couple had changed position. The next shot had Michelle leaning over the table with the man behind her.

I should be turned on, the managing editor thought, surprised by his lack of emotion. *In one way or another, these should have an effect on me.*

He glanced through the rest of the shots quickly. They were all dark and out of focus to some extent. Taken secretly. A white door frame on the right of some of the shots revealed that the photographer had been hiding in a nearby room or space.

In picture number thirty-nine, the outline of another person could be seen. A dark silhouette was present in the upper left-hand corner and the couple on the table had changed to yet another position. The silhouette was closer

in picture number forty and in forty-one he could see who
the person was.

It was Mariana von Berlitz, Carl Wennergren's girlfriend. Mariana had been a summertime extra on the
night shift during the first summer he had worked at the
paper.

She was holding a large revolver.

Anders Schyman felt the hairs on the back of his neck
stand on end. Christ, he had to stand up, he couldn't
believe his eyes. It felt like the camera had grown hot to
the touch – was he holding the murder in his hands?

With slightly trembling hands, he clicked to the next
shot and wound up back at Annika Bengtzon's tipsy
friend again. Square one. He flicked through the pictures
a few times, making certain that he hadn't missed
anything.

Schyman gazed out at the newsroom. No one was
looking in his direction; they were all working for the
company's, or possibly their own, benefit.

What should he do with the pictures?

According to the police, these pictures had no bearing
on the case . . .

No, he corrected himself, *the* camera *has no bearing on
the case. They made copies of the pictures.*

So the logical question was: Who took them?

As far as Schyman knew, no camera had been reported
stolen, which would seem to suggest one of the members
of the paper's staff.

In other words: either Barbara Hanson or Carl
Wennergren.

What the hell should he do with the camera?

He put it on his desk, a potentially explosive lump of
metal. He rocked his chair a bit, concentrating on the
shiny contours of the camera, letting the background
grow fuzzy.

The pictures were unique; they were probably the last ones ever taken of Michelle Carlsson while she was still alive. Publishing them was out of the question. Turning them over to the newsroom staff would be like wall-papering the main square, Sergels torg, with them. Deleting them would be like a journalistic crime.

Schyman leaned back in his chair and covered his eyes with one hand. He remained in this position until he'd made his decision. Then he leaned forward and scooped up the camera. He opened the second desk drawer from the top, tossed the camera in there along with all the paper clips and locked it.

The silence after the drawer closed with a bang echoed in his head. It would just have to stay there – he didn't have the strength to think of another solution right now. He closed his eyes for a brief moment, then surveyed the newsroom and let his gaze rest on Torstensson.

The editor-in-chief was sitting at the foreign corre-spondent's desk, looking vacant and out of place.

He doesn't belong here, Schyman thought, surprised by the sense of certainty that the thought aroused in him.

Annika's knuckles whitened as she gripped the steering wheel.

'Want me to drive?' Anne Snapphane asked.

Annika shook her head and let her gaze sweep across the lake. The shoreline followed the road like a cat follows its mistress during a walk through the woods, taking certain diversions along the way but never straying too far, taking off incomprehensibly, but still present, always close to home.

They had stopped at the Statoil station in Flen and bought a bunch of summer flowers wrapped in plastic for SEK 39.50, checked out from the motel across the road and then headed for Mellösa and Hälleforsnäs.

The countryside was lush with the greenery of early summer, that lovely freshness before an orgy of chlorophyll made the different shades of green merge into one: saturation. The silence in the car was heavy but warm and friendly nonetheless. Anne's tears had subsided, leaving her joints limber and her sinuses swollen. She stared unseeingly out of the window, allowing herself to be rocked and transported.

Annika knew the route without being consciously aware of it. The road and countryside were as familiar to her as if they were carved into her backbone; every last turn in the road, every stone and building had been a daily experience, come rain or come shine, in the heat and in the snow – the route she had taken to school, her childhood's points of reference, her foundation.

'When was the last time you paid your respects at the grave?' Anne asked in a voice that was composed without being tense.

Annika swallowed.

'It's been way too long. When I was expecting Ellen.'

She turned off on the road to Harpsund, crossing the railroad tracks and heading up through the ancient village where the church reposed on the hilltop. She made a left turn at the No Stopping sign and parked next to a pine hedge. She sat still for a few minutes before picking up the flowers, now limp from the heat, and venturing out into the sun.

The dazzling white church was on the left, and Annika noticed a couple leaning on their canes proceeding slowly past the older grave sites. The newer part of the cemetery was on a slope facing the lake, enclosed by hedges of pine and murmuring birch trees. The crunch of the gravel underfoot echoed in the silence. Annika walked carefully, almost furtively. Her gaze swept over the headstones, the old-fashioned Swedish names, the sharecroppers and farmers with time-honoured last names like Andersson, Petersson, Johansson and Eriksson. As she reached the steps, she hesitated and took three deep breaths, watching the sun play a cat-and-mouse game with the shoreline.

It's beautiful here, Gran, Annika thought. *This is a fine place for you.*

She descended the five steps to the next level and went to the left, above the area with the watering cans, plastic vases and garbage cans, passing the grave of the twenty-one-year-old soldier who had died at the Finnish front, on the Svir River, fighting for the freedom of the Nordic countries. There was the reddish-grey granite headstone, polished and lettered with gold: Sofia Katarina. Annika's grandfather rested by Sofia Katarina's side. Annika sank to her knees, the soft grass coating her legs with moisture. Not bothering to use a vase, she laid the flowers, still wrapped in plastic, on the grave.

You would have believed that I was doing the right thing, she thought.

Gran's voice resonated inside her, as strangely youthful and vibrant as when she was alive: *You have to be able to support yourself, you need to have a job. Never let yourself be dependent on a man to put food on the table, do you hear that, Annika? Get a good job.*

'I have a daughter,' Annika whispered. 'I have two children now.'

The next thought she didn't speak aloud.

You wouldn't have approved of me not being married.

She tried to pray: *Our Father Who art in heaven, hallowed be Thy name, Thy kingdom come . . .* But the prayer trailed off, leaving only the whispering of the birch trees, the gentle rustling of the aspen and the rhythm of a train on its way to Eskilstuna.

I miss you, Gran. I miss you every single day. I need you. The loss of your love is like a hole in my soul.

Grief and self-pity shot hot tears into Annika's eyes. She swiped at them impatiently and quickly walked away.

'Do you have time for a detour?' she asked her friend as she got back into the car.

Anne Snapphane was leaning back against the headrest and her eyes were closed.

'I'll go wherever you're going.'

They left the church and made a left turn on the road that wound its way past the log cabins, sweeping past doorways and barns, glassed-in porches and tractors.

Once they had left the village, the country road smoothly accommodated the undulating landscape with its ancient property borders. Red cottages with white trimming nestled on the fringes of the woods, the sun shimmering in handmade glass panes. Thousands of purplish lupins abounded. As they reached the drive leading to the summer residence of the Prime Minister, damp, dark woods enveloped them. Then the surroundings opened up on Lake Harpsund with its famed rowboat, the one that heads of state had gone rowing in. The manor house, done in the style inspired by Sweden's King Karl XII, was located by the road. The cars with tinted-glass windows and the guards posted by the walls gave away the fact that the Prime Minister was on the premises. Annika slowed down, delighting in the view of the grounds.

'Gran was the matron here.'

Anne Snapphane nodded silently.

Slowly, they made their way along the sharply winding road through Granhed and the dark woods by Lake Hosjön.

'And Lyckebo is over there,' Annika said, pointing at a spot higher up on the shore. The farmer had thinned out the trees and the lake was visible from the road.

'Gran's cottage. Well, actually it belonged to the Harpsund estate. She only leased it. And now the place is a hunting lodge.'

They approached Hälleforsnäs. Annika slowed the car down and felt her pulse rev up.

'This is where you grew up,' Anne Snapphane observed, sitting up straight.

Annika nodded. Her throat had constricted. A left turn brought them to the old ironworks, rusting and covered with soot. The plaster was falling away and the gaping windows were boarded up. She stopped by the gate and the barbed-wire fence and stared at the piles of junk and the crumbling exterior of the buildings.

'The blast-furnace?' Anne asked.

Annika nodded again and averted her gaze, not wanting to see the chimney that had channelled smoke and fire from the depths of the furnace. The asphalt at her feet was scarred and patched, the potholes in the road still filled with water.

There was no conscious plan in her mind as she left the car, its engine idling, and took a few steps uphill. A breeze swept past smelling of exhaust fumes and long-forgotten industrial waste. The wind turned sharp and oppressive, stinging her eyes.

Anne came up behind her. Annika pointed.

'They call that development "Gypsy Hill". That's where my mother lives. And my sister.'

The anonymous narrow buildings dotted the hillside above them, red-painted houses built in the 1940s, surrounded by weeds and plastic outdoor furniture, all sharing a view of the ironworks. The wind continued to spiral upward, caressing the empty exteriors and peeling paint. Back in the 1960s the place had been crawling with children but now many of the homes had been abandoned and there was no one in sight. They listened to the emptiness. Somewhere a fan was running, and music could be heard in the distance.

'Where did you used to live?'

Annika looked up at the sun-drenched houses, so cold in winter and unbearably hot in summer, and took a deep breath, making a decision to let her pain surface.

Only it didn't.

There was nothing but the cracked sidewalk to her right and the advancing dandelions to the left of the asphalt.

'Let's go,' she said, abruptly turning and heading back to the car.

As soon as Anne Snapphane was seated Annika put the car in first gear and drove up the hill, remembering the time she had been here, back when she had first met Thomas, and realized that someone had moved into her old apartment. She recalled the mixed feelings of sadness and relief. A chapter was over, someone else was taking care of what had once been hers.

'My apartment was over there. The window with the crocheted lampshades.'

Annika pointed it out and was filled with a sense of unreality. Had she really ever lived here? The windows were sparkling clean and displayed potted plants. That reality belonged to someone else now, it was a part of someone else's life.

'I've seen more cheerful places,' Anne Snapphane commented.

They went right, passed the church and reached the Co-op supermarket, where bicycles were parked out front. Pansies and marigolds were crowded together in large planters by the entrance; they fluttered in the breeze, their gaudy colours crying out for attention before it was too late.

'Isn't this where your mother works?'

'At least she did the last time she called me,' Annika said, tearing her gaze away from the flowers.

They drove through the community, passing *Folkets Hus*, the community centre, the miniature golf course, the rest home, the lamp store and the railroad station. Annika looked around and remembered. The sleeping houses and the swaying trees, the heat of the asphalt and the paving stones. And the huge street that split the whole town in two, it had frightened her so. Now it struck her as narrow and short. The big road, always watch out when you cross the main road – she had been afraid to cross the street on her own until she was in fourth grade.

By now, Anne had lost interest and was resting her head against the window, her eyes closed.

They passed the railroad crossing right by the Hållsta intersection and passed the Erlandsson place. Annika shifted into fourth gear.

As soon as the town disappeared from view, it ceased to exist. The brittle feeling of being locked in the past burst like a bubble; it vanished and was forgotten. Something else began to prey on Annika's mind.

Thomas hadn't called all day. Back at his childhood stomping grounds he wasn't thinking about her at all. The children were creating their own points of reference without her. She wasn't a part of the foundation.

'Don't you want to marry Mehmed?' Annika asked.

Anne Snapphane looked up, dazed and a bit surprised.

'Get married? Are you out of your mind? Why would I want to do that?'

'The two of you have a child together.'

'Come on, we don't even live together. Does this have anything to do with your grandmother?'

Annika rolled up her side window, closing it entirely.

'I want Thomas and me to get married,' she said. 'I really do.'

'Why?'

She shrugged and braked when she caught sight of a deer at the edge of the forest. Then she accelerated once more.

'To show the world that we belong together.'

'You still do, even if you don't get married. Has that gossip got you down?'

'Maybe.'

They sat in silence as the fan stirred up a new-car smell. The surrounding woods were reduced to a green blur as they sped along.

'What was it like?' Annika asked in a low voice.

Anne Snapphane looked out of the window on her side for a few seconds.

'Awful,' she finally said. 'Pretty shitty, to tell you the truth.'

'What was the worst part?'

Anne stared out the window again.

'The guilt,' she said. 'The feeling that it was all my fault. The suspicion.'

Then she turned her head and studied Annika's face in profile.

'For a while there, I thought they were going to arrest me. That they thought I had done it.'

Annika glanced over at Anne.

'Why would you think such a thing?'

Anne Snapphane took a deep breath, filling her lungs with resolve.

'My prints were on the murder weapon.'

'Oh, my God,' Annika exclaimed. 'Why?'

'Because I held the damn thing. Only so did practically everyone else.'

Anne Snapphane looked at Annika.

'In case you were wondering, I didn't do it.'

'Of course I don't think you did it.'

They reached Bäckåsen and turned right, in the direction of Malmköping.

'From what I hear, the whole session was pretty rough going,' Annika said.

Anne Snapphane swallowed.

'A hostess and a researcher,' she said. 'It was humiliating. I deserved a promotion, but right before we got started on the series, I was demoted instead.'

'But you know the reason for that,' Annika countered. 'It wasn't personal. It was because of the cutbacks.'

'I've been a member of the editorial staff for years. The next step should be producer, not hostess, damn it! I should have quit last spring. Guess what I'm supposed to do all week? Label the tapes, take note of the time codes, name cards and junk like that. It's totally insane. Thank God they impounded the damn stuff.'

'I've just got to have some sweets,' Annika said. 'Want some?'

They went into the service station in Malmköping and bought some papers, some cola and a half-kilo of sweets.

'Do you think they'll air the shows?' Annika asked as they pulled out on the road to Strängnäs.

'I should think so,' Anne Snapphane said as she chomped away at a salty licorice treat called *häxvrål*, 'howling witches'. 'I can't imagine that TV Plus would can this golden egg. What did Highlander say?'

'That he would have to confer with the head office in London and delineate the policy regarding the com- memoration of Michelle's memory, and a lot of junk like that.'

Anne Snapphane groaned and smoothed her hair.

'He really knows how to spout bullshit. Did he say confer? He's just a mouthpiece, he can't do a damn thing without a go-ahead from London. Did you know that he fired her on the night that she died?'

Annika was amazed and stared at Anne.

'He *fired* her?'

The wheels of the car's right slipped off the road and she had to turn hard on the steering wheel to get back on track.

'Take it easy. She was too old – she turned thirty-four last Monday.'

Annika eased up on the accelerator, rattled by the close proximity of the ditch.

'What a hypocrite! "Our most esteemed associate" – like hell she was. All right if I use that?'

'Not if you quote me. You see, I only heard it second-hand. Check and see if someone else can confirm it.'

They sat next to each other in silence, Annika gripping the steering wheel firmly with both hands, the bottle of cola like an icy erect penis between her thighs. Oblique rays of sunshine filtered down through the treetops, at times blinding her left eye. She pulled the visor over to the side window and glanced over at her friend. Anne Snapphane had her eyes trained on the landscape, but her gaze was focused inwards. Annika could sense what her friend was seeing in her mind's eye.

'Mariana mentioned a documentary,' she said quietly. 'Michelle was supposedly making a film about her own life, produced by her own company. Do you know anything about it?'

Anne Snapphane blinked a few times.

'It's been a major bone of contention all week. Most people felt that she had exceeded the final limits of conceit. It was all right if anyone else made a documentary about Michelle Carlsson, but she shouldn't do it herself. Some people disagreed, but not many. There was Sebastian Follin, of course, and Bambi. Why shouldn't a public figure be able to profit from their own celebrity? Why did it just have to be everyone else?'

'What do *you* think?' Annika asked, the dancing sunbeams making her squint.

Anne Snapphane fished around in the bag of candy, making a choice between salty licorice gummy fish and cola-flavoured gummy rings.

'Making a tribute to yourself is kind of silly,' she said. 'From a journalistic standpoint it has no credibility whatsoever. I mean, who would dare criticize her?'

'Was she really going to make the film herself?' Annika asked. 'Or would it be made by an independent producer and Michelle's production company would just release it?'

Anne popped a sweet in her mouth and chewed for a while.

'Would it make a difference?' she said eventually, picking her teeth to remove the lingering licorice and preservatives. 'She would still be making and marketing a movie about herself, making money from the fact that she was famous. Now, isn't that kind of lame?'

Annika slowed down as they passed Björndammen, looking at the log cabin that housed a café, at the people who had stopped there for a cup of coffee and some home-made baked goods down by the lake.

'What's so lame about it?' she asked. 'If she used an independent producer who didn't kowtow to her, then it wouldn't really be a problem that the film was produced by her own production company. If the same reasoning applied to everyone else in the media world, it would be impossible for insiders to write about the business.'

'That isn't the same thing at all,' Anne said.

'Yes, it is,' Annika countered. 'Just take the family that owns *Kvällspressen*. They own the largest trade paper too, and the biggest TV network, along with radio stations and Internet companies. Let's say the paper was going to fold

– shouldn't their network or their trade paper be able to cover the story?'

'You just don't get it, do you?' Anne Snapphane said.

They dropped the subject and the ensuing silence was stiffer. Annika fiddled with the car radio, but only managed to get static.

'This Sebastian Follin person,' she said, changing the subject. 'What's the deal with him?'

Anne Snapphane laughed wearily and put the bag of sweets on the floor of the car.

'Oh, my God,' she said. 'Of all the useless people on earth . . .'

Annika shot Anne a quizzical look.

'I thought he booked Michelle.'

'Sebastian Follin was on the payroll as Michelle Carlsson's most avid supporter. His job was to always be there, waving a little flag that said "Michelle is the greatest".'

Anne waved an imaginary flag.

'Why?'

Anne Snapphane shook her head.

'I guess Michelle needed it. She could never get enough applause. Sebastian Follin's job was to give her an overdose.'

They both laughed, briefly and wistfully.

'What other clients has he represented?'

Anne sighed and leaned back against the headrest.

'I don't know, I've never heard him mention anyone else.'

After they passed the works at Länna, Annika made a right turn, taking a short cut through Åkers Styckebruk, the ancient gun factory, along a narrow and winding road.

'Did you ever meet Michelle?' Anne Snapphane asked.

Annika shook her head.

'I don't think so. But somehow it feels like I know her anyway. You've told me so much about her over the years. And then there's all those articles too . . .'

'You have met Karin, though. Karin Bellhorn. At the Christmas party. What did she say?'

Annika mulled it over for a few seconds.

'She seemed pretty exhausted and sad. Talked about how fame does strange things to people, how it's as addictive as a drug. And that once you've had a taste of fame, you would do anything to have more.'

Anne Snapphane nodded.

'Karin would know. She hosted shows back in the 1970s.'

'She did?' Annika said. 'Like she was the hippie equivalent of Michelle Carlsson?'

Anne smiled a little.

'Not exactly, but she had to deal with critics and gossip too. Back in those days her name was Andersson. That was before she married that English rocker, Steven Bellhorn, and left the country.'

'That's right,' Annika said. 'Didn't they get divorced a few years later?'

'Yeah, he ran off with a twenty-three-year-old blonde. Some people say she hasn't got over him yet. What else did she say?'

'That fame was like having a wounded soul. The wounds can heal, but they leave scars. And anyone who's been there will pick at the scabs, they won't be able to leave them alone. She claimed that Michelle was like a bleeding wound. Was she?'

Anne Snapphane didn't answer. She sat quietly while Annika drove out on the highway.

'Did you meet them all?' she asked interested. 'The neo-Nazi girl? Mariana? Wennergren? Stefan?'

Annika swallowed.

Anne shot her a puzzled look.

'That little Nazi girl,' Annika said. 'What an airhead. She knew who I was, which was pretty damn unpleasant.'

'What do you mean?'

Annika's breath was coming out in puffs. She pictured the transfigured features of the girl.

A predator showing its teeth. *What's it like to kill someone? Tell me. I've always wondered what it's like. Was it hard? How did it feel afterwards?*

'She told me she'd heard that Thomas had left me. Mariana and Wennergren drove off without talking to me. So did Axelsson. Bambi Rosenberg did a little scene, but she seemed genuinely devastated.'

'Michelle was her ticket to all the opening-night specials,' Anne Snapphane commented. 'Of course she's upset.'

'Well, these days she gets her own invitations, doesn't she?' Annika protested.

Anne looked out the window and didn't reply. The highway traffic was slow and moved in surges. They were stuck next to a family in a minivan for kilometres on end. A girl who looked like she was around two waved at them the whole time.

'Gunnar Antonsson,' Annika said when they had left the family behind them, 'he didn't really count, did he?'

'What do you mean?'

'Karin said he was easy to forget, and he didn't seem to include himself in the group of journalists.'

'Of course he wouldn't, he's a driver and an engineer. But I like the guy. He really knows his stuff. Did you talk to Stefan Axelsson?'

'I tried,' Annika said. 'He definitely didn't want to talk. How did he feel about Michelle?'

'They had an affair,' Anne Snapphane said. 'A short

one, a couple of years back. After it was over he was really hard on her. Did you meet everyone?'

'Apart from John Essex.'

'So, what do you think?'

Annika shook her head and was quiet for a long time.

'I really don't know,' she said at last.

'Do you think it was one of us?'

A brief pause.

'Probably.'

'Who did it?'

Silence enveloped them. The surrounding cars braked and came to a standstill. They had reached Södertälje, the junction for the freeways heading south and west. There were endless lines in both directions.

'It wasn't you,' Annika said as they waited in the exhaust fumes. 'I don't think it was Gunnar either. But it could be any of the others.'

The newsroom was sharply lit and the night editors were still hyper after a day of sleep. They picked up coffee, laughed, made calls and played pinball on their computers, getting in one last game before the night tied them to Quark Express and the art of the even margin.

Annika couldn't see any of the supervisors at the desk, Schyman's fish tank was empty too. They were probably in a meeting, handing over the day's business somewhere. She went over to her desk and pulled out her laptop. She rested her forehead against her knuckles and took a few deep breaths, then listened to her answering service – nothing. Her cellphone – you have . . . no messages.

According to the original plan they would be coming home tomorrow, on the *Cinderella* in the afternoon, and be back right before six. She picked up the phone on her desk and dialled Thomas's cellphone number. The service picked up and she listened to his distant voice, her chest constricting. Without saying a word, she hung up and pulled out her phone book to find the number of her in-laws' summer cottage. She'd tried to memorize the combination but for some reason Annika could never remember that number, despite having a good head for figures. Once more, she put her hand on the receiver, letting it remain there until her fingers prickled.

He's walking along the shore in the sunset, and he's not missing me.

Annika jumped up and walked over to the coffee machine, leaving images of red suns and blue-tinged beaches behind, and selected a cup of extra-strong coffee. With her back to the wall, she drank the hot liquid as she gazed out over the sharp lines of the newsroom, hearing the echoing sounds and laughter, and tried to banish her throbbing sense of loneliness with controlled breaths.

I'm never going to forgive you for this. Damn you!

The plastic cup crumpled in her hand, the sharp edges cutting the skin. With her gaze fixed on the floor she returned to her desk.

What was she going to write?

Pad and pen in hand, she sketched out the body of the story.

One of the articles should certainly deal with Michelle's final hours.

Annika sighed. The true course of events couldn't be described without dishonouring the deceased; Michelle Carlsson had been roaring drunk, had screamed at her associates, and had reeled around semi-nude while brandishing a gun. She had been fired, she'd fired her manager in turn and she'd been generally out of control.

Still, this had to be suggested somehow – Annika knew it was relevant in some way. Michelle Carlsson's death was a public affair, just like her life had been. The scandals would inevitably leak out. Even if the Swedish press refrained from dishing the dirt, the English tabloids would pull no punches, especially since John Essex was involved.

Annika made a few notes and continued.

The quarrels. The trouble when the shows were taped. They were easier to describe.

The mysterious car that drove up to the castle at a time when the murder could have been committed, probably to pick John Essex up. That was easy too.

The witnesses had been released, but they were expected to hold themselves available for additional interviews.

This was a more delicate situation. Annika chewed on her pen and pondered for a while.

All she had to go on were the cryptic words of Q:

'We cannot rule that out.'

That doesn't really mean anything, though, she thought. Or then again, maybe it meant: any one of them could have done it, or not.

'Bengtzon!'

She jumped and looked up in confusion.

The managing editor was standing in the doorway of his fish tank, waving at her. She picked up the pad with the lists of different items and headed for the corner office.

'Shut the door,' Anders Schyman said and sat down on his creaking chair.

Annika studied him. Her boss looked hot and upset. There were spots on his collar and his eyes were rimmed with red.

'I haven't discussed all the material with Berit yet,' she said, 'but I've tried to set down the basic structure—'

'Discuss that with the guys at the news desk,' Schyman said, interrupting her, his voice hollow with fatigue.

She stopped in mid-explanation. The managing editor was sitting slumped in his chair with his hands over his eyes.

'Is there something wrong?'

Quickly, Schyman leaned forward, his forearms falling on the desk with a thud.

'Will you be working at the beginning of next week?' he asked.

Annika hesitated.

'Why do you ask?'

'You've been at work during the entire holiday. When were you planning to take some time off?'

'As soon as possible. I'll be taking a whole week . . .'

The managing editor made a dismissive gesture with one hand and rubbed his brow with the other.

'I might need your help on Monday with an extremely delicate matter. You aren't allowed to mention it to anyone here at the paper, not even to Berit.'

A sense of surprise bubbled up Annika's spine like a cold carbonated drink, forcing her to sit and lean forward.

'What's it all about?'

Annika studied her boss, trying to find what was hidden behind his bushy beard and his pale eyes.

'What kind of trip is it? Don't the news-desk editors know about it?'

'It's not a trip,' Schyman said. 'This concerns a private matter, one that I need help with.'

Not sure what to think, Annika leaned back.

'I hope I still have a family after this is over,' she said. 'If I'm going to work for you as a personal favour, maybe you could—'

'Forget it,' he said. 'I'll take care of it some other way. Go write your stories.'

Schyman bent over the papers on his desk, indicating

that the conversation was over. Annika studied her boss again. He looked stressed out – there were dark circles under his eyes and rings of sweat under his arms. He seemed tired at times, but this was different.

'What's happened?' she asked.

'Nothing.' He cut her short again.

Annika cocked her head and looked out over the newsroom. The news-desk gang was back, but someone else was there too, a small elderly man in casual clothes, leafing through a magazine.

'Oh my God,' she said. 'Is Torstensson here, on Midsummer's Day?'

Schyman didn't answer. He just stared at his papers without reading them.

'I'm not the only one who has a say when it comes to making up for overtime,' Annika said slowly. 'Now that Sjölander's in New York, I'm supposed to coordinate my schedule with the news-desk editor or the managing editor. If you'd like me to work on Monday, I'll work on Monday.'

Silence filled the room.

'Listen,' Annika said, 'this murder is presenting a problem. My best friend is one of the suspects. Does that disqualify me in some way?'

'How?'

Tired and uninterested.

She hesitated and looked at her fingers clutching at the hem of her shirt.

'Is it possible for me to cover this story in an impartial manner? What if she did it? What would I do?'

Annika looked up and met Schyman's gaze.

'Two of my reporters are suspects,' the managing editor said in a resigned voice. 'I can't spare any more reporters.'

'It's a bit unethical, sort of like the Jesus Alcalà

Amnesty International debacle,' she said, noticing herself becoming evasive.

Anders Schyman sat up straight.

'Some old friends of mine are suspects, too,' he said. 'Karin Bellhorn. We worked together for a short time on the news team for the public service network.'

Annika felt her eyebrows lift in surprise. Was Schyman that old?

'What was she like?'

The managing editor leaned back heavily and stared into his bookcase.

'Well informed,' he said. 'Feisty. A bad case of the camera jones.'

Annika blinked in astonishment.

'The what?'

'The camera jones. She was addicted to being on the screen. I was affected myself, but it's wearing off now.'

Deep in thought, Schyman tapped a pen on the edge of the desk.

'There was some gossip going around about her,' he said. 'Having to do with her last days on the job. I don't know how true it is.'

His stare was still trained on the bookcase and his mind was focused inward.

Annika waited silently.

'Karin circulated a love letter written by a male TV show host to an office trainee. Back in those days you had to sign for any copies you made, and Karin was the only one who had been there the night before this happened. The next day, everyone had received a copy of that love letter in their mail compartment. Karin swore that she hadn't done it, but sources insisted that it couldn't have been anyone else.'

Annika jotted down a few items.

'What happened to the man?'

'It was a feather in his cap.'

'And the trainee?'

'She was immediately dismissed.'

Feeling annoyed, Annika got up.

'Of course,' she said. 'There's a different set of rules for women. And I don't believe that story for a second – people are always putting successful women down.'

'You're quite a feminist, aren't you?' Anders Schyman said.

Annika thought she detected a tinge of derision.

'Well, I've got a brain, haven't I?' she retorted.

Once the glass door closed behind Annika Bengtzon, Anders Schyman let his breath out in an audible sigh. She would do it. She won't ask any questions. No doubt she would understand what was up, but she wouldn't tell. For the first time that day, he felt a flicker of satisfaction. Even though she had been a bit tactless and upset, Annika Bengtzon had been the right horse to back.

He walked up to the glass door and looked out over the newsroom, at the desk where Torstensson had established himself, right at the heart of operations, yet still all alone. The conversations zipped past over his head. Schyman saw how subjects were lobbed back and forth between editors and the night-desk editor, between reporters and the picture editor, between proof-readers and the rewrite people – an organic flow reminiscent of waves, gentle ripples exerting more force than was apparent to the eye. In the middle of this sea the editor-in-chief was like a pile driven into the seabed, rigid and stationary, made of some other stuff. Unaffected by laughter or urgency, unable to contribute to discussions overloaded on adrenalin or possessing any complexity. At times he looked up, always with the same lack of comprehension. His vulnerability was enormous, and

Schyman was struck by a great wave of genuine compassion.

Maybe things will be all right anyway, he thought. *He's too uninformed, that's all. It's a good thing that he's out there tonight, it's a good omen, maybe he'll start cooperating.*

Anders Schyman hesitated momentarily, then locked his door. He went back to his desk, sat down and unlocked the bottom drawer. He considered its contents; it was practically empty. The only file was a red, well-thumbed folder: his contingency plan, armaments for ethical and moral warfare. The volatile material had been stored there, like anthrax or mustard gas, for months, possibly even years, his journalistic weapons of mass destruction. Using this material would be risky, maybe even dangerous. If he went public with this, it could rebound like biological warfare and contaminate him as well.

I don't have to make my decision tonight, Schyman thought.

He picked up the folder anyway and weighed it in his hand. It was pretty thin.

He let it land on his desk; no problem, the material was only dangerous if it came into contact with other journalists. Off came the elastic band, exposing the photocopied sheets within the cardboard folder. He traced the top sheet with his fingers. It was dry and rough. The minutes from the board meetings of this paper for the past three years. Obviously he wasn't supposed to have them, he wasn't even allowed to read them. He didn't have access to the boardroom run by the family that owned *Kvällspressen*.

But Torstensson did. The editor-in-chief attended the board meetings as a co-opted member. He couldn't vote, but he was present in order to pass on pertinent information and participate in discussions. This explained why he received one of the few existing copies of the minutes, documents he presumably kept under lock and key. They weren't. Torstensson put them in a binder marked 'Board meeting minutes'. This was something that Schyman had discovered late one night when he was on his way home. On his way to the garage, he'd suddenly had to take a leak and had used the closest restroom. When he came out he realized that he was facing the editor-in-chief's spacious corner office, and without further ado he walked up to the door and tried the handle. It wasn't locked. Without making a sound, he had entered the dark room and closed the door behind him.

For the next hour Schyman inspected the entire room. Every last document, newspaper and magazine, every binder, the channels on the TV set. The folder with the minutes was in a bookcase behind the desk. Without a qualm he made copies of every single page, in addition to a few other papers that he threw away later on.

But he saved the minutes. Since then, whenever he worked late, a commonplace occurrence, he would generally check out the editor-in-chief's office, sometimes finding it locked. But not always. When it was possible, he took stock of whatever he felt he needed to know, which amounted to almost everything. At the present time he had access to all the documents that had any bearing on the future of the paper.

Am I being presumptuous? he thought as he leafed through the minutes. *Why do I feel as if I'm responsible for the welfare of this paper?*

Because I know the ropes, he answered himself. *I see things. Making observations and figuring out the consequences is what I'm good at. That's why I'm here. I have an obligation to act on my convictions, even if it means using public exposure as a weapon.*

Some of the minutes were earmarked. Schyman picked them out. Two sets of minutes, that was all.

The first set concerned the apartment. Eighteen months ago, Torstensson had asked to be included on the board of the real-estate company owned by the Party. According to the minutes, the other members of the board saw no impediment to this request. The union representative, whose presence was tolerated only because it was required by law, had protested, and this was duly noted. He had felt that such an assignment was unsuitable for a member of the press whose job was to promote the freedom of the press and to question those in power. So an editor-in-chief should not be involved with a political commitment of that nature.

After he had read the minutes, Anders Schyman had contacted the Patent and Registration Office to obtain a list of the board members of the real-estate company. As anticipated, Torstensson had accepted the slot on the board, a fact that Schyman had underlined in pencil in the margins.

Nearly a year later an extremely distraught elderly woman had called Schyman. She had intended to talk to the editor-in-chief, but since Torstensson wasn't available, the operator had put her through to the managing editor.

She introduced herself – her last name evoked the ranks of minor nobility – and told him a rather incoherent tale about how she used to live in a three-bedroom apartment on Floragatan in the fashionable Östermalm district of Stockholm, an apartment that she and her husband had moved into when they were married back in 1945, right after the war, did he remember the war? He didn't? Well, in any case, her husband was no longer alive – the grief was frightful, absolutely frightful – and now her home was being taken away from her as well, she had been forced to move, which was frightful as well. The landlord had remodelled the building and she had been offered another apartment somewhere else – was that really legal?

Slightly annoyed, Schyman had listened to her tale with little interest until she mentioned the name of her landlord. It was the Party's real-estate company. The reason why she was calling Torstensson was that his son now had possession of her old apartment, while she had been packed off to a smaller place on the outskirts of town, in Skärholmen. She didn't want to live there, not at all, there were so many foreigners and you know what they're like, violent terrorists, every last one of them, and the architecture was just frightful. She had been forced to buy a condo in Östermalm, and felt entitled to compensation from the real-estate company.

Schyman had cross-examined the old lady and came to the conclusion that she was telling the truth. Torstensson's son had been listed as residing at that address two months prior to the lady's call, and the apartment was on the same floor. In addition to this, the building was in the process of being turned into a co-op, and Torstensson's son was the chairman of the association.

This might have been good enough, Anders Schyman thought with a sigh, but it wasn't. He fingered the papers that he had collected and assessed their strength. The old lady wouldn't do. Journalistically speaking, she didn't cut the mustard. No one would feel sorry for a filthy-rich upper-class racist who could buy her own place. Sure, it was morally questionable of Torstensson to let his son cut to the head of the line, bypassing the countless hopefuls registered with the housing authorities of Stockholm. But Torstensson would cling to his position no matter what, and if he didn't resign or get fired with a great deal of hue and cry the whole affair would only hurt the paper, not save it.

He had to find something dirtier.

One way of getting rid of Torstensson would be to let the paper botch things up royally, make a mistake that would be condemned by the entire population. If such a thing were to happen, the board would have to consider declaring a vote of no confidence. But Schyman would never go that far. His primary mission was to save the paper, not to send Torstensson to the gallows. The point was to target the editor-in-chief without harming anyone else, which made things much harder and required greater precision.

Schyman didn't want any collateral damage. And he would probably be dismissed as well if the paper got into trouble.

So, it looked like the stock-market transaction was the key, along with Annika Bengtzon.

Schyman pulled out the papers at the very back: one set of minutes, a press release and two clippings from the business paper *Veckans Affärer*.

The first clipping was an inventory of the media corporation controlled by the family that owned *Kvällspressen*, mapping out the financial ties between the different companies. Practically all the different companies were connected in one way or another. The corporate group included newspapers, periodicals, radio and TV networks, Internet services and manufacturing companies that made sanitary pads and nappies, among other things.

The newspaper *Kvällspressen* formed a modest blue brick in the graphic overview of the corporate group. For the time being it was there, but if the economy took a nosedive and there wasn't enough advertising revenue, this could mean that it would be curtains for the paper. Since the circulation didn't look like it was on the rise, advertising revenue was what kept the bottom line nice and black. There was a definite risk that that pale blue brick would soon cease to exist.

Schyman scanned the figures, his attention drawn to the lower right-hand corner and the section for New Media. This article had been published back in 'The Good Old Days', when the future held salvation and the possibilities were endless. The family's proud flagship on the seas of the Digital Age was called Global Future, their Internet company for digital-technology ventures, a team of consultants that would do business with the Market and build the Future. The newspaper *Kvällspressen* was a little blue brick in the Global Future pedigree as well. Somewhere, sometime, their cutting-edge website would be constructed, the site that would win the war in cyberspace and bring *Kvällspressen* into Tomorrowland. It never happened. The paper was still stuck with a hopeless site – a few news flashes and TV guide selections – while their competitor had created the most prestigious portal in Europe.

Schyman sighed loudly, weariness pounding through his system. He leaned back, rubbed his eyes, and fitted the pieces of the puzzle together in his mind.

Most of the family's businesses were public companies, as was Global Futures, and the IPO had been a very costly affair, along with being a bit premature. The family had wanted to ride on the Tech Wave, float in the bubble that brought the stock markets of the world to unrivalled heights, and what was wrong with that? The market spoke and made decisions regardless of whoever was listening. At first, the venture was successful. Global Future was a major comet on the Stockholm Exchange in those days. The CEO was an enterprising young man who had political ties to the Party. He drew up the guidelines for the future, made numerous TV appearances, participated in seminars, and held lectures on the subject 'The Promise of the Future', exploring what life would be like when broadband technology was fully implemented and the virtual household was a reality.

However, the company never actually made a profit. Still, the high market value was a part of the Future and the return on this venture would be so great for so many in the long run. In contrast to other venture capital-based companies, such as boo.com and Framfab, the parent company would assure Global Future's stability.

Torstensson had been wild about it. He had waxed lyrical on the subject of 'The Future' and he had promoted several series of articles about the Promise of the Future that had helped inflate the value of the Internet companies, including Global Future. The generous options provided by his contract allowed Torstensson to be in on the market from the very beginning, and he had bought substantial shares in the company. This was something Schyman had deemed inappropriate in itself, but the Internet department of the paper was to be created and maintained by Global Future, which let Torstensson off the hook. Who could blame an editor-in-chief for believing in his own project?

During the heyday of the Tech Bubble and the raging bull market, Torstensson occasionally revealed how much money he had made by going in on Global Future from the beginning. Schyman estimated that he had made roughly five million kronor, chicken feed in those days but a huge fortune for ordinary people.

He picked up the minutes dated 27 June of last year, fingering one of the dog-eared corners. He had read this many times, pondering on its significance. It was a summary of the meeting held right before summer when the chairman had informed Torstensson that Global Future would no longer be contributing to the paper's digital project. From now on each individual newspaper and periodical within the group would be financially accountable for their own ventures into new media. A serious profit warning was expected in the financial report for Global Future's second quarter that would soon be made public.

Schyman dropped the minutes and picked up the press release dated 20 July.

In stark contrast to previous financial forecasts, Global Future was still not generating a profit. In fact, the company was doing worse than ever, its losses far exceeding those in the preceding quarterly reports. In itself, this shouldn't have alarmed the market – if it hadn't been for the fine print.

The biggest difference in the race between Global Future and the companies with venture capital backing was that the parent company had agreed to allocate funds to the company, as long as – and this was the clincher – the company showed a profit during the now-impending third quarter. Everyone who had done their homework realized the impact of this clause, and unloaded their shares, causing the price to drop 28 per cent on Thursday, 20 July of last year. It went from a peak rate of 412.50 kronor to 297 kronor, and this was only the beginning.

Three months later the parent company announced that they would no longer be able to supply Global Future with any more money, since the company was deeply in the red. During the autumn, the stock price dipped to practically rock bottom, landing at 59 kronor at the beginning of the new year.

This dramatic scenario paralleled that of the other Internet companies. Some companies' valuations had been in the range of one thousand kronor a share. After the bubble burst they might only be worth a mere fraction of a krona, eighty öre. It wasn't the decline as such that was so remarkable, it was the transaction described in another clipping from *Veckans Affärer* that presented a problem.

Or, possibly, a solution, Anders Schyman thought as his gaze lingered on the date: 27 February of this year. He browsed through the long columns, the list of influential people and the stocks they owned.

There he was: Torstensson, editor-in-chief, *Kvällspressen*, owner of the following: No shares.

He had sold them all.

This was an excerpt from the most recent yearbook of the Securities Register Centre. At some point before the end of the year, Torstensson had unloaded something like ten thousand Global Future shares.

The only question was when.

Schyman's investigation had progressed to such an extent that he knew that the transaction had not been reported to the Financial Supervisory Board. On the other hand, there was no reason why it had to be registered there. Torstensson was not obliged to report his transactions.

Still, the thought nagged at the managing editor.

Had Torstensson sold his stocks too early?

The issue had bothered him for quite a while, but Schyman hadn't been able to pursue it any further. Going to the Securities Register Centre would mean having to show some ID, and this information would be recorded on their log. It would leave a trace that would be easy to figure out and to follow. Someone else would have to do the digging, a reporter used to going through files.

Resolutely, he gathered the documents, counted them, put them in the folder and then replaced them in the bottom drawer. He locked the drawer and checked that it was locked.

Then Schyman leaned back in his chair and studied the newsroom team through the glass partition, rocking gently, much more at ease now than he'd been all day.

I don't have to decide just yet.

SUNDAY, 24 JUNE

*D*ear readers, get nice and comfy now, 'cause do I ever
have a story for you! This was absolutely the worst
*Midsummer Eve ever – just imagine getting all dressed up in
your best summer dress and sandals to take part in a grand
show, and then what happens? You get to see the show being
taped and it, pardon the expression, stinks. Our little
scatterbrain was all over the place, pretending to conduct
interviews, and when it's finally over and you sigh with relief,
and have a little champagne to celebrate that you're still alive,
that's when all hell breaks loose! I've never been party to such
machinations in all my life – it was impossible to get any sleep
and people were shouting up a storm, but I swear I didn't hear
a gunshot . . .*

*That's right, my dear readers, I was caught in the midst of
what the hyenas here at the paper refer to as the Midsummer
Murder. Michelle Carlsson was shot in a car that was parked
under my bedroom window, imagine that. Not that I know what
she was doing in that car anyway, maybe she was planning to
leave – even though she had no business driving, considering
the amounts I saw her drink that evening. But then again,*

maybe she couldn't sleep either, seeing as the pillows and the
mattresses at the castle were exceedingly uncomfortable . . .

'What the hell is this?' Anne Snapphane demanded,
letting the newspaper drop on the duvet in a crumpled
heap.

Mehmed peeled off his jeans and underwear and got
back into bed with her again.

'Schyman's certainly got something to sink his teeth
into today,' he said as he flicked his tongue over one of
Anne's nipples. She swatted him lightly on the head and
picked up the paper again.

'This shows a monumental lack of judgement,' she
said. 'It's absolutely disgusting. How can they let that
bitch get away with crap like this?'

'Yeah, it doesn't make sense,' the man agreed, his head
resting on her chest.

'Seriously,' Anne went on, 'isn't this defamation of the
deceased, or something like that?'

'It's hard to get a conviction on counts like that,'
Mehmed said, lifting his head and looking into her eyes.

She stroked his hair, so black and shiny, and traced his
stubbly jaw with one finger, triggering the familiar wave
of desire.

'Why is that?'

He let her finger slip into his mouth and mumbled:

'The chapter on defamation and libel, item four.
"Involving an action which is offensive to the family of
the deceased or constituting, with regard to how long ago
the individual in question was alive along with other
circumstances, a breach of the peace accorded to deceased
personages." She didn't have any relatives, did she?'

'Her mother, the Latvian hooker,' Anne Snapphane
whispered and shifted under him. Effortlessly he slipped
inside her. They lay there without moving, drinking in

each other's breath, exchanging gazes that made them both giddy.

'Oh, Lord,' she moaned quietly, leaning back and closing her eyes, his weight covering her everywhere at once. She took him in, hard and silky.

'Mommy? Look!'

Their barely perceptible movements, motions that they were hardly aware of making, came to an immediate halt. Anne noticed the pungent aroma of newsprint as she opened her eyes and stared into Annika Bengtzon's picture byline.

'What's the matter, honey?' she asked, pushing away the paper and lifting her head from the bed.

'Read book,' her two-year-old demanded, putting the story of Max and his potty on her dad's back.

Mehmed let his head drop and nuzzled into her neck. His heated breathing drifted down under the sheets, causing the hairs on the back of her neck to stand on end.

'Not right now – Mommy and Daddy are resting.'

'It's all right,' Mehmed said softly, close to her ear. 'She's been asking for you all week. We'll continue this later.'

Anne stroked his broad back and swallowed.

'Have you had breakfast, sweetie? Did Daddy make you a sandwich?'

'Daddy sammich,' the girl confirmed and climbed up on the double bed.'

Mehmed slipped out of Anne, leaving a monumental void, followed by warmth and indolent desire.

'Miranda,' Anne Snapphane said. 'Miranda Izol, come and kiss Mommy.'

The girl, with her dark curls and dark eyes, snuggled up to her mother like a freezing kitten to a radiator.

'Mommy,' she said. 'Mommy.'

Anne threw her arms around the child and gently rocked her.

'Has Mommy been gone for a long time?'

The girl nodded.

'But you've had a good time with Daddy, haven't you?'

Another nod.

'Want to hide under the covers?'

Anne Snapphane pulled the covers over her daughter and herself. In the darkness, the air was close with the scent of their bodies. She felt the mattress sway as the springs were released on Mehmed's side of the bed and heard his bare feet pad off towards the door.

'Coffee?'

'Love some,' she replied, her voice throaty.

'Go home?'

Anne looked at the contours of the curled-up toddler and stroked the little head that had immediately got sweaty.

'We *are* home. At Daddy's house.'

The girl snuggled closer and wound her hand in her mother's hair.

'You're going to spend the day with Daddy today. Mommy has to work, but then you and I are going home to Lidingö. Would you like that? To go home to your dolly carriage?'

The girl waved her arms around to let in some air and Anne Snapphane kicked off the covers. The bedroom air hit her like a cold draught, damp and piercing. She shivered.

'Schyman has been trying to get in touch with me on the cell,' Mehmed said as he brought the coffee in and set it on her night-stand: milk, no sugar.

The girl jumped off the bed and Anne propped herself up in bed and leaned back against the pillows again.

'What did he want?'

She picked up the cup and warmed her hands on the china.

Mehmed sat down and caressed her calf.

'He wanted to know how long our team worked during the summer season.'

'Why?'

'Beats me, he just left a message. Was the coffee good?' She smiled at him over the rim of her cup.

'You wouldn't happen to know if something's up at the paper, would you?' he asked.

'If there was,' Anne said, 'why would Schyman tell you?'

Mehmed Izol, host and producer of the most prestigious in-depth news programme at Sweden's public service network, ran his hand up her thigh.

Berit Hamrin slapped the paper down on Annika's desk. She was out of breath and her face was blotchy.

'Have you read Barbara's column?'

Annika stuffed the last morsels of a jam doughnut dusted with sugar in her mouth and licked her fingers before she picked up the paper.

That's right, my dear readers, I was caught in the midst of what the hyenas here at the paper refer to as the Midsummer Murder.

'What the hell . . .?' Annika exclaimed and swallowed the greasy treat. 'Who okayed this?'

'That's exactly what I was wondering,' Berit said, perching on Annika's desk, still wearing her raingear. 'Something's up. Why else would Torstensson be here all night?'

Annika wiped her mouth with an old napkin and thought about Schyman's peculiar private assignment.

'It was a mistake to bring her back from Lisbon,' Berit

declared, studying Barbara Hanson's column again. 'At least she couldn't do any harm over there.'

'She didn't do a darn thing in Lisbon besides run up bills,' Annika said.

Berit Hamrin got up and took off her jacket.

'It might cost us a lot more to let her do as she pleases in print. This is libel, for goodness' sake. What do you think of the rest of the paper?'

Annika picked up her own copy of *Kvällspressen* and opened it to the news pages. Assisted by Jansson, the night editor, she and Berit had pieced together the entire layout last night. Torstensson had been seated nearby, looking preoccupied and uneasy, and his presence had caused them to keep their voices down and hold back on the cynical banter. The results had turned out more or less according to plan: Michelle's final hours, the difficult taping session, the mysterious driver and passenger, and the feature about the suspects, as tricky as a walk on a tightrope, that had the headline 'Tightening the net'. Other pages featured reactions from the entertainment community, a discussion of the future of TV and speculations about if *Summer Frolic at the Castle* would now be aired. Berit and Annika had sifted through all the material, they had edited each other's pieces and all their articles had a double byline.

'It looks fine,' Annika said.

'Check out the next page,' Berit said.

The entertainment section had sent a team to Cologne to cover the John Essex concert. They had managed to get a shot of him getting into his limo in front of the hotel but they didn't get a statement.

Annika studied the picture: the man's wary body language, the anonymous faces of the girls in the crowd, made blurry by the distance and their fervour, the jungle of clutching hands, the silent screams.

It was a suggestive image, backlit and shadowy, yet still striking and expressive. Questions popped up in her mind.

How does he stand it? What could possibly make up for the lack of privacy? What price are people prepared to pay for approval?

'Who took this?' she asked.

'Some new guy, an extra photographer for the entertainment section. His name is Henriksson. Have you talked to Q yet?'

'I was just going to call him.'

Berit Hamrin got up, picked up her jacket, her paper and her bag and went over to her desk, located a few desks down from Annika's.

Annika picked up their competitor's paper, leafing past the op-ed and culture sections to reach the news spread on pages six and seven. She saw his picture byline.

Bosse, looking serious and a few years younger than he actually was, gazed up at her from the pages of the paper. She recalled the heat, the giddiness.

She dismissed the feeling and picked up the phone, dialling the number from memory.

The policeman answered.

'Where were you yesterday?' she heard herself demand. 'I called you like crazy all night long.'

The line crackled and there was a soft rustling sound in the distance.

'I'm kind of busy. What do you want?'

Realizing that she wasn't really prepared, Annika scratched her head and rifled through her notes.

'The forensic investigation,' she said. 'You've identified a shitload of prints found on the murder weapon, right?'

'I told you that yesterday.'

She bit her lip.

'How many?'

'None that can be attributed to a particular assailant.'

'Prints from all of them? All twelve?'

A split-second pause, the sound of the wind whistling.

'Actually, all thirteen of them,' he said.

Annika's eyes widened.

'Michelle's prints too? Could she have shot herself?'

'The thought has occurred to us,' he said dryly. 'But the evidence doesn't support it. No letter, no talk of suicide. We believe someone else pulled the trigger.'

'Who?'

He laughed, almost sadly.

'Think before you ask stuff like that.'

She grew silent and skimmed her notes.

'The weapon,' she said. 'What do you know about it?'

'I told you that yesterday as well.'

'It was big, a heavy ornate piece. Was it an antique?'

'Nope. It was new.'

'So, it was a copy. Of what?'

'I don't know. The original replica wasn't lethal. The barrel's been drilled, and the girl who owned it wasn't very forthcoming.'

'So what does she say?'

'Nothing. We're going to pull her in again. A patrol's on its way.'

Annika raised an eyebrow in surprise and jotted this information down.

'You're going to arrest the little Nazi?'

'That's right.'

'For murder?'

'Illegal possession of a weapon. Don't make too much of it.'

'Will she be remanded in custody?'

'I shouldn't think so, but you never know.'

Annika paused briefly and then asked:

'It was one of the twelve guests, wasn't it?'

The policeman didn't reply.

'Well, it wasn't Anne Snapphane or Gunnar Antonsson,' she said.

'Do you expect me to play *Ten Little Indians* with you?'

The poor connection diluted the sarcasm of his tone. Annika didn't intend to let him off the hook.

'You told me yesterday that you had a picture of the events . . .'

'That's true.'

'And that someone is lying. Who?'

'If only it were that simple,' he said. 'Every last one of them is lying about something. They all claim that they didn't touch the revolver, for example. And what makes you exclude Snapphane and Antonsson?'

'Do you really want to know, or are you being sarcastic again?'

She heard him light a cigarette, inhaling and sighing.

'Tell me,' he said, exhaling a stream of smoke, a gust in her ear.

'I know Anne,' Annika said. 'She would never do such a thing, and all that. And Gunnar Antonsson is too . . . conscientious.'

'I see,' the policeman said, no longer hiding his scorn. 'Who else can we cross off the list?'

'The little Nazi,' Annika said. 'She doesn't know what it's like to kill someone, but she would like to.'

'How do you know that?'

His voice was grave now.

'What's in it for me?'

The detective took a drag on his cigarette and exhaled audibly. It sounded as if he was walking around while he took another greedy drag as he considered his next move.

'The shot to the head killed Michelle Carlsson,' he said. 'There were no other wounds on the body. Semen was found in her vagina. There was no sign of a struggle in the control room. There were traces of vaginal fluids on the murder weapon. What makes you think Hannah Persson is innocent?'

Annika froze in her chair, a sheet of ice covering her head and back.

'Traces of vaginal fluids on the murder weapon? Is *that* what you said?'

'The whole butt, the barrel and the trigger. She can't have had the whole gun inside her, that's anatomically impossible, so someone must have plunged it in and out of her at different angles – either another person or she did it herself.'

'Was it . . . loaded during these . . . escapades?'

'As far as we can tell, yes.'

Something stirred in Annika's gut, a wave of nausea. It filled her belly and her chest, almost making her vomit.

'That's disgusting,' she said.

'Hannah Persson,' Q urged.

Annika closed her eyes, put her hand on her forehead and started breathing with her mouth open.

'Hello?' the policeman called out. 'You still there?'

Annika cleared her throat.

'She pounced on me in the parking lot and asked what it was like to kill someone.'

'She knew who you were?'

'Absolutely. She asked me if it was hard, what it felt like afterwards and she told me she had always wondered what it was like.'

'Maybe she wanted to compare notes?'

'No,' Annika said. 'She was curious. She didn't know. She had toyed with the idea without daring to go for it. I know that's the truth.'

'The stuff about the bodily fluids won't go down well in a family paper like *Kvällspressen*,' Q said.

'It's all in the phrasing,' Annika assured him and the conversation was over.

She held the receiver for a few seconds, choking back her sensation of disgust.

'How did it go?' Berit called out.

Annika hung up.

'Let's go and have some coffee.'

Bambi Rosenberg picked her way carefully up the hill to the offices of Zero Television. Sharp gravel slid under her feet and cut into the thin leather soles of her ankle boots.

Her jeans rode up uncomfortably. She had gained weight.

It was difficult to move and she stopped. Breathing was difficult, simply existing was difficult. She squinted to study the row of windows on the third floor, trying to make out Michelle's. The cloudy weather eliminated that possibility.

Now there was no one around who could understand.

There was no way she could ward off this insight. It was as if it had been rammed down her throat and had got stuck there, making her want to throw up.

She was alone again. Oh, dear God, she was on her own again, the closeness was over, gone.

A cold wind nipped at Bambi's stomach and she pulled the leather jacket tighter.

How was she going to survive without Michelle?

Now things would go back to the way they used to be.

Feeling lost and vulnerable, too much wine, too many different groping hands on her body. Just like in the old days.

She hurried up and stumbled along.

The door was as heavy as if it had been a stone slab. Bambi had to dig her heels in to yank it open. One of her heels slipped and the strap of her shoulder bag shot down to her elbow, causing the bag to slam into her knees and the flap to fly open. Mascara, lip gloss, a caramel chocolate bar and a few stray tampons rolled out on the gravel and tears stung her eyes. She looked for something to prop up the door with, but she was out of luck. Bending over and keeping the door open with her behind, she gathered up her belongings. One of the tampons had landed in a small puddle where it had blossomed to four times its original size, so she left it there.

Bambi had never liked Zero Television.

She took the elevator even though she should have taken the stairs. *Get in shape, start thinking.* Michelle's voice came to her, a ghostly echo under the fluorescent lights. *Don't skip lunch, it ruins your metabolism. Lose the potato crisps, they're pure fat and starch. Orange-peel thighs, now how much fun is that?*

Gingerly she walked into the newsroom, so stark and deserted, computers and papers, dust and coffee stains. She stopped right next to the door. Someone had to be here, the lights were on everywhere, so she listened. The air-conditioning was on, humming with frigid air, but she couldn't hear anything else.

Quickly, Bambi walked over to Michelle's office.

As soon as she had reached the lounge, she saw his back. A short grey jacket covering a shapeless chubby form.

The rush of adrenalin made her feet fly.

'What are you up to?'

Sebastian Follin looked up, his forehead glistening with sweat and his hair on end from standing bent over.

'Oh, it's you . . .'

He turned away again and continued to remove papers from the bottom drawer. Michelle's files.

Bambi Rosenberg went up to the desk, placing her

hands protectively over the disorder on the desk and pushed past Sebastian Follin.

'This stuff belongs to Michelle. What are you doing to Michelle?'

'The police have already searched through it all. There isn't anything of value here for them. It's my property now.'

Bambi stared down at the balding spot on his crown.

'No, it isn't!' she said. 'This is Michelle's stuff, her private possessions. You don't have any business messing with it.'

With considerable effort, the manager got up, his left hand supporting the small of his back.

'Come on, toots,' he said in a slightly reproaching voice, his eyebrows arched. 'This material concerns Michelle's business, and since I'm in charge of her business I want to make sure it won't wind up in the wrong hands.'

'But,' Bambi Rosenberg protested, 'that's not true. You don't have a claim on her. You aren't entitled to her things now that she's dead.'

The man's features were contorted. His chest had sunken in and he looked even chunkier. His hair had flopped into the eyes that had narrowed into slits behind his glasses. He raised his hands.

'Get out of here,' he hissed. 'Beat it. I'm in charge now.'

Bambi Rosenberg blinked a few times, noting the man's aggression but still not registering it.

'You're out of your mind,' she said. 'You don't have anything to do with Michelle any more. She fired you last Thursday.'

Something happened to Follin, a movement that sharpened his contours. A hardness came over him.

'What was that?'

His voice was reduced to a hiss.

'She told me, and she told me she'd told you too. And her word is legally binding . . .'

Sebastian Follin stood utterly still. Bambi could see herself reflected in his glasses.

Suddenly she realized the significance of her words.

She gasped and took a step away from the man.

'You,' she said. 'You did it. She was your whole life, and she took it away from you. If she had been alive the next morning, you would have been out of a job. But now that she's dead, you think she's going to be yours for ever . . .'

The shove came from nowhere, striking Bambi at shoulder height, right above her armpits, and making her tumble backwards with a scream.

'What are you doing, you lunatic?'

'Shut up,' Sebastian Follin bellowed, coming up to her, pressing his body against hers, his head reaching no higher than her cleavage, his hands reaching for her neck.

What little hold her heels had on the wall-to-wall carpeting disappeared. Bambi Rosenberg crashed to the floor, biting her tongue as she banged her head on the glass wall, the manager on top of her. She fought for air and managed to scream.

'Shut up, you little slut . . .'

Oh, dear God, I'm going to die, he killed Michelle and now he's going to kill me, we'll both die by the same hand . . .

'Help, he's crazy, he's trying to kill me . . .!'

Bambi worked one of her arms loose and raked Follin's puffy face with her fake nails, enjoying the drag of her fingers against his skin.

'What on earth are you doing?'

A startled Mariana von Berlitz stood on the threshold.

'Help,' Bambi managed to say. 'He's trying to strangle me.'

The pressure on her body disappeared, leaving her

reeling. Sebastian Follin got to his feet with amazing speed, smoothed his hair and tried to regain control of his breathing.

'She accused me of murder!' he said, pointing a finger at her. 'That's unlawful threat – she threatened me!'

Shocked and in pain, Bambi Rosenberg burst into tears. She felt around for something to support herself on, but couldn't find anything.

'He tried to steal Michelle's stuff. Tell him he's not allowed to take Michelle's stuff!'

She saw Mariana von Berlitz enter the room warily, giving the crazy man a wide berth, and approach the desk.

'Nothing is leaving this room,' the editor said. 'Everything on the premises is the property of Zero Television.'

Swaying, Bambi struggled to her feet. The manager opened his mouth to say something, and his hand went instinctively to his smarting cheek.

'Blood . . .' he exclaimed. 'I'm bleeding.'

To prove this statement he held his hand out, showing it first to Bambi, then to Mariana. Unconsciously, Bambi stepped back and noticed that the editor did the same thing.

'You aren't taking anything away from this office,' Mariana repeated. 'I'm in charge here, this is company property.'

Bambi's rage returned with a vengeance, white-hot.

'It is not!' she heard herself roar and noticed that her hands were shaking. 'Neither of you has the right to take any of Michelle's possessions. She told me to take care of everything if anything ever happened to her. I know what to do. You aren't going to get a thing!'

The man and the other woman suddenly regarded Bambi with a different look in their eyes – supercilious, suspicious and slightly wary.

'You?' Mariana von Berlitz said. 'Why on earth would she ask *you* to take care of things?'

Astonished, Bambi stared at the woman. Was she stupid or something?

'Who else would she have asked?'

'At any rate, the documentary is mine,' Sebastian Follin said. 'Michelle's documentary of her own life is mine, and I have the papers to prove it.'

Mariana the professional stiffened and turned to face the manager.

'Oh, really?' she said. 'As far as I know, TV Plus owns the rights to it.'

Bambi looked back and forth between the two of them as she felt the room start to sway.

'No,' Sebastian Follin said. 'The contract hasn't been signed, and according to *my* contract as a manager it falls under my jurisdiction.'

'There is a letter of intent written by Michelle to the network. You can't bypass—'

'There's nothing legally binding there.'

Bambi Rosenberg had to sit down, so she sank down on Michelle's office chair and tuned out the bickering going on above her head.

I promise, she thought. *I will take care of you. I'll make sure everything's done right.*

The lack of sleep had left Torstensson pale as he stole into the newsroom dressed in a suit jacket without the matching trousers. No one noticed him as he stopped in front of the news desk and gazed around, looking for a seat, staring past Spike whose ear was glued to the phone and the daytime editor playing computer games. Then he went over to the desk belonging to the foreign correspondent. It was on the edge of the fray, but still close enough for him to be involved.

What is his driving force? Schyman wondered from his vantage point in the fish tank.

It can't be the creed of journalism, because it's not something he lives by.

Maybe he likes to influence the issues presented to the public, or he enjoys being in a position of power. Could it be the approval of the family that owns the paper that spurs him on, or the salary, the potential political openings, or the acknowledgement of the Rotary Club?

The editor-in-chief put a few newspapers and a china coffee mug on the desk, pulled out the chair and settled in. Out of the corner of his eye, Spike looked at him, but made no effort to put the phone down or take his feet off the desk.

Schyman went to dial the in-house number to the foreign correspondent's desk and saw Torstensson jump when the phone rang.

'Could you step into my office?' Schyman asked the editor-in-chief. Torstensson complied, his gait defiant.

'What do you want?'

The editor-in-chief stood at the door, on the defensive and suspicious.

'I've already received three calls about libel and possible suits with regard to the contents of today's paper,' Schyman said and sat down on his desk.

Torstensson folded his arms across his chest.

'What do you mean?'

'I'm sure you know what I mean,' the managing editor ~~ed. 'I don't agree with your decision, but of course I
~~t it. Would you like to call Michelle Carlsson's
~~ourself, or should I refer them directly to our legal
~~tive?'

~~held out a few slips of paper. The editor-in-
~~ke them.

'You can't scare me,' Torstensson said. 'I can see right through you.'

Anders Schyman let his arm drop to his side and sighed loudly.

'It's a shame that this has happened,' he said.

'I agree,' Torstensson said and headed back to his seat. Schyman watched him go, studying his receding back, taking in the overly padded shoulders and the thinning hair.

Talk about poor judgement, he thought, and he didn't mean the publication of Barbara Hanson's tasteless column.

How did you ever get involved in this business without having the expertise or the right weapons?

Schyman went over to the phone again and dialled Annika Bengtzon's in-house number.

'Go to the paper's morgue,' he said when the reporter picked up. 'I'll be there in a few minutes.'

He sank back down in his chair, unlocked the desk's bottom drawer and pulled out his 'Anthrax file'. It went straight down into his briefcase. Then he threw on his jacket, left the room and headed for the garage.

'You can reach me on my cellphone if you need me,' he told Spike as he passed him. 'I'm going out to grab a bite.'

The news editor gave him the thumbs-up. Schyman left the newsroom through the main entrance and said hello to Bertil Strand on the way to the garage. Once the photographer had entered the office building, Schyman changed direction and went over to the outdoor entrance to the cafeteria, opened it with his pass and took the elevator to the second floor. The long corridor was cloaked in a bluish darkness, dimly lit by a few blinking fluorescent lights at the end of the hallway.

Annika Bengtzon stood with her back to the wall right next to the entrance to the morgue.

'The police are going to arrest the neo-Nazi kid from Katrineholm,' she said.

'Let's go inside and sit down,' Schyman said, moving on to the next door.

'Where is Carl Wennergren?' Annika asked, coming up behind him. 'Has he left on vacation a week early?'

'I sent him home. It's bad enough that one of the suspects is spewing garbage in our paper.'

'I saw him at the Stables,' the reporter said. 'In the trashed room I wrote about. It seemed like he was looking for something. Has he said anything about it?'

'It was a camera,' Schyman said. 'The police have already returned it – it had nothing to do with the murder investigation.'

Annika Bengtzon glanced up at him, almost disappointed.

The smell of dust and evaporating developer hit them, a cold draught from the filing cabinets loaded with thousands of pictures. Light came in from a window at the far end of the room, back-lighting the cabinets with their drawers labelled in such a cryptic way that no uninitiated person would ever be able to find what they were looking for.

'This is about a suspected insider deal,' the managing editor said as he sat down at an old wooden table by the windows and pulled out the red file from his briefcase.

The reporter silently sat down across from him, attentive and puzzled.

'Substantial stock holdings of an IT company were sold some time during the second half of last year,' he continued and removed the elastic-band closures. 'I would like you to find out when this transaction took place, the exact date.'

'That shouldn't be difficult,' Annika Bengtzon said.

'Transactions like that are supposed to be reported to the Financial Supervisory Board.'

'This case is a bit more complicated,' Anders Schyman explained, picking up the minutes, the clippings and the press release. 'The individual in question wasn't obliged to report his transactions, he wasn't a member of the board and he didn't belong to the management of the company he owned stock in, so his business transactions were never registered.

'So what's the problem?' the reporter asked.

The managing editor looked at the woman with a wary expression.

Oh, my God, he thought. *What am I doing? She could bring me down, just get up and leave and make sure that I get fired before lunch.*

Despair engulfed him, this new sense of powerlessness that was beginning to be a habit.

'I don't know,' he said, leaning back and rubbing his eyes. 'I don't know how to explain it.'

'This has something to do with Torstensson, doesn't it?' Annika Bengtzon asked. 'He's letting this paper go to the dogs and you don't know how to stop him. Is this some old dirt you want me to root around in?'

Anders Schyman stopped holding his breath, letting it out in a lengthy sigh that ricocheted against the metal cabinets.

'You do like calling a spade a spade, don't you?' he said. 'Can I trust you?'

'That depends,' she replied.

Schyman hesitated momentarily.

'You're right,' he said. 'Torstensson has to go, and he won't go willingly.'

'What about the board?' Annika said. 'Can't they budge him?'

Schyman shook his head.

'Herman Wennergren won't play. If we want him out, we have to get rid of him ourselves.'

'How?'

He showed her the minutes from last year's meeting on 27 June that clearly showed that the board of *Kvällspressen* had received prior knowledge of Global Future's impending profit warning. According to these minutes, Torstensson had been present as a co-opted member. At some point during the following six months, Torstensson sold his shares.

'That isn't necessarily a crime,' Annika said.

'No,' Schyman conceded. 'But it might be. It all depends on when the transaction took place. If he unloaded his holdings before this information was made public, he's guilty of insider trading.'

'Even if he wasn't on the board of the company?'

'If a cab driver overhears a conversation in the backseat of his cab, and uses that information to make a profit on the stock market, that would make him guilty of insider trading.'

'That would be hard to prove, though,' the reporter countered, a bit tartly.

'This ought to be easier. Could you check up the facts for me?'

Expectantly and with a slight feeling of misgiving, Annika studied Schyman.

'And if I find something, what do I do? Write a piece for tomorrow's paper?'

He had to smile.

'Not exactly. Just tell me what you find.'

'So what's the magic date?'

'The report for the second quarter, the one that included a profit warning, was made public last year, on 20 July.'

Annika got a pen and a slip of paper out of a back pocket and made some notes.

'So, all sales transactions taking place after 27 June but before 20 July would mean that Torstensson had exploited confidential information regarding the poor returns of Global Future,' she said, summing things up.

Schyman sighed as weariness wrenched at his soul.

'Actually, it's worse than that. He knew that the family was going to bail out, which means that the company would be more or less worthless.'

Annika took some more notes and stuffed the paper back in her pocket again.

'Why me?'

'Anyone making inquiries is going to leave a trail,' he said. 'So I can't do it myself.'

'The Securities Register Centre,' Annika said. 'They keep a record of their visitors, right?'

'That's where you've got to start, but I don't think it'll be enough. You'll need to pound the pavement to get anywhere.'

'Why me?'

Schyman licked his lips and chose his words carefully.

'There aren't many reporters on this paper who have the capacity to get hold of this information.'

Annika made a sound somewhere in between a laugh and a snort.

'And I'm the easiest one to persuade?'

He smiled a little.

'If that's what you think, you have a strange perception of yourself. You know exactly why?'

'No, I don't,' she said as she got up and brushed the dust off the seat of her jeans. 'Tell me.'

'You think like me,' he said.

For a brief moment the reporter was caught off guard and the astonishment she felt was clearly displayed on her face. Then she regained her composure and said in her usual bantering tone:

'I could choose to see this as an assault on my integrity,' she quipped. 'Or an acknowledgement of my capacity. So, I'll choose the latter. You'll be wanting to keep those documents, I guess?'

Schyman shooed her away, his throat dry as dust.

When Annika reached the doorway she suddenly turned around, looking very petite and delicate.

'Wennergren's camera,' she said. 'What happened to it?'

All at once Anders Schyman could picture the shiny contours of the camera, could sense its weight in his hand.

'It was impounded,' he said. 'But it's been released.'

She remained where she was, her hand on the door.

'Where is it?'

'Why do you ask?'

'Are there any pictures in it?'

The numbness he had felt when he saw the sex scenes overcame him again, the secret shame of the voyeur. He jumped up, shaking off the unpleasant sensation.

'You go first,' he said. 'Then come over to my office.'

Five minutes later Annika saw Schyman sail through the main entrance. She let him take off his jacket and sit down at his desk with a paper before she got up. Moving swiftly, she walked over to the fish tank and tapped on the door. He motioned her to come in.

'My name is Bengtzon,' she said, pulling the door partially closed behind her. 'Annika Bengtzon. Shaken, not stirred. Is the camera here?'

Filled with hesitation, Anders Schyman looked at her.

Her mouth went dry.

'Close the door properly,' he said finally and unlocked one of his desk drawers. He pulled out a shiny device that looked more like a Walkman than a camera. A blipping sound signalled that it was being turned on, and he

checked to see that it was working before wordlessly
handing it over to Annika.

The display was lit up from within. Anne Snapphane
was laughing up at her, definitely in party mode.

'How do I flip through the pictures?' she asked and he
pointed out the button.

She pressed it, *blip*, Sebastian Follin's tongue. She
made a face. *Blip*, Carl Wennergren, grinning away in the
lounge of the Stables before it was vandalized.

'Are there only pictures of tipsy party people?' Annika
asked, glancing at the managing editor.

'Go to number sixteen or seventeen,' he said.

She flipped through the pictures, *blip, blip, blip*, then
heard herself gasp and felt a tingling between her thighs.

Michelle Carlsson and John Essex, screwing on the
dining-room table. Legs, shiny thighs, white buttocks. For
a few seconds she stared in fascination, then moved on to
the next picture. *Blip*.

Annika felt her pulse start to race and her crotch grow
hot. Her mouth half-open, she continued to go through
the pictures, *blip, blip*, increasingly conscious of the
throbbing sensation between her legs.

She looked up at Schyman, ashamed of her reaction.

'Oh, my God,' she exclaimed theatrically. 'This is really
something.'

'Go on,' her boss said and waved.

She tried to look at the pictures from some other
perspective. They grew progressively fuzzier. The
photographer appeared to be having a hard time holding
the camera steady.

'He was probably hiding in the kitchen,' she said,
shattering her mood.

Anders Schyman made a rolling motion with his hand.

When she reached the final shot Annika gasped
again.

Mariana von Berlitz was holding the murder weapon.

'Christ,' she said. 'What are you going to do with this?'

He walked up to Annika, took the camera, switched it off and put it back in the drawer. Which he locked.

'I don't know,' he said. 'The pictures are spectacular and unique. They need to be used judiciously.'

Annika felt her jaw drop.

'You can't be serious,' she exclaimed and blinked. 'Are you thinking about publishing them?'

The managing editor sat down.

'I don't know,' he said again. 'I haven't made up my mind yet.'

Rebellion exploded through her and anger coloured her face.

'What the hell,' she demanded. 'Is this a porno magazine?'

'The pictures do have other merits,' Schyman quickly countered, pressing his fingertips together.

Completely taken aback, Annika flung her arms outside.

'Like what, for instance? It damn well isn't the sharp focus and the lighting. How can you even *consider* going public with these shots?'

'The timing,' he said. 'The moment in time. The two stars together – she's dead and he's a suspect. Actually, it's pretty amazing.'

Annika backed away towards the door.

'Sex shots taken on the sly,' she said. 'Could there be a worse assault on the subject's integrity? Would you like someone to publish stuff like this after you'd been murdered?'

She regarded him with astonishment and doubt.

First this unpleasant spying mission.

Now this.

'What about Mariana?' she said. 'What do the police

say?'

'I don't know.'

Thoughts and reactions pitched around the room for a few seconds.

'Listen,' she said, opening the door halfway and lowering her voice. 'No matter what you're involved in, don't lose your good sense, for Christ's sake.'

Annika went back to her desk and noticed that her hands were shaking. The people in the pictures danced in front of her eyes: sex, booze and guns. She was ashamed of her own reaction.

As she sank down on her chair she looked up and saw the managing editor yank open his door with a bang and walk over to Pelle Oscarsson at the photo desk.

'Could you delete the pictures in this camera?' she heard him say. Out of the corner of her eye she saw him place the camera on the picture editor's desk.

'What?' Picture Pelle said, his eyes glued to the screen in front of him, his voice partially drowned out by computer fans.

She quickly got up, feigning a trip to the lavatory.

'It's filled with a load of junk that I don't want to have spread around the newsroom,' Anders Schyman said as she walked past. He shot her a stern look.

The picture editor looked up, a somewhat vacant look on his face.

'You want this done in a hurry? I'm busy with these graphics right now.'

'As soon as possible,' Anders Schyman said, looking at Annika again before returning to his office.

Dumbstruck, she kept walking. Her palms were sopping wet.

*

'Coffee?'

Anne Snapphane shook her head and Sebastian Follin

poured himself a cup instead. He had two scratches on his cheek, Anne noted, but it didn't seem to bother him. The broken-heartedness she had seen in him after the murder was starting to disappear. It had been replaced by determination: there was a task to be undertaken, a memory to honour.

In death, she thought, as in life.

'The next step is very important,' Follin whispered in confiding tones, leaning towards her while the heat from his coffee cup made his glasses steam up.

Anne backed away slightly.

'What do you mean?'

'You've got to protect the brand. People are going to want to use Michelle Carlsson to make money, but these things must be handled with dignity and an eye to the long term.'

Anne stared at the man, unable to accept the meaning of his words.

'Are you listening to yourself?' she said, her voice too shrill and too loud. 'You're talking about her as if she was a logotype.'

The manager collapsed. His lower lip began to quiver.

'I just want to do the right thing,' he said.

'Only who is it right for?' Anne said, suddenly uncomfortable.

She turned away, gazed around the room, through the glass walls and out over the newsroom.

Karin Bellhorn sat in the sofa next to her desk. She was leaning forward and talking to Mariana von Berlitz and Stefan Axelsson in a low voice. Anne Snapphane hurried over to them. She could feel that she looked pale.

'I can't get over the feeling that this is all a trick,' Mariana said to the others as Anne appeared beside the sofa. 'Any minute now we'll hear the theme from the show and she'll come bouncing out, thinner than ever and with a brand-new look. Just imagine the ratings!'

Anne Snapphane looked at her colleague with astonishment.

'You can't be serious,' she heard herself say.

'What?' Mariana said. 'Can't I admit that it feels like I'm on *Candid Camera*?'

Anne noticed that her mouth kept talking, that she couldn't stop herself, and she didn't want to.

'Now that she's dead, do you have to keep picking on her? How much did you hate her for being the one on TV?'

Mariana von Berlitz blanched.

'What . . . what was that? Are you out of your mind?'

Anne Snapphane felt the attention of everyone in the room shifting to her. Regardless of the sheer mystery of the fact that they had been uttered at all, her words hung in the air, stunning them all with their truthfulness. The blood rushed to her chest and throat, making her cheeks burn.

'Why don't you have the courage to admit it? You've always been jealous of Michelle.'

Mariana had got to her feet. She was shaking and held on to the armrest of the sofa for support.

'I've known Michelle Carlsson so much longer than you have,' she said in a hoarse voice. 'And I'll have you know that my reservations against her are based on completely different issues.'

'Quit pretending! I'm not one damn bit better than you. I've been pissed off at Michelle for years because she got the job on screen and I didn't,' Anne continued, the words streaming out of her. 'You weren't even considered. Is that why you're always so condescending? Because I had been in the running?'

'There are scads of things that are way more important than being on TV,' Mariana von Berlitz said emphatically and sat down again. 'There's eternity, for instance, and Michelle Carlsson never did anything but spoil other people's chances of finding a meaningful existence.'

Anne Snapphane couldn't help but snort.

'Jesus Christ,' she exclaimed. 'Did Michelle steal customers from God?'

Mariana chose to ignore the blasphemy.

'I think it's awful that people like Michelle Carlsson are promoted as role models for young women,' she said. 'What good did she ever do? As long as I've known her all she's done is drag other people down into the mud with her.'

'And you would set a better example? A person who passes judgement on others, just because you think you're so superior? Because you're "to the manor born", or could it be because you have the Holy Spirit on your side?'

'I don't judge people. That's up to the Lord.'

The words were harsh, but Mariana's eyes looked frightened. Anne Snapphane knew that she was right: the truth had shattered the other woman's protective veneer of contempt, making Anne feel even headier.

'You can say what you like about God, but it would be great to have some of his PR people on your side,' she murmured, on the verge of tears.

'I'd buy it – at least when it comes to you,' Stefan Axelsson suddenly said to Anne. 'You pretend to be a free spirit, a liberated lady, but in truth you're the most conservative one of us.'

Rage swept through her like a red-hot flood.

'What the hell do you mean?'

'You flaunt your liberated relationship, how you and your boyfriend share a bed and have a child without any strings attached, acting like some kind of role model, letting the tabloids into your home . . .'

The savageness of this attack cleared Anne's mind, helping her make connections that she'd missed previously.

'Holy shit,' she said, her eyes wide. 'You're jealous too. Not only of Mehmed, who gets to be on TV, but it irks you that I was featured in the Sunday special as an example of the New Family. Poor Stefan.'

'You're out of your tiny little mind,' he said. 'I'm talking about duty, obligations, not letting others down . . .'

'You were in love with Michelle,' Anne murmured, taking a few steps closer to him. 'You wanted to leave your wife and family for her, and she just laughed at you, didn't she? All she really wanted was your respect, she wanted you to stop making fun of her in the control room, so she did the only thing she knew how to do, she used the only method she could think of, she screwed you and wrapped you around her little finger. But it all went wrong, didn't it? You fell for her. Did you tell your wife? What did she say?'

Axelsson had turned pale and stared at her with glassy eyes.

'That's . . . not what happened . . .'

'Wasn't it? Then why are you so damn bitter? You begrudge me a three-column picture spread in *Kvällspressen* and Mehmed his job as the host of a news show. He has degrees in law *and* journalism, and he's a prizewinning journalist to boot – twice over! And you know as well as I do—'

'Listen to me!' Axelsson shouted, getting up with a strength that his lanky frame belied. 'I saw you! I saw you by the bus at 3:15! What the hell were you doing there?'

Speechless and breathless, Anne Snapphane stared at Stefan Axelsson.

'Well, where were *you* at the time? And what were *you* doing?' she asked.

The technical director held up his hands.

'Come on, people,' Karin Bellhorn said in a voice that commanded attention. 'That's enough. Let's all calm down. We're talking without thinking. It's up to the police to conduct the investigation. Being suspicious and blaming each other won't do any good. What do you say?'

They all looked in different directions, down at the floor, out through the windows, up at the ceiling or at the walls.

'Today, all we're going to do is take it nice and easy, discuss the upcoming memorial service on Tuesday and try to split up the work. For starters, does anyone need to see a psychologist? A therapist? A counsellor?'

Everything had come to a standstill. Sebastian Follin stood in the doorway leading to the lounge, grey-suited and clutching a cup of coffee. Mariana von Berlitz, in a brazenly red dress, stood next to the sofa. Stefan Axelsson, in jeans and a sweatshirt, had rings of perspiration under his arms. The colour was slowly draining from Anne Snapphane's face.

'No takers? It's nothing to be ashamed of. I think *I'm* going to talk to someone . . .'

The producer closed her eyes for a moment and smoothed back her hair in an unconscious habitual gesture. Anne, her mind clouded by the heady quest for the truth, studied her for a few seconds. She realized that Karin Bellhorn was wearing much more make-up than usual. Her complexion was grey under the foundation. Her eyes had bags that no cosmetic in the world could conceal.

She feels awful, Anne thought. *She seems to be in the worst shape of us all.*

'Why are you acting like nothing's happened?' she said.

Karin swallowed and tried to smile.

'I just offered to get help—'

'Shut up!' Anne screamed, flinging out her arms so that Sebastian Follin's cup smashed into the glass wall. 'Michelle's dead! She's on a gurney at the Medical Examiner's office, being cut to pieces, and one of us probably put her there!'

The ensuing silence was deafening. The air had turned frosty. The drip, drip, drip of Sebastian's coffee filled the room. Finally expressed, the words remained suspended in the air.

Anyone. One of us.

'Have you started without me?'

Highlander came walking from the direction of the elevator, freshly showered and swinging his briefcase.

'I've been talking to London, and we've come to an agreement.'

He smiled, sat down on an office chair, put the briefcase in his lap and unlocked it with twin clicks. He pulled out some papers, closed his case with a bang and put the stack of papers on top of it.

'We're going to kick off with a long show com-memorating Michelle,' he continued, his voice level but light-hearted. 'It will include clips from her entire career, feature guests with testimonials, friends telling about her deep commitment to . . . to whatever she was committed to. We can make it long, use entertainers and actors, maybe a poem or two, or a short play . . . Only use commercials Michelle would have approved of. How about John Essex, Karin? Do you think he would consider making an appearance?'

The atmosphere was tense when the CEO of TV Plus paused. The foundation could no longer conceal Karin

Bellhorn's true complexion. No one could bear to look anyone else in the eye. Shoulders were tensed, throats were dry.

'Highlander,' Karin said in a weak voice. 'Who dreamed this up? The Big Boss in London?'

The CEO's smile faltered but didn't die.

'I just want to move on,' he said. 'To take the next step.'

'Not so fast,' Karin said, getting up, her ample form swaying as she walked up to her boss. 'We've been talking this over – how we saw Michelle, sharing our thoughts. What do you have to say?'

His smile evaporated, leaving Highlander's face as vulnerable as it had been the day before. Sweat beaded his forehead, soaking his bangs.

'About what?'

'About Michelle!' Karin Bellhorn exclaimed.

'Now calm down,' he said. 'All I want to do is make the best of this situation.'

'He fired Michelle,' Karin informed the others, pointing at Highlander and looking each of her associates in the eye, one by one. 'He fired her after the last show was taped, and now he's pretending that it didn't happen.'

Mariana von Berlitz got up slowly, her stare fixed on Highlander.

'So that was it,' she said. 'That's why Michelle was going to say—'

'Shut up!' Highlander shouted, trying to get up. But the briefcase in his lap stopped him.

'She was going to say that the two of you had been involved,' Mariana continued, unstoppable. 'And we know what would have happened to you then.'

Silence descended on the group again, with even greater force this time. Highlander had been kicked upstairs when his predecessor had had to leave quite suddenly. The reason for this quick exit was that numerous people had caught the man concerned in the act of having sex with one of the network's celebrities during a Christmas party.

Anne Snapphane stared at the CEO's sticky hair and sensed his anguish, his fear of being caught beyond the pale.

'She was lying,' Highlander managed to say. 'I would never, ever . . .'

'It doesn't matter,' Mariana said in a flat voice. 'She would have gone to the press and that would have been the end of you.'

Moisture dripped down the inside of the kitchen windows. The potatoes for Sunday's lunch were boiling like mad and no one had turned down the heat.

Thomas hurried over to the stove, as if it would make a difference. He yanked the saucepan off the hotplate and lifted the lid. Nearly all the water had evaporated and the fluffy new potatoes were partially burnt, sticking to the bottom of the pan. He swore under his breath. Somehow this would turn out to be his fault.

'Oh dear! Thomas, what's going on?'

Leaning hard on her cane, his mother limped into the kitchen. There it was, more veiled criticism, now that she'd been so busy with the children and all.

'Someone put on the potatoes and forgot all about them,' Thomas said as he scraped the contents of the pot into the recycling bin for organic matter. 'Are there any more potatoes?'

'Now they won't be ready on time,' his mother complained as she sank down heavily on a chair by the kitchen table. 'Could you set the table, Thomas?'

'Sure,' he replied, sticking his head into the pantry and locating a bag of tiny golden new potatoes. Under a stream of cold water, he scrubbed them in the sink and tossed them into the pan. 'How many for lunch?'

'Eleonor and Martin have left, but Sverker will be here. Where are the kids?'

'They're with Holger, in the boat.'

'Goodness, are they with Holger? Are they wearing life jackets?'

Her hands fluttered with worry. Thomas forced himself to remain calm.

'Yes, they are, Mother. Just you rest. Which plates would you like me to use?'

'Take the East India set, it's a summer lunch. Have you checked the roast? It should only reach seventy-five degrees, you know.'

'Yes, Mother . . .'

He grabbed a pot-holder, opened the oven door and saw that the meat thermometer setting had reached ninety-two degrees.

'It's done,' he said whipping out the thermometer and rinsing it quickly with some cold water. 'Would you like me to make some gravy?'

'Yes, please, dear. And fix the salad too . . .'

Thomas set the roast on the range to cool off a bit. The burnt bits could be trimmed away. Next, he added water to the baking dish, then transferred the pan drippings to a saucepan, thickened the mixture with cream and corn starch, then added beef stock, thyme and garlic.

'You've turned into quite a good cook, Thomas,' his mother said.

'I always have been,' Thomas said as he selected some vegetables from the fridge.

His mother didn't answer. She studied him with weary eyes from her vantage point by the kitchen table.

'I wish I could help you out more,' she said as he drizzled olive oil over the salad.

'I'm almost done,' he said.

'You know what I mean.'

He sighed gently and put down the bottle of olive oil.

'Mom,' he said. 'I'm fine. I don't need to be saved.'

The old woman slowly shook her head.

'Thomas,' she said, 'the one who always has to do everything his own way. Sometimes I'm afraid that you're in over your head.'

His adrenalin level rising, Thomas put down the balsamic vinegar with a bang.

'What do you mean?'

'Nothing,' she said quickly. 'Only you seem to have so much to do, with the kids and the apartment, and all . . . By the way, do you know if you get to keep your job?'

Thomas placed his palms on the counter, feeling the coolness of the slab radiate to his forearms. His breathing became more rapid.

'No, but I might find out this coming week.'

'Isn't it peculiar that they don't let you know such a thing in time?' his mother said indignantly. 'I mean, people have to be able to plan their lives. Particularly when you have a family.'

He really shouldn't have got angry. Her words could have been considerate and supportive, but he knew better.

'If there's something I really don't need,' he said in a rather aloof voice as he put the gravy boat on the table, 'it's to worry about unemployment.'

'But how would you support yourself?'

Her quavering voice expressed so much more than a fear of insufficient funds.

'Well, Mother,' he said cheerfully, 'I might have to settle for a job as an accountant with Social Services again. That wouldn't be so bad, now would it?'

He knew that his mother would love to see him back at a nice secure job like that, particularly in affluent

Vaxholm, in a position as the chief financial officer, the man in charge of public funds.

'Jobs like that don't grow on trees, you know,' she said, a bit indignantly.

Thomas laughed.

'If you only knew what offers I've had.'

'You don't have to pretend, Thomas.'

Something burst inside him, all the countless dammed-up protests he'd suppressed, and he was suddenly livid, slamming the roast on the table so that the china rattled. He shouted:

'I'm satisfied with my life! I love my children and I love Annika. She's real, not a dried-up old pussy like Eleonor . . .'

'Watch your language!' his mother said, shocked.

'Why should I?' he roared. 'You never think before you speak, you say whatever you damn well please. Haven't you noticed how much you hurt Annika with your carping? When you compare her to Eleonor? When you compare our apartment to the house? When you talk about our vacations? You criticize our kids, too – they're never good enough for you, are they? Because Annika is their mother and not Eleonor. Well, guess what, Mother? She didn't want to have any! Eleonor didn't want to have kids! I never would, have been a dad, and you wouldn't have been a grandmother . . .'

The colour had drained from his mother's face. Her cheeks were ashen and she clutched at her chest as she tried to get up.

'I think . . .' she stammered. 'I think . . . I'd better go and lie down . . .'

Thomas caught her as she fell, supporting her around the waist.

'Holger!' he shouted. "Holger!'

'What a ruckus,' his brother said from the hallway.

Holger looked into the kitchen, quickly assessed the situation, and rushed to his mother's side. The two of them carried their mother to the living room and set her down on the sofa. Holger's partner Sverker, a physician, bent over the older woman to check her pulse and her breathing.

'What happened?' he said.

'We . . . had an argument,' Thomas said, suddenly dizzy and faint.

His mother made a gesture in the air with one hand. Her eyelids fluttered and she moaned.

'You've got to be careful, you know,' Sverker said, not bothering to conceal his disapproval.

Thomas walked past his children and headed outdoors, into the rain.

The phone receiver had become all slippery with perspiration. Annika dried her ear off between two calls.

'It wasn't like she wasn't smart. On the contrary. Restless, maybe, and a bit too loud. But I never would have dreamed that she would buy into the white-supremacy movement.'

Annika took notes as she listened to Hannah Persson's junior high school teacher describe the girl: her solid family background, the brother who became a skinhead, her inability to concentrate and the lack of social skills that isolated her from the other girls.

'I think she wanted attention,' her teacher said. 'She wanted to be acknowledged and get some kind of response, and you know what they say, if you can't be loved, you crave admiration; if you can't be admired, you demand respect; if you aren't respected, you choose to be feared . . .'

'That's no excuse,' Annika said.

'No, it isn't,' the teacher said. 'But it could be an explanation.'

Hannah Persson's classmates were less charitable and the conversations were less pleasant in tone. 'Bland,' one person said. 'So needy that she seemed spineless. A loner that nobody bullied – she acted out without inspiring others to join in.'

She was dismissed as stupid by one of the boys in her class.

'Ugly as sin,' said another.

'A royal pain,' one of the girls declared.

Annika studied the class picture taken in ninth grade, the only old picture of the neo-Nazi girl that the newsroom staff had been unable to unearth. A tiny girl with a slouch, a grinning mouth and frightened eyes. She compared it to the picture that Bertil Strand had taken yesterday; in just a few years Hannah's face had gained character and definition. If it hadn't been for the disfiguring swastika, she might even have been pretty. She stood tall and there was a challenging expression in her eyes.

Well then, she found herself an identity, **Annika thought.** *Anything's better than being homeless.*

The girl had studied various subjects in high school, but had quit school without graduating. At present she was the secretary of the Katrineholm Nazi Party. She was listed as residing at her mother's address, but she probably didn't live there. As far as anyone knew, she didn't have a boyfriend. Somehow she had got hold of a replica of an antique revolver made in the US.

Berit had already completed her presentation of the neo-Nazi movement in Sweden today and was reading a fax as she walked up to Annika.

'TV Plus sent over an invitation to a press conference and memorial service for Michelle Carlsson on Tuesday, 26 July, in the conference room over at Zero Television. At this time we will be notified as to the airing of *Summer Frolic at the Castle* and other programmes pertaining to

Michelle Carlsson's career in journalism. This event will be broadcast live on TV Plus.'

Annika rolled her eyes.

'I've been talking to the DA,' Berit said, lowering the fax. 'She's lifting the impound order on the bus and its equipment – the cameras and tapes and all that.'

'When?'

'Tonight or tomorrow morning.'

'Then maybe I should pay a visit to my pal Gunnar Antonsson,' Annika said.

Berit nodded.

'Will you be going to the memorial?'

Annika stretched and yawned.

'I guess I could. Are you taking the day off tomorrow?'

Berit smiled, her eyes weary, and handed the fax to Annika.

'Yeah, right . . . No, I'm flying out to Berlin tonight, it's time to get a statement from John Essex. Not that I can figure out how that's going to happen. The British tabloids have got wind of the story, and if he wasn't in hiding before that, he certainly is now.'

Annika reached for the paper and looked at her colleague, hesitating briefly before saying:

'You can always blackmail the guy,' she said.

Berit looked at her.

'An interview in exchange for keeping mum about where that gun had been.'

'Do you think he . . .?'

The silence, tainted by the unmentionable, hung over them.

'Have you heard about Carl Wennergren's pictures?' Annika asked in a low voice.

Berit looked at her uncomprehendingly.

'What do you mean?'

'Remember how I told you that Carl Wennergren was

looking for something over at the Stables? It was a camera. I've seen the pictures. Michelle Carlsson and John Essex, sex every which way, from the rear, from the front, from above, from below . . .'

Wide-eyed and sceptical, Berit asked: 'Who knows about this?'

'I don't know,' Annika said. 'Just Schyman and me, I guess.'

They looked at each other and considered the situation.

'His fans are like twelve years old and up,' Annika continued in a low voice. 'The word "detrimental" is way too mild to describe what would happen if those pictures and the information about the revolver were published.'

'This paper would never . . .' Berit said.

'He doesn't know that,' Annika countered.

Silence descended again.

'When did Carl take those pictures?' Berit asked.

'He took them over at the Stables. On the sly.'

Slowly, Berit nodded and Annika put her feet up on her desk.

'Who are you going with?'

'I'll be joining Henriksson, the new guy, in Frankfurt.'

Annika leaned back and studied her colleague as she walked through the newsroom. Berit looked so resolute and straightforward, calm and at home in her surroundings as she exchanged a few words with Spike, laughed and patted Picture Pelle on the arm, and greeted Tore Brand on her way out.

She had been married to the same man for twenty-three years, Annika thought. How could that be possible? Where did you find the patience and the sense of security, the conviction that you had made the right choice? How did you find the strength to put your faith in love?

Anne Snapphane walked quickly to the exit. She wanted to get away from the newsroom, away from Karin Bellhorn's words, and she tensed her shoulders to shut out the woman's voice.

To no avail.

'Anne? Could you wait up? It won't take long.'

She stopped in mid-step, letting her arms drop and sighing. With a great effort, she turned around and saw Karin Bellhorn waving to her. Mariana von Berlitz and Sebastian Follin were also on their way to the lounge.

'I've got to go home,' Anne said. 'I've got to pick Miranda up at day care.'

An excuse.

'We covered a lot of ground today, didn't we?' the producer said. 'The whole season is outlined, the memorial is planned, the press release has been issued . . . I think the meeting went very well.'

No one answered, so Karin Bellhorn decided to get to the point.

'Let's discuss Michelle Carlsson's estate,' she said over her shoulder as she poured herself a cup of coffee.

Making her point, Anne Snapphane remained in the doorway, leaning against the frame and keeping her jacket on. The producer took her time settling on the counter, then started the fan running and lit a cigarette.

'When I got in this morning there was quite a squabble going on in Michelle's office,' she explained to Anne. 'That's why I want you all to know a few things.'

Mariana pulled up a chair and sat down on the other side of the door. Sebastian Follin was fussing with the coffee.

'At the present time, no one is allowed to touch the contents of Michelle's office. We have taken on a lawyer to go through all the contracts and figure out exactly who is entitled to what, who owns the rights to her material, and who will be paid for the use of previously published material, new material and reruns. In addition to this, the lawyer will review Michelle's personal assets, find out if there is a will, and figure out who her heirs are.'

'Why should we pay for a lawyer to review her personal affairs?' Mariana asked, her voice still sharp in spite of her fatigue.

Karin Bellhorn took a long drag on her cigarette and expelled the thin stream of smoke in the direction of the fan.

'We'll deduct it from your salary,' she said with a wan smile.

Mariana pursed her lips.

'At any rate, the documentary is mine,' Sebastian Follin said.

'Leave that to the lawyer,' the producer said.

The manager downed his coffee in one gulp, set the cup down on the counter and picked up his briefcase.

'I've got a meeting to attend,' he said as he headed for the exit. 'Good to see you.'

No one responded. Anne stood up to follow him to the door when Karin Bellhorn's cellphone rang.

'Could you please wait a minute,' the producer said to Mariana and Anne as she studied the display. 'I've got to take this call, but there's something I really would like to discuss with you. I'll be right back.'

She vanished in the direction of the smoking lounge, a cloud of cigarette smoke trailing behind her like a wispy silk scarf.

The coffee lounge remained oppressively silent. Anne Snapphane sighed aloud, then perched on a table and rested her chin in one hand. Mariana von Berlitz concentrated on smoothing the skirt of her red dress until she could no longer stand the silence.

'You have no idea what Michelle put me through over

the years,' she finally said.

Anne didn't respond, trying to study Karin's trail of smoke as long as she could before it dispersed.

'We had a good thing going at high school before she turned up,' Mariana continued. 'People were involved in music societies, drama groups, the temperance movement, several political parties had youth leagues at school, and several Christian societies were active too. Everything fell apart once Michelle turned up.'

Anne Snapphane glanced at Mariana, then tried in vain to locate the grey veil again.

'What do you mean?' she said. 'Did Michelle spoil your tidy little world?'

'She never threatened *my* world,' Mariana von Berlitz said with conviction. 'But not everyone's faith was as strong.'

Anne let out a loud sigh and craned her neck to see what Karin was up to in the smoking lounge.

'She came to our school the second year of high school,' Mariana went on, her voice coloured with stale nostalgia. 'Michelle Carlsson smoked, drank and arranged school dances. As far as I knew, she had at least four boyfriends in less than two years.'

Anne Snapphane rolled her eyes.

'Spare me the details,' she said. 'I don't want to hear them.'

Mariana von Berlitz sat up straighter, two red spots on her cheeks.

'Why not? Can't you take the truth? You were so concerned about the truth before the meeting. Michelle had no class, no morals. She ran around informing freshman students about contraceptives and had a really bad influence on the entire class. The societies and clubs had a hard time keeping their members – the kids went to bars, discos and hockey games instead. Michelle changed the standards of what was acceptable and respectable. I think it's a dangerous thing when people like her have too much influence.'

Anne couldn't sit still any longer.

'Come on,' she said. 'Get real. She was just an ordinary kid. You're making her out to be the Antichrist.'

Mariana remained seated and cocked her head a little.

'I believe that there should be a common foundation of values, and these values need to be preserved for the good of society. Turning a person like Michelle into a role model is outrageous, it's actually dangerous.'

'I can't bear to hear another word,' Anne Snapphane said.

She bent down to pick up her bag.

Mariana von Berlitz got up.

'You ought to watch your step too,' she said. 'Making derogatory remarks about God, like you did earlier, won't do you any good.'

Rage made Anne's head pound like it had before the meeting, rubbing out boundary lines and causing reality to tilt.

'Do you mean that he would strike me down?'

She took a step closer to Mariana.

'You know what?' she said. 'I feel so damn sorry for you. You've been stiffed. Your God is only Jahveh, an ancient Jewish tribal god. Did you know that the old tales say that he used to live in a volcano? He was just one of many gods – there were male *and* female deities. The only difference is that the others are forgotten now, and so is the volcano.'

'Don't be too sure of yourself,' Mariana said, backing away.

'Jahveh has been transformed into God and Allah, an almighty god, just because it suited the purpose of the male-orientated society. Every last female deity was overthrown and then women could be enslaved. In the name of your tribal god, our joy and sexuality were stripped from us, and that's something you go around and *celebrate*?'

'Watch it,' Mariana von Berlitz warned her.

But Anne was still furious.

'Are you threatening me? Is that what you're doing? Is it my turn now? Do you plan to get rid of me, expel the next wicked lower-class whore from your sight?'

Karin Bellhorn shut the door of the smoking lounge and sailed over to them, cellphone in hand.

'Actually, all I wanted was to ask you to not fight,' she said.

Anne slung her bag over her shoulder and left the newsroom without another word.

Annika put her feet back down on the floor. She got her stuff together, sent off her article on the computer and put on her jacket.

'The night shift will have to fill in the details from the police interview with the neo-Nazi kid,' she told Spike, barely slowing down on her way to the exit. 'Ask them to check in with the police and see if there are any new developments. You can reach me on my cellphone . . .'

'Why aren't you taking your calls?' Tore Brand asked her in an irritated voice as she passed the newsroom lobby.

'Because I'm here,' Annika said. 'What is it?'

'You've got a visitor,' the man said, pointing at the sofa.

It took a few seconds before Annika recognized him.

'Sebastian Follin,' she said. 'What can I do for you?'

The manager quickly got up, adjusted his glasses and stretched out a hand. Annika took it gingerly, remembering his damp, limp handshake.

'What a pleasure,' the man said. 'I'd really like to have a word with you.'

'Actually, I'm on my way out,' Annika said, pulling back her hand.

'I'd have thought it was important to get the facts straight when you write for a paper,' Follin said. 'That's why I wanted to tell you the real story.'

Annika studied him uncertainly, not sure if his presence pleased or irritated her.

'Of course. We can sit here,' she said.

She took off her jacket again and sank down on the sofa, noticing how Tore Brand opened a paper and pricked up his ears.

'I would like to start by informing you that I will be taking over all of Michelle Carlsson's interests as of today,' the manager said as he sat down again. 'If you have any questions about her business activities and her estate, come to me.'

Politely, Annika picked up her pad and pen and let them rest in her lap.

'How would you describe the taping session of *Summer Frolic at the Castle*?' she asked as a diversion.

'As very successful,' the manager said. 'Well, apart from the weather, that is. This type of programme really suited us – it's what we do best, family entertainment with a broad appeal interspersed with serious journalistic segments. No one can top us there.'

Annika looked down at her lap, carefully choosing her words.

'It must have been quite a blow,' she said, throwing out a feeler and opening her pad.

'It was dreadful,' Follin said, mopping his brow with a handkerchief. 'When someone close to you dies suddenly, it's always a shock, but then there are all these additional aspects, all these people out to make a profit. In the future I'm going to guard our rights.'

Annika sharpened her attention and studied the man more closely. The pale eyes had sprung back to life and his complexion was rosy. He had bounced back quickly.

'Why is this your job?' she asked.

Follin blinked with surprise.

'We were a team,' he said. 'I'm her manager. Well, more than that, we were confidants, we were each other's only friend. We were a team,' he repeated, 'a couple, it was us two against the world. I won't let her down now.'

'I thought Bambi Rosenberg was Michelle's best friend,' Annika said.

The man's expression changed. He leaned close to Annika, staring at her. His coffee-laden breath was in her face.

'I have to warn you about Bambi Rosenberg,' the manager whispered, his eyes wide. 'If she tries to contact you, remember that she is totally untrustworthy. Totally untrustworthy!'

Annika pulled back to get out of the range of the stench of coffee but kept looking him in the eye.

'In what way?' she asked calmly.

The man leaned in even closer, raising his voice.

'It doesn't make sense that Michelle would want to associate with a nobody like her,' he said. 'They can't have had anything in common. Michelle was a natural, truly and uniquely talented. Bambi Rosenberg is a surgically enhanced dime-a-dozen bimbo who hitched a ride on Michelle's star. I tried to talk to Michelle about it, but she wouldn't listen.'

Feeling uncomfortable, Annika shrank back against the backrest.

Trying to open another avenue she said: 'That last night at the castle appears to have been rather rowdy.'

'A little parasite, that's what she is. A little slut who

won't let go. But the documentary is mine now, mine! And I've got the paperwork to prove it.'

Annika stared at Follin, feeling herself grow increasingly uneasy.

'What documentary would that be? The one that Michelle was making about herself?'

'I'm not sure I'll let TV Plus air it. There are quite a few other interested parties, and my job is to take care of Michelle's assets and negotiate the best possible contract for us.'

'I thought she had terminated your contract,' Annika said and waited for the reaction.

And there certainly was one. Follin stopped short as if he'd been slapped, his mouth open, ready to say something. Gasping for air.

'If you only knew what I've been through,' he said, his back rigid. 'Michelle could be impossible – we'd agree on something and a second later she'd change her mind and turn everything upside down, and I'd have to start all over again. She was capricious, as irresponsible as a kid, and just issued commands.'

He leaned back and suddenly began to mimic Michelle in a high voice.

'"This doesn't feel right, Sebastian." "Do something about this, Sebastian." "I can't take this, Sebastian . . ."'

Follin leaned closer again.

'Not to mention all the men,' he hissed. 'I was the one who had to clean up her messes. I'm the only one who really knows everything.'

Trying to conceal her astonishment, Annika stared at the man.

'All right,' she said. 'So who shot her?'

Follin turned his head. The fluorescent lights of the lobby lit up his lenses, turning him into an insect. A telephone began to ring at the service desk, persistently and insistently. Tore Brand made no attempt to answer. He was waiting for Follin's reply.

'Someone who was fed up,' Sebastian Follin said.

He picked up his coat and his briefcase, then got up and headed for the stairs, his shoulders slumped.

Tore Brand reached for the phone.

The apartment hadn't cleaned itself during the weekend. Annika emptied the wastebaskets and opened the windows to air out the place as she took the rubbish downstairs to put it in the garbage bins in the courtyard.

The haze of the newsroom was banished from her mind, work receded, the sticky imprints left by Sebastian Follin dried up and were dismissed from her thoughts.

In the kitchen, the remnants of the children's breakfast cereal had dried up in the saucepan on the stove. Despite her intentions to soak the pan in water last night, Annika had forgotten all about it – she hadn't had the energy to deal with it.

Leaving the mess to stew a while longer, she stopped in the doorway to the children's room, trying to gain some kind of perspective from what she saw there: Ellen's crib in the corner, Kalle's bed with the safety rail by the window, the sweet-and-sour odour of formula and dirty nappies. Her children, the meaning of her life, the whole purpose of being a human being. A damp breeze whispered through the rooms, slamming the bedroom door shut.

Annika turned her head, rested her forehead against the door frame and breathed in and out.

It's going to work, she thought. *It has to.*

Then she pulled herself together and switched off her brain – work was the easy part of her life.

An hour later, the worst of the mess had been cleared up. The toys had been put away, a load of laundry was in the machine, the floors had been skimmed over with the vacuum cleaner, and the overloaded dishwasher chugged away, china clanking. Annika went over to the super-market, Rosetten, and bought milk, butter, eggs, green onions, bread, fish and canned goods. Not having brought enough cash, she was allowed to buy some of it on credit.

As she was lugging the groceries upstairs she could hear the phone ringing, so she dropped her bags, breaking the eggs, and tried to unlock the door though her hands were shaking badly.

'All right if I drop by?'

Annika sat down on the floor, resting her head in one hand, her cheeks burning and quivering with disappointment.

'Of course it's all right,' she told Anne Snapphane.

'You sound pretty blue – is something wrong?'

She tried to laugh.

'I thought it was Thomas.'

'Sorry,' Anne said. 'I'll bring some chocolate pastries.'

Thomas hadn't called once the whole weekend. She didn't even know when he planned on coming home. A sense of failure reverberated throughout her system and her entire being howled out at the breakdown in com-munications between them. Her longing for her children was like a pain in her gut.

Annika got up and put the groceries in the fridge, her body as sore as if she'd been through a tough workout. Acting like a sleepwalker she made coffee. The image of Bosse, the reporter from the competition, suddenly flashed on her retina. She recalled his unselfish kindness.

The doorbell pierced a hole in the pleasant sensation.

Anne Snapphane handed Annika the bag from the bakery and sank down on her couch, limp and shaky.

'I feel like I have a hangover even though I haven't had

a drop. This is truly shitty.'

Annika poured coffee into the mugs and set out a carton of milk.

'We had this meeting at work,' Anne said as she reached for the milk. 'This business has really brought out the worst in us.'

The two young women sat next to each other on the couch, both holding a mug of coffee, and felt the liquid's warmth.

'So it was rough?' Annika said and took a sip.

Anne made a loud swallowing sound.

'Mariana has always been a bit of a Jesus freak, but before today I never realized what a fucking fundamentalist she is. It's scary. Highlander has the sensitivity and intelligence of a tank, Follin is nuts, and Karin hides behind a fussy mothering attitude.'

'Sebastian Follin came to the office today,' Annika said. 'Right before I left for the day. I can't quite figure out what he wanted.'

Anne snorted.

'Try jockeying for position,' she said. 'He wants the world to know that Michelle lives on through him.'

Annika stirred her coffee and looked out the window. The grey daylight leeched all the colour from the surroundings.

'One of you guys might have done it,' she said.

Anne Snapphane drew a deep breath, a sigh that verged on a sob.

'Why do people kill? To be able to go on?'

Annika let her spoon sink down into the mug of coffee.

'Power,' she said. 'People kill for the sake of power, in one way or another. Power over another person, over a family, to obtain the power that money or political influence will provide . . . Power is the all-time number one motive for murder.'

'Envy,' Anne said. 'Begrudging someone something. Feelings of injustice. Cain and Abel.'

'Those things are also a kind of power play,' Annika said, her eyes fixed on the greyness. 'If I can't have it, you can't. Taking a person's life is the ultimate show of power. End of story.'

'That's all, folks,' Anne said. 'No more Michelle Carlsson on TV.'

'As I was saying before, Sebastian Follin came to see me at work,' Annika said as she tried to fish out her spoon again. 'I asked him who shot Michelle, and he said it was someone who got fed up. Who could that be?'

Anne shrugged.

'Everyone, I guess.'

'Did you know that they arrested the neo-Nazi girl?'

'When was that?'

'This morning. But she didn't do it.'

'I don't think so either,' Anne said.

They sat in silence for a while. Annika felt the coffee spreading warmth and tranquillity to her wounded senses.

'Are you going to the memorial service on Tuesday?' she asked as she put up her feet on the coffee table and snuggled back against the pillows.

Anne Snapphane shook her head, took a long, slow sip of coffee and rested her mug in her hand.

'We'll be getting access to the impounded tapes tonight and I've got to start going through the damned things and add time codes. It's extremely tedious work and it'll take days.'

Annika closed her eyes and rubbed her forehead.

'Thomas hasn't called since Friday.'

Anne bit into an almond-and-chocolate confection.

'Would you have wanted him to?'

'Of course I would.'

'But you've been working around the clock. Would you have had the time to chat?'

'I'd have made time. I don't even know when he'll be coming home.'

'That, on the other hand, is pretty rotten,' Anne Snapphane said. 'Is he leaving you in limbo?'

Annika sighed and set her mug down on the floor.

'Oh, well,' she said. 'I brought it upon myself. I've never seen him as angry as he was last Friday.'

Wide-eyed and sceptical, Anne stopped chewing.

'Please tell me you're joking.'

'About what?'

Annika tried to back away and pushed herself further into the cushions.

'It's not your fault that Thomas gets angry. How could it be? He has the right to get angry, but how does that make you the guilty party?'

Annika was thunderstruck, feeling as if she had her back to the wall.

'I was the one who made him upset.'

'Annika,' Anne Snapphane said gravely and leaned towards her. 'Stop doing this, you're creeping me out. Thomas's emotional life is not your responsibility. What is this, the S&M world cup? The World Guilt Championship?'

The air in the room ran out. Annika gasped for breath.

'We're responsible for each other,' she countered.

'I really don't understand why you cater to Thomas so much, you're certainly not a wimp in other situations. Have you always acted like this around men?'

Annika was breathing heavily as she pulled her legs up and wrapped her arms around them.

'And now you're assuming the foetal position too,' Anne Snapphane said. 'Have a cookie so you don't waste away.'

She handed her friend a cookie, and Annika took it mechanically, popping it in her mouth and chewing without tasting it.

'What do you mean by "catering"?' she said, crumbs of baked almond paste escaping from her mouth.

'Thomas can stand living with you, so you have to forfeit your life. You turn into a shadow, running around and slaving away, taking care of everything. You've been on maternity leave for a few years now, but now that you're back on the job it just won't work.'

'Come on.' Annika could barely conjure up the strength to protest. 'That's not how it is, is it?'

Anne flung her arms out and said:

'You're a prize, don't you realize that? He should be so damn grateful that he was lucky enough to catch you. You deserve flowers every single day, and kisses and shouts of joy, and lots of good sex for dessert . . .'

Annika felt laughter bubble up inside. The warmth made her body relax and her feet drop to the floor once more.

'Well, if you say so . . .'

'By the way, do you know what Schyman's up to?'

Anne Snapphane leaned back and munched on her second cookie. Annika felt her muscles tense again.

'What?' she said. 'Why do you ask?'

'He called Mehmed and asked how long they'll be doing the news show this summer.'

The pieces of information clicked into place like a jackpot on a slot machine. Annika could hear the *ka-ching*. She smiled. *The wily old bastard . . .*

So that's what he had up his sleeve.

Anders Schyman could sense the tenseness of the newsroom, the electricity in the air. It was much too quiet; too many men were gathered around Spike. He studied them out of the corner of his eye as he headed for his fish tank, noticing that Carl Wennergren had ignored his request to take his vacation earlier. Schyman took off his jacket and shook it out a bit before hanging it up. It had started to rain again. He had taken a walk along the shore of Lake Mälaren. It wasn't possible to take the time to travel to his home by the sea; come summer the roads leading to the seashore were jammed every single weekend, and traffic moved as slowly as a rolling protest action by French farmers.

He took off his soaking wet shoes and realized that he didn't have another pair here at the office. In one of the filing cabinets he located a pair of dry socks, which was better than nothing.

Then Schyman studied the group at the desk more closely, noticing the excited and fascinated expressions on the men's faces. Only Torstensson stayed aloof, sitting at the foreign correspondent's desk, wearily leafing through a foreign paper.

Schyman sighed, opened the door and walked over to the group. The men looked at him, the identical expression of uncertainty flashing briefly on all their faces.

'Wennergren has a new job,' Spike said, grinning. 'He's a porno photographer now. All he has to do is learn to focus the camera.'

The men snickered, their eyes slightly glazed.

'Turn that screen in my direction,' Schyman said.

The image on the computer was underexposed and grainy, but you could clearly see what was taking place: a man and a woman having sex on a dining-room table.

'Michelle Carlsson and John Essex,' Spike said. 'Wennergren shot these the night she was murdered.'

The excitement tingeing his voice had a duality: fascination with this outpost of the journalism of the macabre mixed with a dose of prurient sexuality.

The silence was palpable. All eyes were on Anders Schyman. Even Torstensson stopped leafing through his paper, even though he didn't look up. The managing editor tried to sort out his impressions and emotions and quickly assessed just how angry he would be.

'What is this picture doing in the paper's computer?' he asked, keeping his voice under control.

'It's not on the computer,' Spike said. 'Wennergren has the pictures on a disk.'

'Eject the disk,' Schyman said. 'And give it to me.'

'I don't think so,' Wennergren said. 'It's my property.'

The managing editor looked at the reporter: a carefree smile, thick blond hair and broad shoulders – one of the boys, a role model. He could sense how the other editors sided with Spike and Wennergren. Without being able to explain it, he knew Torstensson did too.

'Eject that disk,' Anders Schyman said emphatically. 'Before anyone decides to transfer those pictures to a server. We don't want garbage like that in our system.'

The silence intensified.

'Why not?' Wennergren asked, seemingly playful but with an undercurrent of aggression. 'We could post them on some hidden page of our lousy website, and then we could leak the address to a few choice hackers. For the first time in history, our site would have more visitors than our competitor's gets and it would only take a few hours.'

Mouths twitched and shoulders shook. This was what they had found so amusing.

'Would you like me to do it?' Schyman asked coolly.

Spike sighed dramatically, removed the disk from the drive, and handed it to Carl Wennergren.

'Then again, an issue like this should really be decided by the executive editor,' Spike challenged.

Schyman stopped thinking and lunged.

'That's a load of bullshit,' he roared and banged both hands on the news editor's desk. 'This isn't some damn porno rag, and if you don't know that you can leave at once.'

The agitated fluttering of Torstensson's paper scratched the surface of the razor-sharp silence. Spike gaped and blinked a few times.

'Hold your goddam horses,' he said, removing his feet from his desk and turning away.

'Wennergren,' Schyman said. 'My office.'

He waited until the reporter stood up. Then he forced himself to stride smoothly towards his office.

'What are you doing here?' he asked as he closed the door behind Carl Wennergren.

'I'm writing an article about Michelle Carlsson's murder,' Wennergren said in a somewhat less confident voice, one that held no trace of cockiness.

Anders Schyman stood in front of the young man and held Carl's pale-eyed and evasive gaze with his own. The silence grew, and Carl Wennergren shifted his shoulders slightly.

'What of it?' he finally said. 'I was there, wasn't I? It's a scoop. And I know a bunch of stuff that hasn't been published yet.'

'You are not going to write a single line,' Schyman responded, unpleasantly aware of how tense he sounded. 'As long as you are a special witness in a murder investigation, you aren't going to cover the cause for this paper.'

'I should be entitled to write about my own experiences. Barbara got to!'

A spark went off in Anders Schyman's brain, igniting the volatile mass of thoughts that had expanded to dangerous proportions due to fatigue and stress.

'Do you think this is some kind of goddamned kindergarten?' he roared into the reporter's face. '"Barbara got to . . ." Christ!'

He covered his eyes with his hands and turned away. He had lost control, lost some authority. Forcing himself to breathe calmly and think, he looked at the reporter again and noticed that the man's nose and cheeks had gone pale.

'Right now, Sjölander's on a plane crossing the Atlantic,' the managing editor said in a gravelly voice. 'Tomorrow he will be able to interview you about your experience, as a witness, under the exact same conditions as the other witnesses. Naturally, the decision to be interviewed is yours. The resulting article is not under your jurisdiction. Have I made myself clear?'

Something had crumbled in Carl Wennergren's gaze. His eyes had an expression that Anders Schyman had never seen before: an illusion had been shattered – Carl had gained a certain insight about life that had never entered his mind before.

'What kind of interview?' he managed to ask.

'Our reporter tells all about the night of the murder at the castle,' Schyman said, suddenly drained. He had to sit down.

'That makes me sound like a real wuss,' Carl Wennergren said.

'Have you ever figured out how many articles you've written on a similar theme?' Schyman asked.

The reporter stood by the door, started pulling the sliding doors open and paused.

Bristling with defiance and contempt, he turned to face Schyman.

'Just for your information,' he said, looking straight at the managing editor, 'I saw Barbara by the bus right before three o'clock in the morning. She could very well have murdered Michelle. Would you like me to tell all about that as well?'

'This paper's computers are off limits to those pornographic pictures,' Schyman said.

Carl Wennergren left the room, silently closing the sliding doors and then floating off towards the sea of people over by the news desk.

Anders Schyman held his wet socks in one hand and the scissors from his desk drawer in the other. Working methodically and keeping his hands out of sight, he cut the socks into thin ribbons.

Annika's first thought when the children came in was that their features were so clear-cut. Their eyes were round: Kalle's were glad to see her again, Ellen's reflected a one-year-old's sense of betrayal. Their bodies were so warm, so simultaneously hard and soft, and their scent was so distinctive. Sitting on the floor in the hall, she rocked them both with tears in her eyes.

'Can you help me out with the stuff?'

Thomas's voice was commanding and flat.

Annika hurriedly let go of the children and went to the elevator to drag in backpacks, the beach bag, the stroller, sleeping bags and blankets.

'Dinner's ready – it might be a little cold, though,' she said, closing the door and feeling overwhelmed by the situation: her little kids, clinging to her legs, the man who came home, home to her, the life they shared.

Dinner was a bit tense; the children were over-tired and all wound up, and Thomas avoided meeting Annika's gaze. By the time she had put the kids to bed, Thomas had parked himself on the couch to watch a movie on TV. She sat down next to him, close but still so very far away.

It wasn't until they had gone to bed, and both of them were lying there staring up at the ceiling, that she could manage to talk to him.

'How was it?'

He swallowed hard.

'Well, they wondered why you hadn't come along.'

'How did your mother react?'

'She's not a narrow-minded person, you know,' Thomas said. 'She accepts Sverker, calls him her son-in-law, and that's pretty impressive. People may gossip behind her back, but she holds her head high.'

Annika felt hot tears sting her eyes and swallowed to hold them back.

'I know that,' she whispered. 'Don't you see how that makes things even worse? She's not a snob or a bigot, she just doesn't accept me. Do you know how much that hurts?'

Her tears spilled out, heavy and salty, and rolled down into her ears.

'She's disappointed, that's all,' Thomas said without looking at her. 'Eleonor was the daughter she never had – they still call each other several times a week. But their relationship doesn't have anything to do with you. Just let them do their thing.'

'She feels sorry for you because you live with me,' Annika said in a small voice as she stared at the ceiling.

Thomas snorted.

'That's bullshit. Her frame of reference is different, that's all. A house is nicer than an apartment, being a chief financial officer for Social Services is better than doing research on welfare cases, and sure, being a banker is fancier than being a journalist. But let her have her opinions. After all, it's a free country.'

He turned away, his back to her. Annika stared at his shoulders, her tears silently streaming down on to the pillowcase.

'I want us to get married,' she whispered.

He didn't reply.

'In church,' she went on. 'And I want to wear a white gown, and the kids can be our attendants . . .'

Thomas yanked off the covers, his back rigid and forbidding in the summer night, leaving her hurt and longing in their bedding.

'Thomas! Please!'

Annika's voice pierced the air, small and reedy, anxiously waiting for a response that didn't come. She struggled to free herself from the damp tangle of bedding and followed him into the darkness before he switched on the kitchen lamp. She stood in the doorway, naked and shivering.

'People can see you,' Thomas said as he sat there in his robe at the table with a newspaper.

'Why don't you want to marry me?'

He looked up. His eyes were expressionless.

'I've been married. Believe me, there's no difference.'

'It would make a difference to *me*.'

'Why?' he said, pushing back his chair. 'Because you could publish a wedding picture in your home-town paper, *Katrineholms-Kuriren*?'

Annika stood there, blinking away the verbal slap in the face.

'I do everything for you,' she pleaded.

Thomas got up and walked towards her, fire and ice in his eyes. She backed away, another image intruding, another face approaching her. She heard the echo of her own voice, the words she'd said before, 'I do everything for you', and the approaching form with icy fire in his eyes.

'You want a ring on your finger? Is that it? You can have a ring, we'll buy one tomorrow.'

She turned away and ran, escaping through the darkness, panic like a piercing shriek in her left ear.

'Annika.'

His voice behind her, tired, flat.

'Annika, I'm sorry. Annie, come here.'

His arms around her shoulders, his breath on the back of her neck.

'I'm sorry, I didn't mean to . . .'

Annika's eyes were wide open, hot and dry, and she stared blankly at the wall.

I've heard this before. This has happened to me before. I've been ever forgiving, forgiving, forgiving . . .

She twisted out of his arms, grabbed a duvet and a pillow and headed for the children's room.

'Where are you going?'

'That's none of your damn business!'

The complex housing the Securities Register Centre was located on a street behind Sergels torg, one that used to be known for its hookers. It was a metal and glass structure from the 1970s, filled with mirrors and ornate concrete walls. Annika paused as she entered the building and closed her umbrella. The fastidiously official atmosphere made her uncomfortable; it clashed with the reason she was there. She wasn't here as a journalist – she was a snoop, a secret agent, possibly even a traitor.

Slightly nervous, she took the escalator upstairs. On the second floor she encountered an artificial garden, the glass ceiling floating some twenty metres overhead. There were mosaic fountains and marble floors, and a footbridge lined with white stylized lanterns was surrounded by brown stucco office buildings. Annika tried, unsuccessfully, to blink away the surrealistic haze in her mind and stared at the glass sky instead, detecting rivulets of rain, sensing the moisture.

It's only a standard procedure, nothing to make a fuss about.

The reception desk was on the right-hand side of the

lobby. With a fixed smile on her face, she introduced herself. Her name, her personal ID number, the ID card serial number, and the date were noted in a large ledger. While the receptionist was busy writing this down, Annika glanced at the names of the previous visitors, recognizing a reporter from the financial paper *Veckans Affärer*.

'The computers are over there, on the right. Let me know if you need any assistance.'

Two Philips flat-screens were humming with eternity's journey through the universe, and Annika let her jacket, her bag and her umbrella drop to the floor between two chairs. She hit *enter* and a window with three small icons appeared. A click on *Share Register* produced a form to fill in: the issuer, a personal ID number or corporate registration number and the owner's name.

She typed in Global Future as the issuer and Torstensson as the owner. A new window popped up next to the first one, with the heading 'Search results for public ownership listing'.

No data accessed.

'Excuse me,' she said to the receptionist. 'I have a few questions about how to search the database.'

The woman leaned over and said something that Annika didn't quite catch into the intercom.

Annika stared at the computer screen and, just for the heck of it, tried to see how many members of the family who owned *Kvällsposten* also had MTG shares, seeing as they were their competitor.

Three hits.

She smiled wryly.

'You're doing just fine,' a man said behind her.

Annika's heart lurched. The carpet was so thick that she hadn't heard the guy approach.

'Oh, hello,' she said. 'How does . . . this work?'

The man smiled at her. There was a gleam in his eye that made her cheeks grow hot.

'The share register is updated every six months,' he said. 'The version you have here is a record of public ownership as per 31 December of last year.'

Annika blinked a few times. There really wasn't anything underhand about her business apart from its objective.

'How would I go about finding the exact date when a certain holding was sold?' she asked.

'That can't be done,' the man said, still smiling. 'Transactions are reported on a semi-annual basis.'

'So no one would know?' she continued, feeling relieved but also obligated to pursue the matter.

'Yes, someone would,' he said. 'We register all transactions that exceed five hundred lots. Three working days after the transaction, the changes will be on the record.'

'Only that information isn't available to the general public.'

His gaze remained locked on hers. It spoke a different language to the officialese issuing from his mouth.

'We conduct analyses. It's a service we provide for reconciliation companies and certain foreign issuers so that they will be able to analyse the ownership structure of their company. Among other things, they can observe daily updates with regard to the directly registered shareholders.'

Annika looked down.

'They can pay to see who buys and sells their stocks?'

'That's right, they can observe the registration process here.'

'But I wouldn't be able to obtain that service?'

She stole a glance at the guy and saw him shake his head. Then she took in his thick mane of hair, broad shoulders and khaki slacks.

'Okay,' she said to his shoes. 'Say that I would like to find out exactly when a certain individual sold their holding of a particular company last summer or last fall, how would I do that?'

Annika met his gaze again, feeling shy and surprised by the warmth.

'Why don't you ask him?'

She smiled back.

'I'm the kind of girl who likes to find out things for herself,' she said.

'I bet you are,' the man said, grinning. His teeth were white and a tiny bit crooked. 'You could always contact the company. I doubt that they would tell you, but you never know.'

'Who should I ask to talk to?'

'Try the Principal Financial Adviser or the person responsible for investor relations. Only many companies don't have someone exclusively in charge of this type of business; it's usually taken care of by some ordinary administrator or clerk.'

Annika got up, put on her raincoat, picked up her bag and umbrella, and ended up way too close to the man in the confined space.

'Thank you,' she murmured.

'It was my pleasure,' he said. 'Let me know if I can help you in any other way . . .'

The man let the sentence trail off and handed Annika his card without moving to let her pass. She met his gaze, strangely affected by his show of interest. Forcing herself to laugh to relieve the sensation, she took his card.

'In that case I'll let you know.'

Annika stood under the roof by the entrance for a while, feeling assaulted by the sounds of the city: tyres hissing on the rain-slick asphalt, water rushing along the gutters, engines throbbing. She stuffed the umbrella in her bag and walked out into the rain, letting the lukewarm droplets sprinkle her face and hair as she headed for the subway station. Exhaust fumes were trapped at street level, a grey pungent haze that was impossible to keep at bay. Feeling disgusted, she stopped a cab, told the driver to take her to Zero Television, and leaned back against the leather upholstery in the back seat. The fogged-up windows hid the streets from view, protecting her from their ugliness.

I don't have to live like this. I deserve something better.

Annika closed her eyes. Her body and her clothing still retained the scents of her children: Ellen's slightly sour odour from her breakfast of yogurt and cereal and Kalle's more full-bodied aroma of bread and cheese. Her hands remembered the sensation of their silky hair, the warmth of their cheeks.

She had dropped them off at day care that morning. Ellen had accepted day care amazingly well. Kalle had been fussier – he had been older than Ellen when he'd started going to the centre, more aware. There were times when Annika had ended up crying by the door while her son had been crying on the other side.

She shook off the memory. Her children were in good hands. The community day-care centres were a blessing; she wished she could have attended one as a child.

Thomas would be picking the kids up today, since she had dropped them off. They tried to keep their hours to a minimum, generally picking the kids up at three and never coming later than four. This meant that they took turns working late when they weren't going to pick up the kids, making up for supposedly lost time.

Lost in what way, Annika wondered. The absence of her children made her body ache. She opened her eyes, gazed out across the leaden grey surface of Riddarfjärden

Bay and choked back her longing.

The Söderleden tunnel extinguished the grey light. Through the fog on the windows she saw the ancient black granite walls flash past.

I can make it, she thought. *Everything will be all right.*

The place where Anne Snapphane worked was located in a commercial area to the south of the city, close to the ski slopes in Hammarby, where the Olympic arena was being put up. Annika paid the taxi fare with a credit card, stuffed the receipt in her wallet and hoped that the paper would reimburse her for the trip.

The gate was in front of her, marking the outer limits of the television compound, tall grey concrete buildings that disappeared in the mist. On the left there were flat buildings, resembling hangars, that housed the broadcasting buses. She walked past the loading docks and wooden pallets and found the entrance.

Rows of vehicles were in there, all decked out in the same colours – white, with colourful logos – and in a range of different sizes and models. Two men were loading a small van. They looked at her briefly and she raised her hand in greeting.

The largest vehicle of them all was parked almost at the other end. In an indoor setting like this, and next to all the other vehicles, Outside Broadcasting Bus No. Five seemed positively gigantic. She approached it carefully, her footfall echoing on the concrete floor. There were piles of technical equipment by the bus, some of which was packed into metal cases labelled Sony BVP, Cam B Obl, Camera support No. Two.

The left-hand side of the bus had been expanded, just like it had been at Yxtaholm. The same perforated metal steps led up to the control room.

'Hello? Excuse me . . . Gunnar?'

The Technical Operations Manager stuck his grey head

out into the hallway. Annika put one foot on the steps and smiled.

'Hi. It's me, Annika Bengtzon – the train station at Flen, remember? May I come in?'

Gunnar Antonsson came out of the cubbyhole he'd been working in, wiped his hands off on his trousers and came to greet her.

'Sure,' he said. 'Sure, come on in.'

He extended a warm, dry hand, and shook hers firmly.

'Thanks for the ride, by the way. I caught a train fifteen minutes later.'

She smiled at him, then gazed at her surroundings and raised her eyebrows.

'Impressive,' she said.

The impression of being inside a vehicle was gone. This was a technically advanced office, tastefully decorated. The electronic equipment gently buzzing, an isolated universe of tiny shimmering lights and murmuring monitors.

The man's face suddenly came to life. He lit up.

'Want to take a tour?'

Annika nodded, slightly ashamed of her morbid curiosity.

Where was she found? Have you cleaned up the mess?

'This is the sleeping quarters,' the man said, indicating a recess on the right with a broad sweep of his arms.

Annika walked past a window with curtains on one side and a large distribution box on the other, looked into the tiny room and nodded knowingly.

'And what goes on in here?'

Gunnar Antonsson made a sweeping gesture over the screens, controls and keyboards.

'CCUs,' he said. 'The camera control units that the editor uses. It operates the cameras, regulates aperture settings, stuff like that.'

He turned around and continued.

'Technology Row,' he said, opening a door on the right.

Annika poked her head inside. There were millions of cables.

'Everything's in nineteen-inch racks,' he said. 'It's standard equipment.'

He closed the door after Annika had moved away. Her gaze shifted to the opposite wall, which was covered with maps and wiring diagrams.

'This is the editing area,' the man said, already having moved on to the next recess. 'It's where they do the assemblies and other editing. Here are the beta tape machines, the digibetas, the VHS recorders for reference tapes and our profilers . . .'

Annika left the thin red lines of the diagrams and hurried on.

'When we fixed up this bus two years ago, recording images on a hard drive seemed like science fiction,' Gunnar Antonsson continued. 'Now it's reality. A few months ago we had to redo all the racks and put in profilers down here.'

He pointed at the space below the compact editing console, and bent down and picked up a cable. Annika cleared her throat.

'I'm sorry, but what does that mean?'

The man, who was already on his way to the next section, stopped in surprise.

'Editing,' he said. 'This is where you put the show together.'

'On what?' Annika persisted. 'On actual tapes or on computers?'

'You've never worked with TV?' the man asked, shooting a quizzical look at her.

Annika tried to smile.

'No, I stick to words. It's easier to work at a paper.'

Gunnar paused and gave her a searching look as he wound the cable into a tight ring.

'Why did you write so much about Michelle all the time?'

Annika felt her cheeks grow hot. She made an effort to look positive.

'She was a very exciting public figure. An unusual mix of controversial and glamorous. Obviously, that was why the press liked to write about her.'

His expression remaining quizzical, Gunnar let the cable drop.

'But why was she so much more important than everyone else?'

Annika coughed, managing to avert her gaze.

'Michelle sold papers,' she said. 'It's that simple, I guess. She wasn't more important, really – she was commercially viable. Like she was for TV Plus. Someone who appealed to everyone, a person who stood out in the global village. She was nice to look at, nice to read about . . .'

Gunnar Antonsson opened a metal door and put the cable away. 'You always make broadcast-quality tapes,' he said, moving further inside the bus. 'That is, you use beta tapes or digital beta tapes nowadays. It's a kind of videotape that uses another format and the quality's much better. During this shoot we had four machines running simultaneously, just in case something went wrong – damaged tapes and stuff like that. Better safe than sorry, you know. But we didn't use any profilers – computerized recording, that is. Regular videotapes, VHS cassettes, are only used for reference tapes.'

Annika followed him, studying the back of his head. Thin hair, grey. Neatly trimmed.

'What's a reference tape?'

The man cocked an eyebrow and said:

'One is for the host – Michelle always wanted to check how she came across – then there's one for the producer and one for the researcher. The idea is that you don't need to make copies of the betas. The editor can use the time codes.'

Annika surveyed the wall of recorders, monitors and microphones with dozens of yellow markings – VTR 08, VTR 07 and so on – and felt more and more dazed.

'Wow,' she said. 'There sure is a lot to keep track of around here.'

'There sure is,' Gunnar Antonsson agreed, turning away from her and entering the production area.

The corridor opened up on a control room like the ones she'd seen Anne work in. An entire wall covered with monitors displayed the images from the various cameras, and there were buttons, lamps, controls, microphones and a large screen for the outgoing image. The walls were covered with blue and white patterned fabric, counter tops and floors were made of grey laminate, and the rounded wood trim had a shade reminiscent of cherry; Annika's fingers traced the grain.

'She was found lying between the slo-mo and the directing console.'

Annika took her hand away from the wood trim and followed Gunnar's gaze to the floor, to a narrow space between the front and rear production consoles, right in front of the seat used by the technical director. There was a trapdoor in the floor. It had shiny handles and metal strips.

'The directing console and . . . what?'

The technician stood up straight and put his hand on the rear console.

'The guy who operates the slow-motion machine for hockey sits here, and we call it the slo-mo. We call the console up front the directing console: that's where the whole team is, them editor, the technical director, the script girl, the graphics engineer . . .'

'Which direction was she facing?'

Gunnar folded his hands protectively, like a fig leaf, over his groin and rocked slightly back and forth on his heels.

'She had her head by the wall,' he said finally, nodding towards the opposite narrow end of the room. 'Her legs were here, on either side of the trapdoor. Her arms were reaching up, like this.'

He raised his hands, like gangsters do in the movies when the police arrive.

'Her head – well, what was left of it – was resting on the baseboard over there . . .'

Gunnar let his arms drop to his sides and went on to the compartment at the far end of the bus.

'Here's the sound studio. Here you've got the switches, the patches, the ninety-six-channel twin-layer console which provides twice the capacity you see here, and it's all digital . . .'

Gunnar Antonsson pointed out this and that with a wealth of detail. This, Annika knew, was characteristic of a person in shock. She followed him, her mouth dry, and tried to memorize certain words: patches, channels, digital.

'The diversity receivers for the wireless microphones are over here, the communications system that lets the bus communicate with the people outside like the camera crew, the planners and the reporters . . .'

Gunnar grew silent. They had reached the darkest corner of the bus.

'How are you? Is it rough going?' Annika asked in a low voice.

Gunnar Antonsson looked down at the floor and smoothed back his hair with one hand.

'Yeah,' he said. 'It's so strange. You find yourself wondering . . . well, if there's anything left . . .'

He stopped talking and shot her a quick look.

'If there's anything left of Michelle in here?' Annika asked.

'Everything's been thoroughly cleansed,' he said quickly, backing away.

'I guess that's up to you,' Annika said. 'If you want her to stay, she'd probably like to. And if you want her to leave you alone, then I think she'd respect your decision.'

'She liked being in the bus,' Gunnar said. 'She's welcome to stay.'

Annika smiled.

'Then you'll have some company on your drive down to Denmark. When are you leaving?'

He sighed with relief.

'Tomorrow, after lunch. I was planning to go to the memorial service, then I'll take off.'

Gunnar Antonsson looked at his watch and rubbed his stomach.

'Time for a coffee break,' he said. 'Would you like to join me?'

Annika smiled.

Thomas paused outside the section supervisor's office. His palms were all sweaty. His collar chafed. He had got out of the habit of wearing a tie during his years at the Swedish Association of Local Authorities, but today he had one on and he'd forgotten how uncomfortable it was.

He listened quietly outside the door. Did he hear voices in there?

It struck him that he couldn't stand there eaves-dropping, someone might come along. Raising his hand, he knocked firmly on the birch-veneer door.

The voice telling him to come in was sharp and surprised.

Thomas opened the door to be greeted by the aroma of coffee and pastries. He turned pale.

'What do you want?'

The section supervisor for Family Care and Nursing was in a meeting with the person in charge of negotiations and the supervisor of the Developmental Department. A secretary was taking notes. They all looked up at him, their eyes alert. They'd been interrupted.

'Excuse me,' Thomas said. 'I wasn't aware . . .'

Everyone apart from his own supervisor looked down at their papers again, unwilling to share in his embarrassment.

'Anything in particular?'

His supervisor's tone was curt and dismissive.

'It can wait,' Thomas said and quietly closed the door.

For a while he just stood there in the corridor on the ninth floor, his face getting progressively hotter.

He should have known better.

Once they had made their decision, management would get in touch with him. It was not like he could force their hand by asking if they'd made up their minds yet.

Thomas still hadn't received any feedback on the welfare project he'd been researching, but since it had been expanded in scope several times, he presumed that they were satisfied with his work. For the past three and a half years he had looked into issues of poverty, squalor, guilt, contempt and social drop-outs, trying to figure out how society could alleviate these drawbacks in spite of repeated cutbacks.

He had earned a shot at something bigger. He was qualified to take on the regional picture. As far as he could tell, the position of shaping the future development of Sweden's different regions would go either to him or to a woman at the Federation of Swedish County Councils, and she had already spent three years working on the subject. When it came to facts and figures, she had a massive advantage, while Thomas knew the ropes here at the Association – and he was already working here, too.

An older woman from some other section appeared further down the corridor, and he quickly headed back to his office. He trembled as he sank down at his desk, the wheels of his chair squeaking as he pulled himself in closer.

His gaze fell on a diagram that was fastened with a paper clip to a sketchy assessment. To be honest, he hadn't really completed the interim report, but it no longer bothered him. If management didn't give him more work they would just have to accept the inconclusive analysis, and if they did, he could finish the report on the side. He gathered up the papers on his desk, deposited them in a blue folder and put it away in the bookcase behind his desk.

Thomas looked around the room: typically Scandinavian blond birch bookcases, greyish-blue textiles, a dark blue carpet on a hardwood ash floor. It could be that he wouldn't be spending much more time here. His contract expired on 30 June, which would make Friday his last day at work.

He took a deep breath and tried to fight back the feelings of vertigo, the sensation of being sucked down into a vortex of failure. He raked his hair off his face and began to concentrate on practical issues.

There wouldn't be much to pack.

Unless someone protested, he'd be taking his files and material. The plants on the windowsill were company property, just like the furniture, the pictures, the computers and the rest of the technical equipment. As a matter of fact, Thomas hadn't brought in a single personal item. No crayon drawings, no postcards, no pictures of Annika or the children.

If he didn't have his job, what did he have?

Thomas's life had changed in every respect after that day three and a half years ago when Annika had picked him up out at his old home in Vaxholm. Going with her hadn't been an active decision, it had simply been the easiest way out. She had offered him an escape route, and he had taken it, leaping into the great unknown just to get away.

Not heading towards anything, just leaving things behind.

It hadn't been fair to Annika, and it definitely hadn't been fair to Eleonor.

The thought of the other man, the one who had taken his place by his wife's side, was unbearable.

Martin is one of the partners. Aren't you happy for me? I'm so happy, Thomas.

Gripping the edge of the desk, he took a couple of deep breaths.

If he didn't even have a job, then what *did* he have?

Thomas let his gaze sweep across the cemetery that he could see from the window, the churchyard of Mariakyrkan, St Mary's: the waterlogged grounds with their rows of grey granite crosses and headstones criss-crossed by rivulets of rainwater. Self-pity made his chest ache.

This wasn't the way his life was supposed to be.

'Here's your mail.'

Thomas was startled by the cheerful announcement.

'We're almost there,' the mailman said enthusiastic-ally, handing over a small bundle of mail. 'I'll be taking my vacation as of next week. How about you?'

'Me too,' Thomas said, his mouth dry as he took his mail.

The busy mailman vanished as quickly as he had appeared, leaving Thomas dazed as he regarded the pile of manila envelopes. Mechanically, he picked up his paper-knife and slit the top one open. It contained information that he'd requested from the town of Pajala way up north about its implementation of welfare benefits. The next item was an in-house newsletter encouraging everyone to join in on Friday and play boules at Humlegården. Then there was his payslip, looking the same as it had every month.

The next envelope was thicker, glossier. He turned it over. It had been sent on from the city of Vaxholm. The upper left-hand corner displayed a large logotype, IG, followed by a row of Asian characters and the words in English:

Institute for Global Economics.

He hefted the letter in his hand, assessing its thickness: more than a centimetre.

This wasn't anything he had ordered.

With a single flick Thomas tore open the envelope with his finger, not bothering to use the paperknife. A folder in English landed on his desk.

The International Next-Generation Leaders' Forum was established by the Institute for Global Economics and the Korea Foundation with the main purpose of providing an opportunity for international next-generation leaders to meet their counter-parts from all over the world to get acquainted with each other for their future cooperation . . .

He leafed through a few more pages.

Facing New Challenges – Luncheon Address at the 4th International Next-Generation Leaders' Forum, Seoul, South Korea.

What the . . .?

Then he found the cover letter.

Dear Mr Samuelsson, he read. He quickly skimmed through the rest of it.

The Institute was extremely honoured to invite him to represent Sweden and attend the Fourth International Next-Generation Leaders' Forum, in Seoul, South Korea, during the period 2 September through 12 September this year. The forum would be attended by a delegate from each of the sixteen western countries that had been chosen, along with sixteen prominent young South Koreans. The Institute and the Korea Foundation would sponsor the trip, paying for room and board, seminars, field trips and tours of model factories. Unfortunately, the deadline was pressing and he was requested to reply no later than Tuesday, 26 June.

Thomas lowered the letter. Was this some kind of joke?

Quickly, he leafed through the rest of the papers and found a handwritten missive at the bottom of the stack.

Of course.

Kim Sung-Yoon, the forward from his old team back in Åkersberga. Sung-Yoon, the son of the South Korean ambassador, played ice hockey. Thomas, the captain of the team, had made sure that he was included as one of the guys.

Thomas stared at the spidery letters.

Holy smoke. Kim Sung-Yoon, he'd totally forgotten him.

But the Korean had obviously remembered *him*.

Dropping the letter on the desk, Thomas looked out over the cemetery and thought back to the old days: Sung-Yoon, a short and cheerful guy whose eyes almost disappeared when he laughed. They had spent a lot of time together for a year or so. Thomas had been the one to get Sung-Yoon drunk for the very first time. Naturally, the ambassador had been furious, and he had forbidden Thomas to associate with his son, a command that the young men had ignored.

When his father's diplomatic career was over, the Kim family had returned to South Korea. Sung-Yoon got a job with the organization that had arranged the Olympics in Seoul back in 1988. He and Thomas had lost touch seven or eight years ago.

Thomas picked up the letter again, reading the impressively correct Swedish.

It seemed that nowadays Sung-Yoon was an under-secretary of state at the Department of Sports and Athletics in Seoul. He was the one who had proposed Thomas as Sweden's representative at the Fourth International Next-Generation Leader's Forum.

Sung-Yoon would be attending the symposium himself, as one of the sixteen South Korean delegates, and he hoped that they would be able to get together and talk about old times.

Thomas turned the letter over. The paper was blank on the other side. He glanced through the rest of the papers: suggested flight routes, a preliminary agenda for the ten-day stay in Seoul, a description of the dress code for the different events – business attire for meetings, casual dress for tours, no jeans at Panmunjon. A tour of the Hyundai and Samsung plants, and a trip to the tunnels under the demilitarised zone at the Thirty-eighth Parallel, meetings with the Korean president, lunch with the Secretary of the Treasury, dinner with the Defence Secretary, lectures by several professors and a Nobel Prize-winner.

This can't be happening, Thomas thought and realized that he needed some air.

He got up, grabbed his lunch vouchers and made a getaway. When the door to his section supervisor's office opened, Thomas was waiting for the elevator. The three bosses left the room. His supervisor caught sight of him and stopped short, no longer laughing along with the others.

'There you are,' the man boomed. 'What did you want to discuss?'

Thomas squared his shoulders, felt in a jacket pocket for something that wasn't there and spoke in a calmly informative tone of voice:

'All I needed was some information, really,' he said. 'You see, I've been invited to represent Sweden at an international forum for leadership in Seoul this fall so I'll be out of town for the first two weeks of September. I realize that this may have no bearing on your plans for the autumn, but I wanted you to know.'

The entire group had come to a halt. All eyes were on him.

'A leadership forum? What does it involve?'

Thomas's boss had lost his jovial look. His mouth was slack.

'The Fourth International Next-Generation Leaders' Forum,' Thomas said. 'It's arranged by the Institute for Global Economics and the Korea Foundation. Are you familiar with them?'

The elevator bell dinged and the doors opened smoothly. Thomas got in.

'Anyone going down?' he asked the supervisors.

They all shook their heads and Thomas raised his right hand in a farewell gesture as the doors closed. When the cage started to descend he leaned his head back against the wall.

Holy smoke, he thought again. *I'll be damned.*

The heap of black plastic garbage bags practically reached the ceiling, blocking the entrance to the editing room like a sandbagged firing trench.

'Are you in here somewhere?' Annika asked in a low voice, trying to find a chink to peek through.

The response was a groan from the other side of the heap.

'Go around to the right. There's a passage behind the monitor rack,' Anne Snapphane said.

Annika left her jacket and her bag in the doorway, then picked her way over cables and electrical cords. The air in the room was characteristic of editing rooms, crackling with dryness, and the wall-to-wall carpeting was charged with so much static electricity that her hair stood on end. The atmosphere was dusty and greyish. The screens and energy-conserving bulbs gave off a blue, flickering light.

'What's this?' Annika asked, waving in the direction of the bags.

'It's the material from the show, the stuff that was impounded. Isn't this dandy? The police gave it to us like this, in one hell of a mess.'

Annika looked down into the half-full bag at Anne's feet. Videotapes of different formats were mixed up with printouts of schedules and other junk.

'What are you going to do?'

'Catalogue the stuff, categorize it and file it. I've got to make a note of the time codes of each tape, so we can start editing the show, and we're in a tearing hurry, too. It won't be made official until tomorrow, but we're going to start airing the shows on Saturday, just as originally planned.'

'Michelle hasn't even been buried yet,' Annika exclaimed.

'Tell that to the Big Boss in London,' Anne Snapphane said. She pressed the eject button of the portable editing console by her knees, removed the tape with her right hand and put in a new one a second later with her left. While the machine was busy loading the tape, Anne filled out an adhesive label, slapped it on the recently ejected tape and stored it in a box. A moment later the screen started to flicker and Michelle Carlsson appeared on the monitor screen in front of them.

Both women went rigid, struck by the definition of the image. The dead woman was standing there, tense, ready to go, apparently listening to something in her earpiece.

'No, I'd like to put the anarchists on first,' she said into her body mike, talking to someone in the control room, answering a question that was probably stored on some other tape in some other bag.

The woman didn't move from the spot while a make-up artist came into the frame and closely inspected her appearance. Michelle didn't notice her, she was listening so intently to the voice in her ear.

'The anarchists first, then the Nazi – I want a close-up, shot from the left, so that the swastika on her cheek fills the screen.'

The make-up artist dabbed at the woman's forehead with a huge pink puff, picked up a brush, filled in an eyebrow and then backed away.

'Okay,' Michelle Carlsson said and nodded, mouthing a thank-you to the make-up artist. Then she waved, adjusted her earpiece, turned forty-five degrees and gazed into the camera with vacant eyes.

Annika studied those eyes, the blank look, and felt her chest constrict. There was no joy in their depths, no satisfaction, no presence in the moment, only despair and a crushing sense of obligation.

Then Michelle Carlsson nodded again, took a step back and turned on her inner light.

The transformation was immediate, fantastic and dramatic. The woman's face changed: her eyes came alive, gleaming and sparkling, and a sense of warmth reached out through the screen, embracing Annika and Anne like a hug, making them smile.

'Welcome to *Summer Frolic at the Castle*,' Michelle

Carlsson said, her voice like warm honey, her hair like silk, her eyes like crystals. 'This is our last night here at Yxtaholm castle, in the province of Sörmland, this summer, and our guests . . .'

She stopped short and put her hand to her ear. The warmth died out.

'All right,' she said. 'One-two, one-two, can you hear me? One-two . . .'

'What tape is this?' Annika asked.

'I expect it's a tape of the last session, taken with camera two,' Anne Snapphane said and started to fast-forward the tape. The soundtrack turned into gibberish, voices squawking like Donald Duck. Two stripes appeared on the screen and the people moved around like silent-movie stars on speed. Annika kept looking, fascinated by this kaleidoscope of reality.

'Yup,' Anne Snapphane said a few minutes into the actual show. 'This is from camera two.'

She set the machine at a higher speed and now seven stripes streaked the screen instead of two. The sound was reduced to mere high-pitched squeaks, barely audible.

While the tape rattled away, Anne reached for the next one, weighing two in her hands and choosing one. She whipped out the labels again, slumping slightly while she waited for the tape to finish running. Three Michelles started to laugh and talk on different monitors at the same time. The guests and crew members in the background couldn't take their eyes off the TV star. Michelle smiled, sparkled, wrinkled her brow slightly as she listened, welcomed guests and moved on to other segments. The camera clung to her: every last move was important, every expression had its significance.

'It's amazing,' Annika said, 'this is so powerful.'

'It's even mentioned in the Bible,' Anne said, fingering the labels. 'The fourth chapter of Genesis.'

Annika, well aware of Anne's childhood experiences of Lutheran Sunday school at Pitholm's Evangelical Society, waited silently for her to continue.

'Acknowledgement,' Anne Snapphane said. 'It's a basic human need. Not getting the appreciation and recognition we deserve tears us apart. You can't live without it.'

'Are we back to the story of Cain and Abel again?'

'The very first documented motive for murder in the history of the world,' Anne Snapphane said.

'Sorry,' Annika said, 'I'm not really familiar with the details here.'

Anne kicked off her shoes.

'Cain was a tiller of the ground while Abel tended the sheep. Both of them came to the Lord with an offering. Cain brought the fruit of the ground while Abel brought the firstlings of his flock. But God only saw the gift that Abel had brought – he paid no attention to Cain's gift.'

'In other words, the Lord was a total wash-out when it came to parenting skills,' Annika said.

'Exactly. And according to the Bible, Cain was enraged when he wasn't acknowledged, and his countenance fell. And God, the old sadist, asked Cain something like this: "Why are you so angry, and why has your countenance fallen? If you do well, will you not be accepted? And if you do not do well, sin is lurking at the door. Its desire is for you, but you must master it."'

'What a bastard,' Annika said. 'First he says that we are all equals in his sight, that we're created in his image, then he assigns us to different sets of circumstances, and finally he admonishes us when we react to his lack of fairness.'

'Abel was acknowledged and lauded,' Anne said, 'while Cain was supposed to swallow being left in the wings and still be good-natured about it.'

'Abel got all the credit and Cain was supposed to labour away without a complaint,' Annika said, summing it up.

'I guess you know the rest of the story,' Anne Snapphane said, walking over to a bag next to the hard drives.

'Cain lured Abel out into the wilderness and killed him?'

'Right,' Anne said from the depths of the bag. 'Could you hold these tapes? Thanks. God had seen the whole thing – apparently he had some kind of spy cam – so he knew what Cain had done.'

'How was Cain punished?'

'He lost his job: he was no longer allowed to till the soil. He was doomed to be a fugitive and a wanderer on the earth.'

Anne Snapphane sank back down on her chair.

'Are you supposed to look at every last tape?' Annika wondered.

'Not quite,' Anne said. 'But I do have to find out what segments are on each tape, sort them out and make sure that there are no technical glitches.'

The images disappeared and darkness reigned on the monitor screen for a few seconds until the machine switched off. Anne Snapphane sighed and switched tapes with the same rapid-fire precision as before, affixing a label and filing the most recent tape away.

'God didn't care about the results of Cain's work,' Annika said slowly.

'Well, lambs are undeniably cuter than grains of wheat,' Anne countered.

'Cain worked his fingers to the bone, ploughing and sowing, weeding and harvesting,' Annika said, picturing the rocky field. 'Abel spent his days resting, chewing on a blade of grass, while the sheep got it on and had babies.

And yet, baby brother's job got the recognition. Cain couldn't live with that.'

'Abel came across on God's screen, while Cain didn't,' Anne Snapphane murmured.

'It's amazing,' Annika said once again, 'that this stuff is so powerful. Want to go out and grab something to eat?'

Anne made a face.

'No, but a cup of coffee might be nice. Put on a fresh pot and I'll be right out, I just have to . . .'

Annika worked her way out of the cubbyhole and took greedy gulps of air once she got out in the hallway. She went to the lounge and turned on the coffee-maker.

The lounge was really only a glassed-in cubicle in the middle of a large room that had once housed a factory and was now the Zero Television newsroom. White-laminate kitchen cupboards lined one wall, plus a range, a fridge, a sink and a counter-top with a coffee-maker. A stale greasy smell indicated that the fan didn't work very well.

On the other side of the glass wall there were desks, computers, telephones, and a few sofas. The desks were more crowded together than they were at *Kvällspressen*, and the women were younger and prettier. They spent most of their time persuading people to be guests on different network shows: always on the phone, convincing VIPs to sit in on their TV debates, coaxing household names to let themselves be humiliated by their trendy talk-show and game-show hosts, and flattering hip artists so that they'd plug their latest recordings on one of their shows, preferably as an exclusive.

Annika knew that one of the channel's personalities, Sweden's unofficial talk-show king, would only do exclusive interviews. Celebrity guests weren't allowed to do shows with anyone but the 'king' all season, that was the deal, take it or leave it – if you wanted to be seen with the best, it would cost you – and here were the women who did the job, who made sure that the show would go on, who would bring on the clowns . . .

'Thank God!' Karin Bellhorn exclaimed as she zoomed in on the coffee-maker. 'We really should get one of those vending machines, but the coffee's never as good as the drip kind, is it?'

She sailed over to the counter, took out two china mugs from a cupboard and handed one to Annika.

'Are you here to see Anne?' the producer asked as she poured the coffee.

'Just to grab a quick cup of coffee,' Annika replied and looked around for some milk.

'Reporters are calling non-stop,' Karin Bellhorn said, looking intently at Annika. 'Very few reporters have access to the entire menagerie of murder suspects, you know.'

Annika felt the woman's gaze: it was burning and alien. Suddenly uncomfortable, she squirmed.

'Would you like me to leave?'

Leaning against the counter, her arms crossed over her ample bosom, Karin Bellhorn took a sip of coffee and sighed, suddenly sagging with fatigue.

'No,' she said, 'not on my account.'

Annika tried to smile and, feeling uncomfortable, searched for something to say.

'You know what?' the producer suddenly said. 'You're the kind of person that people notice.'

There was nothing ingratiating in the woman's tone, but Annika blushed violently and looked down.

'It's funny,' Karin Bellhorn continued, 'that certain something that makes some people noticeable. A small portion of it is physical beauty, but it's not only that. Michelle wasn't a classic beauty, but I've never seen anyone pop out of the screen like her.'

Annika nodded, thinking of the tape in Anne's office,

the effect when Michelle switched on and became so vibrantly alive.

'Is it true that everyone was envious of her?' Annika asked.

Karin shot a surprised look at Annika.

'Envious?' she said. 'Well, that would depend on how you define the word. Everyone who isn't satisfied with what they have wants more. And that would include the publicity aspect.'

'Why is that so attractive?' Annika said.

Karin Bellhorn laughed.

'That's a funny question, coming from a newspaper reporter.'

She set her mug down on the counter. 'I suppose you're aware of the principles at work here?'

Annika shook her head.

'Celebrity is power. The better known you are, the more powerful you'll be. And you'll rule over more space, more territory. It's all about fighting for your territory, choosing your mate.'

Annika was taken aback.

'Is it really that simple?' she asked, amazed at the naïve brutality of the producer's words.

Karin Bellhorn shrugged and attempted a smile.

'We haven't progressed much further than the dinosaurs, really.'

She looked down at her hands. 'I used to host shows on TV,' she said. 'Did you know that?'

Annika nodded hesitantly. 'A magazine?'

'The first of its kind in Sweden. I belonged to the editorial staff too. Back in those days everything was supposed to be so nice and democratic, but they walked all over me every day. All my suggestions were junked while the subjects that the men wanted to cover made the cut.'

Karin smiled sadly. 'You know the drill. Things change less than we think.'

'Didn't you leave the country?'

Karin Bellhorn cocked her head. 'I married Steven, and then I got as much attention as anyone could ever desire. It wasn't all good. I don't think people here at home in Sweden realized what a huge star Steven was in England. The tabloids were parked under our bedroom window around the clock.'

Something in the producer's voice piqued Annika's interest. The words were critical, but the tone suggested a pride that was kept in check.

'That must have been a hassle,' Annika said.

Karin sighed, raising her eyebrows momentarily as she laughed. 'Being as famous as we were was an unusual experience,' she said. 'You had to deal with all the different kinds of attention you received, even the positive kind. It was difficult to get things done when you were splashed out in the papers or in the headlines.

'It scatters your energies. You get spread out in pieces, you become everyone's property, you belong to everyone on that particular day. It wears you down, I don't know how else to describe it – it's like bits of you are chopped up and spread to the wind. It's extremely difficult to pull yourself together and get things done.'

Annika looked around for Anne Snapphane, but didn't see her anywhere. 'The media were all over Michelle,' she said. 'That must have been awful.'

Karin pulled out a pack of cigarettes from the depths of her cardigan and squeezed it speculatively.

'Well, you have to acknowledge the true nature of gossip and malicious rumours. They're entertainment. What one person perceives as intolerable injustice is simply a brief escape from the daily grind for others

while they're having their hair done. You need to keep
your sense of perspective, though gossip can obviously
be extremely hurtful. Particularly if it's an attack on a
loved one. All famous people have that particular
Achilles heel in common: family. An attack on family is
devastating.'

'Family is the most overused excuse for wriggling out
of an uncomfortable situation,' Annika countered.

'Yes and no,' Karin Bellhorn said, placing a cigarette
between her lips. 'Bad press will always affect the family.
Some old mother or some poor child will always suffer, so
there's a modicum of truth in what you see as a tired
excuse. Would you like some more coffee?'

Annika shook her head.

'Come with me to the smoking area,' Karin said, and
forged ahead through the newsroom.

Annika followed in her wake, crossing the room to
enter a cubicle that reeked of smoke and boasted a view of
the half-finished Victoria Stadium.

'Do you think they'll finish it in time for the games?'
Annika asked, nodding in the direction of the Olympic
arena.

'Of course they will,' Karin Bellhorn replied, taking
such a deep drag on her cigarette that her airways
squealed. 'There are three years to go.'

Uncertain of the producer's intent and of her own role,
Annika didn't comment on this. She had gone from
unwanted to confidante in about eight point seven
minutes. She studied the producer's profile: the deep
lines around her mouth, the nicotine-stained fingers that
fingered her chin. The grey light of day gave her
complexion an unnatural cast.

'Do you enjoy your job?' Annika asked.

Karin Bellhorn shrugged a little and kept gazing off
into the distance.

'We're trying to do something good,' she said. 'We're trying to show society from a female perspective, and that's certainly not bad.'

'Even if it means knuckling under to the powers that be?' Annika wondered.

'Well, we can be grateful for those powers, after all,' Karin said, flicking some cigarette ash into a sand-filled tray.

'If it weren't for those powers there wouldn't be any programmes directed at a young, female audience. You have to grab the attention of consumers before they reach the age of thirty; after that people don't change their habits and preferences. When it comes to household items, women do most of the buying, that's why commercials cater to them. And just look at public service television – they're standard-issue to the max.'

Annika smiled; white middle-aged heterosexual men with a car and a steady income were a group that had been defined and categorized in debates over the past year, ruffling some feathers. They were used to defining the human condition and being suddenly classified as a distinct group offended them.

'That's true,' Annika said. 'On the other hand, commercial television shows are only there to fill in the slots between advertisements.'

'Who cares?' Karin Bellhorn said. 'As long as we get the chance to do something that makes sense, we're going to do it. In addition to this, it creates jobs for women, in front of and behind the camera.'

'Only the wheels don't always run smoothly, from what I gather,' Annika said. 'Mariana von Berlitz and Michelle didn't have a good relationship, did they?'

'It was lousy,' Karin Bellhorn replied curtly, putting out one cigarette and immediately lighting another. 'Things were damn tense. Mariana was here before

Michelle, and she could never accept how Michelle rose to where she did.'

'So Mariana was envious?'

The producer took a deep breath and looked up at the grimy ceiling for a few seconds.

'I'd say she begrudged Michelle her glory,' she said, nodding slowly in acknowledgement of Annika's words. 'Mariana insisted on being screen-tested a few times, but she came to the conclusion herself that she didn't fit the bill. It wasn't really traumatic for her. What she objected to was that Michelle had so much say in the shows. Since she was the host, Michelle could obviously make changes in the script or ask the producer to rearrange segments. And Mariana felt that Michelle didn't possess the know-how or the experience to deal with that level of authority.'

'Was that true?'

Karin Bellhorn greedily inhaled enough nicotine to create a huge hanging ember at the end of her cigarette.

'No,' she said in a low voice. 'Not at all. Michelle was a natural when it came to timing and effect. Mariana is no good at it, she just doesn't have it in her.'

Annika tried to fan away some cigarette smoke.

'What about Stefan Axelsson?'

The producer gave Annika a sideways glance.

'I don't know much about the guy. He's a freelancer.'

'Hasn't he been involved in most of Zero's productions during the past four years?'

Karin Bellhorn shrugged and Annika dropped the subject.

'Then what about Sebastian Follin?'

Karin Bellhorn sank down on an armchair and rested her chin in one hand.

'Sebastian was doing consultant work for the National Road Administration in Växjö when he dedicated his life to making Michelle Carlsson famous. That's all he wanted in life: when he succeeded, he was satisfied. Of course, he was an albatross around Michelle's neck. She had this implicit sense of being indebted to Sebastian. It didn't matter how much money he got, he was always entitled to something more. He was entitled to *her*. He wanted to share the spotlight with her. Sebastian didn't see himself as a manager, he saw himself as an extension of Michelle, a part of her.'

'Is he a little unbalanced?' Annika asked.

'Not at all. That's just my point. Famous people can have that effect on their associates, particularly if you knew the person before they were famous. If a group starts a project together, it's always going to generate a lot of friction if one person reaches critical mass.'

Confused, Annika blinked.

'Critical mass?'

The producer smiled again, carefully balancing her cigarette between her lips.

'When they make a name for themselves,' she said. 'Gain recognition and public acclaim. The best examples of this are in the music business – garage bands that have slaved away for years, say, and become so-called overnight sensations and the singer is seen as the star. Bands like that often split up, and that's due to the mechanisms that control fame.'

Annika smiled.

'The better known you are, the more powerful you'll be. And you'll rule over more space, more territory. Like you said.'

Karin nodded.

'An imbalance in distribution,' she said.

'What other clients did Follin represent?'

The producer took another long drag on her cigarette and waited in silence while the nicotine was being absorbed.

'There are no others,' she said as she exhaled the smoke. 'At first, he pretended there were, but the pretence died out pretty quickly. How frankly should I put this? He had no desire to grow, to expand his business scope. All he wanted to do was show off.'

Annika flushed and changed her tack.

'What really went on that last night?' she asked. 'Why did he go crazy over at the Stables?'

Karin Bellhorn's eyes flashed. She stubbed out her latest cigarette and got up.

'What do you know about that?'

Annika hesitated for a second.

'I saw the mess,' she explained. 'Did it have anything to do with Michelle and John Essex?'

The older woman gasped, the colour draining from her face, from her hairline to her chin. She put out one hand against the wall to support herself.

'What?' she said. 'What?'

Alarmed by Karin's response, Annika took a step towards her.

'Are you all right? Do you need any help? Would you like me to go and get someone?'

The producer stared at Annika for a few moments. Then she closed her eyes while her complexion slowly regained its flesh-tone.

'It was just a drop in blood pressure,' she said. 'I'm sorry. What did you say?'

'I have reason to believe that Michelle and John Essex got it on that last night at the castle,' Annika said. 'Could that have made Sebastian Follin jealous?'

Karin shut her eyes and placed a hand on her forehead.

'I found Sebastian afterwards, in the middle of the mess,' she said. 'He was sitting on the floor, bawling his eyes out, absolutely devastated.'

'Because of John Essex?'

The woman shook her head, sighed, and looked at Annika with glazed eyes.

'Michelle had told him she was terminating their contract. She didn't want him to be her manager any more. He couldn't deal with it – his life fell apart. You've got to understand the guy.'

'Understand him? What do you mean?'

'He was losing his place in the spotlight, his slice of fame. His territory was being snatched away from him, he was being shut out. Without Michelle, who was he?'

'Could that really make someone so desperate?'

A harsh, rattling laugh made Karin Bellhorn's body shake, a reaction so out of control and aggressive that Annika recoiled.

'You have no idea,' the producer said, pushing herself off from the wall and leaving the nicotine-reeking gas chamber.

Annika didn't move, just followed the TV producer with her gaze through the glass partition, breathing in the nauseatingly stuffy air of the room. There was something about the shapeless form of the woman that was echoed in the smoking area: the outdated materials, the lack of freshness.

Stress and shock make people act strangely, Annika thought.

Then she caught sight of Anne Snapphane over by the coffee-maker.

'Where did you go?' Annika asked as she poured the last drops of coffee into a yellow mug embellished with polka dots.

'Karin wanted to talk.'

Anne sniffed at Annika's clothes, wrinkling her nose at the cigarette smell.

'I thought she was going to have a heart attack,'

Annika said, looking apprehensively in the direction of the elevators. 'Is she always like that?'

'Yesterday we were all borderline psychotic. You know, I've really got to get back to work, this is my week with Miranda and . . .'

Annika went to pick up her raincoat and her bag, taking her time as she walked to the elevator. As the elevator rattled down the shaft, her mind was chock-full of impressions but still felt strangely empty. Her thoughts were disjointed, a hum of swirling words.

The lobby was crowded, but Berit Hamrin could immediately locate John Essex's road manager. He was standing in front of the fireplace, rocking back and forth, gently swinging a bottle of French mineral water. His Italian suit was a bit snug at the waist. Armani was designed for athletes, not businessmen.

Berit hurried over to his side. The man chose not to see her.

'It was nice of you to take the time to see me,' Berit said, smiling sweetly, reaching out and shaking his hand before he could withdraw it.

The man turned towards her. His expression conveyed unveiled contempt and irritation. He looked her up and down, assessing her middle-aged body and dismissing her as a person.

'I really don't see the point of this,' he said and looked over at the exit, ready to leave.

Berit lifted up her chin a bit, realizing that the manager wanted to shake her self-confidence by rejecting her as a potential sex object.

'Could we go somewhere and talk in private?' she asked.

The man didn't reply. He just sat down on a leather couch next to the fireplace and put the bottle of water on the floor. Berit walked past a group of German business-men and sat down next to him. She placed a pink cardboard folder in front of them, letting it remain unopened. People swished past at close range, with hushed voices and swinging briefcases.

'I work for a tabloid that's in tailspin,' Berit explained. 'Our circulation is down, our advertising revenue is down and our resources are drying up, which means that people are leaving the paper and the standard of reporting is deteriorating. Our management is very anxious to turn the tide.'

The road manager was about to get up and leave, totally uninterested in anything to do with a lousy tabloid from the North Pole.

'That's why,' Berit continued in a grave voice, 'it's very important that we discuss the situation at hand. I would greatly appreciate dealing with this in a professional manner.'

The man looked at his watch.

'To be honest, I really don't see why my assistant insisted that I should see you,' he said, once again preparing to get up.

Berit forced herself to stay seated and keep her cool.

'She realized how necessary it was to explore the conse-quences of the material that my paper has at its disposal.'

The road manager stopped short, his behind hovering some ten centimetres or so above the leather surface of the couch. For the first time he became truly aware of Berit, realizing that she had them by the balls.

Slowly, he lowered himself back down on the couch.

'Obviously, we don't wish to harm Mr Essex in any way,' Berit continued in a sincere voice, cocking her head slightly to one side. 'On the contrary, all we want is to tell our readers about his impressions of that night at Yxtaholm Castle.'

'That's totally out of the question,' the man said. 'John is in the middle of a world tour. He doesn't have time for this kind of thing. We've put that unfortunate affair behind us.'

Berit studied the man, noting the age spots on his hands and the tanning-bed shade of the skin beneath his beard, trying to find in herself a smidgen of guilt or shame for what she was about to do. There wasn't one.

'That's too bad,' she said, 'because that's not the case for us, nor for the Swedish police. And as I've already informed you, my paper has a duty to keep its readers up to date when it comes to matters of general interest such as this. In addition to this, the owners of the paper demand a return on their investment. We're not in a position to throw out commercially attractive material just to be nice.'

Distrustful, but now attentive, the road manager blinked a few times.

Berit picked up the pink folder and hefted it in her hand.

'My paper is in the possession of photos of John Essex with the recently deceased TV personality,' she said, with a slight wave of the folder.

'Really?' the man said.

'They are pretty sensational,' Berit said, fixing the man with her stare.

His gaze darted around the room and he leaned closer, not particularly ruffled. His breath smelled of cigars.

'So we're talking about sex pictures, then. We can deal with that. It's no news that John screws around.'

'That's only a part of what we've got. We also have a copy of the forensic analysis of the murder weapon.'

Fear took hold of the road manager. His posture became rigid and he avoided Berit's stare.

'John didn't shoot her.'

Berit shrugged.

'That's possible,' she said. 'But he used the loaded gun for other purposes.'

She let her words sink in, seeing the coin drop in the man's mind.

'Kinky sex?' he asked in very hushed tones.

'About as kinky as you can get,' Berit replied equally softly.

'And they're sure it's him?'

'There are fingerprints stuck in the coating of vaginal fluids. On the handle of the gun, the barrel, the trigger . . .'

The road manager held up his hand to stop her, leaned back against the low backrest of the couch and watched a pair of honeymooners as they passed through the lobby.

'This isn't the right place to discuss a matter like this,' he said quietly.

'You picked it,' Berit said, sensing victory in the air.

The rain had stopped, leaving the ground cold and wet. Mud oozed down the asphalt drive leading to the gate.

'Annika? Annika Bengtzon . . .'

She had made it to the bus stop outside the television complex when she heard someone calling out to her.

A woman was hurrying down the hill along with the muddy run-off, carefully picking her way and lurching a bit in her high-heeled boots. When she got closer, Annika recognized Bambi Rosenberg, hollow-eyed under her make-up.

'Boy, am I lucky to catch you,' the woman said as she staggered up to Annika, out of breath.

'Is it true that they're having a memorial service for Michelle over at Zero tomorrow?'

The soap-opera actress was extremely upset. Her lower lip quivered and she had lipstick on her teeth.

'Yes, as far as I know,' Annika said, trying to catch the woman's darting gaze.

'This is just terrible, terrible! Are they allowed to, just like that? Don't they need some kind of authorization?'

Something was bothering the young women. She was wringing her hands, smoothing her hair frantically and shuffling her feet.

'I don't think so,' Annika replied. 'She did work there, after all.'

'They're going to turn it into a tasteless publicity stunt. TV Plus and Sebastian pushed her around and used her while she was alive, and now that she's dead they're going to exploit whatever's left.'

Bambi Rosenberg's pupils were enlarged, practically covering up her irises. She licked her lips and picked at her face.

'That's not really the whole story, is it?' Annika said. 'TV and Sebastian Follin opened the door, made her famous.'

Bambi was walking very close to her now. Her breath smelled sour.

'All Michelle tried to do,' she said, 'was to live up to everyone's expectations. No one ever asked her what she wanted, what she really dreamed of doing.'

'So she was forced into becoming a TV star?'

Annika could hear how sarcastic she sounded.

'Of course not,' Bambi Rosenberg said. 'Michelle was very aware of what she was doing, and for increasingly shorter periods of time she was convinced that she had made the right choice. But you can always fool yourself with logic. This is the best course, because I'll be famous and loved and wealthy, and that's got to be the best thing life has to offer, right?'

'You mean that's just a lie?'

The actress gave a sob.

'Of course it is. The only thing that really matters is people, love, and relationships.'

Annika felt irritation well up inside her head, causing her to purse her mouth even though she knew she wasn't being rational. What right did she have to dismiss Bambi Rosenberg's truths as platitudes?

'How did you get to know Michelle?' she asked, trying to keep her arrogance in check.

The woman answered in a flat voice.

'It was in Playa de las Americas. We were both vacationing alone, only I had arrived the week before. I thought Michelle seemed really nice, only she seemed pretty sad too.'

Bambi paused and looked up at Annika.

'This was before she was famous, you see.'

Annika nodded and tried to look encouraging.

'So you became friends?'

Bambi Rosenberg nodded too.

'It was like we shared the same dreams – we both wanted to make something of our lives. Mickey got a job at Zero after we got home, and I got a modelling contract, so you could say we were in synch.'

'What was she like?'

'Super-nice. She really wanted to help people with problems. She couldn't see needy kids on TV without crying. She signed every list around about refugee kids who were petitioning to be granted asylum, and so did I.'

Well, hallelujah, Annika thought, and decided to play hardball.

'Then you loved it when Michelle became a superstar while you were only an actress in the soaps?'

Bambi's eyes widened to the size of saucers.

'Of course I loved it! It was great. Mickey was a journalist, I'm an actress. I don't like politics and all that stuff, I like to portray human emotions. We helped each other out.'

'Did Michelle *need* help? From you?'

'Mickey needed a lot of help, she needed someone to take care of her. Someone who listened, who talked about everyday stuff. A lot of times she would call at four in the morning, when she couldn't sleep. That was when she needed to talk, because she was lonely. Now I'm the lonely one.'

Bambi Rosenberg rummaged around in a pocket of her jacket, pulled out a handkerchief and blew her nose, then proceeded to totter over to the bench by the bus stop.

Annika looked around and tried to hear the sounds from the nearby commercial area.

No bus.

'She was famous and admired and rich,' Annika said as she walked over to the bench and sat down next to Bambi, kicking at a dandelion that had erupted through the asphalt.

'What about the other stuff? Love, relationships?'

'For short periods of time,' Bambi Rosenberg said, flicking back her mane of hair and putting away the hand-kerchief. 'Friends were the hard part. Lots of her girlfriends let her down when she started hosting TV shows; they spread nasty rumours about her, bad-mouthed her, just out of spite. Once she was a star, some of them came back, drooling and fawning all over her, and wanting to be friends again. Naturally, she cut them dead. And she felt she couldn't really trust her new friends.'

The actress stopped talking and sat silently for a while, staring at the stadium on the other side of the builders' emporium without seeing it.

'What about men?' Annika asked.

Bambi Rosenberg's chest heaved in an unconscious sigh.

'She could have whoever she wanted.'

Bambi looked up at Annika. There was too much mascara on the actress's lashes.

'Naturally,' she said. 'Michelle could just take her pick. Only the guy she really wanted could never be hers.'

'Why is that?'

The question popped out before Annika had thought it over. She bit her cheek, but realized that she really wanted to know. She could feel her eyes sparkle: she was curious.

'He was married, and had kids. It was Stefan Axelsson, the technical director, you know. They had a brief affair a few years back, before Michelle was really big, and it was awfully hard on her.'

Annika blinked, picturing the enraged man, hearing him shout, 'Leave me alone, leave *her* alone!' There was something there: he'd wanted to protect her, even in death.

'Did *he* love *her*?'

Bambi didn't reply. Her eyes had filled with tears. Behind the silence between them, Annika could hear the rumbling of the Stockholm Transit Authorities bus approaching.

'I had an affair with a married man once,' Annika said, trying to keep the conversation rolling.

'You did?' Bambi Rosenberg said, turning to face her, the teary eyes growing even wider. 'What happened?'

'I got pregnant and he moved in with me,' Annika said, hearing a note of pride in her voice.

'Are you married?'

Her pride was wiped out in a second.

'No, but we have two kids now.'

'Michelle got pregnant too,' Bambi Rosenberg said, looking at the builders' emporium again. 'Stefan went crazy, started screaming that she had to have an abortion. She cried for two weeks, then she did it. The next day he did a complete turnaround, he came back to her, told her that he had told his wife, that he wanted to live with her and the baby. Only then it was too late, it was too late for them. They couldn't get past it. Michelle never got over it.'

Annika saw the bus pull up behind Bambi Rosenberg's professionally streaked head.

'That's terrible,' she said in a low voice.

'I don't know what Michelle ever did to deserve such a rotten life,' the actress said.

The crowded bus stopped and Annika got on. She wriggled past baby carriages and bags of groceries, found a seat located over one of the rear wheels, and saw Bambi Rosenberg disappear from view as the bus accelerated away.

The commercial area was drab, its grey buildings sprouting like mushrooms from the ground. Annika closed her eyes for a few minutes, her belly tense with unshed tears, and immediately felt carsick.

So very unfortunate. So tremendously unfair. The words of the soap-opera actress rang in her ears:

I don't know what Michelle ever did. To deserve. Such a rotten life.

She could have had a child, a man who loved her, a home and a family.

Then it hit Annika.

Like I have.

Opening her eyes wide, she forced back the tide of sentimental salt water.

The bus pulled up at another stop. A large older man wearing a cap and an oilskin coat pushed his way to the back of the bus and sat down next to Annika. She pulled her raincoat tighter around her and stared out the window. The wind caused the rain to pelt her side of the bus, sketching psychedelic patterns of dirt and grime on the window.

The man gasped, coughed, and cleared his throat. Annika wrapped her raincoat even tighter around herself. She closed her eyes and saw the negative image of the stripes of rain dance on her eyelids. The driver headed for Gullmarsplan. Squirming passengers rubbed damp fabrics against each other and Annika closed her nose off to the smell of unwashed humanity.

'Excuse me,' the man in the seat next to her said in a commanding voice. 'Could I ask you something?'

The bus swayed as it ran a yellow light. Annika had to grab on to the seat in front of her to avoid being tossed against the man who'd spoken to her.

'Sure,' she said, looking at him quizzically once the vehicle was back on an even keel.

'Aren't you on TV?' the man said and smiled, displaying a set of yellow teeth.

Annika tried to smile back and then had to hang on again when the bus braked sharply at the junction between the bridge at Johanneshov and Nynäsvägen.

'No,' she said. 'I'm sorry, you're mistaken.'

'But I recognize you,' the man insisted. 'You sit on that sofa, with all the women.'

Annika took a deep breath and looked out over Gullmarsplan.

'Sorry,' she said, picking up her bag to indicate that she was getting off.

The man's smile died. He muttered something inaudible and moved his legs a mere millimetre, indicating that Annika should climb over him. Rage exploded behind her eyes, intense and sudden.

'What the hell? Now move it, let me out,' she said in a loud and aggressive voice.

The old man's eyes flew open in surprise and, befuddled by astonishment, he got up.

Annika got off by way of the rear exit, stepping out

into the wind. A gust grabbed hold of her raincoat, finding its way under her sweater, wetting her stomach. She let the wind have its way with her for a few seconds, feeling the goose bumps rise on her skin. She looked up at the glass structure that housed the subway station, at the red steel girders around the glassed-in entrance, not wanting to go in. Not wanting to go to the newsroom.

She went over to the news-stand instead, got out of the wind and pulled out her cellphone. She called information and got the number for Global Future, breathing heavily while she waited for them to pick up.

'I'd like to talk to the person in charge of investor relations,' she said to the switchboard operator.

'We don't have anyone like that around here any more,' the girl replied.

Annika moved to let an elderly lady with a walker get past.

'What don't you have? The investors or the people who coordinate their relations?'

The girl giggled.

'We don't have the one or the other.'

There was a flight of stairs on her right, in front of the health-food store.

'What about the executive manager?'

'He was fired last week.'

Annika hurried over to the staircase and raced downstairs, stopping on the landing in the middle to get out of the rain.

'Are you the only person left?'

'More or less,' the girl said. 'What would you like to know?'

The stairwell smelled of piss and damp concrete. Annika swallowed and decided to go for it.

'I have a question about the analyses that the Securities Register Centre does for you . . .'

'I take care of that at the moment,' the girl said, 'so you can see how far down on the list of priorities *that* particular job has fallen. You see, we don't exactly get good news.'

Annika kicked away a few dented soft-drink cans and an empty bottle of drinkable yogurt, and looked out over the subway tracks below her. 'How much is one of your shares worth today?'

'The last time I checked, half an hour ago, the price was SEK 38.50.'

'That's pretty lousy, isn't it?' Annika asked.

The girl at the other end laughed again, this time sadly.

'You're not exactly a business wiz, are you?'

With a squeal of brakes, a train pulled up on a side track.

'That's right,' Annika said. 'I'm no good at playing the market, but other people like to see themselves as smart investors. People who have caused companies like yours to go belly-up. I'm investigating a story like that.'

'So, what are you looking for?' said the switchboard operator cum investor relations coordinator cum general manager of Global Future.

Residents of the southern suburbs of Stockholm filed past Annika, a damp grey crowd issuing from blue metal trains. She turned her back on them.

'The date for a certain transfer of shares,' she replied in a low voice.

'I'm not at liberty to divulge information like that,' the girl said.

'I'm aware of that,' Annika said. 'And I'm not asking you to. I figured I'd tell you what I've dug up, and you can check it out if you like.'

There was no response at the other end. A subway train roared into the station somewhere on her right, causing the concrete to vibrate.

'What's it all about?'

'An insider deal, but not one that involves any members of your board or your management.'

The train came to a stop, the stream of people dried up and Annika's head was filled with a ringing silence.

'When did this take place?'

'Right before that disastrous second-quarter report last year . . .'

'The one dated 20 July, I know. Who is it?'

Annika took a deep but silent breath while a bus headed for Tyresö started up with a loud rumble above her.

'A man by the name of Torstensson,' she said, hunched over her cellphone. 'A pretty sizeable transaction: 9,200 shares.'

'Hang on.'

This was said in a whisper.

Annika looked up the stairs. The graffiti and the power lines laced into a framework of steel reminded her of monsters from a nightmarish video by Pink Floyd. The wind whistled through the perforated metal, making the lines sing. Holding her breath, she listened.

'9,200 shares,' the woman said. 'I've got it right here.'

Annika closed her eyes and felt her pulse rate go through the roof.

'What date was it?'

'24 July.'

She pulled her chin down to her chest, closed her eyes tight and felt her jaws clench until her molars squeaked.

'All right,' she said. 'Thank you very much.'

'You won't tell, will you?'

'Tell anyone that the information came from you? No way.'

Annika hung up and gazed out at the traffic, the sanitation units and the trucks, a steady stream of metal on its way downtown. After taking three deep breaths she dialled Schyman's number.

'No luck,' she said. 'According to the analysis by the Securities Register Centre, Torstensson sold his shares on 24 July. Four days after the report went public.'

Not a sound was heard from the other end. Annika looked at her phone.

'Hello?'

'Are you sure of that?'

'About as sure as I can be,' Annika replied.

'Okay . . . Thanks.'

Schyman's disappointment seared the line.

'I'm really sorry,' she said, feeling strangely ashamed.

'That's all right.'

He hung up on her. Her cheeks burning, Annika switched off her phone. Why did she take Schyman's failure to heart?

She pictured Anne Snapphane's puzzled face when she'd wondered why Annika couldn't seem to ask the men in her life for anything.

Was her boss one of those men? Did they have a relationship that could be defined as close?

Annika shook off the thought and made another call, easing into the concentrated state of mind that she needed to talk to Q.

'Hannah Persson is listed as a resident of her mother's household in Malmö,' she informed the policeman when he answered the phone. 'Only she doesn't live there, she lives somewhere in Katrineholm. That's where you picked her up, right?'

'What is this, twenty questions?'

She ignored his bantering tone.

'It doesn't seem like she has many childhood friends left, so she probably lives with some of her Nazi buddies. Am I right?'

She could hear him chuckle.

'Go on.'

'She shares an apartment with some of her Nazi buddies—'

'Well, that's not entirely correct,' the lieutenant said, interrupting her.

Annika leaned back against the wall, noticing too late that someone had wiped off a glob of snuff there.

'Fucking hell,' she swore, flicking off the disgusting mess.

'What?'

'Not an apartment, but close. She lives with her Nazi buddies in a room somewhere . . . She lives in the offices of the Nazi Party!'

'Bingo! But as far as we know, she's the only one living there.'

Wanly, Annika smiled into the phone.

'Okay. Now where would we find such a place . . .?'

She shut her eyes and concentrated.

'There aren't very many suitable places in Katrineholm where you could have an office for the Nazi Party without being noticed,' she said, thinking aloud. 'My guess is that it would be out at Nävertorp, if it weren't for all the immigrants there. I don't think that Nazis would like it there, and the residents wouldn't leave them alone. So, maybe the east side – yes, that's it: the east side, right?'

'I don't know the local names for the different neighbourhoods.'

'The east side is where the hospital is, lots of grimy basement-level rooms and weird video shops. I once did a story exposing a secret porno shop when I worked at the local paper. Am I right?'

The detective gave her the address.

'Which is on the east side,' she said, grinning. 'Thanks.'

Annika hung up, once more aware of the smell of piss and

concrete, and felt overwhelmed by Anders Schyman's defeat.

It would have been nice to do something for her boss.

Dirty words built up to a roar inside the managing editor's head. *What a hellish mistake.*

24 July, four days after the report had been made public. Torstensson had waited – the bastard hadn't cheated. Curses sizzled through Schyman's mind like grease dripping on hot coals, creating unmentionable uncharitable thoughts about the editor-in-chief:

The guy was too stupid to understand what the board had discussed.

Too dumb to use the information for an insider deal.

Too chicken to bail out.

Too loyal to let the others down.

Too honest, perhaps, to commit a crime.

The final conclusion forced Anders Schyman to get up, get away. His chest was starting to constrict and it was getting hard to breathe. What had he done? What can of worms had he opened? What forces had he set in motion, and how far had they gone? Would he be forced to resign?

Schyman looked out through the closed glass door. The newsroom pulsated on the other side, a living organism that required support, nourishment, and pruning. Torstensson was the wrong man – or was Schyman himself the wrong horse to back? Challenging the editor-in-chief had been a mistake. Oh dear God, he was struck full force by just how much he had counted on his anthrax file. He didn't have anything else up his sleeve, no power over the newsroom, no backing from the board, just orneriness, the abuse of power and deceit – all he'd had was the one weapon: public exposure. Now his ammunition was gone, running out in the silence after

Annika Bengtzon's call. He was defenceless, out for the count, caught with his pants down.

He clenched his fists tightly, saw Spike on the phone over at the news desk, feet up and clutching a pack of cigarettes.

Why do I even care? he thought. All I have to do is let go, let the place go to the devil. It's not my problem – I can go back to broadcasting, sit in on different boards, get into information technology.

Schyman slumped, feeling his spine strain against the fabric of his shirt.

It was all over. That was it. He might as well accept that he couldn't stay on. There was no way he could stand another day with Torstensson as his boss, another day full of frustration and antipathy. To be honest, there was no reason he should prolong his agony.

Anders Schyman returned to his seat. The air was hard to breathe. His forehead broke out in a sweat and his hands were shaking. He got his contract out and read items six and seven. According to its terms, he could leave today, walk out and never come back, just by claiming a conflict of interest, that he was going to compete in the same sphere. They would throw him out and lock the door behind him. His time at *Kvällspressen* would be a mere interlude, a brief footnote. He caught himself wondering what they would say about him, what adjectives they'd use to describe him and his work.

Hot-tempered. Surly. Possibly pretentious, ignorant. Definitely ignorant – they used to love to bombard him with printer's terminology. No good at delegating work, played favourites, that Bengtzon gal . . .

Schyman had almost reached his own obituaries when the phone rang, making him jump.

'Listen,' Annika Bengtzon said. 'I just figured something out. According to the Securities Register Centre, the shares changed hands on 24 July.'

The room was utterly silent. Schyman unbuttoned his shirt and loosened his collar with a jerk.

'You told me that already,' he said, his hand going to his brow.

'So I called this guy I met at the centre this morning, and he confirmed my hunch.'

The line crackled and a vehicle roared in the background.

'What?' he said, barely capable of making a sound.

'It takes three days to register a change of ownership.'

Schyman sagged and had to conjure up the strength not to just collapse on his desk.

'It's still not good enough,' he said. 'That would make it the twenty-first.'

'Three business days,' Bengtzon said. '24 July was a Monday. The transaction took place the previous Wednesday.'

Time came to a halt. Silence enveloped the earth, the sudden void creating a piercing echo in the managing editor's head. Anders Schyman lifted his gaze and looked out over the newsroom.

'That means . . .'

'That Torstensson sold his shares on 19 July, the day before the report was made public,' Annika Bengtzon said. 'There's something else: I've dug up an address for the little Nazi, and I figured I'd try to talk to her. Is that okay?'

Schyman's powers of deduction were gone. They had been switched off.

'The nineteenth? 19 July? Is that true?'

'Absolutely. It was summer vacation time, which might have even delayed registration a day or so. But the transaction took place no later than the nineteenth.'

Relief gushed through Schyman's system like a thundering waterfall, making him gasp.

'And you're positively sure?'

'As sure as can be. What about the little Nazi?'

'What?'

'Is it okay if I go to see Hannah Persson in Katrineholm? She was released this morning. The X2000 train only takes fifty-six minutes to get there. I figured a little talk about life and death might be in order.'

He would cheerfully have sent her to Hawaii.

'Go,' he said.

In the silence of his room Schyman was filled with a sense of elation so great that it threatened to make him explode. *That bastard!* He thought he was so smart – or maybe he was just a coward who had dithered to the last minute.

The odds were that Schyman would never know for sure. He reached for the phone, dialled the direct line to the host and producer of the public service TV channel's news magazine, a show devoted to investigative reporting, the scrutiny of elected officials and giving abusers of power the third degree.

'Mehmed? Hello there. Well, I'm doing just fine, thanks. Damn nasty business with Michelle Carlsson . . . No, that's not why I'm calling – I've got something for you. Can we meet? Say, thirty minutes from now?'

His vigour restored, Anders Schyman made a quick gesture with his left arm and looked at his watch.

'Excellent.'

Yet another deep sigh escaped from Anne Snapphane's lips. How the hell was she going to get through this crap before the weekend? Even if she had the machines on fast-forward there weren't enough hours left in the week to go through all the material.

A beta tape came to a halt. She finished filling out the slip and switched tapes.

And now that Miranda was staying with her, she couldn't spend the nights working.

Time for the next tape, a master for the second, somewhat inferior, show of the series. Anne pressed the play button. Michelle was fine, but the guests weren't up to par. Once she was certain which show it was, Anne put the machine in fast-forward mode, revving up the tape. Like a sleepwalker, she saw the characters cavort their way through the show, their voices, barely audible, coming out in treble squeaks.

There was no point in complaining, Anne knew that. She was so far down on the food chain that she was absolutely and utterly replaceable. If she so much as breathed her task was impossible, she knew that she wouldn't be a part of the next production.

Things had been different for Michelle. She could make the strangest demands and everyone would accommodate her. In fact, they'd bow down and suck up to her.

Michelle couldn't deal with the green set decor. It was too oppressive, it deprived her of oxygen. She had something more easygoing in mind – blue, maybe, or yellow.

The sets were changed and Michelle earned herself yet another sworn enemy, the set designer.

'Knock-knock.'

Anne looked up in surprise. Gunnar Antonsson was standing in the doorway, peering over the sacks of films.

'Well, hello there,' Anne said. 'Come on in, if you can figure out how . . .'

The man's grey head ducked in behind the monitors. By the time he made it into the editing cubicle, his face was red with exertion.

'Oh,' he said, 'they stuck you with this.'

'They sure did,' Anne said and shrugged. 'Do you think I'll ever manage to get finished?'

'You always do,' Gunnar Antonsson said, sitting down on a filing cabinet. 'The main thing is that you do a good job.'

Red-eyed and exhausted, Anne smiled. Like Gunnar, the man who never slipped up, she was meticulous.

'You know what?' he said, 'I have something on my mind.'

Something in his voice made Anne Snapphane pay attention. She looked at him more closely, noticing the shadows under his eyes, the chapped cheeks.

'When you woke me up,' he said, and Anne immediately knew what he was referring to, the events they would never forget. 'Who knocked on my door?'

The adrenalin exploded in her brain, preparing her body for fight or flight.

'I did. Why do you ask?'

The tone of her voice signalled retreat, but Gunnar, blinkered by his own insecurity, didn't notice.

'Do you know if my door was unlocked?'

The tape had finished and the machine started to rewind it. The Donald Duck chatter was replaced by an electronic whine.

Anne Snapphane felt her pulse throb.

'Um, no, I don't,' she said. 'Why do you ask?'

Gunnar Antonsson squirmed, nervously running his hands through his hair.

'I feel so guilty,' he said. 'I know I locked the bus that evening. I always do, and I did it last Thursday too, I'm certain of that. But I'm not sure if I locked the door to my room – sometimes I don't, you see, in case of fire, and that means I leave the road wide open . . .'

The man's agitated words calmed her. He wasn't out to

get her, he simply wanted to find out what his own part in the drama had been.

'Oh, Gunnar,' she said, leaning towards him and putting a hand on his knee. 'Don't go thinking you—'

'It's true,' he said, interrupting her. 'Someone went into my room during the night and stole the keys to the bus. If I left the door unlocked, it's all my fault.'

'But,' Anne protested, 'that couldn't have happened. You unlocked the bus door. You were the only one who had the keys, and they were in your pocket, just like always.'

His response was a quick shake of the head. His eyes were filled with tears.

'No,' he whispered. 'They weren't where they were supposed to be. They were in the right pocket.'

Affected by his misery and despair, Anne stared at the man.

'What?' she said.

'My slacks – the keys were in the *right*-hand pocket. I always keep them in the *left*-hand pocket. Someone took my keys and put them back again, figuring they wouldn't be noticed. That's why I'm asking you if you remember whether my door was unlocked.'

Anne Snapphane closed her eyes and sifted through her drunken recollections of that night. She had banged on Gunnar's door, sure. They had figured out that Michelle must be hiding in the bus, since that was the only place they hadn't checked yet. She remembered her rage, how she had wanted to settle the score; Michelle had some answering to do, damn her! Anne had banged on the door yelling 'Wake up, Gunnar!', trying to make herself heard over his loud snores. Then she had tried the door. The handle went down and the door had swung open. The room had smelled awful, sweat and stale air, and the occupant of the room was a hump under a thin duvet.

'Yes,' Anne said quietly. 'The door was unlocked.'

Gunnar's sigh was heavy but still relieved.

'Now I know,' he said, patting her on the shoulder as he got up. 'You're a good kid, Anne.' Then he left the same way he'd come in.

The long, straight street was lined with a variety of three-storey apartment buildings from the 1940s and 1950s: yellow brick, grey stucco, balconies with iron railings.

The damp oily-smelling wind whipped at Annika as she passed a boat service centre, a satellite-dish store, a tanning-bed salon with the blinds down, a club for people who liked to build scale models, and a karate club.

The courtyard that supposedly housed the offices of the Nazi Party was interchangeable with the other yards on the block: sheet-metal garages, a large dumpster, a platform for beating carpets, posts to hook up engine pre-heaters, a few drastically pruned birch trees and some patched asphalt. A flight of stairs led down to a metal door at basement level. Annika cautiously made her way along the uneven concrete floor and knocked firmly on the door. No reply.

She tried the door, pulling on the handle. It opened. Music welled out of the depths of the room, a poor-quality recording of something heavy-metallish, a hoarse youth shouting: 'Fight the system, fight the system, fight the system, knock it down, burn it to the ground, politicians don't work for the people, they're only in it to rip us off, they're sticking it to us in the ass.'

Annika stepped into the gloom, feeling the bass line hit her in the gut, and felt her way down a dusty passage, a smell of mould in the air. Further down, on the left, a door stood ajar, emitting waves of light and sound. It was metal, painted black, and icy cold to the touch. The squeal of the opening door drowned out the white-supremacy anthem, causing the young woman inside to stop in her tracks. Annika walked into the room and met the girl's gaze, black as outer space, her rigid body ready to run.

'All right if I come in?' Annika shouted to be heard over the music.

Hannah Persson sprang to life, turning around and switching off the stereo, the sudden silence producing a surreal impression of a deafening echo in the room.

'What do you want?' she said, the feral expression back in her eyes again. She had been crying. Her eyes were glazed and her eyelids were swollen.

'To talk, that's all,' Annika said.

'About what?'

Hannah Persson's hostility was too forced to be convincing. Annika walked into the room and looked around. The windows were nailed shut and the walls were plastered with racist propaganda posters.

'All sorts of stuff,' she said. 'About you, why you're a Nazi, what it was like to be arrested, what happened at Yxtaholm . . .'

'Why should I tell you anything?'

Annika stood in front of Hannah Persson, face to face, looked her in the eye and realized that the girl had probably been drinking.

'You asked me a few questions,' Annika replied calmly. 'Still interested in an answer?'

The girl's eyes went slightly out of focus and she took two steps back.

'What do you mean?'

Annika looked away and walked over to a bookcase containing a few slim volumes and pulled out *The Destiny of the Angels*. On the back cover the following prodigious questions were posed: Does a race, the Nordic peoples, have the right to exist, the right to live? Are they entitled to claim the conditions they need to exist?

'Read this?' Annika asked, holding up the book. Not getting a reply, she then picked up the next one. *The Treatise on Race*, by the same author, purported to contain a proclamation of racial rights, racial purity and racial independence.

'That's a deeply philosophical book,' Hannah Persson said.

'In what way?' Annika asked.

'It discusses what happens when a race is subjected to living conditions that can lead only to their gradual destruction.'

The girl's face had become animated. Two red spots flamed on her cheeks. Under the influence of booze but still lucid, she turned to Annika.

'So what conclusions does it reach?' Annika asked.

'That we cannot escape our obligation: choice. Do we, the Nordic peoples, have the right to acknowledge our racially unique features? Do we have the right to be cognizant of the physical and spiritual beauty that would be lost for ever if we were deprived of the conditions we need for our survival?'

Annika was stunned by the blatant racism, its rankness hitting her like a gust of fetid breath.

'My guess is that this book says the answer to those questions is yes,' she said.

Once again the predator, the young Nazi smiled at Annika's dismay.

'In the midst of a culture and a dominant moral doctrine that says no,' she added, walking up to Annika and taking the book from her hand.

'Ever considered why society and your book have different answers?'

Deep in thought, Hannah Persson leafed through the book reverently, the forced smile still in place. Choosing to read aloud from the book instead she intoned:

'Due to several unfortunate factors, ranging from altruism and self-sacrificing generosity to the hazardous objectivity that places the non-vital interests of others before the vital needs of their own people, the Nordic peoples literally throw away their wealth, their culture and civilization, their material welfare, and, above all, the natural richness inherent in their unique racial and genetic characteristics on a physical, mental, aesthetic and spiritual plane.'

Hannah closed the book and looked Annika in the eye.

'Discussing issues like these is seen as being immoral,' she went on, the predator just barely kept below the surface. 'Northern Europeans who try to raise them are defamed and called evil. All over Scandinavia, the media as well as the cultural and political establishments actively thwart the vital interests of the Nordic peoples. Lots of ignorant people such as yourself contribute to a self-destructive process that you don't even understand.'

Fascinated, Annika asked the girl: 'How did you come by these opinions?'

The insolent teenager was back now and the girl merely shrugged.

'I do have a brain, you know, even though nobody seems to think so,' she said. 'I do my own thinking. In school, they claim to teach you to think for yourself, but then they get pissed off if you do. We're supposed to come to our own conclusions, just as long as they're identical to everyone else's.'

'Why Nazism?'

'Because of one of those survivors,' she said, her voice thin and grating as she went over to sit down on a mattress next to the wall.

'This old biddy came to our school and showed black-and-white pictures from the concentration camps, and they were awful, of course – all the girls cried but me – but everything was kind of vague. I never figured out where the old lady fitted in. Afterwards there was supposed to be a panel discussion, and not much happened until some patriots sitting up front started to question some of her facts.'

Hannah Persson leaned back against the wall, pulled her feet up, wrapped her arms around her legs, and rested her head against her knees.

'They called it "Democracy Week", and we were supposed to listen to this survivor person. But when the patriots started to ask questions, the principal stopped the debate and threw them out. What kind of democracy is that?'

The little Nazi rocked jerkily back and forth on the mattress.

'And you know what? *Katrineholms-Kuriren* wrote that the patriots had caused a riot during "Democracy Week", and that just wasn't true! The paper lied! I was there – there wasn't any riot, the patriots were only trying to join the discussion, but they didn't get a chance!'

Her eyes were huge and wide, and filled with artless indignation.

'Did these . . . patriots go to your school?'

'It was an open forum held at the school auditorium. Lots of other people were there.'

Annika put the deeply philosophical tome back on the shelf and looked at some of the others: *Twilight of the Norse Gods, Sturm 33, Land of Our Fathers and How to Protect It.*

'Do you do a lot of reading?' she asked the girl.

'Pretty much. It's just that the books are so expensive. You can't exactly get the paperback versions over at the local news-stand.'

Hannah Persson grinned apologetically, not with her predator's expression this time.

'When we met in the parking lot, you asked me a question,' Annika said again, determined to press on despite her shaking hands.

The young Nazi's eyes gleamed.

'Yeah, I remember,' she said.

'I killed my boyfriend,' Annika said. 'I hit him with a piece of pipe. He lost his balance and fell into a blast-furnace.'

Hannah Persson's eyes had changed. Now their expression was rapt and alert.

'Why did you do it?' she asked, in the same pretty childlike voice as when she had stood by the police tape at Yxtaholm.

'Otherwise he would have killed me,' Annika replied. 'It was either him or me.'

She swallowed hard.

'Actually,' she said. 'It was because he killed my cat.'

The Nazi blinked, causing the swastika on her face to twitch.

'What a bastard,' she said. 'He killed your cat?'

'He slit its stomach open. Its name was Whiskers.'

'Why?'

The unsteadiness of Hannah Persson's voice revealed how upset she was.

'Because it rubbed up against him. Or because I loved it. Or just because it was in the way, I don't know. Sven didn't need a reason to get violent. All he wanted was power. If he didn't have it, he took it.'

The girl nodded and swallowed.

'The master race has always done that, oppressed the weak. How did you feel afterwards?'

Annika tried to steady her breathing.

'Not really that much, at first. I didn't realize what I'd . . . Later on I was miserable for months, could barely manage to stay alive. For years after that I lived in a void.

Life had no colour, everything was either black or white, somehow. Meaningless.

'Have you ever regretted it?'

Annika stared at the bright-eyed young woman and was overcome with the same sense of nausea as she had felt in the parking lot at Yxtaholm.

'Every day,' she said in a low, hoarse voice. 'Every single solitary day since then, and I'll keep on regretting it until I die.'

'The oppressed have to be able to defend themselves, though.'

'Do you feel for them? The oppressed?'

Hannah shot back her answer in a tinny voice.

'Of course I do.'

'In what way?'

The girl flinched and shrank away.

'Why did you get a gun?' Annika asked.

The young Nazi's stare met hers. Hannah's eyes were still bright, but now they were suddenly filled with tension. She opened her mouth to speak but held back. Annika persisted.

'Who did you want to kill?'

Hannah Persson's eyes filled with her tears and she sucked in her lower lip, making herself look like a mere child.

'No one,' she whispered.

'No one? You went to the trouble of getting a gun, but there wasn't anyone you wanted to eliminate?'

The answer was barely audible:

'Just myself.'

Stunned, Annika looked at the girl. Hannah was crying, her chin pressed to her chest and her hair spilling down into her lap. Once her shoulders stopped shaking, she looked up and her expression was somehow simultaneously blank, immature and knowing.

'There was this candlelight vigil last winter,' she whispered. 'This young guy had been murdered by a group of ethnic intruders, and we gathered at the railroad station one afternoon to show our sympathy and respect.'

She sat up straighter, swiped away a few tears and it was as though the light of the vigil torches was reflected in her eyes as she gazed at the boarded-up window.

'We weren't carrying any flags or banners, just torches and candles. All of the national groups supported the demonstration and had sent officials; it was so tasteful, so dignified and really nice. We walked together, all of us, the boy's family at the head of the procession, and we put down flowers and lit candles. It was really sad. I cried the whole time, and it felt so good, you know?'

The girl looked at Annika, tears streaming down her face.

'We grieved for our patriot, together. Can you see what a powerful experience that was?'

Annika nodded. Her throat was dry and she tried to clear it.

'Yes,' she said, 'I can see that it would be. And you wanted them to do the same thing for you?'

Hannah nodded again. Then she dissolved into tears, crying with the ease that alcohol provides.

'Where did you get the gun?' Annika asked her a few minutes later, her voice gentle.

'I sent away for it, got it from *Soldiers of Fortune*. It's their anniversary-edition revolver, celebrating twenty-five years of freedom fighting, only it's been remodelled. The original is only for decoration.'

'How did you smuggle it into Sweden?'

'I didn't. It was the postal services. "Global Priority Mail." It said "CD records" on the package.'

'Have you told the police?'

She hesitated and then nodded.

'I squealed,' she confessed.

'What do you mean?' Annika said. 'It was the postal services. They deserve it.'

Hannah Persson chuckled and dried her tears.

'So what actually went down over at the castle?'

Hannah Persson shook her head in contempt.

'At any rate,' she said with the superiority of one who knew it all, 'the papers got it all wrong. The whole crowd was drunk and they started fighting. Michelle Carlsson was running around with no clothes on, screwing that pop star all over the place. People were crying and hitting each other and none of that was in the papers.'

'You don't always put everything in the paper,' Annika explained in a serious voice.

'Why not, if it's the truth?'

'Well, there's personal integrity to consider.'

'But you couldn't care less about the integrity of patriots. You write bad stuff about us all the time – lots of lies, too.'

The words came out as a knee-jerk response. There was no aggressive edge to them. Annika managed to smile.

'Well, since you're in the know, enlighten me.'

'About everything?'

'Take it from the top. How did the staff of *Summer Frolic at the Castle* get hold of you?'

Hannah Persson twirled a lock of hair between her thumb and her middle finger.

'They e-mailed our website,' she said. 'I'm in charge of the site, so I wrote back. They wanted one of our people to have a debate with an anarchist on TV, at least that's what they wrote. It turned out that they had invited two radical feminist anarchists, the worst kind . . .'

'How was the atmosphere when you go there?'

'Everyone was pretty stressed-out. They were wet, too – it rained like nobody's business. They put some make-up on me, only not on my cheeks, they wanted the tattoo to show.'

The young Nazi grinned, a satisfied little girl's smile.

'And that pop star was there, John Essex. I saw him up at the castle, in a room on the second floor.'

'What were you doing up there?'

Hannah Persson's face turned bright red.

'Checking out the place, that's all.'

Annika nodded. The girl had probably been looking for something to steal.

'Was it exciting to be on TV?'

The girl shrugged.

'I should have known,' she said. 'There weren't looking for a democratic debate, they just wanted us to get in a fight. And those dykes attacked me, look . . .'

Hannah tilted her head up, showing her chin. Annika politely inspected the partially healed scratch.

'It got real rowdy. People came running from all over, they had to stop taping and everything.'

As far as Annika could tell, the girl seemed pretty pleased about that.

'When were you done?'

'Like around 8:30. Everyone else left, only I wasn't supposed to leave at the same time as the anarchists. Later on no one seemed to care that I was still around.'

'Did everyone else leave?'

'Not the pop star. The band and the rest of the guys left, but he had his sights on Michelle Carlsson, so he stayed. On the top floor they served food and drinks, awesome food. I ate loads of it.'

'Did everyone else eat a lot too?'

'Some people did. The cameramen and the sound engineers sat together at one of the tables; they ate for a long time and then they split. One of them stayed on, a chunky guy in a plaid shirt. He sat around watching TV in one of the wings later on, and it really bugged him that everyone was so loud that he couldn't hear what they were saying on his stupid old show . . .'

'Did you see Michelle Carlsson?'

'Of course I did. She was there, but she didn't eat a thing, all she did was drink. She was flaky and super-touchy and kept picking fights.'

'Who did she fight with?'

'First of all with Anne, one of the girls who worked on the show. They argued about money, salaries, about who deserved to earn the most. If it's right to make a lot of money on the stock market, boring stuff. It was like they were talking about themselves, only not. Finally, the girl got really pissed off and started yelling at Michelle, saying she was greedy. For a while there, I thought they were going to start fighting.'

The little Nazi kept twirling her hair, a faraway look in her eyes. The silence was filled with a growing sense of that troubled evening; it seemed to move right into the room.

'That bitch of a reporter was there too, you know. She was drunk while they taped the shows and she kept calling Michelle "our little scatterbrain". I saw Michelle go up to her and kind of hiss something at her.'

Hannah Persson got up, walked a few steps away from the mattress, peered out from under her bangs and mimicked Michelle:

'"You're a fat, alcoholic has-been, who lives off that high-and-mighty family of yours!"'

She stood straight and went on:

'The bitch went crazy and chucked a bottle of wine at Michelle, aiming for her head and missing it by just a centimetre or so. Then she tossed back three drinks in a row and passed out on the couch.'

'What did Michelle do?' Annika asked, enthralled by

the unfolding spectacle and picturing the scene in the dining room.

'She left the room and the pop star went with her. They went to the lounge in the wing where everyone was staying and made out in an easy chair. Then everyone else came in and the old guy wanted to watch TV. Michelle and the pop star took off somewhere. The old guy complained so much that everyone got irritated and we went back to the castle.'

'When did you show people that gun of yours?'

The girl shot Annika an evasive look.

'I guess it was then,' she said. 'I went to my car and brought it in and let everyone hold it. They were really interested. I tried to tell them about the patriots, but they didn't listen. Then the staff came in and said they were going to lock up the castle, so we went over to the Stables instead.'

'Just who are we talking about?'

Hannah shrugged.

'I don't know – a group of guys and girls, there were six of us, maybe eight. Everyone was pretty wasted. Michelle was in the worst shape, she kept shouting things and laughing really loud, and even started crying a few times. Up at the castle, one of the women, the one with the fancy titled name, she bawled her out, saying that everything in Michelle's life revolved around her career, that she was so stuck-up and insensitive, and then she said . . .'

In her mind's eye, Annika pictured the Stables: Mariana and Michelle, both drunk and overworked.

'"I was here before you,"' Hannah said, now portraying Mariana von Berlitz. '"You always luck out even though you don't know a darn thing, and to top it off, you demand respect. The only thing you're good at is pushing people around, and people let you do it because of your visibility. But actually you're nothing but a cardboard cut-out, all surface flash and no substance. The rest of us supply the contents, fill you with significance, and you just use us."'

'What did Michelle say?'

'That the other girl didn't have a clue, that she would never understand what a rough time she had and how pressured she was. The girl said something else and Michelle started screaming that she was a jealous vindictive nobody who could go fuck herself.'

The Nazi miss grinned at the thought.

'How did the rest of the group react?'

'That other girl, Anne, she agreed with Mariana.'

She adopted Anne's expression:

'"I taught you everything when we started out doing *The Women's Sofa*, but when they made you the host, I no longer existed. You used me up and threw me away. I can't forgive you for that."'

'Didn't anyone defend Michelle?'

'That blonde girl, the one on *Broken Promises*, she did.'

'Bambi Rosenberg.'

'Exactly. Do you watch her show?'

Annika shook her head.

'I used to see it all the time, but now I don't have a TV set. I think Bambi's a really good actress.'

And an Aryan too, Annika thought, but didn't say so out loud.

'Bambi stuck up for her, but later on all she did was cry.'

Hannah Persson sat back down again, slumping slightly, a distant light in her eyes. Annika waited; she detected a shadow play in the girl's eyes.

'I think Bambi had borrowed something from Michelle, money or something kind of major. "There's no way I can pay you back," Bambi said to her. "Then I guess you'll have to sell," Michelle snapped back. They fought about whatever it was, screaming "you greedy bitch" and stuff like that. Then Bambi ran out of the room.'

The Nazi girl sat up straight.

'And the tall guy with the greying hair,' she said. 'He defended Michelle too, only that was later on, when she had taken off and they went to look for her . . .'

'When did she take off?'

'After that lunatic trashed the dining room. Everyone was so darn upset, they sat around in groups, grumbling. And they drank, and drank. Almost like the patriots . . .'

Hannah grinned again.

'Who had the gun?' Annika asked.

The corners of the girl's mouth turned down and she bit her lower lip as she considered the question.

'I saw it outside the Stables,' she said. 'That manager guy had it.'

Annika felt the hairs on the back of her neck stand on end and had to force herself to keep her voice steady.

'When was that, and what did he do with it?'

'He stood out there in the rain, by the dining-room window, looking in.'

'What about the gun?'

The young Nazi raised her eyebrows indulgently.

'It happens to be a revolver, you know. He was holding it, but then the girl with the fancy name came up and took it away from him. Then she went indoors and talked to some people and a while later the manager guy went inside and trashed the place.'

Finally getting a clear picture of the evening, Annika looked at the girl.

'What about the car? What was that all about?'

'They came to pick up the pop star, he was so wasted.'

'You said that the others went to look for Michelle. Why was that?'

'They were all talking in the kitchen in one of the wings,' Hannah Persson said. 'The fat lady, what's her name?'

'Karin. She's the producer.'

'She was telling this story about when Michelle was up for the job as a talk-show host. They were going to screen-test Michelle and Anne, and one of them would get the job. The problem was that Anne showed up an hour late, so she didn't have time to prepare or to be made up.'

Annika nodded. She remembered how frustrated and furious Anne had been, how she had cried and cursed about the idiot who had told her the wrong time.

'But that couldn't have anything to do with Michelle, could it?'

'Oh, yes, it did,' Hannah said. 'That night, the fat lady told Anne what had happened. Michelle was the one who had put the note with the wrong time in Anne's mail compartment, and the lady said she had done it on purpose, just to eliminate Anne from the running. Anne went crazy, she started crying and screaming that she was going to strangle that little cunt . . .'

Hannah Persson burst into a fit of nervous giggles. Annika stared at her.

'Did Anne say that?'

The girl nodded.

'Every one of them had a bone to pick with Michelle, they were all upset about something. So they went looking for her. And they found her in the end . . .'

Once the spectre of Michelle Carlsson's death emerged in the two young women's minds, a cloud of silence descended on the official headquarters of the Nazi Party of Katrineholm. The shadows grew longer in the corners, and Annika shuddered. The walls closed in and it felt as though the swastikas scratched her skin. A car accelerated outside the boarded-up windows, passing right behind her head and making the concrete vibrate.

Suddenly she felt overwhelmed. She couldn't stay another second.

'Is it okay if I write an article about you in tomorrow's paper?' Annika asked as she rose and picked up her bag.

Hannah Persson's widening eyes reflected her loneliness.

'Are you leaving?'

'I've got to go home. I have two little kids,' Annika said, missing them so much suddenly that it was like being stabbed in the chest.

'Um, will you be coming back?' the Nazi girl asked.

Her face was as open as a child's and her eyes were clear and trusting. In the poor light, her skin appeared to shimmer.

'No,' Annika replied quietly. 'Probably not.'

Hannah Persson stood up and her eyes changed, becoming narrow and dark.

'Why did you come here?'

Annika took a step closer to the young woman and looked her in the eye.

'You don't need to live like this,' she said. 'You could have a job and a real place of your own if you just—'

'Don't you tell me what to do!'

The girl's shout was deafening. Annika backed away, banging her heel on the threshold of the door, perplexed by the aggression of the outburst. Hannah Persson had bared her teeth again; the predator was back.

'I have the right to live wherever I damn well please, and I'm entitled to my opinions. You can stuff your fucking lectures! Go away! Beat it!'

Hannah picked up a book from the stack of Nazi propaganda and hurled it at Annika's head.

Annika ducked. She managed to open the door,

stagger down the hall and escape upstairs. The music was unleashed again, stalking her: fight the system, fight the system . . . She slammed the front door, turning the bass line into distant vibrations in the concrete. For a few seconds, she remained standing in the street, catching her breath. Faint light seeped through the cracks in the boarded-up windows.

She'll do whatever she wants to do, Annika thought. *She is responsible for herself, just like I'm responsible for myself.*

A few drops of rain landed on the back of her neck. She hunched her shoulders and turned her back on the place. Slowly, she started to head for the station, her mind filled with conflicting impressions.

Hannah Persson's destructive course, so obviously self-inflicted in other people's eyes, was such a basic part of her personality. How could she be so blind to her own inherent potential? Why did she end up on the wrong side of accepted society? What kind of experiences were so shattering that they could lead a person to choose to become an outsider?

Annika coughed and steeled herself for the next item.

Anne Snapphane had missed the opportunity of a lifetime and Michelle was to blame. What responses had been triggered by this awareness? Her spontaneous reaction had been to shout that she would strangle Michelle. How intense was her need for revenge? Strong enough to act on her words, to pick up a weapon and fire it?

Annika shuddered and walked faster. It just wasn't possible, absolutely not. She closed her eyes and let the impact of each step radiate throughout her body.

Not Anne, it was impossible.

The limits and taboos that human beings live by change over time and from culture to culture, but killing out of envy or for revenge was invariably forbidden.

Anne would never do it, Annika thought, like an incantation.

Her cellphone rang and Annika paused, sure that it was Anne, that telepathy had prompted her to call.

Puzzled, she saw that the number on the glowing display wasn't one that she recognized.

'Hello? Is that you, Annika? It's me, Bosse.'

She stared at the street where there were no shadows, frantically searching her memory.

'Who?'

'Bosse – I work for the competition. How are you?'

She inhaled sharply and felt a rush of blood to her face. Anne was suddenly light years away from her thoughts.

'Oh, I'm fine,' she said, weak at the knees. 'Everything's great. How about you?'

'A few of us are going out after work to grab a beer and I wondered . . . if you wanted to come along?'

Annika stopped breathing. Her mouth was open but nothing came out.

What she wanted to shout was 'Yes! Yes! I want to drink beer and laugh and be acknowledged; I want to discuss the headlines and Michelle Carlsson and the clowns on Studio 69; I want to listen to time-worn media anecdotes and accounts of the state of the world; I want to look into eyes that give me warmth in return, I want to sit close to someone, I want to be a part of it all. I want to have fun!'

'I'm sorry,' she said curtly. 'I have to go home.'

She swallowed hard. Something warm flowed through her body, blazing alive.

'I see . . .'

The voice on the other end couldn't conceal its disappointment.

Annika pressed her lips together hard, holding back the joy she felt.

'Oh well,' Bosse said, trying to laugh. 'That's life. Some other time, maybe?'

She closed her eyes and felt the tears coming on.

'I don't think so,' she whispered.

'You don't . . . It was just . . . You sounded so pleased when you answered.'

An oppressive silence mushroomed between them.

'I'm sorry,' she said finally. 'I've got to go.'

'Okay. Take care.'

Annika clicked off her cellphone.

She kept her gaze fixed on the road. It was straight and narrow. The scattered raindrops turned into a shower. She would be soaked by the time she reached the train.

Annika pulled up the hood of her jacket and ran.

Exhausted, Thomas sank down at the kitchen table with a brandy and a magazine. His head was buzzing with thoughts and voices. He gulped down the liquor to quiet them.

South Korea, the Fourth International Next-Generation Leaders' Forum. *Holy shit.* He'd been chosen to be a leader of the next generation.

The crass voice in his head protested immediately. Sung-Yoon just wanted to talk about old times, that was all.

He opened his magazine and rubbed his eyes. The English words were hopping like bunnies.

2–12 September. He would be going – just let Annika try stopping him.

Irritated, he turned the page and tried to read the next article.

'I'm scared.'

Thomas looked up and saw the little boy standing in the doorway, clutching his blanket and his teddy and sucking on a finger.

A tremendous sense of resignation wound itself around him.

'Come on, son,' he said. 'You've got to go to bed now. We've already talked about this.'

'But I'm scared.'

For a brief second, Thomas struggled with his fatigue and gave up.

'I've tucked you in three times now, Kalle. Go back to bed. Go on.'

Then he made a great show of going back to reading his magazine.

'I want Mommy. Where's Mommy?'

Thomas kept his gaze fixed on his magazine.

'Kalle,' he said. 'Now that's enough. We've checked under the bed several times and there isn't anything there. Go. To. Bed.'

The boy went away and shadows took over the doorway.

Thomas rested his head in his hands, slumped a bit and listened for sounds in the hallway. Grey, cold silence. The landlord had turned off the central heating for the summer and the dampness from the rain had seeped into every single corner.

Feeling irritated, he pushed away the magazine. This was what it was like living in a fucking apartment, you had no say, some lousy bureaucrat decided whether you were going to be hot or cold. At least if they had lived in a condo, then he could have been on the board and had some kind of influence, but not in this fucking rental.

He downed the rest of his brandy, went over to the cabinet to get the bottle, and poured himself another one.

Taking care of kids really drained the hell out of you.

Thomas slumped against the counter and swirled the amber liquid in a sturdy Duralex glass.

Maybe that's why he hadn't had the energy to work as

much as he should have. Time and energy had gone elsewhere. If it weren't for the kids, he might have already received a new assignment, he would have been immersed in the regional development of Sweden's social services. They might have wanted to keep him on if he could have put more effort into his work.

A noise from the hallway caught his attention. He got up, walked over to the door, opened it and turned on the light.

The little boy was huddled in the far corner, shuddering with sobs, his eyes wide with reproach and exhaustion. The feelings that assaulted him were conflicting and obscure.

'What's this? Why are you in the hallway?'

Thomas tried to keep his irritation in check and conjured up some patience. He went over to the three-year-old and kneeled down to his height. The boy turned away and face the wall.

'Hey, Kalle, you've got to get some sleep, you're going to nursery school tomorrow, you know that.'

He put his hand on the rounded shoulder. The child pulled away, shuddering with sobs.

'No! I want my mummy!'

'Okay,' Thomas said, picking up his son. 'Now that's enough.'

The boy howled, his body rigid as a bow, and pulled his father's hair.

'Stop it!' Thomas yelled back and yanked the boy's hand away, scattering a flurry of hairs over his face.

'No-o-o!' the boy screamed as he kicked and twisted in his dad's arms.

A sudden draught of air made Thomas stop in his tracks. Annika was standing in the doorway, the bright light of the stairwell turning her shape into a dark silhouette.

'What are you doing?' she asked in a subdued voice as she shut the front door.

'He won't go to sleep!' Thomas shouted, setting down the boy. Kalle let go of his teddy and his blanket and hurled himself at his mother. Thomas saw her drop her jacket and bag on the floor, get down on her knees and open her arms wide and let the boy tumble into her arms. She sat there, rocking him, murmuring words of comfort, and his crying subsided in a matter of minutes. A few seconds after that, the boy giggled, a golden chirping sound that he never shared with Thomas. Annika chimed in with a soft chuckle and gently smoothed his hair.

'I'll go with you, and you and I will tuck Teddy in,' she said. 'Now, where's Teddy?'

The boy pointed sulkily in his dad's direction.

Annika looked at Thomas steadily as she walked over to her son's bedtime buddy and picked it up from the floor without averting her accusing gaze.

'You're spoiling him,' Thomas said.

'Shut up,' Annika said in a quietly dismissive voice.

He gritted his teeth and flushed. But Annika was already gone; she was in the nursery, whispering and joking with the boy.

Thomas returned to the kitchen, gulped down his brandy and poured himself some more.

'Now that's mature,' Annika remarked as she walked in and saw him knock back the brandy. 'That's terrific. Booze it up, now that's a sure-fire way to make things better.'

She took a glass, filled it with tap water, and sat down at the kitchen table.

'Do you know what time it is?' Thomas asked.

Annika drank without answering him.

'So, you figured it was time to come home now, did you? Do you have any idea how rough it's been taking care of everything around here? You've got a lot of nerve, leaving all this to me.'

'Stop it,' she said, her voice devoid of emotion.

'Stop what?' he said as he downed the rest of his brandy, choking on it. 'Exactly what should I stop doing? Taking care of your kids? Your apartment? Your dirty laundry?'

'It's time you cleaned up your act,' she said, walking right up to Thomas. 'You have everything a person could ask for, and all you do is complain. Why don't you stop wallowing in self-pity, for a change?'

'What do you want?' he asked, way too loud. 'Do you expect me to stop working and be a household drone? You might get what you want sooner than you think. I'm all washed up, in every way.'

'Christ, you're such a baby,' Annika said, her eyes flashing with contempt. 'We brought two kids into this world, and it's our goddam obligation as parents to make sure that they grow up and have a reasonably good environment. Stop feeling so fucking sorry for yourself just because you don't live in your fancy old brick house by the sea any more. This is where you live now, so pull yourself together and make the best of it. For God's sake, grow up!'

Thomas shrank back, edging up against the counter.

'Don't you tell me what to do,' he said in an unsteady voice.

She stepped up to him.

'Well, who else is going to do it?' she shouted. 'You're totally incapable of making decisions, for Christ's sake. How the hell can you be in charge of a project? Everything is too much trouble. You've been so over-indulged, I swear you're almost lazy!'

He pushed her away and headed for the hallway.

'I'm not going to listen to this,' he said.

'Great!' Annika called out to his retreating form. 'Do it, run away, go and find someone who will stroke that goddam super-sized ego of yours'

Thomas staggered out into the hallway and, with shaking hands, put on his boots and his raincoat.

Then he slammed the door shut behind him.

The newsroom was at rest, the morning light painting it a delicate shade of blue. The night desk pulsated like a living organism. Its human occupants had gone, but the room still echoed with the sound of chairs being pushed back, computers powering down, and pens rolling away and dropping to the floor.

At this moment, the Knights of the Night Desk were probably sitting in the canteen two floors down, red-eyed and wired, trying to wash the excess adrenalin back down into the darkest recesses of their brains with beer and tea.

The morning team sat further away, concentrated and silent. The next deadline was seventy-five minutes away, one and a half eternities away, all the time in the world.

Anders Schyman took in the sight, tucking it away in his soul. It was a sight he might never see again.

He went to his room, set his mug of coffee on his desk and tossed the first edition, the one sent out to the provinces, next to it. The newsprint was still slightly damp; a half-hour earlier it had rolled off the presses.

Schyman was always in early, since only two

possibilities were available to him: he could spend hours in traffic on his way in from Nacka, or he could risk a ticket or even losing his licence by cruising in the bus lanes.

This particular morning was nothing like the usual grind. The air was charged with electricity, and he knew why.

It was always easier to get up and go into battle.

Peacetime was so much less inspiring.

His body felt supple as he sat down, opened the paper and started to read it enthusiastically.

The front page was terrific: a soulful close-up of John Essex, sad and devoid of make-up, taken at a hotel room in Berlin the day before. The pop icon had granted Berit Hamrin at *Kvällspressen* an exclusive interview about his friendship with the murdered TV star Michelle Carlsson, telling everything about the events of that fatal night and what it was like to be interrogated by the Swedish police. Fabulous stuff.

The editorial dealt with a consumer issue, an article that had been produced as a front-page back-up during the holidays but which hadn't been used due to the murder of Michelle Carlsson. An article somewhere else in the paper covered the story of hazardous medications: the entire list.

The editorial demanded that drastic measures should be taken against the jaded giants of the pharmaceutical industry. The piece wasn't very good.

The managing editor rolled his shoulders restlessly and flipped through the pages of the paper.

The Lifestyle section, on the other hand, contained an astute observation of the future of TV, a timely blow straight to the solar plexus, a clear-headed and talented analysis by one of the paper's own reporters.

The interview with the pop star was splashed across

pages six and seven. The Entertainment section had felt that it should be featured in their section, but Spike had insisted on this location. Schyman smiled and brushed his hand lovingly over the words.

'Michelle Carlsson was a wonderful woman,' John Essex had told *Kvällspressen*'s representative.

'We only met on that one occasion, but we bonded immediately. She had vitality, a sparkling intellect, and we got along very well. Her death is a great loss, both on a personal level and with regard to European TV audiences. She had so much left to give.'

'Do you think your friendship would have continued?' Berit Hamrin had asked Essex.

'I would have enjoyed getting to know Michelle better. Very few people understand where I'm coming from right off the bat, but she did. We could get right down to the important issues, which was unusual. In addition to all that, she was incredibly lovely. I haven't met many women who could hold a candle to her, and I've known quite a few.'

The whole world would be wanting to copy the interview and buy the pictures. When Schyman asked Berit how she had pulled off such a feat she simply made a reference to *The Godfather*, something about making an offer that John Essex couldn't refuse. He hadn't pursued the subject.

Schyman carefully sipped the hot coffee from the automat, turned the page and caught sight of Carl Wennergren striking a pose in front of Yxtaholm Castle. *Kvällspressen*'s reporter tells all about the tragedy that rocked Sweden's entertainment community. Sjölander had written the piece, and, to be honest, you could tell that he had been affected by jet lag. The article wasn't Pulitzer Prize-winning material, but at least now they had run the story.

Schyman continued to leaf through the paper and got caught up in Annika Bengtzon's piece about the neo-Nazi girl in Katrineholm living in a dismal basement. His restlessness was submerged for a while as he drank in the description of the young woman, her past and her views. He was transported to that fateful night at the castle and saw the shadows dance.

Afterwards he blinked a few times before landing back in his own chair again.

Good story, well written too; it had depth and perspective. It was sheer perfection.

Then there was a review of the investigation, based on information from the police, a professor of criminology and one of the country's most famous defence lawyers.

Schyman learned that investigations of this kind generally consisted of a puzzle with two ingredients: the testimonies of the witnesses and forensic evidence. In this particular case, the different testimonies were contradictory and inconclusive, possibly due to the fact that the witnesses had been inebriated or overworked, or because they hoped to protect themselves from some consequence that had nothing to do with the murder. However, it appeared to be more and more certain that the assailant had been one of the twelve people who had spent the night at the castle. The police were confident that the solution could be found among the material they had obtained, but as yet there had been no arrests.

The professor of criminology assured the public that the reason why the police were not very forthcoming with information was because they were hard at work. Time was always a major adversary in cases like this, which was why the police focused all their resources on the investigation. The defence lawyer explained the importance of thorough investigation prior to any arrest. Unless there was a confession, the indictment would be based on a chain of circumstantial evidence that would have to be supported by forensic evidence.

The managing editor sighed. There was something about the slight vagueness of the wording that made him suspect that the solution to this crime was further off than anyone would like to admit.

The next spread was dominated by the pharmaceuticals story. It was ambitiously conceived, with explicit diagrams and a great case study of a young mother who had died after taking over-the-counter pain relievers. The headline was an eye-catcher: *Lethal Relief*. It was almost like a jingle. Schyman smiled and didn't notice Torstensson until he knocked on the glass door.

'The TV team is here,' the editor-in-chief said, his eyes a bit bleary this early in the morning.

Anders Schyman forced himself to don his most neutral expression as he looked up from the paper.

'So soon? I thought they were coming in at eight?'

Torstensson rubbed his clean-shaven chin and straightened his tie.

'They're setting up cameras in my office.'

'Have they mentioned what this is all about?'

The editor-in-chief rocked on his heels impatiently.

'No,' he replied. 'And I'd like to get this over with as quickly as possible. I'm on vacation.'

'You're the one they wanted to interview,' Schyman pointed out, aware that he was stirring things up. 'Why do they want me to be present?'

'If this has anything to do with journalistic ethics, I'm not going to cover for your mistakes,' Torstensson said curtly. 'You'll have to field any questions about them yourself.'

Then he turned and walked across the newsroom, his overly padded shoulders bobbing like floats on a lake.

This isn't about journalistic ethics, Anders Schyman

thought as he rubbed his forehead, pushed in his chair and looked around.

He walked out, leaving the door to his office open.

Thomas held on to the door frame. The entire kitchen felt like it was pitching.

'Is there any coffee?'

'In the pot,' Annika replied in a neutral tone of voice without looking up from the morning paper. She was holding a spoon in one hand and a napkin in the other and was sitting between the children. Kalle was eating a cheese sandwich and Ellen was covered with yogurt.

Suddenly Annika realized that she was always up by the time Thomas walked in for breakfast, that the kids were dressed and fed, the coffee was ready and the papers were spread out on the table.

Thomas staggered over to the cupboard and pulled out a mug, noticing that his hand was shaking.

He wasn't used to drinking alcohol on week nights.

'When did you get in last night?' she asked, still not looking at him.

'Late,' he said as he poured himself some coffee.

'Where did you go?'

She looked up and her eyes were filled with anger, disappointment and sadness.

He licked off a used spoon and stirred his beverage.

'I went to a pub not far from here.'

She nodded and looked back down at her paper.

'I'm sorry,' he said.

'Why don't you sit down?' she asked, indicating the chair on the opposite side of the table with her gaze.

'Mommy, I'm done,' Kalle piped up to her right.

Ellen pushed away the spoon on her left.

'All righty,' Annika said. 'Now go and wash your face and brush your teeth.'

With an efficiency born of habit, she lifted Ellen out of the high chair, wiped the baby's sticky hands and face and sat her down on the floor beside her. Ellen scooted after her brother using the special crawling style she'd developed, with one foot under her.

'She'll be walking soon,' Thomas said in a doting daddy's voice as he sat down.

The morning light illuminated the woman sitting across the table, his woman, the ruthless rays revealing how tired she was.

'I'm sorry,' he repeated as he covered her hand with his.

She let his hand remain there, but she avoided his pleading gaze.

'You scared me the other night,' Annika said.

Thomas looked down at the table without making any comment.

'It wasn't only what you said,' she continued. 'It was my own reaction too. I keep running in circles, I've behaved the same way when I'm with you as I did with Sven . . .'

'Stop it!' he demanded. 'Don't compare me to him.'

'I have to,' Annika said, looking up, both her gaze and her voice steady. 'Not because the two of you are alike, but because I haven't changed. I still act the same way, I haven't learned a damn thing. I've grovelled, I've danced attendance on you, and I've tried to make amends. It's not your mother's fault that she can't accept me. I'm the one who's felt sorry for you for choosing me. I don't approve of myself.'

She took a sip of her orange juice. Her hand was shaking.

'But that's over now,' she said. 'Either you choose me for real, or we forget the whole thing.'

Thomas slumped, looking at her in shocked surprise.

'What do you mean? What did you have in mind?'

'We'll get married,' she said. 'We'll have a church wedding with all the trimmings, invite every last relative, all the friends we ever had, and rent a big hall, book a cover band and dance until dawn. A real wedding and a big picture in *Katrineholms-Kuriren*.'

He sat up straight, then leaned back and rolled his eyes.

'You're hung up on the petty details,' he said. 'The major issue isn't the church or the party.'

Annika looked out of the window and studied the courtyard with its bicycle stand and its garbage cans.

'In any case, that's the way things stand,' she said.

She pulled her hand away from his.

'Hello? Alide?'

Bambi listened to the fuzzy connection, sensing someone on the other end who seemed much further away than they actually were. A faint moaning sound emerged from the static that didn't bode well.

'Alide, how are you? Were you asleep?'

Something that might have been a sob floated west across the Baltic Sea, following the Latvian coast, passing Ösel, crossing to Gotska Sandön, landing in Sweden on the tiny distant island of Landsort and travelling along the telephone lines all the way to Solna.

'No,' the Latvian woman said. 'I was awake.'

Bambi Rosenberg sighed in relief. It sounded like Alide was sober. Possibly hung-over, but still in the possession of her faculties.

'Everything's been taken care of,' she said. 'I saw the lawyers yesterday, and we went through all the papers and things like that.'

The woman didn't make any comment and Bambi thought she could detect the sound of crying in the silence. She sank down on the dresser in the hallway, and looked up at the ceiling to keep her own tears in check.

'Don't be sad,' she said in a choked-up voice. 'Listen to me, Alide, we've got to be strong now.'

'I miss her,' the woman said in her heavily accented English. 'I've missed her all my life, and now it's too late.'

Bambi closed her eyes and surrendered, letting the tears course down her cheeks.

'I know,' she said in a whisper. 'Michelle missed you, too. But she did forgive you, Alide, she did. You know that.'

A deep sigh came over the phone, one that might even have held a trace of relief. Bambi stared at the dark wallpaper, content with her half-truth. Michelle had forgiven her mother, but she had never been able to deal with the sorrow caused by her deceit.

'What do the police say? Have they arrested anyone?'

Bambi Rosenberg shook her head at the wall.

'No. I don't know what's taking them so long.'

'Have you heard anything about the funeral?'

'No date has been set yet. It will take a few more weeks. The network is conducting a memorial service today – I'll tape it so that you can watch it when you get here.'

'I don't want to stay at Michelle's place,' the woman said in a whisper that was barely audible over the buzz of the connection.

The actress wiped her face with the back of her left hand.

'You can stay here,' she said. 'You know that. Just tell me when you'll be arriving and I'll pick you up at the boat terminal.'

They shared a silent moment of bonding across the sea.

'Do you know what's going to happen?' Michelle

Carlsson's mother asked after a while. 'With the allowance, I mean?'

'You won't be needing one,' Bambi replied. 'She didn't have a will. You inherit everything. The apartment, the business and all the rights, the furniture and the jewellery. You're her sole heir.'

Alide's voice was very weary as she said:

'Michelle wouldn't have liked that,' she said. 'I don't deserve it.'

'Oh, yes, you do,' Bambi said, selecting the appropriate reassuring tone of voice from her repertoire. 'Michelle wanted you to be all right, you know that. She wouldn't have sent you that allowance if she didn't. She wanted you to be comfortable. The only reason she doled money out to you like that was so that you wouldn't blow it all at once. You know how things used to be . . .'

'You should have some of it,' Alide Carlsson declared.

Bambi Rosenberg's face flushed and she was glad no one could see her.

'I haven't paid back the loan for my breast implants yet,' she said. 'I have no claim on her estate.'

'You took care of the things I should have done,' Michelle's mother said. 'I'm going to make sure you get what's coming to you. Trust me.'

Her words conjured up a dizzying sense of déjà vu, making Bambi Rosenberg start to cry again.

'No,' she said, shaking her head. She had heard those kinds of promise before and knew that she would be let down. 'You're not my mother, Alide, you don't have to do anything for me. But call me when you get here and we'll get together.'

After she had hung up, Bambi Rosenberg sank to the floor, curled up in the foetal position and fell asleep.

*

Mehmed had seated Torstensson on his executive chair with the painting by Anders Zorn in the background. Schyman stood in the doorway and surveyed the scene, trying to figure out the layout by studying the equipment. He unobtrusively observed the people at work, busy with cords, cables, headsets, microphones, and sheets of paper for balancing whiteness. Two cameramen, a sound engineer and the host; a fair-sized operation.

One camera was stationary and focused on the editor-in-chief while the other was mobile and would follow Mehmed. This meant that they expected Torstensson to sit still while Mehmed would be able to move around. Okay.

The editor-in-chief was already sweating under the spotlights. They weren't really necessary, but their hot glare could certainly come in handy when you were putting someone on the spot – so to speak. Torstensson fidgeted a great deal, running his hands through his hair, bumping up against the body mike he was wearing on the lapel of his jacket and clearing his throat.

Schyman understood more or less what would take place. Mehmed's problem would be to get Torstensson to admit to selling his holdings on 19 July, the day before the disastrous second-quarter report was made public. This meant that he would probably focus on something else at first, something he already knew, such as when Torstensson was made privy to this confidential information, and in what circumstances. The date of the transaction would be obvious, and if the editor-in-chief didn't stay on his toes, he would get all tangled up in a web of excuses.

'When it comes to journalistic ethics, I'm not the only . . .' Torstensson started to say, but no one took any notice of him.

Anders Schyman saw that the technical end was

complete. He shut the door and stood next to one of the cameramen.

'All right,' Mehmed Izol said. 'Shall we get moving?'

The host sat on a chair in the middle of the room, about a metre away from the subject of his interview, crossed his legs, and let his hands rest calmly in his lap.

A thought flashed through Schyman's mind: *He is so good.*

'Editor-in-chief Torstensson,' Mehmed began. 'Could you please tell me the stance you take at *Kvällspressen* on economic crime?'

Torstensson settled back in his chair and cleared his throat. On a small monitor by the cameraman's feet, Schyman saw how the ample nude in the Zorn painting floated right above the editor-in-chief's left ear.

'Crime is a blot on society in every democracy,' Torstensson replied. 'One of the most important obligations of the press is to investigate criminals at all levels of society and expose them.'

Oh, really? Schyman thought. *And here I thought that's what the police are supposed to do.*

He folded his arms across his chest and forced his pulse to calm down. If anyone could pull this off, it would be Mehmed.

The wall of bags in Anne's editing room had possibly shrunk a smidgen.

'Come on in and listen to what I found,' Anne Snapphane said on the other side of the wall.

Annika walked around the plastic bags, silent and somewhat apprehensive. Worry made her feel weak and shaky.

'At first I thought it was just some old junk, since there aren't any pictures,' Anne explained as she turned up the volume.

'Now, listen to this.'

Annika stood behind her friend and breathed in the electronically desiccated air, the dust making her sneeze. Then she listened to a tape played on an ordinary VHS player at Anne's feet. There was a lot of static and background noise, but somewhere in there you could hear panting and moaning.

'What's this?'

'I'm not sure,' Anne Snapphane replied, rooting around in the depths of a plastic bag standing next to her.

'Is it only a sound recording?' Annika asked.

'Yup. I've been listening to it for about fifteen minutes. Sounds like people screwing.'

Anne Snapphane sat up again, her face red from the exertion of bending over, and held up a bunch of tapes.

'It seems to belong to the *Summer Frolic at the Castle* sessions, probably from the last night.'

She put in a new tape on one of the other machines, one of the beta players. The monitor in front of her flickered and then displayed the rain-drenched exterior of Yxtaholm. The lovemaking soundtrack was rolling in the background while cameras were balancing whiteness and sound was being tested on the beta.

'Listen,' Annika said. 'There's something I've got to ask you.'

'What?' Anne said as she set the beta on fast-forward.

Annika swallowed and looked down on the back of her friend's head, her tousled hair.

'Is it true that Michelle made sure you got the wrong time for that screen test a while back?'

Anne Snapphane's back went rigid and her shoulders hunched up. She turned around and stared at Annika, gaping.

'Who told you that?'

'Is it true? *Did* she sabotage your audition?'

For a few seconds, Anne just stared at her. Then she turned abruptly and put a new tape in the beta player. The moans and groans continued to roll at her feet.

'I don't know,' she said. 'Karin Bellhorn claims that's what happened. I have no idea why she would lie about something like that.'

Anne lowered the slip she was holding and stared out over the plastic bags.

'On the other hand, I don't know why she never told me this before.'

She looked over her shoulder at Annika.

'So I really don't know,' she said. 'Why are you asking me this?'

The question hovered over their heads.

'Is it true that you . . . threatened to strangle Michelle when you heard what she'd done?' Annika asked, her voice brittle.

Anne's own voice was wary as she challenged her friend.

'Right, so you're wondering if I killed her?'

She turned around again and calmly met Annika's gaze.

Annika swallowed audibly.

'No, that's not it, it's just that you didn't tell me this yourself. It felt weird hearing about it from someone else, that's all.'

Anne looked down at her hands.

'You see, I'd forgotten all about it at first,' she said. 'Then, later on, I guess I felt ashamed.'

She looked up at Annika again.

'Almost every single one of us wanted to kill Michelle at some point during the evening.'

They looked at each other and Annika knew it was the truth. The tense silence between them was filled with the moans from the tape, and both Annika and Anne were startled when the sounds suddenly ceased. There was a whooshing sound as if an unexpected breeze had blown in and a man's voice filled the room.

'Did someone come in?'

The faint whooshing continued, accompanied by static.

'No, no one, come on . . .'

The sounds of sex returned: whispers, laughter, panting and moaning.

'Have they talked before this?' Annika asked, surprised.

Anne Snapphane shook her head, looking somewhat paler.

'Could it be Michelle and John Essex?' Annika asked.

Anne hesitated and then nodded.

'At the beginning of the tape there was a lot of intercom chatter – you know, what they say in the control room, like five seconds to go, ready, camera one, cue theme song, start video number two . . . Michelle introduced John, so this is the right evening.'

'Who recorded this?'

Anne Snapphane's breath was coming out in puffs and she shook her head.

'I have no idea. It was in that jumble of reference VHS tapes, but it isn't something we need for the show.'

The couple on the tape continued to moan and carry on. Annika stood there and listened to the sounds, and after a minute or two Anne put the tape in fast-forward mode, turning the sound into cartoon chatter, speed-fucking. Annika swallowed, her pulse beating hard at the base of her throat.

'We missed some talk,' Anne Snapphane said and rewound the tape.

'How's it going?'

Karin Bellhorn's face peered through the stack of bags.

Anne switched off the sex recording. The producer's eyebrows were raised as if she was standing on tiptoe. The expression in her eyes turned cold when she caught sight of Annika.

'What are you doing here?'

Annika tried to smile.

'The memorial service,' she said. 'I thought I might . . .'

But Karin Bellhorn had already lost interest in her.

'Have you located all the material for 101 and 102 yet?'

'More or less,' Anne replied, diving back down in the bag again. 'All the time codes are noted on the tapes I've found, and as far as I can see, they're ready for the rough-cut assembly.'

'Could you do it?' the producer asked, her voice roughened by stress and smoking. 'Could you make an edit-decision list, list the in and out codes, and have it on my desk before you leave today?'

Annika saw Anne grit her teeth.

'There's a lot left to—'

'It doesn't matter, you can do that next week. You know the schedule, so put together the tapes we need to make a final cut. That's great.'

Karin Bellhorn turned and left.

'That bitch!' Anne hissed as the heavy footfall of the producer faded down the hall. Tears of rage were in her eyes. 'I'll be stuck here for the rest of the summer. Well, I can forget about going to any damn memorial service, that's for sure.'

Annika fidgeted uncomfortably, knowing that she was in the way.

'Listen,' she said, picking up her bag. 'I'll go and take a walk.'

Anne Snapphane bent down and removed the sex tape.

'It's so fucking unfair,' she said. 'This company treats me like a lousy . . .'

She wiped away the wetness on her face.

'Take this,' she said, handing the tape to Annika. 'Go and ask Gunnar what it is, who recorded it, and why.'

Annika took the tape, stuffed it into her bag and wriggled past the monitors.

Thomas recognized the footfall approaching on the thick carpet, simultaneously springy and heavy. He yanked out his top desk drawer and tossed some reports on his desk, assessed the distance of the steps and counted down: three seconds, two, one . . .

'Could you please come to the section supervisor's office for a minute?'

He looked up, surprised and busy.

The secretary was leaning against the doorway on one hand, a slightly pained expression on her face due to her uncomfortable insoles.

Thomas smiled.

'Of course.'

He picked up the reports, rearranged two of them, put them in the drawer and locked it. Then he followed the secretary down the corridor, crossing the lobby, passing the coffee lounge and reaching the corner office.

'Coffee?' she asked as she opened the door.

'Yes, please,' Thomas replied. 'I'd like some milk in that.'

He swallowed and looked inside.

All five section supervisors were present. So was the head of negotiations and the director. They were all lined up on the other side of the conference table. Thomas's hangover made his head throb and caused his movements to be somewhat jerky. He walked straight up to the table, pulled out a chair, sat down and leaned back. There was a faint buzzing in his ears. The seven supervisors were wearing inscrutable expressions as they gazed at the table and the ceiling.

Thomas had a crystal-clear flash of insight: he wouldn't be getting the job. They were going with the woman from the Federation of County Councils.

The head of negotiations, seated at the head of the table, said: 'Thomas, we would like to start by saying that we are very satisfied with the work that you have done on the welfare project.'

Thomas swallowed and folded his hands in his lap, noticing that they were cold and damp.

'As you know, we have explored various avenues with regard to regional planning and development in Sweden,' the head of negotiations continued, glancing quickly around the room. 'This has become a somewhat sensitive issue for us here at the Association of Local Authorities, since we have always claimed that the issue lacks merit. Our position has always been that there is no need to discuss *regional* development, only *local* development. Now the tide has turned: we need to appear to have had this issue on our agenda the whole time, and this needs to be taken care of quickly. I guess you could say it requires a balancing act.'

Thomas leaned forward, put his folded hands on the table and nodded appreciatively at the secretary as she brought him coffee.

'That's right,' he said, realizing that he wouldn't be able to drink his coffee anyway because his hands were shaking too badly. 'I've given this matter some thought, and I have a suggestion as to how we can get around the problem.'

The five section supervisors looked at him for the first time since he had taken a seat at the table, surprised and curious expressions on their faces.

'It's vital that the Association forges ahead now that

this issue has come to the forefront,' Thomas continued. 'We haven't been overly enthusiastic about the initial phases of this project, the allocation of the regional parliament to the province of Skåne, and the merger of several counties into the region of Västra Götaland. But, on the other hand, we have not taken a critical stance either, so we're still very much in the running, as I see it. However, it is imperative that we clarify our position and display well-defined objectives that will be effective throughout our operations, objectives which are also shored up politically.'

The head of negotiations regarded him expectantly.

'What did you have in mind?'

They're asking me, Thomas realized. *I've got the ball and they're listening.*

'In my opinion, we should take this course of events very seriously,' Thomas said, leaning back again and letting his hands drop back into his lap. 'This is not merely a cosmetic issue for the Association, it will become a concrete reality to deal with in the years to come. Regional influence will increase dramatically and we need to adapt to the change in climate. I suggest that we team up with the Federation of County Councils in a joint venture placing regional development at the heart of our efforts – along with the continued development of the local authorities, of course . . .'

His voice gave out, his throat was parched. The silence in the conference room was pregnant and electric.

The head of negotiations cleared his throat.

'What section should have jurisdiction over this . . . joint venture, in your opinion?'

'Naturally, it should be the Developmental Section,' Thomas said. 'There shouldn't be any hard and fast boundaries between local and regional development. From this day forward, our policy will be to treat these two routes like Siamese twins; they will be intertwined and mutually supportive.'

Several of the section supervisors nodded – this was the right stuff at the right time.

'But how will we persuade organizations and authorities to accept this new direction?' the supervisor in charge of Family Care and Nursing asked.

'It's not a new direction,' Thomas countered quickly. 'On the contrary, the Association has always promoted the same regional policy, only now we will broadcast it in a much more forceful manner.'

The silence at the table, an atmosphere of expectancy and doubt, made Thomas break out in a sweat.

'Printed matter,' he said, raising his voice to the point of hoarseness. 'A series of informative hardcover publications, a handbook for everyone involved in regional development: history, research, assessments, analyses. Huge open seminars and discussion forums, a series of lectures, financial incentives for locally based developmental models. The Association will be in the forefront, we'll set the agenda and the others will follow . . .'

'And would you be prepared to accept such an assignment?' the head of negotiations asked.

Thomas quietly cleared his throat before answering.

'It would be the most stimulating task I could conceive of at the moment.'

The section supervisor for the Developmental Section leaned forward, his eyes now gleaming. If this plan were implemented, his department would receive significantly increased resources, not to mention an increase in clout and prestige.

'It's an interesting proposal,' he started to say, but was cut short by the head of negotiations who had turned to speak to Thomas again.

'What are your personal circumstances? You have a family, and you live here in town?'

'I have a wife,' Thomas said, attempting to smile. 'We have two children who go to a community day-care centre and we rent an apartment in Kungsholmen. Prior to taking on an assignment here, I spent seven years working for the city of Vaxholm, a city that was a fore-runner when it came to privatization and restructuring.'

Not quite able to continue, Thomas's voice trailed off. He was struck by the feeling of being a whore selling her body from a window in Thailand. Here he was, bragging about living in an apartment, which he detested, and that his kids went to a day-care centre that he wasn't thrilled about, and topping things off with a reference to the city he had run out on.

He looked down at the table.

'Your proposal is interesting,' the head of negotiations remarked. 'We'll discuss it and get back to you as soon as possible, possibly later on today.'

That concluded his audience. He got up, almost tipping over the chair. The secretary caught it and removed his untouched cup of coffee with her other hand.

Thomas turned and headed for the door. His knees were shaking and a phrase was reverberating in his head: *Judgement Day.*

Gunnar Antonsson tightened the strap around the chair, securing it so that it wouldn't roll around. He stretched and then rubbed the small of his back while his eyes performed their ritual check-off procedure. The zinc cases were stowed and secured, the control panel was set on standby, and the furniture had been tied down. Outside Broadcast Bus No. Five was almost ready for take-off. Once he had cut off the outside power and closed up the hydraulics he could hit the road to Denmark.

Gunnar straightened his collar, smoothed his hair and suddenly felt light-hearted. It was a windy day – fresh breezes would make the entire countryside shimmy as he drove down through Sweden. Cool air, almost like autumn even though there hadn't been any real summer weather yet, and autumn was his favourite season.

He was walking towards the exit when a face appeared in the doorway. Her eyes were large and beautiful and he smiled instinctively. It was that tabloid reporter, the girl who had been interested in the technical equipment, Annika Bengtzon.

'On your way to the Continent?' she said.

Gunnar Antonsson smoothed out his slacks.

'Ready to go,' he said.

'It must be great to just get up and go like that,' she said.

Gunnar studied the girl. She was excited and slightly out of breath. Something about her was familiar, there was something about her that he recognized, but he couldn't quite put his finger on.

'Can I help you?'

She paused, flushing slightly.

'Actually, Anne Snapphane sent me. She's busy with the time codes and didn't have time to do this herself.'

'Well, give my best to Anne,' Gunnar said.

'I have this tape,' Annika Bengtzon said, locking her gaze on Gunnar. 'It's one of those regular videotapes, and there's a lot of technical jargon on it, from the last sessions at Yxtaholm. Do you know what's on it?'

'Come on in,' he said, with a welcoming motion. 'Technical jargon? What exactly do you mean?'

Annika Bengtzon entered and started rooting around in her sizeable bag. A good-looking woman, sexy, big breasts. Gunnar felt a rush of heat to his groin.

'I'm not quite sure,' she said, looking a bit embarrassed. 'I didn't hear it myself, but Anne told me that someone said: Ready, five seconds to go, camera, cue theme song, start up the video . . .'

'Oh, that would be the squawk box,' he said. 'That's how the crew talks to each other on the set. I've stowed and secured all the equipment, but I could activate a VHS player and listen to it, if you like.'

Annika didn't move, just shifted her weight back and forth, not really wanting to let go of the tape.

'What is it you want to know?' he asked her carefully.

She looked so extremely concerned that Gunnar Antonsson felt uneasy, overcome by a nagging sense of guilt. Had he overlooked something?

'I want to know who taped this, and why,' she explained.

'We make some behind-the-scenes shows, and then we tape the intercom communication too,' he said calmly.

'What do you mean?'

'Well, we did a special about the Eurovision Song Contest, for example, and to illustrate the work behind the scenes we needed access to the dialogue between the control room and the people on the set, the director's orders to the cameramen, what was said during the editing process, the stuff you never hear when you see a show. The soundtrack from the show is there too, only it's submerged in the background.'

'And it's a pretty common thing to do?'

Calmer now, Gunnar Antonsson smoothed his hair back. She was a reporter, they were always curious, he certainly knew all about that.

'We've done it for the *Who Wants To Be A Millionaire?* series,' he went on. 'For various benefits, a few documentaries . . .'

'Michelle,' she said, her eyes widening. 'Michelle

asked you to tape the intercom dialogue for the last show of the *Summer Frolic at the Castle* series, so she could use it in the documentary she was making of her own life.'

Gunnar Antonsson felt his neck flush.

'I was a little bit late,' he said. 'But that was only because there was a sound glitch up in the music room.'

'What?' Annika Bengtzon said and blinked.

'Michelle wanted to tape the entire session, but I missed the theme song. I'd forgotten about that.'

Gunnar Antonsson squirmed a little and felt his back break out in a sweat.

'It wasn't an official order,' he went on, 'and I wasn't going to bill anyone for it either. I just pushed a button, that was all there was to it. It's not like I was going to bill anyone for my services . . .'

The reporter held up her hand.

'Absolutely,' she said. 'I realize that. But you see, Gunnar, there's a conversation on this tape, it's at the very end. How could that have happened?'

The Technical Operations Manager gave the young woman a searching look and noticed how intensely focused she was. So that was what she wanted to know. His uneasiness increased.

'What do you mean?'

He took a step back as he said this, and he could hear how dismissive he sounded. Annika Bengtzon countered by taking a step forward.

'At the end of the tape, some people are talking to each other,' she said excitedly. 'I would like you to explain how that could have been recorded.'

Something in her eyes made him continue to back away.

'It's just not possible,' he said. 'The whole set was struck. Every last mike and intercom device was packed. It must be something left over from an old recording.'

The woman looked at him intently.

'When did you start taping?'

Gunnar Antonsson shut his eyes for a moment, recalling the sound engineer's cry for help seven minutes before they were scheduled to start the session: 'Gunnar, there's a glitch in the music room. Gunnar!' He had dropped everything and got up there as fast as he could, and the two of them had managed to locate the culprit, a shorted-out cable in the grounds. Afterwards he had hurried back to the bus, soaked through and in a foul mood.

'We had been taping for twelve minutes by the time I popped a tape into one of the reference machines. I set it for long run and let it roll.'

'That would make it 7:12 p.m.,' Annika said. 'So, did you turn it off?'

He swallowed audibly and scoured his memory.

'I probably didn't,' he said. 'It stops automatically after eight hours.'

Annika Bengtzon did some calculating and her eyes widened.

'Those last minutes on the tape took place right after three in the morning! How could those voices have ended up on the tape?'

Puzzled and intrigued, she stared at him. A wave of relief soothed the ache in his gut: he hadn't done anything wrong. The young woman was obviously just interested in the technical solution to her problem. He turned around and headed for the control room, for the console with all its buttons, levers, lights, mikes and monitors. His gaze swept over the walls, his brow was creased and he felt the back of his neck grow moist.

'It's just not possible,' he said. 'There must be something wrong. Everything had been dismantled and put away. There wasn't anything left that could transmit sound. The power had been cut off, the batteries were being recharged . . .'

'But there was some kind of power on in the bus?' Annika Bengtzon asked. 'I mean, the tape was rolling.'

Gunnar shot her a glance. She was no dummy. Stroking his clean-shaven cheeks with one hand, he looked around. Suddenly he caught sight of a tiny red light in the middle of the rack on the wall. He moved in closer, coming up against the console, and pointed.

'See that?'

'See what?' the young woman said. He could see her eyes scanning the rows of red, green and extinguished miniature lights.

'The four-wire unit's on.'

Slowly, he turned. She was standing very close to him.

'That's it. The squawk box was on, so the miked sound went into the general. It happens all the time. Sometimes you get to hear really embarrassing things.'

Annika blinked in confusion and moistened her lips.

'See all the mikes on the console? The control room crew uses them to communicate with the set. You have to press this button to talk . . .'

He bent over and indicated a centimetre-long black switch located next to one of the microphones.

'Then the mike transmission will be run through the console, through the general command circuit, and everyone can hear what's being said. When you're done, you just release the button and the circuit is broken.'

Gunnar stood up straight and tried to disregard the ache at the small of his back.

'However,' he continued, 'the technical director's mike is always on. He talks all the time and everybody needs to hear him. You're supposed to switch it off when the session's over, but that generally doesn't happen, so the most amazing comments leak out.'

'Like what?'

He shifted his stance, planting his feet further apart.

'Directors often reserve the right to go crazy after a wrap. They speak their minds about stupid guests, worthless cameramen, silly show hosts, you name it. It can get pretty sticky. Stefan can be very mean. He said terrible things about everyone.'

'So what's on the tape?'

'It could only be something that came in over the director's mike in the control room.'

'Events that took place in here, around three in the morning on Midsummer Even?'

He nodded.

'Thank you so much for your help,' Annika said and whirled out of the bus.

Gunnar Antonsson watched her disappear and listened to the silence that she had left him with, trying to figure out the emotion she triggered in him.

Chills ran up and down his spine when it hit him.

She reminded him of Michelle Carlsson.

Morning was usually a slow time at the newsroom but today was different. There was more whispering, heads were closer together, eyes were wider. Everyone knew that something was up, but they weren't sure what. Everyone seemed to know that Torstensson had done a TV interview early that morning, but no one knew what it was all about. Every single person employed by the paper *Kvällspressen* had received a whispered account about how the editor-in-chief had locked himself in his office and was refusing to take any calls, everyone could see that the managing editor was sitting in his fish tank reading newspapers, apparently untroubled, everyone had heard that Herman Wennergren, the chairman of the board, was on his way in.

Anders Schyman sat on his chair, drained and immobile. Leaning heavily against the backrest, he had spread out a paper in front of him to make it look as though he was busy reading. His digestion was shot; he had already been to the bathroom ten times this morning.

For the fifth time in fifteen minutes he looked at his watch. There was nothing left that he could do. His anthrax file had to have some kind of effect; he could only hope and pray that it would be the right one.

Suddenly the phone rang, a piercing and demanding in-house signal, and he almost flew out of his chair.

'He's here,' Tore Brand at the service desk informed him, hanging up without waiting for a response.

Slowly the managing editor put the phone down, looked out over the sea of newsroom employees and waited for the chairman of the board.

Only the person approaching him now was his son, Carl Wennergren, a quicker and more agile man than his father. Schyman bent over his paper and started breathing through his mouth.

The knock was hard and aggressive. He motioned with a distracted gesture to the reporter to come in.

'What did you do to Torstensson?' Carl Wennergren demanded with narrowed, icy blue eyes.

'Why don't you ask what Torstensson did?' Schyman said calmly and turned a page. 'What do you want?'

'To make your dreams come true,' Carl Wennergren said, removing a piece of paper from the inside pocket of his jacket. 'This is my resignation, effective immediately.'

Anders Schyman felt his pulse begin to race and prayed that it wouldn't show. He let the paper remain on his desk, not looking at it, not making any attempt to pick it up.

'Why?' he asked in a cool and collected voice.

Carl Wennergren was not that good at acting: his

hairline was sweaty and the hand that had tossed down the resignation had been a little shaky.

'You know why,' he said, his voice strangely both aggressive and subdued.

'No,' Schyman said. 'You tell me.'

He looked up at the tall, blond, broad-shouldered reporter.

A thought flew through his head: *If he starts swinging, I don't stand a chance.*

'You don't respect me as a reporter,' the young man said. 'You have pets, like that Bengtzon girl. You're a coward when it comes to ethics. You don't know enough about the newspaper business. Would you like me to go on? I don't intend to be abused by you any longer.'

Carl Wennergren's chin wobbled when he was done, and the significance of the reporter's words made Anders Schyman's hands and feet tingle.

He's resigning because I'm going to take over, he thought. *Oh, my God – he doesn't want to stay on here when I'm the big boss. I've won, dear Lord, it's over!*

He gasped and covered his face for a brief second, gathering strength.

You might be wrong, he thought. *This could mean any number of things.*

'Carl,' he said. 'You are an enterprising and fearless reporter. Sometimes you're too hasty, and your judgement isn't always as good as it should be, but if you're willing to—'

'No,' Carl Wennergren interjected. 'I don't want to answer to you any longer. I'll be clearing out my desk this afternoon.'

He turned his back on Schyman decisively.

'Not so fast,' Schyman said, his voice almost a drawl. 'According to your contract, you have two, or maybe even three months' notice. I would like to review its terms before I let you go.'

The reporter turned around again, a triumphant smile on his face.

'I'm going to be working with one of our competitors,' he said. 'You can't force me to work here when I've already signed on with another company.'

'That depends on the company,' Schyman said, leaning so far back in his chair that it creaked.

Carl Wennergren thrust out his chin and regarded Schyman with raised eyebrows.

'I'm going to be the new CEO of Global Future.'

Anders Schyman burst into a fit of laughter so intense that he had to lean forward not to fall out of his chair. *Oh my God, the irony of it all.* This was incredible. The reporter was deflated. He blinked a few times and flicked his tongue over his lips.

'What's so funny?'

'I thought Global Future had folded,' Schyman said once he had pulled himself together.

'No, not at all. The company is going to be restructured and I'm buying it. I've got a damn fine plan to get it back on its feet again.'

'Good,' Schyman said and got up. 'Then you can honour your contract. Global Future isn't a competitor of this paper.'

'You're just jerking me around,' the reporter shouted, his eyes flashing. 'You're only doing this to keep me here.'

Carl Wennergren turned to escape from the fish tank, only to discover that his father was standing in the doorway.

'Schyman won't let me go,' he said, pointing an accusing finger at the managing editor.

'It's always a shame when talented people such as yourself choose to leave,' Anders Schyman said, doing his utmost to keep his voice under control. 'But if we can't offer you anything that would make you stay, naturally we will respect your decision to devote yourself to your own company.'

The reporter exhaled in a manner that conveyed contempt and distrust.

'You are such a goddam toady!' he said.

Carl walked past his father and headed for the newsroom. Herman Wennergren pulled the door shut a bit roughly. His demeanour was serious. Anders Schyman had to sit down; his legs refused to support him.

'I'm here at the request of editor-in-chief Torstensson,' the chairman of the board said, his head bowed and his face blotchy. 'He is extremely concerned about certain information that had come to the attention of a TV network.'

Anders Schyman acknowledged this with a slight nod.

'I was present during the interview this morning,' he said. 'It was highly unpleasant.'

The chairman of the board went up to the managing editor and gazed down at him with an eagle-like stare.

'I'll never know how you arranged this,' he said, 'but you should be aware of one thing: I can see your true colours.'

The managing editor looked back at the man, a neutral expression on his face even though his brain had frozen up.

I've got to do something. Say something. React. Immediately.

Schyman conjured up every last particle of strength he had and got up with a bounce, swinging his arms as he rose.

'I'm sure you realize that I have no idea what you're talking about,' he said.

Herman Wennergren, the chairman of the board, took one step closer to him, narrowed his eyes and hissed:

'You are one mean and spiteful bastard!'

'I'm exactly what this paper needs,' Schyman replied.

By the time she reached Anne Snapphane's dry and dusty workplace, Annika was out of breath.

'So, what did Gunnar say?'

'The technical director's mike was on,' Annika gasped. 'There was a reference tape set for recording the internal communications, it was meant for Michelle's documentary, and it ran until 3:12 a.m.'

She picked up the tape. Her entire body had turned to jelly. Anne Snapphane looked up from her monitor.

'The director's mike, on the directing console? But that's right next to the spot . . .'

Annika nodded, suddenly feeling like she wanted to cry.

'Oh, my God . . .' she said.

She met Anne Snapphane's gaze, knowing that they were both thinking the same thing. She handed the VHS tape to her friend and saw her pop it in and rewind it for a few seconds.

The sound came on right at the whooshing noise.

'Did someone come in?'

The whispering male voice.

'No, no one, come on . . .'

More whispering, followed by laughs and moans.

Anne turned the volume down as low as possible. Annika felt her cheeks start flaming and, to her embarrassment, there was a throbbing in her groin.

'We shouldn't be listening to this,' she said in a whisper. 'We really should call the police.'

Anne Snapphane nodded.

They listened for a while longer, still undecided.

Then they heard the man start whispering again, catching something like: 'Someone's in the bus . . .'

This was followed by silence and more whooshing. Anne and Annika gaped at each other.

Then they heard a female voice coming from a distance: 'Your manager is here.'

'Someone else is inside the bus,' Anne Snapphane whispered, her eyes wide as saucers.

'What?'

Scraping and rattling noises, murmurs and giggles.

'John, they're here to pick you up, your manager and the driver.'

'Tell them I'm busy.'

Giggles, the sound of someone drinking followed by a burp.

'It's very late. I really think you should go now.'

This was greeted by a hysterical fit of giggles and the male voice murmured: 'How long has she been here?' The woman's voice, now pitched very high, said:

'You know, I really must ask you to leave now!'

The man's voice again, slurred:

'What's the matter with this bitch?'

Peals of shrill laughter. The other female voice got louder – she must have been closer to the mike.

'What did you call me?' said the other female voice.

'Who cares, let her watch if she wants to . . .'

'What's her problem?'

Something rattled, the murmur of voices rose and fell, and then a rustling sound was heard.

'This is a production area, not a bedroom. It's in the middle of the night and I want both of you out of here. Now!'

Annika's stomach turned over as she recognized the voice.

'Karin,' she said. 'It's Karin Bellhorn.'

'What's wrong with you?'

'This is outrageous! I'm here to let you know that your car is here, and you insult me! Do I have to call security to get you out?'

'What do you mean? This place doesn't have any security.'

'And that's Michelle's voice,' Annika said.

The tape continued to roll. There was a loud crash and the man's voice said:

'Is she always like this?'

'Well yeah, now you know what I mean.'

More giggles, the man said something that they couldn't make out and the woman who must have been Karin Bellhorn started screaming.

'Get out! Get out!'

Anne Snapphane nodded, her face ghostly pale, and said:

'Call Q.'

There was another crash, someone shouted something and then there was a rattling noise followed by the sound of the wind.

'John! Wait!'

'Are you going to run after him? Come on, there's got to be a limit to how much you're willing to degrade yourself!'

The man's voice could be heard in the background, faint and trailing off:

'. . . Fucking crazy bitches . . .'

'Damn you! Why did you do that? Make him go away like that?'

'Pull yourself together . . .'

'What are you doing here, anyway? Why did you come in here?'

'It's her,' Anne said in a low voice. 'Make the call. Now.'

They looked at each other and saw their own terror reflected on the other person's face.

Annika got up, feeling oddly weightless, and floated out into the hallway. The technical crew was rigging a set for the live broadcast in the conference room. A few journalists had already arrived and were hanging up their coats. Annika stopped short, retraced her steps a bit and unlocked an emergency exit. It opened up on a flimsy-looking spiral staircase; it was extremely gusty outdoors and the wind whistled melodies through the perforations in the metal structure.

'I'm busy,' Q said when he finally answered.

'It was Karin Bellhorn,' Annika said. 'Anne Snapphane's found a tape to prove it.'

The line was silent for a few seconds.

'Are you sure of that?'

'I haven't heard the whole thing, but Karin's definitely inside the bus.'

'What kind of tape are we talking about?'

'It's a tape of the internal communications from the bus. It had been running all night and the technical director's mike hadn't been switched off.'

'Why do you think Karin Bellhorn did it?'

'Because she and Michelle were in a fight after three a.m.'

'That must be right before the murder took place. Can you hear any gunshot?'

Confused and embarrassed, Annika paused to think.

'I don't know, I haven't heard the whole tape. What did Karin tell you?'

'John Essex told us that she had been in the bus, so we asked her about it. She admits she was in there, but she claims that she left the bus long before three. However, she told us that she saw Anne Snapphane over by the bus when she went back to her room.'

Annika gasped.

'That's not true,' she said. 'Anne didn't do it.'

Q's voice was very dry as he said:

'We've eliminated most of the suspects. Only three are left: Karin, Anne and John. During our interviews, Anne is the one whose behaviour has been the strangest. She's been the most evasive and she's told us the most lies. In addition to all that, she's exhibited a range of weird physical reactions, like sweating profusely, fainting and acting out.'

'She's a hypochondriac, she always thinks she's going to die,' Annika explained in a feeble and shaky voice. 'Do you think I would protect a murderer?'

The policeman didn't say a word. He just let his sceptical attitude remain in the air.

'What did Karin tell you?' Annika asked.

'That she went to get Essex and that they left the bus together.'

'And what does he say?'

'That he doesn't really remember what happened. Overall, he's been an arrogant son of a bitch. Are you telling me that Karin Bellhorn was in the bus with Michelle after Essex had left?'

'Definitely.'

Q was silent for a few moments.

'Where can I get this tape?'

'Over at Zero Television. I'm there right now. In a few minutes they will be airing some kind of memorial service for Michelle Carlsson, followed by a press conference.'

'Is Karin there?'

'I saw her half an hour ago.'

Q hung up with a click.

For a few minutes, Annika remained on the staircase, letting the breeze ruffle her hair while tenseness made the pit of her stomach clench.

*

The cemetery was bathed in cold sunshine. Gusts made branches shake, the leaves bobbing and shimmying.

Thomas stood by the window, completely unable to do a thing after the morning's meeting. He had skipped lunch and downed three cokes and a bottle of Ramlösa mineral water. Every organ in his body was tied up in a knot of despair and longing.

How had he become so inept at life? Why wasn't he capable of valuing anything consummate and unique? Why was he so blind when it came to seeing Annika and the children in a true light? And how had Eleonor suddenly become the personification of his ideal woman?

He closed his eyes, rubbed the bridge of his nose and forced himself to recall what it had been like.

Her helpless voice: *I don't know how to work the VCR, Thomas. Help me out, what button do you push?* Her reluctance to go sailing: *It makes me seasick.* To go abroad: *The view here at home is so much better.* To have children: *With all our obligations to the community? Thomas, please!*

'All right if we come in, Thomas?'

He turned around, caught in the act of daydreaming.

'I have the same view,' the head of negotiations said, nodding at the window. 'Only my office is on another floor, higher up. It's beautiful, isn't it? And a bit melancholy.'

Thomas smoothed back his hair and indicated two chairs. All three men took a seat. The head of negotiations and the section supervisor for the Developmental Section were facing him on the other side of the desk.

'That analysis you presented this morning was very interesting,' the head of negotiations said. 'We discussed it briefly, and we reached a unanimous conclusion to take this up with the board.'

'I touched base with the Federation of County

Councils,' the section supervisor for the Developmental Section said. 'And their immediate response was very positive. It seems like your proposal will be implemented with no friction at all.'

Thomas hid his shaking hands out of view.

'We will not be able to make a public announcement at the present time,' the head of negotiations said. 'But, as we see it, this project would involve a commitment of four years or more. Your office would be two floors down, in the Developmental Section, and you will also be spending a great deal of time at the offices of the Federation of County Councils. Our proposal is that we take you on as a permanent employee here at the Association of Local Authorities, and when the regional development project has been concluded, you can move on to other assignments. Would you be interested in such an arrangement?'

The head of negotiations granted him a smile. Thomas wet his parched lips and cleared his throat.

'I . . .' he said. 'I just have one thing to say . . . Of course. Absolutely. I'm delighted.'

A bark of laughter escaped him, but he quickly put a lid on it.

The men on the other side of the desk beamed.

'It feels reassuring, Thomas,' the head of negotiations continued, 'to have a man like you aboard. Your feet are firmly planted in reality, you are conscientious and committed, the life you lead reflects those of the people you will be researching. I believe, personally, that these aspects are a prerequisite for success in this business. And it has come to our attention that you have received international acknowledgement for your work as well. To be honest, we had no solution at hand for keeping you on, and we would have deeply regretted having to let you go. So this resolution suits us all extremely well.'

'When will we be able to go public with this decision?' Thomas asked.

'After the summer,' the head of negotiations said. 'We'll have to discuss it with the politicians and you'll start out by setting down the guidelines of our policy. When everything is set, we'll hold a huge press conference. Anyone in Sweden who has ever had anything to do with this particular issue will find out just who is blazing the trail.'

The head of negotiations proffered his hand. Thomas quickly wiped his own hand on his trousers and shook it. He shook hands with both bosses, sealing the deal.

'And you're going to Korea too,' the section supervisor said, impressed.

'From the second to the twelfth of September,' Thomas said, leaning back, a wide smile on his face.

Annika entered the conference room from the back and walked straight into a wall of black-jacketed backs. The door closed behind her. One of the men in front of her stepped on her foot and barely took notice of her feeble protests. She jumped up a few times to see what was going on, to no avail. The wall of men stepped back in unison and she felt panic welling up inside her, the feeling of not having enough air.

Got to get out of here.

Got to breathe. She heaved herself up on a radiator, got up on the windowsill and stood there.

It wouldn't be comfortable, that was for sure.

She turned around, leaned her behind against the window, and held on to either side of the window frame.

The conference room was a black sea. It was hot in there already, the lack of oxygen making the air oppressive. An abundance of white flowers blanketed the room with their scent, enveloping everyone in the room, the perfume going to their heads.

Annika perched in the window, trying to survey the scene.

There were three cameras, one at the front, by the stage; one at the entrance on the other side of the room, and one up by the ceiling at the back of the room. Cables snaked their way along walls and underfoot and microphones appeared in the sea of humanity like periscopes. On stage there was a lectern, even more flowers and a large TV monitor up by the ceiling. Technicians, cameramen, and sound and light engineers fought their way through the crowd, talking into invisible mikes and listening through earpieces. Four chairs had been placed on the stage. Apart from that there was nothing to sit on.

The sun in Annika's eyes made her squint as she tried to see who was present. Almost everyone in the crowd was a familiar face. The people she didn't know personally were the folks who got their pictures in the paper, the beautiful people, TV celebrities and reporters, actors and artists. They had come for various reasons: hoping for work, out of curiosity, or prompted by a sincere sense of loss. The atmosphere was energetic and heightened but the murmuring of the crowd was kept to a subdued roar. A pamphlet had been handed out. Annika looked down over the shoulders of the men in front of her and saw that it appeared to contain press material and an agenda. A lot of people were fanning themselves with the folder.

Annika looked around, holding on so tight that her knuckles turned white. She noticed that Anne Snapphane wasn't present.

Highlander was standing at the very front of the room, on the tiny stage. In an effort to seem calm, collected and serious, he was dressed in a black suit and a silver tie, and

it looked like he was wearing tan make-up. Karin
Bellhorn was seated next to him; their heads were close
together as they whispered to each other. The insistent
quality of the producer's hand movements suggested that
the network boss didn't quite understand the task at
hand. Maybe he needed instruction. Karin's black tent of
a dress swayed, golden threads in the cloth glistening.
Annika noticed that she was heavily made up and her
hair was up.

'One minute to go,' the floor manager shouted.

Highlander raised a hand in protest and waved in
dismissal at the producer. Nervously, he began to shuffle
papers around. Then he walked up to the microphone
and said: 'One-two, one-two', earning a thumbs-up from
a sound engineer who was gazing towards the control
room.

The cameras started whirring softly, spreading an
electronic smog that made your skin prickle. It got relentlessly hotter, Annika wiped her face with her sleeve.

Then she heard Barbara Hanson's voice, shrill and a
tad tipsy: 'Oh, my God, it's so hot in here. Do we really
have to *stand up* the whole time? What kind of an affair *is*
this, anyway?'

On the other side of the room she caught sight of Carl
Wennergren, a frown on his blotchy face, propelling
Mariana von Berlitz forward with a firm hand on her
elbow.

Stefan Axelsson stood at the very back of the room, his
arms folded across his chest, his face white.

And there, of course, was Sebastian Follin. He had
some business up by the stage, and was whispering
something to Highlander.

'Thirty seconds to go.'

Karin Bellhorn retired to the right of the stage. Bambi
Rosenberg had parked herself right in front of

Highlander's lectern and was already crying so hard that her shoulders were shaking. Gunnar Antonsson had stationed himself right next to the door, he looked vaguely confused and seemed ready to pick up and run at any moment.

Everyone was here, Annika reckoned, except for John Essex, the little Nazi girl and Anne.

The journalists and the press photographers huddled by the stage. She spotted Bertil Strand and Sjölander. When she caught sight of the delegation from their competitor, she became more attentive. But Bosse wasn't there. She swallowed her disappointment.

'Fifteen seconds to go.'

Annika's left leg started to shake; the windowsill was too narrow. She looked for somewhere else to stand, couldn't find anything, and braced herself against the radiator. Looking up at the large TV screen to the left of Highlander, she tried to shift her weight to the other foot.

'Seven, six, five, four . . .'

The floor manager illustrated the last three counts with his fingers.

Intro music began to play. A bombastic piece in a minor key spilled out of the loudspeakers at ceiling level, making the walls and windows vibrate. Annika was overwhelmed by emotion. Her chest constricted and she had to breathe with her mouth open, in shallow gasps, to hold back the tears. Bambi's sobs up by the stage grew progressively louder, a jarring sound in stark contrast to the sweeping melody.

As the music faded, Highlander walked out into the spotlights focused on the lectern.

'Dear friends,' he began in a serious voice, 'colleagues and . . . well, friends. On behalf of TV Plus I would like to welcome you to this ceremony dedicated to the memory of our dear friend and esteemed associate, Michelle

Carlsson, and I will also inform you all about how the TV Plus network plans to commemorate Michelle's memory.'

Annika swallowed. The sentimental atmosphere created by the music had been compromised, and irritation took its place.

'We will continue to carry on in Michelle's spirit,' Highlander continued from the screen on high, 'and follow a route we know she would have appreciated. We are also proud to present a new associate: Sebastian Follin, Michelle Carlsson's best friend and colleague will be working full time for this network to commemorate Michelle's memory.'

The manager stepped forward, lit from within by an inner fire, and flung out his arms as if he was expecting a cheering crowd. A smattering of applause made him blush.

'This is why we have decided to air Michelle's final production in its entirety,' Highlander continued. 'The first show of the series titled *Summer Frolic at the Castle* will be aired on Saturday, as originally planned.'

Annika surveyed the audience, trying to interpret their reaction.

They were neutral. Expectant. A bit moved.

Sebastian Follin continued to stand next to Highlander at the edge of the stage, the beams of the spotlights reflected in his glasses.

He won, Annika thought. *He's turned this into a victory.*

'The shows will be aired in the order in which they were taped, just as originally planned. We will be seeing Michelle Carlsson in the way she would prefer it, as a professional taking part in a production that she was committed to.'

The silence grew more intense. The audience was waiting, the cameras were whirring. Highlander cleared his throat.

'I would like to point out,' he said, 'that this decision has been carefully considered. The network management has discussed the issues very carefully with the production staff and, above all, with Sebastian Follin. Our decision is a unanimous and wholehearted one. Michelle Carlsson was one of the driving forces behind this series: she had asked for a chance to increase her repertoire here at TV Plus, and we welcomed her proposal with open arms.'

A reporter by the door left the room, distracting Highlander momentarily.

'We are very proud of this series,' he went on, speaking now in a louder voice, trying to reach even the people who didn't want to listen. 'It is our absolute conviction that this is what Michelle would have wanted. She wouldn't have wanted to see her final production tossed in the waste-paper basket, all that work for nothing. So we made this decision for Michelle's sake.'

'And I'm the King of Denmark,' one of the men below Annika quipped in a hushed voice.

'There is some truth in it, though,' another man said. 'I do think Michelle would have wanted the shows to be aired.'

'I'll grant you that,' the first man said. 'But not two weeks before her funeral. You should be able to expect some decency, even from a TV network, shouldn't you?'

'We are presently faced,' Highlander said on stage, 'with the problem of finding a worthy successor to Michelle Carlsson, someone who can take over the helm at *The Women's Sofa* and carry on in her spirit. This task is painful, but we know that Michelle would not have wanted to see her creation go off the air, a show that she made into a smash hit for that particular demographic.'

'Oh, please,' a third man at Annika's feet protested.

A split second later, Annika caught sight of Q over by

the door. She stopped breathing, wanting to call out to him and almost falling.

The police officer made his way over to the stage, murmuring excuses to the wall of backs that made room for him in surprise. Three cops in uniform trailed after him, rigid and silent. The atmosphere in the room changed. Unease prevailed, and the dominant sound was of people murmuring and shuffling their feet.

'Now,' Highlander continued, unaware of the turbulence in the room, 'I would like to stand down in favour of Michelle's closest friend and associate, Sebastian Follin.'

Anne Snapphane stared at the monitor and saw Sebastian step up to the lectern. The spotlights had made his forehead all shiny. The camera zoomed in on his face, catching the slight twitching of his mouth, the expectancy, the apprehension. The way he held his head signalled that he was affected by the seriousness of the occasion, while the fire in his eyes was that of the true believer. The man cleared his throat, unfolded a piece of paper, adjusted his glasses better, and was leaning closer to the mike when suddenly the image on the TV screen began flickering. Sebastian Follin looked up and scanned the audience, his gaze darting.

'Dear friends . . .' he began. But the camera had already moved away from his face and now swept the room.

Live broadcasts were produced from the control room next to Anne's editing cubicle. The technical director, a consultant, cued another camera, producing a change of perspective. Anne caught sight of Annika, perched in a window, hanging on to the window frame for dear life. The room next door got noisier – people were upset and distracted. What was going on?

A tape stopped at Anne's feet, she heard the sound but decided to ignore it.

Camera three took over, an overview shot of the entire conference room. The crowd, a dark mass with bobbing heads where one particular face popped out at her.

It was Q. *Holy shit*. He was here.

Anne leaned closer to the monitor. The warm sensation radiating from her stomach spread waves of relief throughout her body.

Q was here. It would be over soon.

She looked attentively at the screen. Stefan was at the back, there were Mariana and Carl Wennergren, and Karin Bellhorn was over by the stage, to the right.

The director cut back to camera one, the shot with the stage and the lectern, right when Sebastian Follin stepped out of range.

Anne gritted her teeth, ashamed even though she had done nothing. What a messy and shoddy job.

'Well . . .' someone whose mike was switched on, probably Highlander, said. 'What do we do now?'

Camera three was cued, and the shot of the whole room was back. Q was on his way over to Karin Bellhorn, three policemen in tow. He said something to her and the producer's reaction was immediate and aggressive. She held out her hands and Anne could hear what she was saying in spite of the static and the noise in the room.

'Why? For what reason?'

Q said something she couldn't make out and Karin Bellhorn took a step backwards.

'No way!' she shouted. 'I most certainly will not!'

The woman turned around, away from the policemen, and ran.

Annika Snapphane stared at the screen, her cheeks blazing.

Camera two zoomed in on the back of Karin Bellhorn's head. The plastic comb that held her hair up was bobbing towards the exit. Wide-eyed members of the audience moved to let her pass, blinking in confusion at her, at the police and into the camera.

One of the uniformed policemen caught up with the producer, grabbed her upper arm and said something to her. The woman turned around and slugged the policeman who tumbled into the camera while the crowd drew back . . .

'Take it easy!' Anne heard Q say from somewhere behind camera two, his voice hard and steady.

'Take it easy?' Karin Bellhorn screamed into the camera, the mike picking up every last breath. 'You're accusing me of murder, and I'm supposed to take it easy?'

Anne could hear the crowd gasp. There was more light by the producer now and people were backing away.

'I didn't do it!' she screamed, looking at the crowd. 'I didn't do it, I swear! It was Anne Snapphane, our researcher, I saw her! I saw her go over to the bus, then I heard a gunshot!'

The floor disappeared beneath Anne's feet. She was conscious of the fact that she was falling, but she couldn't stop herself. The air ran out of oxygen and she couldn't breathe.

The frightened eyes of Karin Bellhorn darted back and forth on the screen. She flicked her tongue over her lips and smoothed her hair.

Anne's head was ringing with the words: *It's not true, you're lying, I didn't do it!*

'She did it!' Karin Bellhorn shouted, the loudness of her voice causing distortion.

Apart from the scuffle, everyone and everything was silent. The entire building was holding its breath, and so was the screen.

'Anne hated Michelle, because Michelle got the job, she was the host. So . . . that's what happened. She . . . couldn't stand her!'

Anne struggled to get air and to stay up. The words echoed, reverberating through her feet, her belly and her brain.

'She . . . isn't here! Isn't that right? Well, there you are!'

A triumphant and shaky smile spread across the dry lips of the producer.

'Anne Snapphane hated Michelle so much that she didn't even show up at her memorial service!'

Rage lit up the editing room like a white flash of revelation, burning away paralysis and consideration. Shaking all over, a dry-mouthed Anne got up. Almost hyperventilating, she forced her breathing to steady while her mind occupied itself with wiring circuits and cable connections. She had been involved in Zero's technical development, so she had a fair idea how things worked. Closing her eyes, she came to a swift conclusion.

It could work.

With mercurial speed she threw herself down on the floor, crawled behind the console, and rewired two connections from the mixer to the four-wire, the talk box. Then she crawled back into her cubicle, quickly and breathlessly, picked up the unmarked reference tape and popped it into the VHS player.

She pressed *play*, got to her feet and turned up the volume of Zero Television's internal communications system as far as it would go.

There was a deafening silence in the room after the producer had spoken. No one so much as breathed. Annika felt as though her heart had stopped. She swayed there in the window recess, damp palms making it hard to hold on.

Jesus Christ, she thought, *someone has got to contest this. What should I do? What should I say?*

'Well,' Highlander said as he approached the lectern

on stage. 'This was certainly an unexpected turn of events. Perhaps we should compose ourselves . . .'

The TV monitor up by the ceiling flickered as the outgoing image was replaced by a grey screen. Loud static filled the air and a series of scraping and rattling noises poured out of the loudspeakers in the conference room. This was followed by a voice, hauntingly clear and familiar, a spectral presence in the room.

'What do you mean? This place doesn't have any security.'

'Is she always like this?'

'Well yeah, now you know what I mean.'

The roomful of people froze as Michelle started talking. Annika realized what was going on, even though she had no clue about how it was possible. She looked around to check out the response. Stefan Axelsson was as pale as death: he looked like he was going to pass out. Mariana and Carl Wennergren were wide-eyed and gaping. Gunnar Antonsson had a wary look on his face. Karin Bellhorn's face had gone blotchy with sheer panic.

'Get out! Get out!' she screamed from the loud-speakers.

Q looked around, not understanding where the voices were coming from. The police officer next to him let go of Karin Bellhorn.

Crashing sounds. Shouts. Clattering.

'John! Wait!'

'Are you going to run after him? Come on, there's got to be a limit to how much you're willing to degrade yourself!'

The numbness wore off and the members of the audience began searching for answers in each other's eyes, without finding any.

'. . . Fucking crazy bitches . . .'

'Damn you! Why did you do that? Make him leave?'

'Pull yourself together . . .'

'What are you doing here, anyway? Why did you come in here?'

The room began to buzz, the murmurs of the crowd mixing with the unintelligible words on the tape.

'Michelle, you're acting like a slut. You've got to think of your reputation. When a person's as famous as you are, they can't behave like this, people won't want to see you . . .'

All stares fixed on Karin Bellhorn, who had remained frozen to the spot, stunned.

Drunken giggles spilled out of the loudspeakers. They tipped over into hysteria.

'What are you laughing at?'

Michelle's raucous laughter filled the entire room, rolling along the walls and floors, slapping the audience in the gut.

'What's so funny?'

'You are. You're such a fool. What's the point of making it big, if you never get to do what you want?'

'I'm responsible for a whole crew, and it all depends on you if they'll be able to put food on the table. You have an obligation to behave.'

There was a crash that made people jump.

'Don't you tell me what to do!'

The voice was hysterical. Its owner was coming apart at the seams.

'Everybody's always telling me what to do. You think you can wind me up like a doll and I'll do whatever you want. Do you think I'm some kind of fucking robot? I'm a real live person, you know, and I won't take any more crap. I can't take any more of your disgusting expectations. Highlander can fire me a hundred times over, I would have quit anyway. I can't stand this bullshit any more!'

Now people looked away from Karin Bellhorn and fixed their gazes on the network CEO. Two red spots burned on his cheeks, and he rushed over and whispered something to a sound engineer. It wasn't hard to figure out what he'd said, Annika thought.

What the hell is this and where is it coming from?

'You spoiled brat,' Karin Bellhorn said on the tape in a slightly slurred voice. 'You actually feel sorry for yourself, don't you? Isn't that right?'

The sound engineer pushed his way through the crowd and disappeared down the corridor.

'I've worked my fingers to the bone for people like you my whole career,' the producer's voice continued. 'Egotistic morons who just act on their instincts. I'm the one with the expertise, I do all the work and people like you get all the attention. Do you realize how sick I am of the whole thing?'

The crowd was swirling now, agitated whispers and eyes as big as saucers. One of the policemen went over to stand in the doorway, blocking Karin Bellhorn's route of escape.

'Some people are worthy of attention,' Michelle countered. 'Others aren't.'

The tape buzzed and someone was panting.

'What exactly do you mean? I've been appreciated, I've worked in this business for thirty years now, and I've always been in demand. I was married to . . . He could have had anyone he wanted, and . . .'

Karin Bellhorn turned her back on the crowd in the conference room.

Michelle's laughter rang out through the loudspeakers again.

'That's the greatest achievement of your entire lifetime, isn't it? You caught yourself an English pop star. But guess what? Do you know what he tells people about you?'

More laughter.

'You can laugh all you want,' Karin Bellhorn said, her voice coloured with contempt and pain. 'Steven loved me. They only want to fuck you.'

After this, there was nothing but silence and Annika thought the tape had run out. She locked stares with Bambi Rosenberg. The other woman's eyes were red, smeary with make-up and full of shocked despair. Malice hovered over the room like a dark cloud and Michelle had apparently been rendered speechless. When the voices came back on, Karin was the one to speak.

'I can do your job any day, but you couldn't do mine.'

A snort of contempt billowed throughout the room.

'There's one thing you ought to know,' Michelle said. 'You have me to thank for your job on this show. Highlander wanted to use someone else, only I insisted on having you, but that was a big mistake. You don't have what it takes any more. You make shows for the senior-citizen set. You go around thinking that you make things work, but everyone else has to cover for your mistakes.'

Something in the TV star's voice made the crowd hush. A new note of hardness, ruthlessness, a steely intent to inflict pain and crush her foe. The vulnerable whine in Karin Bellhorn's voice on the tape proved that she had perceived it too.

'That's nonsense,' she whimpered.

'Please, are you telling me you don't even realize it? You're nothing but a goddam has-been who doesn't have the sense to bow out.'

'I'm not going to listen to this.'

'You park your fat arse in the newsroom and lord it over everyone, so sure you have all the answers. You even think you're good enough to be on screen.'

'You'd better be quiet, Michelle!'

'Why do you think I show up on the set even when I'm

running one hell of a temperature? I do it because otherwise you'd sit in.'

Gales of hysterical, drunken laughter.

'Can't you see how pathetic you are?'

'You don't know what you're talking about.'

'You try to be young and with it, but you're so totally wrong, and you take out your bitterness on people like me, the successful ones . . .'

'You watch your mouth!'

'Did you know that Steven goes around telling people about those sponges you used instead of tampons? And how disgusting he thought it was? Everybody knows about it, you're a laughing stock . . .'

'You'd better watch it, you little—'

'John told me you came on to him. I saw it, too – everyone did.'

'Shut up!'

'You tried to get him into bed, and all he could think about was how you rinsed out those bloody sponges . . .'

The shot rang out without warning. The ear-popping sound roared like thunder through the loudspeakers, making the audience jump.

Gunnar Antonsson was still in the doorway. His gaze darted around the room in dismay. Karin Bellhorn had turned around and was staring at the fuzzy TV screen.

In the echo after the shot the sound of breathing could be heard, a heavy asthmatic wheeze.

'Michelle?'

Static coupled with rustling sounds.

'Michelle? Oh, my God – Michelle! Oh, no . . .'

A dull thud, the sound of a heavy object dropping on carpeting. Gasps of hyperventilation, someone moving around. A whoosh of air followed by silence.

Annika didn't move, the sound of the shot still ringing in her ears. The stares of the crowd shifted from the screen to Highlander, to Karin Bellhorn, all flushed and sweaty. Gunnar Antonsson straightened up, then turned away and left. An exalted Barbara Hanson was whispering to the people around her. Not bothering to disguise her tears, Mariana von Berlitz clung to Carl Wennergren.

When the tide of accusing looks grew too strong, Karin Bellhorn shrank back, bumping into the wall.

'What?' the producer demanded as she looked around. 'Do you believe this?'

Bambi Rosenberg's face was all red except for a white ring around her tightened mouth. Her eyes blazed.

'Damn you!' she screamed at Karin Bellhorn. 'Damn you to hell!'

One of the policemen grabbed hold of the woman, restraining her. Sebastian Follin was still standing by the lectern, stunned and confused, his notes clenched in his hands. Highlander was dialling a long number on his cellphone, probably to London, and he moved to a corner of the stage. Stefan Axelsson's head was bowed and he was crying so hard that his shoulders were shaking.

Annika turned to gaze at the producer again; she had suspected as much, but the truth hadn't really sunk in. She hadn't understood the forces at work even though they had surrounded her the whole time.

'For God's sake!' Karin Bellhorn shouted, feeling hot and hunted, her gaze darting around in desperation. 'It's all a fake! Don't you get it? She did it, Anne Snapphane, she mixed this tape, you know how it's done . . .'

The insight Annika had just acquired fanned the flames of her fundamental sense of judgement: that bitch was trying to put the blame on someone else, attempting to finger Anne who wasn't even here! The room faded, leaving the black-robed producer who had her back to the wall highlighted and exposed.

'This is an outrage!' Karin Bellhorn cried on the other

end of eternity. 'She's ruthless! Now why would I want to murder Michelle?'

Annika braced herself against the radiator and tensed her fingers to gain a sure grip. Then she let her voice ring out:

'Cain and Abel,' she said, her voice as clear as a bell. 'The most ancient motive for murder in the history of the world. It's so easy to become what you do. You believe that you are what everyone else sees.'

Heads turned as astonished glances were shot in her direction, Annika could sense them without seeing them, felt their attention, but didn't care. She knew that their minds were wide open, that all the fences were down, that they were ready for anything.

Karin Bellhorn leaned forward, her eyes dark with rage, fighting for her life.

'Are you insinuating that I would kill someone out of simple envy?'

Total silence. The crowd had stopped breathing. The electronic whir of the cameras filled the room in between the exchanges of words. The spotlights made faces flush, while the scent of the flowers was oppressive.

'Absolutely not,' Annika said, the voice from beyond. 'It's so much bigger than that.'

'You don't know what you're talking about,' Karin Bellhorn screamed.

Annika closed her eyes for a moment and found her truth.

'If you don't think you're worth anything, you become what you do. If no one sees what you do, you become invisible twice over. The more you try to be noticed, the more annoying you become, sort of like a buzzing fly. And if someone else should happen to be acknowledged at the same time, and taken seriously, someone who might not deserve it . . .'

'Are you out of your mind?'

The producer's voice broke, while Annika's rang out across the room.

'Karin,' Annika said, 'you have given more thought to the mechanisms that control celebrity than anyone else. I think you reached the end of your tether. Everyone saw Michelle Carlsson, but no one saw you.'

Annika locked stares with the producer across the room, over the heads of the mourners.

'I understand, Karin,' Annika said. 'I know why you did it. I understand Cain too. If you're invisible for too long, you cease to be human. In the end, you'll do anything just to prove that you exist.'

Karin Bellhorn blinked. Annika saw her falter.

'The revolver was on the floor,' Annika said. 'You picked it up. It was sticky, but you didn't know why.'

There was no comment from the producer other than the wheezing of her airways.

Annika closed her eyes and let it come to her, channelling the events, feeling them seep into her.

'You raised the revolver,' she said. 'You didn't feel its weight, only the cold metal. It was weightless, an extension of your arm.'

Karin Bellhorn tried to say something, but words failed her.

'Michelle stood there, her words cutting you to pieces. You knew that you would die if she continued.'

The producer gaped and stared at her.

'It was either her or you,' Annika said. 'And it was so easy to pull the trigger that you hardly felt it. You looked into her eyes as the impact knocked her backwards, and you saw that she didn't get it. She died without understanding a thing.'

Karin Bellhorn's face was now white and she struggled to get air.

'Later on, you heard the bang and felt the gun recoil, and your mind went blank. You knew what had happened, and you knew that it was wrong. Isn't that right, Karin?'

Annika's voice was a whisper floating on the scent of the flowers.

'I only wanted to make her shut up,' Karin Bellhorn said.

Anne Snapphane stared at Annika on the monitor, perched up on the windowsill, the heads turning in the crowd, going from Karin to Annika. Backlit by the sun through the window, her body was outlined with a golden halo. Her hair was translucent and glowing.

Anne took a deep breath and noticed that the cramping sensation in her stomach was slowly easing up. Her legs started to shake instead, so she sat down carefully among the bags of tapes, taking shallow breaths. She felt as if she had escaped being pushed off a cliff, even though she had been in free fall.

'What the hell are you up to?'

Highlander loomed up over the pile of impounded and returned evidence. His face was a mess of make-up, confusion and rage. The silvery tie was no longer on straight.

Anne tried to say something, but couldn't find her voice and cleared her throat. Looking at the floor, she felt tears well up.

'I didn't do it,' she whispered.

'Don't you give me that!' Highlander said in a voice that was dull with rage. 'The guys went through every last source in the control room. You bypassed the regular circuit and ran something through the talk box.'

Anne looked up, tears blurring her sight.

'I didn't shoot her. I walked around outside the bus, looking for her, but I didn't do it.'

She bowed her head, the tears falling into her lap. The sound of a footfall in the corridor made her try to pull herself together. She pressed the back of her hand under her nose, swiped away the mucus and tears, then wiped her hand on her jeans and got up, feeling unsteady.

There wasn't much space by the door, the bags were in the way, and she could see Q's head bobbing impatiently on the other side.

'We've got to move this garbage.'

'Careful now!' Highlander admonished.

The bags flew out into the corridor. Lieutenant Q stood in front of her, pale and determined-looking.

'Annika tells me you found a reference tape of the intercom circuit that had been running in the bus on the night of the murder.

Anne Snapphane felt a new surge of panic spread from her stomach to her legs and shoot up to her shoulders. She swallowed and nodded.

'I presume that the conversation we heard in the conference room was that very tape. Am I right?'

Another nod.

'The engineers have established that the tape was played in this room. I assume that you had something to do with it?'

Anne tried to breathe, bent down, pushed *eject* on the VHS player, and handed the tape to Q.

'This wasn't exactly the ideal way to pursue an investigation,' he said, teeth clenched.

'I'm sorry,' she said, looking down at the floor but still feeling the scorch of his glare.

The policeman bagged the tape as evidence.

'I'll be talking to you again,' he said as he left the room.

Highlander remained stationed behind the monitors,

looking at the jumble of tapes and papers, and straightened his tie. He sighed, smoothed his brow, looked like he was about to say something, but decided not to. Instead, he turned and left the room.

As Anne gazed at his retreating back, she suddenly realized the obvious.

'We don't have a producer,' she said. 'How are we going to put a show together by Saturday without one?'

Highlander whirled around to face her, panic in his eyes. He flicked his tongue across his lips a few times while thoughts shot through his mind like balls of lightning.

'Oh, my God,' he said. 'What are we going to do?'

'I've located most of the material,' Anne said in a dull voice. 'I could run up a rough copy with all the in and out times, and get everything together . . .'

'Why don't you do the final cut?' Highlander asked. 'You can do it.'

Utterly surprised, Anne inhaled sharply and sat down. This was a once-in-a-lifetime opportunity.

'I want a producer's salary and a company car,' she said quickly.

They would never be able to afford to demote her again.

Her boss kept looking at her as he slowly exhaled, expressing contempt.

'Karin always warned me about you, said you'd take over as soon as you got the chance. She was right to keep you in check. How can you even think of using a situation like this?'

'Well, you should talk,' Anne countered.

Annika stopped as she reached the light, resting in the whoosh of the doors closing behind her, sealing in the dust and the air-conditioned air of the newsroom. Relief gushed through her system like a waterfall.

She had eight days off ahead of her.

Exhaling, she blinked up at the sun, feeling its warmth. The wind had died down, having blown the low-pressure zone from the Atlantic elsewhere, opening the door to a heat wave from Russia. She pulled off her sweater and let summertime caress her skin and hair. Hitched her bag up on her shoulder and slowly headed for Rålambshovsparken. There was a smell of hot asphalt in the air, for the first time this summer. She took a deep breath of it and had to smile. Mother Nature responded, delirious with longing, with an explosion of aromas, colours and insects.

The paper and Michelle Carlsson were left behind her, and they faded into a haze. The newsroom had been in a void: Torstensson remained in his room, Schyman had continued to be absent-minded. Rumours were flying around about an extra board meeting.

She hadn't been allowed to write about the memorial service, since she had been involved in the broadcast. Sjölander had interviewed her instead, which was strange, but prudent.

'Why did you cross-examine Karin Bellhorn from across the room?' he had asked.

'Because I knew what the answers would be,' Annika had replied. 'And I wanted everyone else to know too.'

That was the truth, and Anne Snapphane had provided her with another reason as well:

'Thank you,' Anne had whispered in the corridor behind the conference room. 'You saved me from becoming a murderer in the minds of everyone around for ever and ever. It wouldn't have mattered who really did it, people would just remember this: "Hmm, Anne Snapphane, didn't she get accused of murder on TV?"'

Riddarfjärden surged and fell, the water flashing like

the shards of a shattered mirror. Annika rummaged through her bag for her sunglasses. No such luck. As she walked along the edge of the water, positively drunk with joy, she squinted so hard that she missed seeing a poodle on a lead and tripped over it.

Q had been a bit upset, but not as angry as she feared. A public confession was hardly a bad thing, even though it wasn't legally binding.

In the initial interview, Karin Bellhorn had tried to claim that the gun went off accidentally and that it was unpremeditated, which didn't quite make sense.

'She's going down,' Q said when he called from his crummy cellphone inside police headquarters. 'One way or another, she's going down.'

Annika walked along Kungstorget, passing police headquarters and glancing up at the jail, Kronoberg-shäktet, at the top of the complex. Where could Karin Bellhorn be? The thought sent a shiver down her legs and a chill up her spine. Darkness welled up in her chest and she swallowed hard to make it go away. She speeded up, her heels tapping along the pavement and the breeze ruffling her hair.

The children were playing outdoors. Ellen was in the sandbox, dressed in a nappy, a shirt and a sun hat. Kalle was on the slide. His feet were bare and he was in high spirits. She saw both of them at the same time – both of them and only them. Two clear-cut figures. Running up to them, her joy at being reunited with them equalled that of her children at being with their mother. She held them and rocked them, both at the same time. Kissed sandy hands and snotty cheeks, the natural thing to do.

She informed the staff that her children would not be coming in for the rest of the week, and probably not the following week either. They all walked slowly down the sunny side of Scheelegatan in the direction of the Co-op store. Ellen was tired and quiet. She snuggled up in her stroller with her thumb in her mouth. Kalle jabbered away. Soon he would get overtired and become cranky. Annika felt as if her feet weren't quite touching the ground. Utterly present in this moment of being with her children in the summer weather, she floated along. In the cool recesses of the supermarket, she bought chicken and coconut milk, along with ice-cream bars and some beer. Then she raced home to Hantverkargatan while Kalle stood on the kiddy board, crowing with glee. This sense of bliss stayed intact until Kalle dumped fish sauce on the floor and Ellen pooped.

When Thomas unlocked the front door, she felt herself go rigid and the last trace of bliss evaporated. The children had eaten, Ellen had fallen asleep and Kalle had put on his pyjamas. She assessed the kitchen with a quick glance and inspected her son's appearance before she forced herself to stop.

It wasn't up to him to judge her or the housekeeping standards, and she shouldn't hand him the chance to do it.

She was standing in the kitchen when he came in. She saw traces of her own mood surrounding him.

He kissed her on the mouth. His lips were cold.

'Just you wait, I've got lots to tell you.'

'So have I,' she said.

He turned away, grabbed Kalle and swung him up high.

Annika read Kalle a story while Thomas reheated some chicken wok in the microwave. It was the recipe with chilli and pickled coriander, the one he had taught her to make. She tucked Teddy in, kissed her son goodnight and caressed his cheek.

She went into the living room, her body and soul feeling empty, and let the breeze from an open window sweep over her bare arms. Sinking down on the couch next to Thomas, armed with potato crisps and the remote control, she inhaled the scent of the city in the summertime. Birch trees and soot, lilacs and exhaust fumes. The sounds were intermittent, a car had time to disappear before the next one passed by, and somehow the noises were more distinct and incisive than usual.

On TV, the Swedish host of *Jeopardy*, Magnus Härenstam, gave his guests the answers and they supplied the questions.

Annika leaned back and closed her eyes.

'I got the job,' Thomas said.

She looked up at him and smiled.

'I said they'd give it to you – if they had any brains, that is.'

'I wasn't so sure they had.'

'Well, congratulations. First Seoul, then this. So, what happened?'

'I did what you told me to do, talked about hardcover booklets and how we had to convince everyone we had always had this position.'

Annika raised her eyebrows in surprise.

'I thought you thought it was a lousy idea.'

Thomas stared at the TV screen, his face a shade pinker.

'I didn't say, like you did, that it's all in the phrasing,' he said.

She sat next to him, watching without seeing, hearing without listening. Drinking in the nearness of him, nurtured by his warmth.

Not long after 7:30 Thomas switched channels. They had missed the opening headlines and the top story was already in full swing. The camera showed a view of the Russian Embassy, as taken from inside Torstensson's office.

Annika sat up straight and leaned forward. The editor-in-chief came into focus, sweating, and there was a painting of a naked woman hanging behind him.

'Editor-in-chief Torstensson,' Mehmed began, off camera. 'Could you please tell me the stance you take at *Kvällspressen* on economic crime?'

Torstensson cleared his throat.

'Crime is a blot on society in every democracy,' Torstensson replied. 'One of the most important obligations of the press is to investigate criminals at all levels of society and expose them.'

'And here I thought that's what the police were supposed to do,' Annika commented, unknowingly echoing Schyman's earlier thought.

'What's your personal opinion of people who perform insider deals?'

The editor-in-chief's tongue snaked across his lips and he tried to get more comfortable in his chair.

'Crime of any nature should be investigated,' he replied, his eyes wide. 'It's a prerequisite of any functioning—'

'No, that's not what I was asking about,' Mehmed said in a calm voice, interrupting him. 'I was asking for your personal opinion.'

Torstensson paused. He was perspiring profusely.

'Why are you asking this?'

'I have received information that you knew, in advance, about a certain outcome that would be made public in the second-quarter report, that is on 20 July last year.'

Annika felt a bit light-headed. *Christ, here we go . . .*

Torstensson gulped and shook his head.

'No,' he said. 'That's not true.'

'I can assure you that it *is* true,' Mehmed said. 'My source is dependable. And since you sold your holdings on the nineteenth, that would make you guilty of insider trading.'

Annika stared at Torstensson's sweaty face, barely able to breathe. The editor-in-chief's eyes grew even wider. She could see flashes of thoughts and panic rising in them.

'By no means is this true,' he said. 'I had no knowledge of this.'

'Then how come you sold your entire holding, 9,200 shares, on 19 July, the day before the report was made public?'

The editor-in-chief shook his head.

'It was pure coincidence,' he said. 'I had been planning to unload them for quite some time.'

'On 19 July, a Wednesday, you sold your 9,200 shares of Global Future, rated at SEK 412.50, which means you made 3,795,000 kronor. The very next day, Thursday, 20 July, the report for the second quarter was made public and the share price dropped twenty-eight per cent, to SEK 297. That means you would have received 2,732,400 kronor for the same stocks, right?'

Torstensson's face revealed emotions such as doubt and fear while Mehmed was talking. When he answered Mehmed, his voice was full of restrained contempt.

'The whole point is to sell in time,' he said. 'That's what playing the stock market is all about.'

'What a loser,' Thomas said.

'You earned over a million kronor by selling on the nineteenth instead of the twentieth,' Mehmed said.

'That's chicken feed,' Torstensson said.

'I don't think your readers would agree. In addition to all this, the parent company declared that they would no longer supply the company with funds, which meant that the share price dropped to virtually zero. You were aware of this as well.'

'This is slander!' the editor-in-chief exclaimed, moving as if he intended to get up.

'By the first of January, the share price for Global Future was 59 kronor, today it's worth a mere 37 kronor. Your shares would have been worth 340,000 kronor today. Your insider deal made you more than three million kronor.'

'I'm not going to listen to any more of this,' Torstensson said, so upset that it was difficult for him to speak.

At that very moment there was a change of perspective. After being locked on Torstensson's face, the camera moved to an angle that showed Mehmed getting up, walking past the conference table and going over to the bookcase. Another camera came briefly into view, along with a tangle of cables and some people.

'There's Schyman!' Annika exclaimed, pointing at the screen. 'I saw him, he was standing behind the cameraman. Did you see him?'

Thomas shushed her.

'Here,' Mehmed said, pointing at a binder in Torstensson's bookcase. 'This contains the minutes of the board meetings of the *Kvällspressen* board of directors, doesn't it?'

'How dare you?' Torstensson shouted and got up. 'Touch that binder and I'll have you charged with trespassing.'

'Wow,' Annika said. 'He actually knows the legal classification of a crime.'

Mehmed slipped his hand inside his black denim jacket and pulled a folded piece of paper out of the pocket.

'That won't be necessary,' he said. 'I have a copy of the minutes of the board meeting held on 27 June last year, and it details that you were present and that you were made privy to this information. I would like to hear your comment.'

Standing in the middle of the room, Torstensson swayed slightly.

'My comment?'

'What you were thinking? Feeling? What made you risk everything you've built up just to make a killing on the market and earn a million?'

The editor-in-chief yanked off his mike, stepped on it and left the room.

'Christ,' Thomas exclaimed. 'What an amazing scoop! That Mehmed is one hell of a reporter! How did he ever dig this up?'

Feeling sweaty, Annika swallowed.

The news anchor came on screen again and concluded the story.

'Editor-in-chief Torstensson of *Kvällspressen* resigned this evening after this network's in-depth news team revealed the details of his insider dealings. The police are now pursuing the matter. An extra board meeting was called, appointing Anders Schyman, a former employee of this network, as *Kvällspressen*'s new editor-in-chief and executive editor. More coverage of this story will be available after the regular news hour, when we will be airing a live broadcast, an in-depth look at the news.'

The news anchor switched to a fresh piece of paper.

'What a story,' Thomas said, looking at Annika. 'I just don't understand how you people find everything out.'

Annika shushed him. A new segment filled the screen: the conference room at the offices of Zero Television, the thundering gunshot, the jerky camera skipping across the audience, Karin Bellhorn's beet-red face.

'For God's sake,' she shouted. 'This is all a fake. Can't you tell?'

A cut to another angle: Annika could hear her own voice, far away but distinct.

'Cain and Abel. The most ancient motive for murder in the history of the world.'

A close-up of Karin Bellhorn, leaning forward, looking aggressive.

'Are you insinuating that I would kill someone out of simple envy?'

The camera shook and then Annika was on screen, perched on the windowsill.

'Oh, my goodness,' Thomas said, his mouth full of chips. 'That's you!'

'Absolutely not,' the Annika on TV said. 'It's so much bigger than that.'

'Turn it off,' Annika said in a subdued voice.

'Why?'

'You don't know what you're talking about,' Karin Bellhorn screamed on TV.

'Please?'

Thomas turned off the TV.

'Is it hard to look at yourself?'

Annika nodded.

'Karin confessed – she did it.'

'Did you know that she was the one?'

Annika leaned back.

'For a while there I thought it was Anne.'

They sat there for a while, listening to the sounds of summer, drinking in its light, its scents. Thomas took her hand and kissed her palm.

'I'm sorry,' he whispered. 'I really am.'

She didn't say anything, just looked down at her thighs.

'I have behaved . . .' he began, then swallowed, searching for the right words. 'Badly. That's not good. I lost faith in my abilities.'

'You lost faith in *us*,' Annika said, glancing at him, seeing that he was in agony.

'No, it was more than that. Everything – how I should live my life.'

Thomas's long hair spilled on to his face. Annika saw her own hand reach out and smooth it back. Then she met his gaze, so dark and frightened.

'But I've already made my choices, even though I wasn't aware of it. I chose you and the children, I chose you nearly four years ago. If you want to get married, if it's important to you, then let's do it.'

She shook her head.

'No,' she said. 'I want you to want it too.'

'I do want it, only I don't want the blow-out. I've done the traditional thing once, and that's enough.'

She looked up at him and nodded.

'You can get married at the Swedish Embassy in Seoul, you know,' Thomas said. 'I've talked to them, there's an opening for us on 10 September.'

Annika sat bolt upright on the couch and blinked.

'But I can't go to Seoul. There's work and . . . who will take care of the kids?'

'My parents.'

'Would they want to?'

'Well, we're talking about their grandchildren. And work won't be a problem – the president of the USA will be arriving on the twelfth to visit Korea. You can be a part of the press delegation when he goes to Panmunjon and the Bridge of No Return on the 39th Parallel, before he heads for the four-way talks in Peking . . .'

Annika shook her head and smiled sadly.

'It sounds great,' she said. 'But the paper would never let me go to Korea on an assignment.'

'Actually, I called Schyman and involved him in my little conspiracy. He told me you could go to Hawaii if you liked. He must think you're one hell of a reporter.'

Annika blinked, pieced things together and considered the implications for a few seconds.

Schyman wanted to pay her back. A marriage in return for a position as editor-in-chief.

She jumped up.

'Would you like another beer?'

Thomas pulled her close and kissed her.

'Please say yes,' he said. 'I want this.'

The phone rang and she disengaged herself from his arms, then went into the kitchen and got a beer out of the fridge. She listened to the rhythmic whoosh of the dishwasher, the sounds of the courtyard through the open window, fans, crying children, a burglar alarm.

Present in the moment, the day that was today, she closed her eyes.

'Annika? It's for you.'

She took a couple of breaths and returned to the living room.

'Annika Bengtzon?'

The voice was familiar, but she couldn't quite place it.

'We've met a few times during the past few days, out at Yxtaholm and during the service today . . .'

It was Highlander.

'You'll have to call the paper,' she said quickly, glancing at Thomas. 'I haven't written anything about the ceremony. If you have anything to add, you'll have to talk to the night-desk editor.'

'Oh, no, that's not why I'm calling,' the network executive said. 'You see, the boys in London have seen the tapes from the broadcast today. Have *you* seen it?'

Annika cleared her throat quietly.

'Well,' she said, 'just a bit of it.'

'I must say that they were very impressed. It's not often they see a diamond in the rough emerge like that.'

'What?' Annika said, placing her hand on her forehead.

'We're looking for someone to replace Michelle Carlsson, someone who can take over *The Women's Sofa* and carry on in the same spirit. We would like to screen-test you for the job – what do you say?'

'Who? Me?'

Highlander drew a patient breath.

'We think you have a great deal of charisma. You pop right out of the screen, you have presence. Have you ever considered going for a new career?'

Annika rubbed her forehead and gaped like a fish a few times, looking at Thomas who watched her from the other end of the couch, blinking in surprise.

'Is this some kind of joke?' she managed to say.

'Absolutely not,' Highlander said, a touch of irritation in his voice. 'We will be kicking off the autumn season on 10 September, so we need to get moving with the auditions and contracts. By the way, do you have a manager?'

'Um, no . . .' Annika said, feeling more and more flustered.

'Then I could recommend Sebastian Follin, he's available now that . . . You know.'

Annika ran the idea through her system, immersing herself in what fame had to offer.

Hosting a show. TV. Opening nights. Money. Her own production company. An international career. The mechanisms that control fame, reaching critical mass.

'I'm sorry,' Annika said, looking steadily at Thomas. 'It's just not possible. You see, I'm getting married on 10 September.'

Highlander's laugh had a forced ring to it.

'That should be taken care of rather quickly,' he said. 'You'll have time to tape a show too.'

'The wedding's taking place at the Swedish Embassy in Seoul,' Annika explained.

Anders Schyman, his heart full to overflowing, turned around and left the fish tank. He closed the sliding door, unconsciously anticipating the suction sound of the rubber runners heralding that everything was locked up and ready to go.

It was *finito*.

Over with.

Victory was his.

He took a long, deep breath. His lungs felt hard to inflate, they were so filled with relief and the residue of pent-up worry.

He had achieved his end.

Yes. Absolutely.

He exhaled.

Tomorrow, the maintenance crew would be moving his things into the corner office with a view of the Russian Embassy.

Letting his keys drop into his inside pocket, Schyman felt their weight bob by his ribs. Then he looked up at the news desk and the editors.

He met each one's gaze.

Walking at a measured pace and leaning forward just a bit, he headed for the exit. Editors and reporters, sketch artists and picture editors, photographers and telephone operators – the living organism that was the newsroom followed his every move in a new way.

'We made some changes in the corporate heading,' Jansson said as he stood outside the smoking area, holding one arm inside, the cigarette smoke snaking upwards to the fan.

Anders Schyman, editor-in-chief and executive editor, nodded curtly.

'I'll be checking back with you by phone around midnight,' he said.

'Hard to imagine that there will be any changes now,' the night-desk editor said, taking a puff on his cigarette and blowing the smoke aimlessly into the smoking area. 'We'll run Michelle's murder as the header and the top story, Barbara Hanson's interview with you will be on the centre spread, and the editorial will deal with Torstensson's insider-trading deal.'

Another nod, a wave of his hand. His chest felt constricted.

Tore Brand was staring at the blue light of a TV screen as he passed. TV Plus, a newly scheduled rerun of Michelle Carlsson's memorial service.

A thought flashed through Schyman's mind: *I wonder how long she'll live on.* It would be the measure of her greatness, an assessment measured in decades and centuries.

The immortal ones.

Would Michelle Carlsson be one of them?

He laughed at the absurdity of the thought, a short bark that echoed against the tiled walls of the stairwell. He took the stairs two at a time.

The automatic doors ushered him out into the late summer evening, golden and cool. His car welcomed him with its electronic chirp: The doors are unlocked, please get in, remember to fasten your seat belt or I'll be reminding you.

Giants endure, Schyman thought to himself. *They are the victors of power struggles and they write history.* The inventors, changing the agenda for future generations. The perpetually hated dictators and oppressors. The good leaders creating prosperity and legends. The women, the fairest of them all, loved by heroes and celebrated by dead poets.

He drove slowly through the city: asphalt, drunken revelry and neon lights.

I'm a survivor, he thought.

Immortal, at least for one night.

No southbound traffic. The freeway transported him to Nacka and then on to Saltsjöbaden.

At last Schyman reached the sea, shimmering and eternal.

ACKNOWLEDGEMENT

This is a work of fiction. Every last character originated in the mind of the author. Any similarities to real-life figures are sheer coincidence. The newspaper *Kvällspressen* does not exist, which also goes for Zero Television and the network I chose to call TV Plus. They were inspired by a number of existing organizations, but the manner in which they appear in this book is solely a product of the author's imagination.

On a number of occasions I have exercised my right as an author to tailor the details of existing locations, floor plans and routes to suit my purposes.

I would like to take this opportunity to thank everyone who has been kind enough to help me and answer my questions.

They are: Anders Carsfeldt, a mobile broadcasting engineer, cameraman, OB technician and general Rock of Gibraltar at the TV4 network, who explained the technical details of outside broadcasting and television technology and let me study the set-ups.

Team Jelbe Production allowed us to study their buses.

The entire staff at Yxtaholm Castle in Södermanland, with a special nod to Patrik Arneke, the restaurateur, for the fantastic service and his patience when providing information.

Bengt Wingqvist, the head of the Stockholm County Police Department's forensics unit, for his extensive knowledge of crime-scene investigation.

Tor Petrell, detective inspector of the Stockholm police force, for details about police interview procedures and work methods.

Gunilla Bauer, registered nurse and business proprietor on the island of Gällnö, for information about the island and its history.

Henrik Olsson, a solicitor belonging to the firm of Advokatfirman Peter Althin, for help with legal issues and matters pertaining to the freedom of the press.

Per Hultengård, a lawyer employed by the Swedish Association for Press Publications, for explaining and discussing various scenarios with regard to executive liability.

Sakari Pitkänen, editor-in-chief and executive editor of *Metro*, for discussions pertaining to the moral rights and obligations of an editor-in-chief.

Mikael Aspeborg, CEO of OTW Television and my husband, for help with practical details about TV productions.

Peter Svensson, senior press officer for Sweden's military authorities, for information on weapons used by the Swedish Army.

David Lagercrantz, an author and a colleague, for discussions about the stock market.

Nils Liliedahl, the head of information administration at the Stockholm Stock Exchange, for assistance with scenarios dealing with insider trading and its exposure.

Peter Sving, head of operations at the Securities Register

Centre in Stockholm, for information about their procedures and services.

Anna Borné, Mattias Boström, Cherie Fusser, Madeleine Lawass and Anna Carin Sigling at my Swedish publishing company, Piratförlaget, for their supportive and enriching teamwork.

Lotta Byqvist, my associate and press agent: I'd be dead by morning if it wasn't for you.

Karin Kihlberg, who still makes everything work.

Bengt Nordin, my fantastic agent, who sent Annika out to see the world.

Sigge Sigfridsson, a publisher and a journalist, who made it all possible.

Lotta Snickare, the head of leadership development at Föreningssparbanken, for consultations and inspiration.

Jonas Gummesson, CEO of TV4, who answers any strange questions at any hour.

Jenny Nordin, my creative web editor, who keeps lizamarklund.net up to date.

Astrid Sivander and Arne Öström for proof-reading and make-up.

Karolina Olsson, Fredrik Hjerling and Mi Johansson for their work on the photography, design and layout of the book's cover and my make-up.

Johanne Hildebrandt, a journalist, writer and a dear friend, for discussions, criticism and support.

Anne-Marie Skarp, my publisher *extraordinaire*, for her boundless knowledge and linguistic instincts.

And last of all, but foremost, as usual: the dramatist Tove Alsterdal, for reading, criticizing, analysing and encouraging – she accompanies me every step of the way. There would not be any books without you!

Thank you, one and all.

And finally, any factual errors in this book are mine exclusively.